Word on the street about *The Coronation*...

"*The Tales of Tarsurella: The Coronation*, was a delightfully lovely book filled with action, romance, mystery and even some Godly truths that convict! You will be on the edge of your seat to read the next chapter, and will be motivated to trust, praise, and love God more and more because of what the characters go through. It's an amazing road of a novel, with many twists and turns around the bend that you never see coming, but that's the beauty of it."
-Halee, age 15, Texas

"One of my favorite books from now on forever! It is a touching story and I have been able not only to enjoy reading but learning more about God and his precious ways of working and being. This is not only a beautiful novel but a way of spreading God's word and love to the world."
-Amanda, age 22, Guatemala

"This is such a compelling story! It combines fantasy with reality which results in a wonderful fairytale! The characters illustrate the struggles we face in our teen years, and they are so relatable that I can't help but love them! This book is definitely a page turner that I wouldn't hesitate to recommend!"
-Xandria, age 14, Tennessee

"It was a wonderful story with vivid details and lively characters. It was so easy to get wrapped up in the story and wish you were there. I laughed and cried with the characters. I freaked out! I screamed for joy, and I yelled in frustration! At times I was so wrapped up in the story that I had no idea what was going on around me. I fell in love with the characters and began to believe that it was all true. It was a beautiful blend of characters, places, and details

that was easy to get lost in. I enjoyed every minute of reading this book, even when I was yelling at the characters."
-Alice, age 19, Colorado

"The high quality of this book pleasantly surprised me, and I wholeheartedly enjoyed reading it. In a world where good quality Christian fiction is scarce, this book gives me hope that a story can be entertaining and enjoyable while still teaching valuable, Biblical lessons."
-Bethany, age 17, Ohio

The Tales of Tarsurella: The Coronation

By Livy Jarmusch

Copyright 2017 ©

Thank You…(A Letter from Livy)

Thank you. Two simple words. Words that are so casually thrown around, sometimes I fear that they may lose their power. It is my hope that everyone reading these words will hear the genuineness behind my "Thank You"! Writing this Thank You page is a very special moment for me, because before we dive into this story, I'd like to pause for a moment and give honor to whom honor is due. There's only one author name on the cover, but the reality is that there are so many beautiful souls in my life whose names should be on the front as well! *The Coronation* was truly a team effort, and everyone in my world (whether your name is featured on this page or not) has influenced this story and the creation of it in some small way!

Thank You…
Kimberly Snyder. Your editing skills were such a blessing to me! (I still can't believe that you read *The Coronation* three times and didn't grow tired of it!) Volunteering to share your God- given talent and lending your unique giftset toward this project, lifted this story and brought it to a whole new level. So thank you, sister. Thank you for fixing my typos, making lovely suggestions, and bringing another pair of eyes to this project!

Kenya Nicole. My biggest cheerleader, sweetest friend, and never-ending supporter! From the very beginning, when I first decided to creep out of my shell of secrecy and say, "Uhhh…I'm writing a novel," you instantly encouraged me, prayed for me, and inspired me to keep pressing on! Thank you for enduring my dramatic, ranting text messages. Thank you for laughing with me when I needed a break, reminding me to rest and not push myself so hard, and for whole-heartedly encouraging all my crazy endeavors. (Even if you don't always understand them! Haha!) I love you!

My cousins; Noah, Evan, and Jadon. Three people on the planet who have always encouraged and challenged my creativity. You were the first group of ears to hear that first (very) rough draft. I'll never forget reading it out loud on that sweaty summer afternoon, hearing you guys laugh, and thinking, *I wonder if this means someone else out there will enjoy reading this too?* Thank you for all the positive feedback and encouragement, despite this being a very, *very* girly tale. ;) Thank you Noah for helping me zoom in, dive deeper, develop stronger characters, and improve the story.

Sarah. Thank you for encouraging me throughout this crazy journey! Thank you for reminding me to keep pressing forward, even when writing feels like an uphill climb. And thank you for editing *Regal Hearts*, enabling me to work on two projects at once! Score! Love you, sister!

Bella. You are just a gem, through and through! I have to admit that your excitement over *The Coronation* made me a little bit giddy! Thank you for sacrificing sleep and staying up half the night to read! Your enjoyment over this story has made me enjoy everything so much more! As a fellow writer, you know what this writing life is like, and it means so much to have someone walking the journey with me who understands. Thank you for doing the dirty work… formatting and creating my page numbers! *Throws hugs and kisses across the United States.*

Alex. Oh goodness, girl, where do I even begin with you? Easily dubbed as *The Coronation*'s first ever super fan, your excitement over this story has been such a joy. Your dramatic messages make me laugh, and encourage me to keep writing. Your excited feedback caused me to realize that there *just* might be other girls out there who would enjoy this story as well! Thank you for being your fun, mellow-dramatic, over-the-top, passionate self. You're amazing!

The Tarsurella Street Team – you girls know who you are! Thank you for coming along on this journey, for spreading the word about this novel with your friends, and supporting this project! Much love to each and every one of you!

My Mother. Thank you for listening to me chat excitedly about characters and plot twists, even when you're tired and ready to fall asleep! Thank you for all your reading, re-reading, and then re-reading again. Thank you for your prayer, encouragement, and reminding me that I can do all things through Christ who gives me strength! I can't imagine trying to tackle a project like this without parents who support me!

And lastly, but most certainly not least: My Heavenly Father. Jesus Christ. Holy Spirit! My amazing Lord and Savior who loves me, inspires me, and has filled me with His Creative Spirit! Thank You for blessing me with my creative mind, and for teaching me how to take authority over my thoughts, take every thought captive, and use this brain for your glory! It feels so silly to try and write a Thank You note for the King of Kings and Lord of Lords, when all the praise in the universe wouldn't be enough to do You justice! But, I'm going to give you my humble little words and tiny pen anyway. Thank You for reminding me that, "If it's not good, it's not the end." Thank You for Your faithfulness, not only in my life, but in the lives of everyone who reads *The Coronation*.

I pray that You would speak to the hearts of every reader, encourage and strengthen them in their walk with You, bless them with a fresh anointing of creativity, and draw them closer into Your heart. *Your* Kingdom come, and *Your* will be done on earth as it is in Heaven! In Jesus name. Amen.

Character Profiles

Get to know the Royal Family through this fun Q and A with the starring characters of Tarsurella!

Name: Addison

Lineup in the Royal Family: First born

Age: 20

Favorite way to spend a Saturday: Hanging out with my family. Eating pizza, playing board games, and just spending quality time together. As busy as we are, times like these are becoming a rarity in The Palace, so I enjoy every moment I get to spend with my family.

Favorite Movie: Lord of the Rings

Biggest Fear: Disappointing my Dad, my family, and the nation of Tarsurella.

Biggest Dream: To have a peaceful Tarsurella, where every citizen is given the opportunity to live out their dreams and discover their God-given purpose.

If I were a breakfast food I would be: Waffles. Because even though my personality is really steady and reliable, I like to think that I'm a little bit more entertaining than bland old toast. (Haha!) I can be a little square at times, simply because some people can view my faith and values as old fashioned, but I like to think that I still have enough fun elements to splash some syrup on the day and make it sweet. ;)

If I could travel anywhere in the world I would go to: A warm beach somewhere. I'd take a week off and lounge around on the sandy shores with my family, then splash across the ocean waves on a jet-ski...ahh, yeah. Vacation sounds amazing.

♔

Name: Bridget

Lineup in the Royal Family: Second born

Age: 19

Favorite way to spend a Saturday: Shopping in Paris! Or, attending a fashion event, premiere party, regal ball, or just hanging out with my best friends, Kitty and Bailee.

Favorite Movie: A Walk to Remember. (I always cry ugly tears every time I watch it!)

Biggest Fear: Spiders

Biggest Dream: To meet and marry the young man that God has for me.

If I were a breakfast food I would be: Jello. Okay, so I know that Jello is not seen as a traditional breakfast food. (But it should be! Jello is delicious!) My personality is pretty outside the box, so I feel like Jello is the only breakfast food possible for me to be. ;)

If I could travel anywhere in the world I would go to: Somewhere in the United States. Not sure where. Maybe to an adorable little coffee shop in the middle of nowhere!

Name: Chasity

Lineup in the Royal Family: Third

Age: 18

Favorite way to spend a Saturday: Completely immersed in a fantastic novel. Or out horseback riding.

Favorite Movie: National Velvet. (Such a beautiful classic!)

Biggest Fear: Living an unfulfilled life. Not living up to my God-given potential, and missing out on whatever adventures God might have for me.

Biggest Dream: To be the girl that God wants me to be.

If I were a breakfast food I would be: Pancakes. Even though my personality is pretty simple and straightforward, I also have a lot of layers, so depending on whether I'm wearing maple syrup, strawberry topping, or big chunky chocolate chips, I like to mix things up a little bit. ;)

If I could travel anywhere in the world I would go to: Horseback riding on the beach! I don't really care which beach it is–Hawaii, The Bahama's, California...I just think that riding on the beach would be a blast!

Name: Hope

Lineup in the Royal Family: Fourth

Age: 17

Favorite way to spend a Saturday: Sleeping in. Being lazy. Netflix and chill!

Favorite Movie: The Sisterhood of the Traveling Pants. (Haha, I know, it's such a chick flick. But that's one movie I never get tired of watching.)

Biggest Fear: Making an absolute fool out of myself in front of the press. Stumbling down the stairs, stuttering mindlessly into a camera, tripping on the catwalk…but I guess I've already done all of the above, and I survived! So maybe it's not so much a fear as it is the fact that I try to avoid utter humiliation! Haha.

Biggest Dream: To discover and embrace everything that God has for me in this life. You know, to walk out those Jeremiah 29:11 plans. Even though I have no clue what they are.

If I were a breakfast food I would be: Sugar cereal! I am a cereal girl. I love them all! Captain Crunch, Coco Puffs, Fruity Pebbles…okay, maybe not Grape Nuts, but I don't think anybody likes Grape Nuts!

If I could travel anywhere in the world I would go to: A third-world country. Perhaps Uganda, or Haiti. My family has been so abundantly blessed, and it's still hard for me to imagine that other people in the world live in such devastating poverty. I'd love to go visit and make a difference in whatever ways possible.

♛

Name: Asher

Lineup in the Royal Family: Fifth

Age: 14

Favorite way to spend a Saturday: Playing video games.

Favorite Movie: Star Wars, I guess.

Biggest Fear: Having a massive power outage and not being able to play video games for several days. That would be a straight-up nightmare.

Biggest Dream: I guess I don't really know.

If I were a breakfast food I would be: Toast. You can eat it quickly and move on with your life.

If I could travel anywhere in the world I would go to: Again, I really don't know. Or care.

Name: Jillian

Lineup in the Royal Family: Sixth

Age: 11

Favorite way to spend a Saturday: Doing something fun with the family! Whether it's getting my nails done with my sisters; grilling in the backyard with Dad; playing charades; or just all hanging out watching a movie together, popping popcorn and making jokes. Anything when the family is all together is an absolute blast!

Favorite Movie: High School Musical! My older siblings tease me about it, but I don't care. There's just something magical about a school that breaks into musical numbers all day long. I would happily live in that world. ;)

Biggest Fear: Something bad happening to my Dad. Or Addison, or Bridget, or any of my other siblings.

Biggest Dream: Oh my goodness, so many dreams, so little time! I would love to follow in Bridget's footsteps and dabble within the fashion world. Perhaps create my own clothing line, and makeup? I'd also love to do a lot of traveling, attend premiers, get involved with cool charity projects…ahh, so much I'd love to do!

If I were a breakfast food I would be: Oatmeal. I know it might sound a little boring, but oatmeal can actually be really fun and interesting! There are so many different flavors to mix in and try out, and I would say I'm a lot like oatmeal! Always very colorful and constantly changing what I like and don't like!

If I could travel anywhere in the world I would go to: Anywhere! Again, this is such a hard question. I would love to go to Paris, London, Barcelona, Hong Kong, Los Angeles…everywhere!

♛

Name: Millie

Lineup in the Royal Family: Seventh

Age: 8

Favorite way to spend a Saturday: Exploring! Playing in the backyard treehouse, secretly spying on guests at The Palace, fighting dragons and beating bad guys with Willie! Going to outer space, defeating pirates, finding buried treasure, and going camping! I've never actually been camping, but I want to go soon!

Favorite Movie: Ramona and Beezus

Biggest Fear: Lava-Crocodiles! Lava-Crocodiles are crocodiles that live in lava and they won't burn up, and they can actually eat you.

Biggest Dream: To go camping!

If I were a breakfast food I would be: Bacon! I love bacon!

If I could travel anywhere in the world I would go to: Camping!

Name: William (Willie)

Lineup in the Royal Family: Eighth

Age: 5

Favorite way to spend a Saturday: Playing with Millie.

Favorite Movie: Curious George

Biggest Fear: Getting sucked down the drain in the bathtub. Oh, and gorillas. Gorillas are kinda scary too.

Biggest Dream: To be a superhero.

If I were a breakfast food I would be: Cupcakes! We only had cupcakes for breakfast one time on a special occasion, but I would like if we did that every day.

If I could travel anywhere in the world I would go to: Outer space!

Chapter 1 – Unexpected Encounter

Golden leaves sparkled and danced in the gentle breeze, waving sweetly to the bustling city below. The ancient maple trees had lived through many changes. Hundreds of years passed since these European saplings first sprouted from the dirt. They had observed the transformation of dirt paths to cobblestone streets. Horse-drawn carriages were replaced with humming motor vehicles, and women in long lacy gowns now sported skinny-jeans and cell phones. Charming lamp-posts, yummy bakeries, and loud paperboys were the only thing on Main Street that hadn't changed. If the trees could talk, they would tell you the tales. The tales of a noble Kingdom with the regal name of Tarsurella.

The maples would open their wise mouths, and declare the stories of centuries past. But the trees had been subjected to silence, completely dependent on the mercy of men, disposable in their hands. The trees could not control whether they would be chopped down, or defended and preserved, yet they knew that the very pulse and purpose of nature itself, was to change. For without change, new life could not spring forth.

The warm fall air was mixed with a dash of coolness, reminding the Tarsurellian citizens that winter would soon be knocking at their door. But the busy brains below were much too consumed with their hectic schedules and monstrous "to-do" lists, to pause and ponder such truths.

A slightly frazzled young man, nervous about being late for his first day of work, rushed down the sidewalk. A tender leaf fell right in front of his face, but his thoughts were elsewhere. Dressed in a midnight-black suit and classy olive-tone tie, his mother had cried happy tears as he prepared for his new employment that morning. "Oh, Hanson!" she sniffled. "My little boy is all grown up!"

The eighteen-year-old fidgeted in front of the mirror, completely uncomfortable in the wake of his mother's waterworks. He thought the uppity suit made him look like a stiff penguin. Nevertheless, it was the required work attire. Feeling awkward with his current image, Hanson slipped on a black leather jacket and pair of sunglasses, hoping to appear a little bit more casual on his stroll to work.

"My dear boy, I hope you know how proud I am of you." She gazed at him with ardent admiration, and tousled his messy black hair.

Hesitant to show affection, yet tenderhearted toward his mother's emotions, Hanson hugged his mother before leaving. "I love you," he spoke to the misty-eyed woman, "and I never could have done this without you."

"Extra, Extra, Read All About It!" a loud voice cried, grabbing Hanson's stray thoughts and pulling them back into the current moment. He glanced at the perky paper-boy who wore a pair of eighteenth-century knickers and suspenders. It was a familiar sight for Main Street. The historical downtown district of Tarsurella was filled with young employees dressed as characters from the past, a charming little element that gave tourists great enjoyment. "T-Minus Three Weeks and Counting!" The loud voice continued, "Prince Addison's Royal Coronation is on the Horizon! Read all about how The Palace is preparing for the event of a lifetime!"

Hanson continued walking. In the past, he might've stopped to make a joke and tease the little nerd who got weaseled into such an embarrassing job. But not today. He bypassed his favorite doughnut shop and a necessary lifeblood – coffee – determined to arrive at the bus stop on time. If he missed this bus, he was doomed. Showing up late for his first day of work could be detrimental.

As a native Tarsurellian, the city streets were forever mapped out in Hanson's memory. He knew what areas to avoid during prime tourist season. The double-decker bus, which unloaded only a few blocks away from The Palace, would be full this morning. If there were any school groups loading up for a field trip, Main Street would be crammed. Hanson decided to take a back street instead. He turned into an alleyway.

The backside of Tarsurella's beautiful buildings weren't so pretty. Graffiti-splattered walls and smelly lanes were hidden from the eyes of the general public. Hanson was well aware of the fact that many homeless people roamed this particular drag. Some citizens were plagued with an irrational phobia, as if the homeless community carried a freak desire to harm everyone, but Hanson never knew that to be true. There was a time in life where he and his mother were almost homeless. And who was there to help them through that rough patch in life? Some of the very same people on these ugly backstreets.

Hanson anxiously glanced at his watch, he only had nine minutes to -

"Umph!" All at once, without warning, someone plowed into Hanson like a steam-roller. The body smashed into him, pushing him off balance, and knocked him into a stone wall. The unsuspecting attack forced the wind out of him. Hanson gasped for air, trying to realize what just happened.

A strong, burly man had pinned Hanson up against the wall, smooshing him there with his over-weight body. Hanson lifted his knee and smashed it into the offender. That caused the man to fall, stumbling several feet backwards. Hanson quickly readied himself in a fight stance. The previous blow had caught him off guard, but this time the foolish attacker wouldn't stand a chance, now that Hanson was prepared to fight. Hanson's fists pulsed with adrenaline, ready to defend himself, just like he had been trained to do.

The large attacker didn't waste any time and quickly made the first punch. Hanson dodged it, and returned the favor with one in his stomach. The attacker groaned, suddenly in pain from the unwelcome impact. Hanson leaped on the opportunity of weakness, and attempted to pin the man to the ground. But as he dove on top of him, another enemy rose from the shadows and blindsided Hanson. The next few seconds were like a wrestling match, as Hanson kicked and punched and dodged and rolled on the ground, attempting to defeat his foes. But it was two against one, and Hanson found himself pinned to the cement, struggling like a mouse in a trap.

"That's enough!" a voice echoed through the alleyway. Hanson fought to lift his head from the ground, desperate to see who was approaching. But a large hand pinned his head to the pavement, holding him victim by his hair. Hanson winced, ashamed to accept defeat.

"Now, now, we don't want to completely batter the boy before his first day of work."

Hanson froze. His entire body tightened up with rage and

disgust. He recognized the voice.

"Let the boy have some dignity," the voice continued, "Stand him up on his feet." The two attackers obeyed, and yanked Hanson up to a standing position. His dark tan face was scrunched up in anger, as he met the eyes of this despised man.

"I never thought I'd live to see the day…" the man spoke in a belittling tone, "My own flesh and blood, working for the Royal Security Team at The Palace. And everyone said they thought you were going to end up like your old man." He laughed mockingly.

Hanson's breathing quickened, as his estranged father's face drew closer. Hanson hadn't seen the man in close to six years. But he still hated him just as much as the day he left. "Why are you here?" Hanson growled, un-nerved by the fact that he had showed up in town again. Hanson wanted to sound fearless, but the hidden truth was that memories of this man still gave him nightmares.

"Oh, come now," the older-looking version of himself replied, "You don't sound very happy to see your old man! I wanted to congratulate you on your job! It's not every day that a kid your age is offered such an honored position. I know middle-aged men who would kill to be you. Forty-year-old guys back at the academy are struggling to land jobs like that. And look at you! Just barely eighteen, and already offered a position working for the Royal Family." He whistled in amazement.

"Just a tip–" Hanson spat bitterly, "next time you want to congratulate somebody, try balloons and a gift card. It might go over better than attacking them with two hitmen in an alleyway."

His dad chuckled, "I'll keep that in mind." He placed his hand on Hanson's shoulder. "Now listen, I know that you and I haven't had the best relationship over the years…"

Hanson was seething. The hand on his shoulder reminded him of everything he wanted so desperately to forget.

"But at the end of day I'm your dad, like it or not. You inherited my genetics. You have my same charming smile and deep brown eyes your mother fell for. Just like me, you were born to fight. You have all this frustrated, bottled up anger, afraid that you're never gonna be enough in this life. Let me tell you something, you're cut from the same cloth I am. After I ditched this town, I started working hard, going after what I wanted, and I made a life for myself. I don't work for anybody. I do what I want, whenever I want, and I always come out ahead. No bosses, no contracts, no paperwork, and no frilly ties." He paused and flicked Hanson's tie. "Now today, you're gonna go to work, take orders from your commander, work the long hours that he assigns you, and eventually feel restless and unfulfilled. Sure, you'll be excited for a week or two. Heck, maybe even a month. But soon all the nostalgia is gonna wear off, and you'll ache for adventure. You'll want to be free, like I am. So I'm willing to make you an offer. Truth is, I need help with the family business, and you're the only guy I'd trust with the job."

"You're wrong," Hanson hissed, "I am *nothing* like you. And I never will be. So get your grubby hands off of me, take your two morons, and get out of this town."

His dad pretended to be offended, and continued in his teasing tone, "Aw man, how can you talk to your old man like that? I'll admit, I'm disappointed to hear that you don't want me here; I was planning on dropping by the house and giving your mom a visit—"

All at once, Hanson broke free from the men and their iron grips, and attempted to tackle his dad. "Stay away from her!" Hanson threatened with a shout. The large men quickly regained control of the situation and Hanson was again trapped and helpless.

"Or what?" His father chuckled. "You'll send the Secret Service after me?"

Hanson wished with all his might that he could smack this crooked man in the face. He would never forgive him for their violent past. As a teary-eyed ten-year-old he vowed that nobody would ever hurt his mother again. And with every fiber of his being, Hanson intended to keep that promise. "You don't know who you're messing with." He replied with distain, "The past is over. Mom and I are not on your puppet strings anymore. If you touch her, I will destroy you."

"Oh, you wanna make threats, do you?" Dad's tone intensified, "Two can play that game." He quickly dug into his pocket and slipped out a small micro-chip. "I tried to make my offer as nicely as possible, but if you want to be nasty, I can go there. Here's the deal. You have access to something I want. And I'll do whatever it takes to get it. We can either do this the easy way, or the hard way. So I'd recommend you listen closely and get to work. Tarsurella has the most elite security system in the world. Virtually impenetrable. Created by an underground brainiac who excels in the wizardry of computer programing, the processing code for this program is worth twenty-five-million dollars. *Twenty-five mill!* Get me the code on this chip, and I'll see to it that you're set for life. I'm willing to give you a percentage of the profits, since, after all, you are my own son." He smiled wickedly, "Just think of it. No bosses, no orders and no alarm clocks. It's freedom, my boy. Get the code and you'll never have to work another day in your life."

"Yeah sure," Hanson laughed bitterly, "Twenty-five-million dollars and life in prison. I'm not gonna break the law and do your dirty little crimes for you."

"You may want to rethink your position," he spoke as he slipped his hand into Hanson's pocket and took out his cellphone. Hanson tensed up, concerned with what he might do. He took the back off his phone, and placed the micro-chip inside. Then he returned it to its home in his pocket, "Because in case I wasn't clear enough, this isn't a request, or a multiple choice quiz testing your morality. You've got three weeks. If I don't have this chip back, with the code, by the night of Prince Addison's Coronation, it's all over for you."

"I'm not afraid of you." Hanson boldly proclaimed, "You can use all the bluffs and blackmail you want, but it doesn't mean anything to me. I would rather die than stoop to your snaky level, rolling around in the pile of putrid trash that you are."

Hanson's dad placed an angry hand around his neck, offering just enough pressure to invoke fear. Hanson struggled to breathe. Mr. Fletcher lowered his voice to a terrifying whisper, spitting right in his face, "If you fail this mission, your mother will pay the price. I'll rip her apart, piece by piece, and I'll see to it that you are fully alive to endure every hellish moment of it." With one final blow, he threw his son up against the brick wall, and watched him slide down to the ground.

He commanded his evil cohorts to leave. "Our work here is done," he glared at his son who gasped for air, struggling to stand up once more. "You've got three weeks. Don't disappoint me."

Chapter 2 – Royal Fangirls

A nervous hand tapped on his father's heavy oak door.

"Come in." The door opened at his father's command, and the son stepped slowly into the suite.

Dazzling sunlight poured in from the balcony doors. As his eyes adjusted to the light, he could only see the silhouette of his father. Soon the shadowy image of the man was enlightened by the sun, as the King looked almost transfigured before him. Basking in the glory of the day, and in the glory of his majesty, he truly looked like a King, with a golden glow radiating around him. It was moments like these when his dad felt far more like an unapproachable King than he did a normal father.

Addison stood staring at his dad, who was dressed in a black suit, and straightening his tie in front of the mirror. Grey hairs peppered the King's receding hairline. Although the distinguished Royal appeared very vibrant and healthy for his age, he couldn't hide the whispers of grey that had snuck in from raising a family of eight children, as well as from running a nation. His blue eyes kindly smiled at Addison. "Good morning, Son," he greeted. "You slept well I presume? What is it that you wanted to see me about?"

After stepping deeper into the room, Addison shifted his weight uncomfortably on his feet. His sparkling blue eyes glanced at the floor for a moment, praying for courage, then shot back at his father who stood patiently, waiting for him to speak. Addison reached a nervous hand to scratch the back of his neck. How could he fairly express what was on his heart without causing his father disappointment? For twenty years now, he had been shadowing his father, watching the King's every move; and in three weeks, he would inherit the crown. On his twenty-first birthday, Addison's inheritance–

the entire Kingdom—would be handed to him.

As a little boy, Addison often wore his father's shoes, playfully stumbling around in them, emulating his favorite man in the entire world. His hero. Many years had passed since those carefree days of childhood, and now Addison's feet were the same size as his father's. It was time to wear his shoes, in every possible meaning of the phrase. But what if he tripped and fell, as clumsily as when he was a young boy? Addison now had the strong, vigorous body of a man, but deep inside he still felt like a mere child. How could he tell his father of the doubts and fears that plagued his heart and mind? Of the fear of failure that kept him tossing and turning at night? He lost sleep over nightmares of what might come to him, and consequentially to his entire nation. The burden of leading his country weighed heavy on his broad shoulders. He needed to tell someone about the inner turmoil of worry. It caused a crushing load that even the strongest man couldn't carry on his own.

"Dad," he spoke slowly, "it's about my Coronation."

A smile spread across the patient father's face as he placed a proud arm around his son's neck. "Ah, yes. The time is almost here. You were born to be a ruler, Addison. Come, let's step outside on the balcony."

Addison followed his father's beckoning and the twosome stepped through double French doors. On the marble balcony, warm sunlight greeted them. The view which spread out below was stunning. Addison's blue eyes scanned the courtyard which was lovingly cared for and pruned by the King's servants. He let his eyes wander to the vast expanse of green pasture which spread far into the distance. His eyes traveled further. The green rolling hills which had been there for as long as Addison could remember, still lay in place. The sun peeked over the farthest hill, painting the sky with melodious colors of pink, purple, and orange, all blending together in a sweet harmony.

The scene reminded Addison of *The Lion King,* when Mufassa led Simba to the highest rock, and revealed all the land he was to inherit. "As far as the light touches," the regal lion had told his cub.
As a boy, Addison watched that movie to the point of memorizing every line, and eventually the VHS tape broke. Simba's great journey and excitement about becoming King, spoke volumes to Addison as a child. "Oh, I just can't wait to be King!" Addison sang along with the movie, dreaming about the days of his own Royal ruler-ship. But now the moment was near at hand, and he greatly desired to be that little boy again, sitting on the couch in his red and white stripped pajamas, singing "Hakuna Matata."

"You've been training your whole life for this position," the King spoke gently. "Everything you've learned in your studies, and everything you've seen from me, it shall all help you greatly. But, Addison, no amount of training can fully prepare a man for the humbling and sometimes frightening task of being King. Many global leaders foolishly rule, and use their power for their own selfish gain. But my father desired that I do no such thing. He told me, 'Son, you should take pride in your low position. To be a King is not to be the first, but to be the last. For someday you shall have to answer to God as to how you led these people.' I took his words seriously, and pondered them every day. I advise you to do the same. Only God can give you the strength to be King, Addison. Only God."

"Excuse me, Your Majesty?" a careful voice interrupted. She truly hated to break up the sweet father-son moment.

Both men twirled their heads around to see Deborah, their slender secretary, standing in high heels, with her headset, clipboard, and a cup of coffee in hand. "Forgive me for interrupting, Your Majesty, but the press conference has been moved to nine o'clock, therefore we need you for a quick briefing in the Boardroom at eight-thirty, and your breakfast meeting has been moved up to seven-thirty."

The King nodded, and turned to his son, "We will finish our talk later. Deborah, when am I free?"

She glanced at the clipboard in her hand, "After the press conference you have an eleven o'clock hearing with the locals; a one o'clock luncheon with the Ambassador of France; two o'clock meeting with President Rick Johnson from the Going Green Committee; three o'clock meeting with the Security Team; four o'clock meeting with Walt Geffen, our newest financial manager; and your usual six o'clock is dinner. But at seven you have a free time slot."

"Very well. Pencil Addison in for seven."

"Yes, sir," she nodded, and quickly went about his bidding. "Oh! And before I forget, Prince Addison, you're needed in Wardrobe to meet with Victoria who wishes to do a second fitting before the Coronation Ball, just to be safe. That's at ten. And here is your coffee, sir." She handed the King his mug, curtsied, and vanished as quickly as she had appeared.

"Deborah, she always keeps us on our toes!" the King shook his head after her speedy exit, "But she's one of the best we have on staff, and I advise you to never get rid of her."

Addison smiled, "I wouldn't dream of it."

Deborah had been working for them for as long as Addison remembered. He could scarcely imagine what life around The Palace would be like without her. Not only was she their secretary, scheduler, and organizer; but she also brought a motherly touch, which was lacking from Addison's life.

His mother died five years ago while giving birth to his youngest brother, William. The grief in Addison's heart had been tumultuous, as their entire family was forced to adjust to a new rhythm of life at The Palace without their mother. No one could ever replace their beloved Queen, but in some small way, Deborah helped to fill the gaping hole which his mother had left vacant with her passing.

The King went back inside, to head out for his full day of meetings. Addison turned to go inside as well, now that he had been rescheduled. After bidding his father a temporary goodbye, the two took separate paths; one down the hall and the other down the staircase. Addison turned down the hall and headed for The Family Room.

The main floor of the castle still held hundreds of original ancient rooms, which were filled with antiques and old family heirlooms. They hadn't been updated for hundreds of years, and served as honorable memorials of the Kings and Queens who ruled before them. But the second floor of The Palace had been remodeled and transformed into a comfortable, modern hangout.

Addison pushed through the door to see some of his very favorite people residing in the Family Room–his family.

His seventeen-year-old sister, Hope, lay sprawled out on the couch in her purple-polka-dot pajama's, with a bowl of *Captain Crunch* in her hand. Her shiny, blue eyes were fixed on the mounted TV. Hope's bouncy, brunette locks tumbled over her shoulders and down her back. Only faint kinks and loose curls remained after sleeping on yesterday's curling iron-assisted 'do.

Five-year-old William sat cross-legged on the grey recliner, his wide eyes fixed on the TV as well. He was wearing nothing but a pair of red boxers, and his wild mane of red hair was left un-touched, free to jump about in every possible direction. Willie's barbaric hair told Addison that he had just tumbled out of bed.

Willie noticed his big brother's entrance. "Addi!" he called, using Addison's childhood nick-name, turning his face full of freckles away from the TV, "*The Brady Bunch* just came on! Come watch with us?"

Addison smiled, "Not today, buddy." He tasseled the boy's hair, making it worse than it already was, "Shouldn't you be getting ready? Isn't this a school day?"

Eight-year-old Millie jumped up from the couch and launched herself into Addison's arms. Her bright-green eyes danced with excitement. "This is the episode where they go camping! When can we go camping? We haven't been camping in a super long time."

"Tell ya what," Addison playfully tapped his little sister on the nose. Her pale, freckled face had been inherited from her mother. Millie and Willie were the only siblings who possessed this unique characteristic from the Queen. "You go get dressed and ready for school, and I *promise* we'll go camping sometime."

Millie's emerald eyes widened, as excitement pounded through her voice, "Really!? You mean it?"

He nodded, "Uh huh. You and I will go camp out under the stars. Like real adventurers!"

"Oh boy!" she could scarcely contain the excitement as Addison placed her on the floor. "Adventure is out there!"

she hollered. Millie shot her hand into the air and rocketed down the hallway, emulating Ellie, her favorite cartoon character from Up.

"Go get dressed, buddy," Addison admonished Willie, and he reluctantly obeyed.

"Fine, I've seen this episode anyway." He jumped off the chair, and took off down the hall in his red boxers.

"Someone needs to tell that boy he's gotta wear some more clothes," Hope laughed as she turned the TV off and stood up to stretch her long limbs. "The press would have a hay-day if they ever saw him looking like that."

Addison laughed, "And what about you? Don't you have school today, too?"

Hope released a yawn, then looked at her brother with pleading eyes, "I just got back from Paris last night, and I'm totally jet-lagged. Can't I have a day off?"

Addison raised a suspicious eyebrow, wondering how Hope could possibly be experiencing jet-lag after such a short trip to the nearby country. "Somehow, I don't think Miss Christy would go for that." Christy was the family's in-palace teacher and tutor. She taught all six school-aged kids, every grade necessary, all by herself. Addison admired her for taking on such a daunting task.

"Breakfast is ready!" eleven-year-old Jillian announced from the small kitchenette, taking off her apron.

Addison smiled at her as he walked into the breakfast nook. Cheerful sunlight poured through the bay windows. "You fixed breakfast all by yourself?"

Jillian had always acted older than her age. Addison noticed signs of early maturity in her. Even though she was only eleven, she already dreamed of someday running the country, and took her role as a Princess *very* seriously. The spunky little brunette wore a sophisticated, shoulder-length cut which framed her face. Jillian thought it made her look older, but Addison loved the way it highlighted her dimpled grin. Try as she may, the adorable little girl couldn't get rid of her "cute" factor. She was still far too young to wear makeup, go to fancy parties, or fly around the world with her big sisters. She was quite exasperated with her lot in life; constantly being lumped together with the "little kids." Jillian's deep-brown doe eyes desired to be seen and respected as the old soul she believed herself to be. She couldn't wait for the day that her family realized she was finally one of the "big kids."

"I wanted to give the maids a day off." Jillian replied sweetly. "They do so much for us. It's only right that we should do something for them."

"What did you fix?" Addison asked, sitting down, suddenly realizing how hungry he was.

Hope occupied the chair beside him, just as hungry.

"It's a breakfast quiche." Jillian placed the hot steamy tray in the center of the table. "It has eggs, and bacon and, well… just try it. Is Daddy eating with us?" Jillian asked.

"He has a meeting," Addison explained, "but he's planning to join us for dinner."

Millie and Willie came back onto the scene and climbed into their seats. The young adventurers had changed out of their PJ's and into their school clothes.

"What. Is. *That?*" Millie asked, drawing out each word for dramatic effect.

"It's called quiche," Jillian stated simply.

"I've never heard of it." Millie wrinkled her nose, "I don't think I like it."

"Just try it," Jillian replied.

"But what if I can't bear to swallow it?"

"Then you'll be polite, and eat it anyway."

"But what if it's the most disgusting food in the entire world and it makes me feel sick to my stomach?"

"It doesn't matter; you'll still be gracious and eat it."

"But what if—"

"Millie," Addison interrupted, "let's pray. I know everyone isn't here yet, but our food's going to get cold if we wait any longer."

Millie, unsatisfied, sighed her surrender; then they all grabbed hands.

"Dear Lord," Addison's strong voice filled the room as each bowed their heads, "Thank You for this new day. Thank You for the blessing of our family, that we're all safe, and protected under Your care. Bless Jillian for fixing our breakfast, and help us all to make good choices today that honor You. Give Dad the strength to be the ruler and King that You have called him to be. In Jesus name, Amen."

An echo of "amen" arose from around the table. Jillian began to dish up and serve the quiche.

"So, where is everybody this morning?" Addison asked, turning to Hope, who seemed to keep tabs on their large family. The long table was abnormally empty.

"Bridget is sleeping in, because she is no longer confined by the chains of high school and has the luxury to do so." Hope chuckled at her own wit, a half-attempt to mask the jealousy. "Chasity wanted to take an early horseback ride, and I haven't the faintest idea what Asher is up to. Probably playing video games in that dungeon of a bedroom of his."

"Deborah reminded me that we have wardrobe fittings with Victoria at ten," Addison said, "so make sure the girls are ready by then."

"*Another* wardrobe fitting?" Jillian let out an exasperated sigh. "Goodness, by the way everyone's acting around here, you'd think we were celebrating the biggest event ever."

"Jillian," Hope scolded her, "that isn't very considerate of you. Addison's Coronation is a huge, historical, monumental event! You're just too young to understand."

Jillian crossed her arms in protest, "No, I'm not. I perfectly understand the significance of Addison becoming King. I just don't understand why we have to make such a huge deal about it. I mean, is it really necessary to have a guest list with *thousands* of people? We've been rehearsing everything for months. Dancing, curtseying, smiling, and posing for cameras. It's so time-consuming! When can we get back to just being a family again? You know, doing normal things?

Like backyard football, grilling with Dad, or playing charades?"

Addison felt a twinge of compassion for his little sister. Things around The Palace had been extremely crazy lately. Everyone was wrapped up in the excitement of preparing for The Ball. "Don't worry," he reassured her, "the excitement should die down soon. We've only got three weeks left, and after that, life will return to its normal pace."

"Yeah," Jillian starred at the piece of quiche which lay on her plate, "but then you'll be gone."

Addison didn't know what to say. His sister was right. The day Addison becomes King, everything will change for him. As much as he'd love to wrap the little girl in his arms, and reassure her that nothing was ever going to change, he knew that he couldn't. The coming change was inevitable. The days ahead were like an unstoppable, flowing current in which they could only do their best to learn how to swim.

Just then, Deborah came into the kitchen. "Good morning, children. Prince Addison, as soon as you're through with your breakfast, your father requests that you review the guest list."

Addison set down his napkin. "I thought the invitations were sent months ago?"

"They were, Your Highness. But your father had hoped that perhaps while taking a second look at the list of those who will be attending, someone might strike your personal interest. The King thought that by inviting local, single girls from high class families and of good reputation, he might assist you in your pursuit of finding a wife."

Addison felt his entire body tighten up at the last words spoken. *Your pursuit of finding a wife.* It was expected of him to be engaged soon. Everyone was poking and prodding at the subject, urging him to find the right woman. He was advised not to begin ruling without a wife by his side. And though he had been searching, he still had not found the young woman he wanted to spend the rest of his life with. Sure, he had met several beautiful, sweet, and kind young ladies. He enjoyed their friendship. But he had not fallen in love with any of them.

"The single ladies guest list is in the home theater, available to scroll through at your leisure whenever you're ready. It's complete with pictures, short biographies, and family trees. If you have any questions or concerns about a young lady, we can research her more thoroughly; or if you see any whom you desire to meet, we can schedule a get-together with any or all of them."

Addison sighed. It sounded as though his father highly hoped he would find a future mate in one of his guests at The Ball. "Very well. You can tell Dad that I'll look through it."

Addison pressed 'Play' and watched the parade of profiles before him. In this Power Point presentation, he had the ability to stop and take a closer look at any of the girls. Sitting in a comfy, red theater chair, with a cup of coffee in his hand, he watched pictures of possible future "love-interests" pass before his eyes. Thankfully, no one else was in the room. All of his younger siblings had gone off to lessons with Miss. Christy, and no one was there to tease him.

Addison knew he shouldn't complain. Most would envy his lofty position. The fact that he had hundreds of women in the Kingdom who would be more than thrilled to marry him, should've been exciting. But he only half-heartedly watched the pictures flash before him. How much could he *really* know about any of these girls, simply from their photographs? They were only beautiful faces. How could he know what was underneath? He tossed up a silent prayer to Heaven,

Lord? How am I to know who the right one is? Am I crazy for wanting someone with a heart of genuine purity, passion, and faith? Someone with substance? A girl who challenges me to be the best man that I can possibly be? I want to find a diamond in the rough. I want someone special. Someone who loves me for me, not just because I'm a Prince.

Just then, he heard the door open. His nineteen-year-old sister, Bridget, walked in wearing sweatpants and her favorite, baggy *Tarsurella U* shirt which belonged to Dad. One wouldn't know by looking at her that she was Tarsurella's biggest fashion icon, and the world's most-beloved Princess-Celebrity-Supermodel. Right now, she merely looked like an average, tired, blue-eyed girl who had just crawled out of bed. Her lose blonde braids were in a tangled mess.

"Whatcha watching?" she asked, cozying up next to her brother. She had a big, green mug of steaming-hot peppermint tea in hand.

"A list of Dad's favorite 'marriage-material' ladies attending The Ball." There was obvious displeasure in his voice.

They sat in silence as several profiles breezed by, then she spoke, "See any you like yet?"

He sighed, "I dunno. Right now, they all look the same to me."

"I know how you feel." She traced her long pointer finger around the rim of her cup, "That's what it was like for me after the whole fiasco with Jacob. It doesn't matter how handsome, impressive, or charismatic any of these guys are. I'm completely numb to the idea of falling in love *ever* again."

As Bridget sat in silence with her brother, she was swept into a world of unwelcome memories. The memories with Jacob were not ones she wished to revisit. But she couldn't seem to run away from them. They always found her, pushing past the 'Do Not Enter' sign on her brain, pounding down the door, and letting themselves in.

Jacob Linch had inflicted a deep pain upon her soul. Her heart still ached every time she thought of it. Jacob had been her first real boyfriend. Her father, in much wisdom, strongly advised against the relationship. He had a deep gut feeling that the boy was trouble. But Bridget, acting against his wishes and warnings, chose Jacob. What she thought was going to be a whimsical Romeo and Juliet fairytale, where she snuck away, off the balcony with her forbidden love, turned out to be an utter disaster. It was Romeo and Juliet alright; but instead of dying in one another's arms, Jacob struck her soul with a knife and then ditched the scene.

They had met through a network of friends, and the Australian heartthrob captured her heart all too quickly. Little did she know that he was sharing her secrets with an Australian teen magazine. But that wasn't the worst of it.

Jacob constantly flattered her with his lips. He told her how beautiful and amazing she was, and her heart melted beneath the gaze of his warm attention. He adorned her with gifts and complements, and caused Bridget to believe that his love for her was real.

The temptation to kiss him was always strong. But as a young girl, she had made the decision that her first kiss wasn't going to happen until her wedding day. An unpopular and seemingly outdated idea, of course, but Bridget had a strong conviction about her beliefs. Sadly, Jacob didn't feel the same way. He pressured her to break the promise of purity she had made with God. She told Jacob where she stood, and how she strived to live her life according to the Bible. But he was not in the same place as her.

One evening, after a dreamy date, he pressured her again to break her "no kissing" rule. The temptation to give in was tantalizing, but she longed to honor God. When she refused him, he was outraged. He tried to get what he wanted, but she broke free from his strong arms. A security guard witnessed the whole scene, and Jacob was banished from The Palace, never to return again. Later, that same security guard found a video camera hidden in her bedroom. Whatever Jacob had hoped would happen that night, he planned on getting footage.

The cold dagger had nearly destroyed her. Some days were harder than others. She was still healing from the pain. Jacob had completely betrayed her trust, and she doubted if she would ever meet anyone worth her heart. Now, after learning such difficult lessons first-hand, she followed the advice of Proverbs 4:23 and guarded the door of her heart much more fiercely.

"I'd better go get changed," Bridget suddenly jumped up, pulling herself from the place her unbridled thoughts had carried her. "Victoria said the wardrobe fitting is at ten, right?"

"Yup." Addison glanced at his watch. He still had ample time to review more profiles before he needed to head downstairs.

Bridget slowly lifted herself off the couch. "Later, bro!"

As Bridget exited, Deborah entered. "Do you approve of the guest list?"

Addison stood up and poured himself another cup of coffee. "Sure. I mean, they all look lovely and like they're from nice families. But this has to be the most unnatural and awkward way of meeting a potential future spouse, ever invented."

Deborah laughed, "I can only imagine how uncomfortable this must be for you. But finding a wife fit for a Prince is not an easy task."

It could be, Addison thought to himself, *if everyone would pull their nosey selves out of it and let me do this my own way.*

"Well, I'm glad that you approve," Deborah continued, "because the King has suggested that we arrange a meeting with a few of the young ladies this morning."

Addison opened his mouth to protest, but his words drained away. *This* morning? Seriously? But he could not object. It had already been settled. If it was added to the schedule, and onto Deborah's clip board, then it was absolutely happening.

At ten o'clock sharp, Addison was summoned to a downstairs parlor, a space most popularly dubbed 'The Courting Room.' Addison's crystal eyes grew wide as he was ushered inside.

Standing before him was a line of twelve ladies, all varying heights, hair colors, shades of skin, and facial features. When

Deborah told him *a few*, he'd only expected two or three; not an entire room full!

They all curtsied upon his entrance, and Addison smiled politely. He felt as though he had stepped into the middle of a bizarre game show, like the 1970's phenomenon, *The Dating Game*. He shook his head. Dazzling white teeth flashed from each flawless girl. This was too much. He turned to Deborah with pleading eyes begging to find a way out of this mess. But Deborah had her orders. She was to issue a meeting with twelve of the most well-bred, educated, classy, and beautiful young women from the guest list. All the ladies selected were from wealthy families, and believed to be solid wife material. Each girl in the room stood in an honored position. If one of these could capture the heart of the Prince, she had the chance to become Queen.

The nervous energy in that room was unparalleled to anything these young women had ever experienced before. After receiving the mind-blowing phone call late last night, some screamed with excitement, and others fainted. Hands shook in anticipation as they prepared themselves for hours, with curling irons, flat irons, cosmetics, and last-minute, midnight shopping trips. But now, no matter what great stress and torture they had put themselves (and the rest of their households) through before their encounter with the Prince, it was now forgotten. Preparation time was over. This was their moment to shine.

Addison forced a smile onto his face and began making his rounds about the room, welcoming each young lady and properly thanking her for attending. Addison's blonde hair gently brushed just above his ears, making it the perfect length for Tarsurella's swoon-worthy Prince. His strong, chiseled jaw and charismatic grin was too much perfection presented in one package, for the spastic fangirls to handle. But the crowning jewel of Addison's flawless appearance was his sapphire eyes.

"Welcome," Addison shook hands with the first girl in line, "It's a pleasure to meet you."

The girl smelled strongly of hairspray and some kind of putrid, gag-worthy perfume. Addison felt as though he may be sick. He held back the cough that was surfacing.

"Thank you!" she gushed. "I'm so excited to be here! I cannot wait for the Coronation. It's all we've been talking about at home. Edward Stefanick is designing my gown, and it is stunning! I can't wait for you to see it!"

Addison kept the fake grin plastered to his face, "Ah, yes!" He pretended that her words interested him, "I'm sure it's lovely."

He casually inched himself closer to a nearby window and hoped to open it up without appearing too obvious. Perhaps the fall breeze would help dissipate the choking smell.

"Excuse me," Addison smiled at another girl who stood in front of the window, "Do you mind if I just reach in here and—"

The girl's face suddenly turned pale. She grew light headed, tossed a hand over her mouth, another on her stomach, and bolted from the room.

Addison shot a concerned glance toward Deborah. Deborah

hurried out after her. Addison sighed. He felt bad for the poor girl. So many of these ladies had lost their minds over him. As flattering as it was at times to have so much attention and adoration from his female citizens, it was mostly annoying and disturbing. He knew that it came with the territory of being a Royal celebrity, but he blamed pop-culture for all the extra hype. Magazines and the media enjoyed obsessing over the bland details of Addison's life, and reported them on the daily. Did so many people *really* care about what he had for breakfast that morning? Or whether he was a "cat person," or a "dog person"? Apparently so, because the Royal fangirls excitedly ate up anything published about him. The young ladies in his Kingdom had puffed him up in their minds to be some sort of glorious fantasy. The idea of meeting the Prince made some of them go weak in the knees and lose every ounce of common sense they possessed. It was ridiculous.

"Oh my goodness!" A third girl pushed herself into Addison's personal space and started talking, "I can't believe that I'm actually meeting you! This is like a dream come true! When Mother told me that I would be attending your ball, I totally freaked out! I've been to some of your other events, like races and polo matches, and I was even at your sixteenth birthday party, but you've always been so busy mingling with others that we never got the chance to meet! I'm Adaline Shortmyers!"

"Pleasure to meet you," Addison shook her hand, then another girl hopped into the conversation who smelled just like the first girl. But she was short, with jet black hair and snow-white skin. The oriental beauty reminded Addison somewhat of the Disney Princess, *Mulan*. Of all the Princess movies his younger sisters forced him to watch, he actually enjoyed that one.

"My name is Mim," she spoke with a slight bow. "Your Governess, Mrs. Gram, has served my family as well."

The fifth girl spoke up. "I wasn't aware that the practice of having in-home governesses was still a thing in Tarsurella." Addison remembered her from the profiles. Her name was Sapphire, and Addison thought the name suited her well. Her dazzling blue eyes sparkled and danced as she spoke, and she didn't throw her words around nervously like the others had. The British girl presented herself with elegance, and grace. Her accent was quite captivating.

"Of course!" Mim replied. "I would guess that everyone in this room has been greatly influenced by the perks of a governess. At least, those who *know* how to conduct themselves in the presence of Royalty." Mim's comment was throwing some serious shade at the girl who had nearly thrown-up on Addison's shoes.

"Isn't that comment a little harsh?" A brunette from the other side of the room spoke up. All eyes darted across to her. "I didn't have a governess; does that mean I shouldn't be here?" She spoke with a flicker of sass and passion. Addison was surprised by her casual attire. She was the only one in the room who wasn't flaunting a designer dress, high heels, and diamond jewelry. Her simple summer dress looked like something a normal person would wear on any other regular old day. Addison found it refreshing.

"Oh, you poor dear!" Sapphire called to her. "However, then, did you learn to prepare for social events and gatherings such as these?"

The spunky brunette fought back a laugh, but her brown eyes still showed it. "I learned everything you could possibly need to know about attending Royal functions from watching the *Princess Diaries*. Queen Clarisse is like a Royal Jedi-Ninja Master. I took lots of notes." She winked.

Only a few of the girls laughed. The rest of them frowned at her.

Addison cocked his head, not at all sure who this girl was. "Excuse me if I'm being rude," he crossed the room to speak with her, "but I don't think I recognize you from the guest list."

"Oh no, you wouldn't," the girl quickly explained, "I'm actually just visiting Tarsurella. I'm here at the palace on a trip with my parents, as a graduation gift. A few days ago I heard about this fundraiser the King is doing, to open up tickets to the public for your ball, in order to raise money for the homeless in Tarsurella. I thought it would be a really, uh, interesting opportunity, so I bought a ticket. I was about to fly home this morning, when last night someone invited me to this little shindig. So, yeah, that's my slightly long and uninteresting backstory."

"Lovely accent," Sapphire shot a sarcastic arrow in the girl's direction. "Tarsurella is changing so swiftly; it's hard to keep up, isn't it? Apparently, now American tourists can buy a lucky lottery ticket to fawn over Prince Addison for a day— what a charming little marketing plan!"

The American was all too aware of the shot of venom coming from Sapphire's ruthless jab. Several other girls in the room turned their slithery grins upward in agreement. The outnumbered American couldn't help but feel that she had been thrown into a pit of sparkly snakes. "Personally, I thought that a benefit to raise money for the homeless community in Tarsurella was a great idea. I'm sure I'm not the only American who finds it bitterly ironic, that one of the wealthiest nations in the world tragically allows two-and-a-half percent of their population to be homeless and hungry as they roam drug-infested streets. Meanwhile, an abundance of Tarsurellian teens are spending thousands of dollars on their newest designer dresses and paying their uppity governesses."

Addison almost smiled. The young woman's comment of retaliation was brilliant. Addison was presently surprised to hear the passion behind her complaint. "I'm sorry, I didn't catch your name?"

"Vanessa." Her hazel eyes met his gaze. She placed uncertain hands in her flowery pockets, then removed them again, trying to remain respectful. All at once she remembered to state her last name, "Bennett."

"It sounds as if you've done a lot of research about our homeless crisis," he marveled. "What sparked your interest in Tarsurella's humanitarian work?"

"I wouldn't say that I am intrigued by the work you guys are doing, but more like the shamefully embarrassing *lack* of it." Vanessa's reply was cold, "I'm puzzled by the fact that such a wealthy nation hasn't done more to provide answers for and assist those who so vitally need them."

"My, my!" Sapphire gasped, "Those are some lofty opinions from a girl who lives in a country that is *nineteen-trillion* dollars in debt."

"Girls, please!" a girl named Lilly Chesterfield spoke up. Addison recognized her.

Lilly's fair skin was sprinkled with freckles, and her blazing red hair framed her lovely face. "Let's not get into a heated game of 'my country is better than your country'," Lilly laughed. "We are not the sum of the choices our countries make. *But,* I'm sure we are all confident of the fact that Prince Addison is going to do a fantastic job leading Tarsurella. In fact, let's have a toast! To Prince Addison, and the beautiful future that is in store for him and his nation!"

Addison smiled at Lilly, impressed with the gentle yet firm way she changed the subject. Addison had known Lilly for many years. Their parents had been longtime friends. Lilly lived at Chesterfield Manner, a spectacular horse farm just several miles down the road. Their family was known for breeding the most beautiful and strongest thoroughbreds in all of Tarsurella. Lilly had chatted with Addison at many local horse events in the community, such as races and polo matches. Lilly possessed a certain zest and excitement for life, horses, and being outdoors. With a sudden pang, Addison realized that Lilly reminded him far too much of his mother.

Chapter 3 – Paperwork and Papercuts

Hanson Fletcher took a deep breath, attempting to calm his shook-up nerves. His morning had been stressful, to say the very least.

The surprise encounter with his father was shockingly unexpected. It rattled his confidence. After exiting the alleyway, he anxiously raced to the bus stop, concerned that he was now running severely late. But a far greater worry than a tardy slip plagued his mind. The safety of his mother might be in jeopardy.

Hanson could only hope that the morbid man would leave town quietly, without paying her a visit. He desperately wished that he could stay home, lock the doors, and ensure her safety; but he knew what his mother would say if he showed up back home...

..."Hanson Fletcher, how dare you throw your career away over a measly little threat?" He could hear her imaginary voice in his mind.

Hanson's once-in-a-lifetime job opportunity was like a golden ticket to destiny. After too many years of eating canned food and tasteless blocks of surplus cheese provided by the Tarsurellian government, the cruel hand of poverty was about to be lifted from their home. Hanson's struggling mother deserved more than minimum wage and second-hand shopping. After many Christmases with nothing under the tree, cold winters not being able to pay the heat bills, and occasional apartment evictions, it was time for things to change. Hanson wanted more than anything to give his mother the life she deserved; a life of financial security and peace of mind. His job at the palace would provide exactly that. If he threw away his shining, new career over a nagging fear that might only turn out to be smoke and mirrors, both

Hanson and his mother would be worse off than ever before.

Hanson shook his head of black hair, attempting to clear his mind. He had to focus on the task at hand, his first day of work.

The double-decker bus had dumped him off, along with a group of young school children, at The Palace parking lot. They were still too far away from the Palace Grounds to catch a glimpse of the magnificent building. Tourists would have to walk up the steep hill, wait for the tram, or rent a bike in the nearby Welcome Center.

Excited little third-graders chatted, squealed and laughed, thrilled to have the opportunity to tour the legendary castle. Hanson remembered the day when his third-grade class was treated to the very same outing. The thought brought an almost-smile to his face. It had been a monumental day in his eight-year-old life, exploring the impressive home of the beloved Royals. His classmates were gifted with souvenirs from The Palace Gift Shop, and Hanson still treasured his miniature toy version of the castle. Never in his wildest dreams could he have imagined, that someday he would have the honor of working here.

Upon leaving the bus, Hanson quickly leapt into action, weaving through the crowds, to finally approach the gated "Employees Only" entrance. He was instructed to scan his badge. From there, he was deemed permission to use a palace golf-cart to ride up the hilly terrain ahead.

He quickly buzzed up the hill, eager to fly past the maple trees, colorful gardens, and elaborate lawn theming. A boyish excitement gripped his heart. Hanson knew he was only seconds away from catching a glimpse of Tarsurella's finest architectural treasure. He knew what the ancient castle looked like, having seen it on postcards, flyers, and on his third-grade field trip; but no matter how many previous exposures to this grand monument he had in the past, nothing prepared him for the whimsical sense of wonder and awe that cascaded over him once more.

All at once it stood before him. The regal castle stretched heavenward, with pointy watch towers piercing into the clouds. The strong, slim towers saluted with a patriotic spirit, proudly bursting forth from the strong structure. Tarsurellian flags danced in the breeze, like fingertips brushing the heavens. The ancient, white-washed stone stood four stories high, tastefully decorated with medieval windows. The original stone structure was one of the oldest fortresses in Europe. Over the years, The Palace had been renovated and built upon, causing it to grow in both width and height. The front yards had been tailored for tourist appeal, decorated with flowing fountains and fancy gardens.

But Hanson didn't have time to stop and snap pictures. He continued driving his cart to the back of the building, following the signs toward "Security Parking."

Once he found it, he opened a side door reading, "Employees Only," and jogged down a flight of stairs that led him to a carpeted basement. Once his shoe left the bottom step, he was in a large lobby. This sub-level area was a sophisticated space, completely dedicated to the hundreds of palace employees.

A small line of new recruits stood patiently at the front desk, waiting for their instructions. Hanson joined the crowd and breathed a sigh of relief. He had made it on time, with three minutes to spare.

A few moments later, he was ushered into a private boardroom, where he met his Commander, the Head of Royal Security, Jackson Hudson. The man dressed in black sported a stylish bald-spot in the center of his grey hair. Jackson welcomed the new recruits, reminded them of important rules, and handed out their assignments.

"Hanson Fletcher," Jackson handed Hanson a thick manila folder. "We believe you are one of the finest recruits we've ever seen come from the Academy. We were quite blown away by your impressive accomplishments, and everything you've achieved at such a young age. We've never seen anyone this young perform at your level before. We're very excited about your future, and couldn't be more thrilled to have you here on our team. I've assigned you to a case that is very near and dear to my heart, and I'm sure you'll know, by the very nature of this assignment, how much trust I'm placing in you."

"Thank you, Commander," Hanson nodded respectfully.

Hanson opened the file, astonished to see the words:

HANSON FLETCHER: SECURITY, SECTOR A
PERSONAL SECURITY ASSIGNMENT: PRINCESS
CHASITY

He never could have expected such a massive assignment, so soon. People worked their whole lives with only the whisper of a hope of ever getting into Security Sector A. Being entrusted with a personal security assignment for the Royal Family was no small task. He knew the weight of this responsibility. Protecting the Princess would be his number one priority.

"This is a lofty assignment, but we believe you are well-equipped to do it," Commander Jackson spoke words of faith into the newbie. "I'm sure you are well aware of all the rules concerning your interactions with the Princess, but just to be sure that we make things perfectly clear, we have a short video presentation describing in detail what you are agreeing to when you sign this contract. If, after watching this video, you agree to our terms and conditions, we have some paper work for you to fill out. Then we'll bring you upstairs to meet the Princess."

"Yes sir." Hanson nodded.

An hour-and-a-half later, Hanson signed his sloppy signature on the dotted line. His hand cramped up. Thankfully, his mountain of paperwork was now completed. He collected the variety of papers spread across the small table and attempted to put them back in order.

A young man seated beside him, who appeared to be about the same age, collected his papers as well. "Whew, glad that part is over!" He flopped his right hand around in the air to add dramatic affect to his statement, "I think I just signed my whole life away!"

Hanson laughed. He had to agree. The thirty-three pages of paperwork had been intense. "Actually, we did."

"Lance Carpenter," the floppy-haired young man held out a hand. "I'll be working in Security Sector A. You?"

"Hanson Fletcher." Hanson stood up, ready to take his contract of agreement and place it on Commander Jackson's desk. "And, same." Hanson reached an uncertain hand behind his neck, "Looks like we've got our work cut out for us. Not much freedom after signing these papers."

"I know, right?!" Lance agreed, "Gone are the days of sleeping in until ten-thirty! But hey, at least we still get to eat what we want, you know? If they tried to take my tater-tots away, I might have had to turn the job down."

Hanson laughed. He found Jackson's desk and handed over the papers. Lance was right behind him.

"Thank you, Mr. Fletcher," Jackson nodded respectfully. "It's an honor to have you both on our team. Come upstairs, and I'll introduce you to Her Royal Highness."

Eighteen-year-old Princess Chasity resisted the urge to flop stomach-first onto her cozy window seat. The grey fluffy pillows were calling her name. Her favorite time of day had arrived. The hour in which her tutor, Miss Christy, excused her to return to her bedroom, to read a classical novel on her own. The rare luxury of sitting in her sunny bay window was a treat that she enjoyed far too much. She felt like an introverted kitty-cat as she crawled into the seat and soaked in the warm, beaming sunrays.

She sighed happily. She opened her book and allowed the words to transport her to a celestial place of bliss. With her bedroom door securely shut, she was confident that the next hour would be spent in silence. Her chatty little sister, Jillian, was nowhere to be seen. As much as Chasity adored the girl, sharing a bedroom with her could be a bit exasperating at times. Jillian was a bubbly socialite. She thrived on human connection, late night conversations, and hearing herself talk. Chasity respected the fact that her little sister took after Bridget; a flamboyant extravert who got her energy from being around other people. But Chasity wasn't cut from the same social cloth. She needed her space. She had a strange love for quietness. She was a deep thinker and needed moments like these to read and recharge.

Believing Jillian was still in lessons with Miss Christy, Chasity wiggled deeper into the pillows, taking advantage of her sister's absence and embracing the moment of stillness.

All at once the bedroom door opened. Chasity's head snapped up. She felt like a grumpy polar bear being disturbed from her deep winter's nap of hibernation and soul refreshment.

Jillian bounded into their large bedroom.

"Back already?" Chasity asked. She tried not to sound too rude.

Jillian's excited Golden Retriever, lovingly named "Mr. Darcy," followed her in. Darcy's paws pranced across the wooden floors, through the small kitchenette attached to their bedroom, and straight to the red water dish with his name engraved on it.

"I'm heading out for a jog. I need to hurry though, thanks to Lance who *insists* that I be back in time for dance lessons with Mrs. Gram. The guy is so uptight!" Jillian's voice was notably irritated.

"Our new guards are a piece of work, aren't they?" Chasity replied. "Hanson's been like my shadow the entire morning."

"Speaking of our new guards, where is yours?" Jillian opened the closet and hung up Darcy's leash.

"He was called down to the Main Office for his lunch break." She sighed as she glanced at the clock. She knew his break was nearly over. Her moments of precious alone time were quickly evaporating.

Jillian walked over to the small kitchen area, opened the pantry door, and grabbed a water bottle. "Jackson says we need to be patient with them," she called out. "I promised I'd try, but they're so overbearing!"

"At least you were assigned a guard older than you. Mine appears to be around the same age. But in teenager years, an eighteen-year-old boy calculates to acting about age, mmm... subtract six," she pursed her pink lips together, "thirteen."

"I dunno, Chas," Jillian smiled mischievously, moving to the small sink. Jillian filled up her water bottle. "It might not be all bad that Hanson is around the same age as you. He's kinda cute."

Chasity felt her jaw drop. "Jillian!" She was shocked to hear that her little sister would be finding anyone in the male species attractive. Surely she was far too young to be thinking like that!

At that very moment, Hanson announced that he was at the door. Jillian shrugged as if to say, "Just think about it," then turned on her heel for the great outdoors.

As Hanson entered, Chasity wished Jillian hadn't said what she did. Truth was, she *had* found the young man attractive. His chocolate-brown eyes smiled at her from beneath his lightly tanned skin, and his dark black hair wisped gently over his ears. When he smiled, though it was a rarity, she was sure she saw a trace of hidden dimples. He had a childish innocence and joy that danced in his eyes, even though he wore a serious look on his face. He looked quite sharp as he walked across the room dressed in a black suit and tie, yet struck a casual chord of youthfulness with his hands dug into his pockets. Chasity hadn't allowed her mind to dwell on the fact that he was handsome, before this, because, well, he was her *security guard*. And that was just weird. She averted her eyes from him and turned back to her book. Okay, he was cute. Handsome even. She could admit that much. But she would not allow her mind to give him any more than that. He was working for her. And having a crush on staff would be awkward, bizarre, and just totally wrong. They could be friends, if he wanted to, but nothing more.

He sat down beside her on the window seat without saying a word, perhaps a bit too close for comfort. She tried her very hardest to become enraptured with her book, but Hanson's lingering presence was a great challenge to ignore. He twiddled his thumbs, sighed, twiddled them in the opposite direction, and began making popping noises. Yes, he was chewing gum.

"Um," Chasity looked up from her book, unable to focus, "do you mind?"

Hanson appeared confused, not understanding her request. She scooted several inches away from him, hoping that the gesture would not appear rude. He didn't seem at all phased by it, and continued staring forward into space, chewing his gum.

"Please," she said this time, "I'm trying to read."

"Oh!" Hanson's eyes lit up, as though this time he understood. "Sorry, Your Highness." He spit out his gum in the wrapper and stuffed it in his pocket.

Hanson was relieved that the first half of his day at work had gone so smoothly. But now, as he sat here in a flowery window-seat beside the Princess, he wondered if each day was going to be like this one. Long and boring. Was his assignment truly to just sit here and watch her read? *The worst thing that could happen*, Hanson thought, *is she gets a papercut*.

Surely the job would include more than just this. Right?

After years of underground training at the Security Academy, he knew he was preparing for an exciting future. A unique existence. One that all Tarsurellian boys dreamed about, but only a small population of men ever experienced. A job filled with action, adventure, and suspense. He had been trained to track down bad guys, battle against ninja war-lords, defuse bombs, and jump through laser beams. But they never mentioned anything about sitting around, doing absolutely nothing.

For one quick, forbidden moment, Hanson wondered if his dad had been right. Were they too much alike? Would he grow tired of this job, and crave something greater? Could fulfilling his twisted mission and loading up his bank account with an unfathomable amount of money give Hanson and his mom the life they always dreamed about?

Hanson wanted to smack himself for entertaining such a thought. Suddenly, Hanson realized why this job could potentially be maddening—it might allow him way too much quiet time to think. If Princess Chasity intended on reading for hours every afternoon, Hanson would be left alone with his thoughts. The idea made him squirm.

"Would you care for a book of your own?" Chasity suddenly asked, breaking in to disrupt Hanson's inner anxiety.

"No, thank you, Your Highness," he replied.

"I just thought that, perhaps, you may wish for something to do," she spoke quietly. "We don't get a lot of excitement around here. Books can help spice things up a bit!" She laughed.

He shook his head again, "I've never been one for books, Your Highness." He may have said too much. A guard wasn't allowed to express his personal opinions to the Royal Family. He must remember his place. After watching the intense video and signing his life away this morning, the reality was more real than ever. His mission was to be like a fly on a wall. Seen, but not heard, and easily forgotten about.

If the Princess was offended by his voiced opinion she surely did not show it. "Not fond of books?" she sounded surprised. "Why, I can't even begin to imagine what my life would be like without books! The written word causes you to transcend time and geographical locations! Boundaries are broken and every limit is shattered, as suddenly the reader finds herself in an entirely new world!"

Hanson didn't reply. Chasity realized that he was completely un-interested, and so she returned to her wonderful world of reading.

Chapter 4 – Lunch with the Prince

Prince Addison left the Courting Room with a desperate sigh of relief. He had survived the circus.

"Slight change in plans," Deborah told him, "your father has requested that you join him in the Throne Room. He's meeting with the locals today, and would like you to shadow him."

Addison nodded in agreement, "Absolutely."

Over the past few weeks, the King had been requesting that Addison shadow him more often; in board meetings, press conferences, and hearings with the locals. Addison had been theoretically studying and preparing for these scenarios on paper for years, but being right in the middle of them gave him a new and experiential perspective on the reality that would soon be his. In just a few short weeks, Addison would be completely responsible for the entire Kingdom.

The King had always placed his people first, and Addison deeply admired him for that. The King had an extensive list of duties. Caring for his nation meant endless problem solving. He had to keep a balance in the Tarsurellian economy. International relations and maintaining world peace were all on his daily "to-do" list. Protection from terror attacks, improving public school education, defending farmer's rights, and seeing to it that the nation didn't rebel against the Crown, were all part of a hard day's work. Yet, in spite of all these pressing matters on his agenda, the King strived to stay focused on what truly mattered—people.

Tarsurella had an ancient tradition of opening its palace doors to meet with the locals every few months, at least six days out of the year. Everyone who wished to come and speak with The King was invited to share their thoughts, ideas, requests, and desires for a better tomorrow. Addison found that his father's people truly trusted him, because he listened to what they had to say. The fact that he cared was evident. The bond between the King and his loyal nation was unbreakable. Addison could only hope that someday the people would trust him just as much.

This morning, the line to meet with the King spread out of the Throne Room and down the long hall into the West Wing of The Palace. It continued into the foyer, past the front desk, down The Grand Staircase, and into the entrance hall. Hopeful citizens had lined up at the front gate hours before dawn.

Addison sat beside his father, who occupied the ancient throne. Each arm of the regal chair boasted brass images of a roaring lion. Every time Addison entered this room, he could feel the history of his ancestors come alive. The Throne Room had been remarkably preserved and cared for, and really served no purpose other than for Royal nostalgia, Kingdom pride, and fancy press conferences. Still, Addison relished every moment spent in it.

The first in line were ushered in by several security guards. Although they never had issues with visitors in the past, they knew better than to let their guard down.

A man stood at the front of the line in a pair of tall cowboy boots. A faded cowboy hat hid part of his face, as he slowly rocked his way forward to approach the King. He carried a lamb in his arms, which he gave to a staff member in charge of receiving the Royal gifts.

Each visitor would bring a gift, paying homage to His Royal Majesty. Some would bring money, jewels, or gold, and others brought livestock, or gifted horses to the Royal Stables.

The man removed his hat, bowed respectfully, and uttered, "Your Majesty, you have no idea how honored I am to be here, meet'n you like this. You see, I'm an honest hardworking fellow. Ain't never stole anything a day in my life. But nowadays, hard work don't get you very far."

Addison listened closely as the man spoke. Every citizen who entered this room had a different story. Some were poor, others rich. Some came humbly with holes in their clothes, begging for money and lavishing their praise upon the king; while others angrily huffed in, wearing their finest, demanding change, telling the King everything that was wrong with his country.

"You see, I have a wife, and a decent size farm, and a beautiful little daughter named Bella. That girl is the joy of my life. I wanna give her the world, but I'm afraid I ain't gonna be able to give her anything other than a patch of dirt, which is the land we live off of, and a whole lot of love. It's always been my dream to do something real nice and special for her. And the reason I came to you, Your Majesty, is to… is to… ask, if I might find favor in your eyes, to do something special for my daughter."

The King smiled, even though his heart ached. The sad stories that reached his ears were endless. It seemed that everybody always needed *something*. Some came to him out of pure desperation, and others with dishonest motives hoping to receive an easy handout. The King tried to offer his services to those who needed them the most, and this man appeared to be genuine. Of course, the King would send caseworkers to his farm, examine their living situation, their monthly finances, and make sure he really *did* have a daughter, before his request would be granted. The King explained these things to the man standing before him; and Jenna, one of the caseworkers, took his name and address, and said she'd be out to see him soon. "Soon" could range anywhere from a few weeks to a few *years*. The waiting list was tremendously long.

The man left, satisfied with his answer, and the next citizen was ushered in. A tall, dark, chocolate-toned man entered with his young son, who appeared to be about four or five. The little boy, who sported an afro, lit up as soon as he saw Addison.

It was common knowledge that oftentimes one of the Princes or Princesses would accompany the King in his morning meeting with the people. They would sign autographs or take pictures with young children who tagged along with their parents in hopes of catching a glimpse of their favorite hero or heroine.

The little boy was elated. "You're my favorite Prince!" He grinned, "I wanna be just like you when I get big!"

Addison leaped off his chair and gave him a hug, "Hi there! It's so great to meet you!" Unlike the forced smile that he had worn earlier while in the Courting Room, this smile was real. Addison loved little kids, and this boy's toothy grin brought him a rush of joy. He signed an autograph for the boy, smiled for a flashing camera, and spoke with the child's father.

"We've stood in line for hours, waiting to meet you." The man spoke with a grin nearly as bright as his son's, "Today's Javon's Birthday. He's gonna remember this day for the rest of his life."

Addison leaned down to talk to the boy, who hadn't stopped smiling, "Happy Birthday Javon! How old are you today?"

"Six," the little boy spoke, but thanks to some of his missing teeth, the word came out "Thix."

Addison couldn't help but smile harder. Something about little kids always got to him. It didn't take long for them to get him wrapped around their little fingers. As a matter of fact, Millie had it down to an art form. There were days that Addison could do without the fainting girls, but he never grew tired of the little kids who looked up to him. That alone was enough to make him endure, and brush off all the other "thorns in his side" that came from being popular.

"How would you like to hang around The Palace today?" Addison asked. "You can see what it's really like in the life of a Prince. We've got a pretty sweet Birthday Package that includes a V.I.P. tour of The Palace, a meal and cake in The Royal Restaurant, a musical performance in The Royal Theater, and—"

If Javon was excited before, this suggestion sent the little guy through the roof. "For real!?"

Javon's father spoke with concern in a quite tone, "Um, Your Majesty, we don't really have the money right now to do all that."

"No problem," Addison smiled, "I'll take care of it. Deborah, would you please show Javon to The Royal Fashion Studio for his new princely look, and give him the V.I.P. birthday treatment?"

Javon's brown eyes grew wider with every passing second.

Deborah was pleased with Addison's great generosity. "Of course," she summoned the little boy, "follow me, right this way, sir."

"Then have Javon and his father join me for lunch on the terrace," Addison added. "That way we can get to know each other better." He patted Javon on the back, and the little boy let out a victory hoot.

"All right!" he shouted, jumping up and pumping his fists into the air.

Deborah's eyes gazed at Addison approvingly. *Tarsurella has nothing to worry about,* she thought. *Addison will make a splendid King.*

Addison slipped on his sunglasses before approaching the folks waiting for him on the terrace. Little Javon, who was stuffing his mouth full with french-fries and chicken fingers, looked up and his eyes smiled. Javon's dad appeared just as pleased, though Addison poured out his apologies for being late. He hated to keep people waiting.

"Hey man," Addison placed a friendly arm on Javon's small shoulder, "sorry our meeting ran late. How's your day been so far?"

"Awesome!" Javon offered two eager thumbs up, and Addison laughed.

Deborah scurried in. "Prince Addison, one of the young ladies you met with earlier this morning won't be flying out until tomorrow. Vanessa Bennett will be staying at The Palace longer than she anticipated. Would it be too much to ask if the young American may join you for lunch?"

Addison resisted a groan rising from deep within. His staff was trying just a *bit* too hard.
Addison nodded despite his annoyance, "You guys don't mind, do you?" Addison checked with Javon first.

After a reassuring "Nope!" from the boy, Addison spoke,

"Yes, Deborah, that will be fine. You can escort her in."

Deborah scuttled out of the scene, returning shortly with Vanessa Bennett.

Addison stood up to honor her presence, as he was taught to do with all female visitors. He removed his shades, then nodded and greeted her with a smile, "Hello, again."

Vanessa failed to curtsey or bow, and instead approached him with a smile of her own, "Hey."

Vanessa took a deep breath, and looked around her as Addison invited her to take a seat. She could scarcely believe this. Here she was, sitting on the terrace of The Palace, surrounded by enchanting garden scenery, with the *Prince* of Tarsurella.

What began as her desire to help the homeless had turned into something far more exciting. Here she was with possibly one of the most influential people in the world!

The current moment, as uncommon and unthinkable as it was, had all been made possible by her generous parents. Vanessa had been blessed with a special graduation gift from her family—a tour of the Palace of Tarsurella. For the Bennett family, European vacations didn't happen every summer. In fact, this was Vanessa's first time *ever* out of the United States.

While preparing for her highly-anticipated European trip, she did lots of research over the summer. Vanessa was a history buff, and thoroughly enjoyed studying Tarsurella's past. But while digging up Tarsurella's history, Vanessa also discovered some frustrating realities about this present-day monarchy. They had a humanitarian crisis on their hands.

It angered Vanessa to learn that this Royal Family flew private planes and hosted extravagant parties; meanwhile, homeless children went to bed on the streets just several blocks away! She read about the pounds of leftover food from the Royal Restaurant thrown into the dumpster each night, and Vanessa was furious with the waste. She was determined to make her trip to Tarsurella matter. And so, when she learned of the tickets being sold to Prince Addison's Coronation in order to raise funds for the homeless, Vanessa decided she wanted to support that cause. She would fly back again in a few weeks and think of some way to make her voice heard. Perhaps she would create a petition online, daring the jet-set Prince to abandon his family's frivolous expenses and spend their funds on those who actually needed them the most. She didn't know what she was going to do, but she would come up with something. Be it protesting with neon signs or wearing convicting T-Shirts, Vanessa was determined to take action. She would brainstorm something that perhaps might catch the attention of the press, and even of the Royals themselves.

But now, in a wild turn of events, Vanessa had the future King's ear. She didn't need to create a sign or jump up and down in order to get his attention. She was sitting here, eating *lunch* with him!

As if last night's invitation to meet with the Prince in the morning had been surprising enough, she was even more shocked when Deborah insisted that she join Addison again for a meal.

Despite all her previous plans, Vanessa couldn't seem to come up with a single good idea. What should she say to him now? In fact, Vanessa was having trouble coming up with anything much to speak at all.

Addison joked playfully with Javon, who replied with wide eyes in-between mouthfuls of his food. She smiled at the cute kid and his proud, beaming father. Deborah had previously explained that Addison was entertaining Javon as part of his "charity work."

Addison glanced Vanessa, noticing that she hadn't been contributing to the conversation. Earlier she had spoken with such passion and fervor. Why was she suddenly acting so shy?

"How's your stay been at The Palace?" Addison asked, "Have you been to The Royal Restaurant? Does it compare to American cuisine?"

Vanessa's eyes grew wide. "Are you kidding? The food is amazing! I've never tasted anything quite like it. And, since you guys are such clean eaters, I'm pretty confident that it's not loaded with growth hormones, preservatives, and all sorts of nasty stuff like we have in the States."

"So there is something that you approve of in Tarsurella after all," Addison grinned teasingly.

"Of course," Vanessa's gaze softened. "Listen, I'm sorry if I came across as too harsh earlier. Sometimes I drive my parents crazy. I'm just really, um…passionate. At times I can get a little out of hand. I don't know how to explain it, or why I get so worked up, but I actually believe that one person can, if they truly want to, change the world. And I get super irritated when I see people wasting their lives and squandering their amazing God-given potential as human beings."

"Do you think I am?" Addison asked. "Wasting my life, I mean, living less than my potential?"

"Wow," Vanessa was surprised that he would ask such a question, "do you want the truth?"

"Of course," he replied simply.

Vanessa took a deep breath, "The United States media makes you out to be, oh, how should I put this nicely? A spoiled, European brat. In the U.S., you only make headlines because of your new Ferrari, or when you launched your latest line of crazy expensive tuxedos. Not to mention, your toxic perfume line! But they've never talked about this side of you–the Prince who spends his afternoon hanging out with the less fortunate and makes a little boy's dreams come true. Until today, I had not seen this part of you. Now that I've seen both sides, I'm not sure which to believe."

"I would like to think," Addison replied thoughtfully, "that I am *much* more the guy that you're seeing here today, than whatever distorted, self-absorbed image the press is making me out to be."

"Maybe you are," Vanessa said, "I just haven't made up my mind yet."

"Will you let me know when you do?" Addison asked.

Vanessa nodded with a small smile, surprised that the Prince was so down-to-earth and easy to talk to, "Of course." She quickly changed the subject, realizing that the conversation had fallen quiet. "So, tell us Prince Addison, what do you do in a normal day at The Palace? How do you spend your time and energy?"

"Yeah!" Javon piped up, "Tell us! Uh, can we eat ice cream after this?"

Addison laughed, "Sure thing. Just ring for our butler." He winked, before turning to Vanessa, "Well, today I'm spending the day shadowing my dad, which I guess I've been doing a lot of lately. After this, we'll be meeting with the Go Green

Committee, and then we have a meeting with our Royal Security Team. Then..."

Chapter 5 - Looking for Normal

Princess Bridget pushed her way through the doors into The Royal Fashion Studio. Now she was standing in the domain of Victoria Stefan, their head tailor and wardrobe manager. Bridget adored hanging out in Victoria's studio. Bridget had an unquenchable passion for fashion and enjoyed splurging on new accessories just as much as the next girl, but as a Princess, she couldn't just hop in her car and drive down to the mall. She attempted to do so once and was nearly crushed beneath the frenzied mob of berserk shoppers. If it wasn't for her security guards, she might not have made it home in one piece! As much as Bridget was devoted to the art of putting together a superb outfit, it wasn't worth risking her life over a new scarf.

The in-palace Fashion Studio helped bring a chunk of the mall into the cozy comforts of their own home. Bridget's professional shoppers purchased hundreds of possible clothing options for Bridget each month, allowing her to leaf through them; deciding what to keep, and what to get rid of. Bridget tried to embrace every perk of her Royal title, and not focus so much on the overwhelming negatives that frowned at her. In some sort of pretend way, she got to "shop" like any other teen girl, but Bridget was confident that it could never be the same as going to the mall with her friends.

Sometimes she felt like she was stuck in one of those modern Disney Channel Movies, the cliché coming of age tale where a winsome teenage girl wished she could live the life of someone else. She had seen them all…the popstar wanted to be an average girl, the average girl wanted to be a popstar, the book worm who wanted to be a mermaid, the mermaid who wants to be a real girl, bla, bla, blah. Bridget knew that her unique lot in life was predestined and determined by God. In the same way that she couldn't change her eye color, her skin tone, or the terribly off-tune voice that came out when she sang karaoke, she couldn't change the fact that she was a Princess. In each of those movies, the grass was never greener on the other side of the fence. And once the heroine spent a whole sixty minutes enjoying her fish-out-of-water experience, something went terribly wrong, and she would realize that she was foolish to wish for anything other than what she already had.

Bridget knew the ending, and she realized it was probably true for her life as well. Yet, as silly and immature as it was to daydream about life in the "real world," Bridget couldn't help but fantasize. She would give up so much just to know what it was like to walk into a room without being noticed. To enter a coffee shop and talk to the cute cashier without making national headlines. To stroll through the downtown district without buff security guards on her trail, while antique browsing and window shopping. Oh, the unimaginable joys of going to the mall with her besties, ordering cheesy fries, then snapping selfies together in *Forever21*! But the nineteen-year-old would never taste of those simple luxuries.

"Bridget!" Victoria greeted with her usual high-strung energy, "looking gorgeous as usual, pray you had a lovely time in Paris, absolutely enchanting, okay let's get about business! We still must choose between the crème lace evening gown and the stunning violet number. You look gorgeous in the crème, my dear, but the purple is more majestic, matching the mood of the occasion. I fear we shall never choose! Please darling, try them both on and model the runway, so that we may make the best decision."

Before Bridget could object, she was already being scooted toward the dressing rooms.

"Princess Bridget, this crème dress is just about the most beautiful thing I've ever laid eyes on." Shay, her cinnamon-skinned stylist and wardrobe consultant, leaned over to whisper in her ear, "I think you should wear this one to The Ball."

Bridget looked lovingly at the beautiful dress hanging on the rack, "I'm quite partial to it myself as well. Victoria wants me to try it on again and model it."

"Well then, hurry up girl, I'm just itch'n to see you in it again! Don't dally!" She closed the dressing room door behind her, and Bridget found herself standing alone in the large room with her dress. Mirrors surrounded her on all four walls. She slipped off her jeans and sweatshirt.

"Princess," Shay called from outside the door, "You've had three young fellows try to call you since last night. James O'Conner of England, Brandon Frasier of France, and Boneset Renaldo of France. They each left personal messages, about being absolutely enchanted by you, wishing to get to know you better, and wanting to escort you to your next shindig. Would you care to respond to any of their calls?"

Bridget sighed, slipping the gown over her head, "No thank you, Shay."

"Not even James?" Shay's brown eyes sparkled as Bridget opened the door, "My, he was a *fine* one."

"I'm just not ready to start a courtship again," Bridget explained. "Tell each of them that I greatly appreciate their thoughtfulness, but am much too busy, and my schedule won't allow it."

"Yes, ma'am." Shay nodded. "My, oh my, that dress fits you to a T."

"Thanks, Shay," Bridget smiled as she examined the dress in

the mirror. She anxiously pulled her blonde, bouncy curls upward, wondering what style she might try the night of her brother's ball. Her thick lashes fluttered as her blue eyes blinked. "The material is gorgeous. Victoria has completely outdone herself. Again."

Shay nodded in agreement, then gave her a quick briefing of her schedule for the day, "You have a photoshoot with *Elle* magazine, an interview with *Popstar* magazine, a fitting for your next premiere party in the States, and then six o'clock dinner as usual."

Bridget nodded, "Very well."

"Now scurry your little self over to the runway!" Shay urged her. "Victoria is on a tight time schedule. There's so much to be done before the Coronation."

"We're ready for you, Princess!" Victoria called. "Lights! Cue the music!"

A spotlight from above centered on her as the ceiling lights dimmed. A preppy, upbeat song with a strong beat filled the air. She strutted down the narrow catwalk, knowing the perfect time to turn, stop, and twirl. She had been doing this since she could walk. She knew the drill. She always gave Victoria exactly what she asked for on the runway. Several photographers snapped cameras with oversize lenses and monstrous flashes, so that Victoria could review the outfit again later.

From the catwalk, Bridget could see Victoria and several consultants talking amongst themselves, discussing how the dress ebbed and flowed. Would it do for The Ball? It was classy and elegant. Did they need something more bold and flashy? They studied to see if the design would pass Victoria's test. She wanted only her most fabulous work displayed for occasions such as this. Once Bridget wore the one-of-a-kind gown, every young maiden in the land would rush out to buy their own, less expensive version of the show stopper. Victoria Stefan was one of the most popular fashion designers in Tarsurella. The simple fact that the Royal Family wore her designs had sky-rocketed her labels to fame.

From her elevated position on the catwalk, Bridget spotted her best friend Kitty Kittredge. She wanted to wave, but she knew Victoria would frown upon such behavior. So she waited patiently until her run was over.

The music ended, lights filled the room, and Bridget scurried down the steps to embrace her friend.
"That dress is *gorgeous!*" Kitty complemented her after their hug, her green eyes open wide with excitement. "So how was Paris? I'm so jealous I couldn't go. Tell me everything!"

"I've got to keep moving," Bridget explained, heading toward the dressing rooms, "I still have to model another dress. I'll tell you about it over tea?"

Kitty nodded, satisfied with her answer, "Great! I'll tell Bailee!"

Kitty and Bailee had been Bridget's closest friends, ever since Kindergarten. As her hired handmaidens, the young girls were chosen to play with Her Royal Highness. When her handmaidens turned twelve, they were released from their Royal duties, but Bridget remained close with them. She couldn't imagine what life would be like without her two closest companions.

"Sounds like a plan!" She squeezed Kitty's hand before closing the dressing room door between them. "See you then!"

The tea table had been prepared for the ladies in the East Garden. A wicker table was dressed in lace cloth and adorned with a tea set, hand-painted with delicate pink posies. The precious tea set was a family treasure. It had been passed down for three generations prior, and was the late Queen's favorite.

The scene was a lovely little sight to behold. The gentle waterfall gurgled and whooshed in the background, as birds chirped playfully, singing their sweet end-of-summer songs. Surrounded by roses which climbed the brick walls, the terrace was enclosed with just the perfect amount of shade for an afternoon get-together. A dainty plate of petit fours, delicate Queen's cakes, ham sandwiches, and chocolate-covered strawberries were brought out on a silver platter to the young ladies, carried in the steady hand of Monsieur Michael, their faithful waiter.

"Merci beaucoup, Monsieur," Bridget smiled thankfully. Monsieur Michael bowed upon leaving, but left a silver bell to be rung in case they further needed his services.

The Princess sat alone, as she poured herself a cup of hot tea and scooped a lump of sugar into her cup. The head security guard, Jackson, stood a short distance from the table, keeping his careful watch on the Princess.

A voice came through Jackson's headset, announcing the coming presence. Jackson broadcasted the news: "Princess," he properly gave warning to their entrance, "Miss Kitty Kittredge, and Miss Bailey Kittredge."

She heard the sound of high heels approaching on the stone terrace. She turned around to greet her friends with a smile. "I'm so glad you two could come!"

"So are we!" Bailee gave her a quick hug, followed by Kitty. The sisters shared the same big green eyes, and fair, freckled faces.

"It's about time you fit us into your schedule," Kitty poked Bridget playfully with a grin as they took their seats. "You've been much too busy running around Europe with heart-throb superstars, touring romantic cities and visiting exotic sights, while we're stuck here going to community college. Lemme tell you. College guys? Bleh."

"Is *that* how the media paints the picture of my life?" Bridget frowned, "One big exotic fairy tale of romance and luxury? I have been terribly busy, though. And I'm sorry. It's been much too long. We need to catch up."

Bailee nodded as she poured herself a cup of tea, "Don't fret about it Bridget. We completely understand don't we Kitty?"

"For sure," Kitty paused from filling her plate as she looked up, "So tell us *everything*."

Bridget laughed, "Everything? My, I wouldn't even know where to begin!"

"Begin with Paris," Kitty winked, "And James O'Conner."

Bridget looked up from her plate that she had filled with strawberries. She couldn't wait to bite into them. "What? How did you hear about–"

"Someone happened to snap a picture of you two talking at the party last night," Bailee explained calmly, "which the paparazzi got ahold of, and fabricated a story out of. All the gossip sites are buzzing."

"Yeah, it's not that hard to keep tabs on you," Kitty added. "All we have to do is a Google search. There's always a story!"

"The paparazzi needs to mind its own business!" Bridget cried out. "Can't a girl speak to a young man without assuming there must be some big story behind it? Ugh, the media can get so exhausting. Sometimes I wish they would leave me alone, for like a week. Now *that* would be luxury and bliss. But enough about me, how you girls doing? You just started college! That has to be absolutely exciting, right?"

Kitty and Bailee exchanged sisterly glances, then burst out laughing. "Yeah, right! I think absolutely *exhausting* is a better choice of words."

"Oh, come on, it can't be that bad." Bridget smiled, "I know the work load must be crazy, but there's something almost euphoric about the idea of going to college, walking around the campus, and studying with kids who share similar passions and like minds as you."

Bailee's eyebrows shot up, "Yeah, you thought the same thing about high school. Trust me, girl, you are *so* blessed that you don't have to attend a public institution to get your education. Personally, I don't find anything enchanting about classmates who swear like sailors and whistle at you every time you walk by. The only thing these kids are passionate about is partying."

"I get it," Bridget nodded, "I'm sure there are challenges involved. But I still *love* the idea of moving out, going to school, the three us getting a little apartment with a few cats as our roomies, and working as waitresses at some hole-in-the-wall café, just struggling to pay the bills."

"Says the girl who just got back from Paris because she doesn't have to pay bills or worry about money," Kitty laughed again. "You're officially crazy!"

"I'm sure the whole idea of the 'college experience' sounds fun, but trust me Bridge, you're not missing out," Bailee touched her arm reassuringly. "And you're taking courses online, right?"

"Yeah," Bridget sighed, "but that's completely different."

"Our lives are *so* boring and mundane compared to yours," Kitty whined, "so puh-leaze, let's get back to what happened in Paris last night! James, is he as cute in person as he is online? What did he say to you? What did you tell him? Does he like you? Has he asked you out?! Oh my gosh, he seems so perfect. Details! We need details, girl!"

"Kitty, chill!" Bridget snapped. "Goodness, you're just as bad as the paparazzi."

Kitty was surprised by her heated response. Yikes. Perhaps she had been pressing the wrong buttons. Both Bailee and Kitty knew that Bridget was struggling to return to her old self, after jerk-face Jacob broke her heart. But it had been six months now. Wasn't she ready to move on? Kitty wanted nothing more than to see her best friend joyful, giddy, and alive again. But clearly she was still struggling to heal.

"We're sorry if we've offended you, Bridget," Bailee apologized. "We really meant no harm."

Bridget made an effort to smile even though her heart was hurting. She knew that she couldn't take it out on her friends. "I know. It's not you.... it's just," Bridget could feel her thoughts drifting back to Jacob and all the bittersweet memories that they shared. She thought of James, and Boneset and all the other guys who lined up at the front door of her heart. No way was she letting any of them in.

"Sometimes I wish the paparazzi would find someone else to hound."

Just then, the sound of a barking dog was heard in the distance.

"It sounds as though they've found you!" Kitty laughed, humored by her own joke.

The bark was followed by the jingle of dog tags and puppy toes prancing down the terrace.

"Cue, Mr. Darcy's entrance," Jackson smiled as the Royal Golden Retriever made his presence known. Darcy greeted the girls as shockwaves of excitement flowed through his tail. His wet nose sniffed the table, detecting the desired food that was present.

"No table scraps," Bridget scolded the furry face. "Jillian has spoiled you."

"Announcing, Princess Jillian," Jackson spoke. A sweaty and exhausted figure appeared. The eleven-year-old was panting, feeling the burning in her lungs, as she leaned over with her hands on her knees, pausing to catch her breath.

"Darcy!" she called when she finally had enough air to speak. Darcy turned his head at the familiar sound of his name. "You're still faster than me!"

"Are you running from something, Princess?" Jackson asked.

"No, Jack," she responded, standing up straight, able to breathe a little bit deeper than before. "Only trying to keep up with him."

"I pity the man who tries to keep up with the both of you,"

[79]

Jackson said with a twinkle in his eye. "I've just received word that Lance has lost tabs on your location. He's stricken with panic, and nearly beside himself. He fears that I'll fire him."

Jillian tried her very best to keep a straight face, but a laugh was bubbling up inside. It was only Lance's first day on the job. But Jillian had already grown tired of his constant presence. When she decided to go for a jog with Darcy, she was determined to ditch him. Lance tried his very best to keep up with her, but Jillian had been running for years, and could easily jog several miles without feeling fatigued. Lance's forte was sprinting, excelling with quick bursts of energy, not long-distance endurance running. As she took off down one of the many winding trails stretching through The Palace grounds, he eventually lost sight of her. Jillian was secretly pleased with the fact that he was lost in her dust, but she also knew she was in no real danger. There were hidden security cameras mounted on nearly every tree. But Lance, the newbie, took his job very seriously, and the twenty-year-old feared he would be terminated before he ever had the chance to begin.

Several moments ago, Lance had made an emergency call to Jackson. "Big Daddy, this is Little Robin checking in at 3:03 p.m., do you copy?"

"What is your location Little Robin?" Jackson asked, knowing that all was well.

"Uh, sir… I mean, Big Daddy…umm, we have a massive problem. Like, a code *red* problem. I, I mean, I didn't, she did… the Princess, Jillian, uh, I mean Snow White—"

"Speak up Little Robin, you're not coming in clearly."

"I've lost Snow White! Sir, I've looked everywhere! She was just here a second ago and—"

The Main Security Center turned off their microphones as they listened to Lance's stuttering voice coming in over the intercom, and burst out in laughter. They had been watching Princess Jillian on the security cameras, and their carefully-trained eyes had seen everything that happened on the trails–Jillian's running, and Lance's frantic searching. The young man sweated and huffed, and wiped his brow. He had been building up the courage to report his loss. And now that he had, the agents cut off their audio with the young man so he would not hear their laughter. The security guards always enjoyed their front row seat from the Security Tower. Never a dull moment in The Palace!

They were amused with the new guy's antics, but didn't want to hurt the young man's pride. The experienced agents saw a younger version of themselves in Lance. They took pity on him, for they each remembered their first day working for the Royals; how nervous they'd been, and how one of the children had tried to pull the wool over their eyes too. But now, many, *many* years after their first day, each agent knew that life at The Palace only got better, and the job was never quite as terrifying as that terrible, nerve-wracking first day.

"I have the Princess in my sights," Jackson explained calmly to the fearful Lance. "Snow White's location is on the Garden Terrace."

All listening on the intercom heard a sigh of relief followed by a string of thank-you's and, "I'll never lose sight of her again, I promise!"

After a good hearty laugh, the security guards turned their microphones back on, and connected with Lance again.

"Your new security guard," Jillian spoke to Jackson, "is, oh, how can I say this nicely–a tad bit...ridiculous. This morning, he insisted on testing my hot chocolate before I drank even a sip. And he was practically breathing down my neck during lessons with Miss Christy. It was an interesting conversation when I had to explain that I was allowed to go to the bathroom by myself."

Jackson couldn't help but smile, "Lance is one of the best youngsters in his field. I hired him for this job because I believe he has great potential. You'll have to trust me on this one. I wouldn't spend time training him if I didn't believe he was worth it. He'll get the hang of it. Although, it does require patience on our part."

Jillian sighed, "Patience has never been one of my strong points. But I'll try."

"Princess, Princess!" Lance called, suddenly running up to her. The young man had beads of sweat running down his face, mixed with the long brown hair that hung over his eyes like an Old English Sheep Dog. Frequently, he shook his head to move the hair from his sight of vision. But it always fell into the place it was before. Jillian thought he could use a haircut. "You're expected inside for dance lessons with Mrs. Gram."

Jillian sighed, "Come along, Darcy."

Following Lance inside, they entered the glass-ceilinged Greenhouse Room, blooming with flowers and plants; which then led to The Main Hall. When she turned to mount the grand marble staircase Lance spoke, "Uh, Princess, I believe The Ball Room is that way." He pointed down the long hall.

"Yes Lance, I know," she responded, "But I'm going to go shower and change first."

"But the schedule says you're to be in The Ball Room at three o'clock promptly. It's three o'five."

"I'm sure I'll be forgiven if I'm a tad late. But I can't go to wardrobe looking like..." she glanced down at her sweaty shirt, "this."

A confused look played across his young face, "Are you allowed to do that?"

Jillian almost laughed. "Yes. Yes I am. Now if you'll excuse me, I'm going upstairs for my shower." Her tennis shoes began to climb the marble steps, and she heard him coming up behind her.

She twirled around and faced him firmly, "Lance, remember what we spoke of earlier this morning? The restroom is off limits." She pointed down the stairs, ordering him to, "Wait here."

He wanted to argue, but he knew better than to pick a fight with the young Princess. He was already walking on egg shells with his new job, and didn't want to make things any worse. His feet remained glued in place on the bottom step.

Chasity took a deep breath, savoring the sweet smell of the garden. Birds sang their joyful songs of exuberant praise, fluttering from tree to tree, occasionally landing on the ground and skipping across the path as they collected an essential bug or twig for their nests. Chasity walked leisurely down the shaded path, past the fragrant roses, poppies, lilacs, and forget-me-nots. Orange, yellow, red and violet flowers surrounded her on either side. With her book in hand and Hanson following closely behind, she continued down the path. Quite often, when passing through this quiet sanctuary, she remembered her mother, who called this courtyard her Eden.

Chasity was fourteen years old when the Queen had died. Her sweet memories of the nurturing woman were like a bouquet of wild-flowers she had picked and propped up in a vase on the window sill of her heart. But flowers don't last forever, and her childhood memories were slowly starting to fade as well. The memories that she cherished the most all happened in this very spot. She used to take walks with mother, as the Queen would lovingly point out every flower, tree, and bird, explaining how everything was made to worship the Creator. "When I married your father, life in The Palace was so busy!" she had told her. "We were flying around at breakneck speeds, and I had so much to adjust to. With endless demands for my attention, I felt like I was being pulled in every direction. But one afternoon, when I was feeling exhausted and stressed out, Jesus whispered to my heart, 'Come into the Garden. Get away. Spend some time with me.' So I did. Then every morning, and every evening, I would spend as much out here with Him as I could! This is my favorite place to pray and be with Him, no matter how busy life gets."

Now, Chasity felt the same way about this garden. It was her secret place to meet with God and share her innermost thoughts and feelings. Whether she was sitting quietly on the bench reading her Bible, or taking a stroll and singing quiet hymns, she always felt God's presence here.

She passed elegant fountains, which had been strategically placed by landscapers with an eye for beauty, and centuries-old, stone statues which stood in the lawn. Maintenance men on lawn mowers and gardeners with pruning scissors worked diligently to keep the courtyard looking and feeling like a glorious haven. The Royal Courtyard was an elite example to the rest of the country, demonstrating what could be possible in an elaborate dream garden. The Queen's Garden won many prizes from magazines and attention from television shows who drooled over the breath-taking environment. *Better Homes and Gardens* dubbed the Queen's Courtyard "The Most Beautiful Garden in the World!" sixteen years in a row.

Chasity passed by a small waterfall and brushed her hand through the tumbling water, allowing the refreshing wetness to soak into her skin. She crossed an adorable iron bridge, which skipped across a winding stream where large goldfish swam beneath the surface. The next part of the path wove through a maze of waterspouts shooting from the ground on every side. The water sprang up from underground, and shot into the air several feet high. Next, she passed a pond where more goldfish swam beneath the lily pads. Finally, she reached a wall where an iron, courtyard gate stood, with pink roses climbing up.

She opened it, and continued down the path to the stables. For a short while she forgot Hanson was even with her, until he spoke. "Princess? May I ask where you are going?"

She stopped in her tracks and turned to face him. His handsome features nearly took her by surprise, but she kept her voice even as she spoke. "Here's an idea. I've almost finished this book. Why don't you read a chapter or two? You must be frightfully bored, and this will help pass the time while I'm out riding." She spotted the nearest bench, "Sit here. I'll be perfectly safe. The stable hand watches out for me when I ride. I should only be about forty-five minutes or so. And who knows? You might actually enjoy the book."

He could not argue with his boss, so he regretfully sat and watched her continue down the path to the stables.

She smiled to herself as she entered the familiar barn, the first building which housed their Royal horses. The three long, rectangular-shaped buildings housed thirty-five thoroughbreds. These horses had been bred for centuries, and racing these magnificent creatures was a Tarsurellian tradition. Racing was dubbed "The Sport of Kings," but Chasity much preferred to ride them than to watch them run.

The Young Princess owned three horses of her own, and loved each of them dearly. Moss, the stable hand, greeted her just outside the first building where he was bathing several horses with a hose. "Princess," he tipped his cowboy hat, "would you like me to tack up Esmerelda?

Esmerelda was Chasity's first horse, which she received when she turned ten years old. She was a gentle, chestnut mare.

"I think I'd like to ride Nic this time," she replied. "It's been awhile."

Nicholas, her newest horse, was a high-strung stallion who proved to be her greatest challenge yet. His favorite thing to do was run, and sometimes the three-year-old would bolt unexpectedly. The staff was concerned for her safety, but Chasity knew that if anyone could help settle and tame Nic, it would be her.

A look of concern spread across Moss's face. "He bolted last time. We still haven't gentled that free-spirited foal out of him, yet. You sure you don't wanna give 'em a couple more days?"

Chasity smiled, "Aren't you the one who always says we're not to take away their free spirit, but instead direct their high-strung energy in another way? I'd like to make Nicholas my polo pony."

"Polo?!" Moss almost laughed, "Isn't that a lofty ambition for Nic? I mean, every horse has its limits."

"I know, but why not try? Nic is a special horse, I can feel it. He's got a lot of potential. I just need to spend more time with him, instead of giving him time off every time he bolts. Horses are smart. He might be onto the fact that whenever he acts crazy, he gets rewarded with more freedom. And I don't want to reward him for such behavior."

It was his turn to smile, "Okay, you're determined. There's no stopping the two of you now. Just be careful, Princess. I promised your father that I'd always put your safety first. We don't want you breaking any bones."

"Besides," Chasity added, even though she already had Moss sold on the idea, "with Addison's Coronation coming up, Father has invited guests to stay here that weekend. If the Royal British Clan is coming, I'd love to show James and his beloved Bernard that I can beat him in the sport on *any* horse. Their family has way too many bragging rights when it comes to their horses. It's time they are faced with a real challenge."

Moss laughed, "In that case, you'd better get to work right away."

Miss Gram excused the youngest of her Royal students from their dance lessons. Eight-year-old Millie felt like a lioness being released from her captivity in the zoo. She raced out of The Ball Room, eager to leap into her carefree ocean of free time.

"Millie!" Jillian called after her. "Have you forgotten what Miss Gram told you already?! Use your manners. You're a Princess, not a stampeding elephant. You cannot gallivant around here like a wild animal!"

"But I'm in a hurry!" she called back, most definitely not using her inside voice. "There are only so many hours before dinner, and then bed, and I've got *lots* to do!"

Redeeming the lost time, she went bounding up the staircase. When landing on the second floor, she didn't remain there. She continued her voyage up another flight of stairs. After kicking off her red Converse shoes, she released her feet from the restricting confinements of her socks. The red, white, and green-striped knee-high socks were left on the floor like a pile of shed snake skin.

Free at last, she pressed a big, red button on the wall which said "Do Not Press." As she did, a rope ladder descended from the ceiling. She gripped it carefully and climbed up. Once she reached the top, she pulled the ladder up behind her so that no one could follow. She had reached the secret library tower. Tall and dusty bookcases, filled with their treasures, lined every wall. But Millie did not stop there. She kept moving.

Below a bookshelf mounted on the wall was a secret hatch, which she opened. It was large enough for her to squeeze through, but an adult could not have done it. Getting down on all fours, she inched her way through the dark, dusty, passageway that connected this tower to another. Above her was the very top of the castle, where ancient knights had stood guard. She opened another hatch after reaching the end of the tunnel, and hopped into the red tubular slide which carried her into her bedroom. Millie was the only Royal who had her very own tower. The same tower, that used to be the dominion of fearless knights and the highest point in the entire castle, had been remodeled into her very own bedroom. Millie loved to escape to, and play in, her secret room. No one could find her here, and she was allowed the luxury of spending hours lost in her wonderful world of imagination. She could pretend to be a firefighter, a jungle explorer, or a wild dinosaur-tamer.

Landing on a fluffy mattress, she stood up, climbed a rope ladder leading to her lookout tower, and gazed over the Kingdom below. She could see for miles on end. And with her telescope, when darkness fell, she had a breath-taking view of the starry hosts above.

Millie threw on a brown, leather aviator hat and a pair of goggles, then peered through her telescope to scan the horizon. Today, she would be Amelia Earhart, the first woman pilot. "We've got splendid flying weather today!" she reported to her sidekick, Mr. Pork Chops; her pink, stuffed piglet. "There's not a cloud in the sky! I say we fly across the entire ocean!"

Strapping Pork Chops to her helmet, she spread her arms out wide, and imagined she was in a plane. "Ready for lift-off?" she asked her passenger. "Hold onto your bacon!"

She jumped from her lookout tower, landing on the hardwood floor. She zoomed around the room, making a myriad of *swoosh* and *vrroooomm* noises before hopping into a green slide, and landing back on the third floor below. She jumped to her feet and flew down the hallway, waving to a maid who was picking up the socks which she had left lying on the floor.

"Your shoes, Princess?" the maid asked.

"Amelia Earhart likes flying better barefoot," she explained before zooming down the next flight of steps.

Millie knocked on her brother's door, "Captain Willie, do you read me? This is Amelia calling! Over!"

In an instant, Willie opened the door, standing in his checkered boxers once again. It appeared the boy had an aversion to wearing pants and a shirt.

"Pork Chops and I are planning to land in The Main Hall, wanna come along?"

"Sure!" Willie grinned, tying a red blanket around his neck, "I'm Superman! Let's go Amelia!"

"Superman, you're supposed to say *copy that,*" she commanded.

"Copy that!" he echoed, and the two tore off down the hall, then down the staircase and onto the main floor.

In The Main Hall, a group of tourists had gathered together by the front desk, standing behind red ropes. The staff gave daily tours of the Castle, as the tourist industry was booming. The King had made additions to the castle, tailoring it to the tourists' interests. They had built The Royal Gift Shop, The Royal Restaurant, an indoor fountain and garden area, and had added a carousel and miniature petting zoo.

Millie and Willie had been ordered to stay out of that area of the castle, and usually they did as they were told. If they were in The Main Hall when a new flock of tourists arrived, it was time for them to leave. The King didn't want his children to feel like tourist attractions on display in their own home, so that's why they spent most of their time upstairs.

Today, Millie spotted the large company of people with cameras, sunglasses, and vacation t-shirts from The Royal Gift Shop. She pointed them out to Willie, and they quickly ducked behind a large indoor plant, in hopes they wouldn't be spotted. They listened in silence as a young, smiley worker with high energy introduced herself as their tour guide: "Step inside as we embark on the adventure of a lifetime, here at The Royal Palace! Feel free to take pictures of whatever you please, but don't wander off, and stay with the group at all times. Our first stop is The Queen's Ball Room. Built in the early sixteen-hundred's..." the voice trailed off as she stepped into another room with the crowd following her.

"Phew," Millie stepped out from behind the plant, "that was close!"

"Yeah," Willie grinned, "we sure don't wanna get caught!"

"I've got an idea!" A lightbulb suddenly went off overtop Millie's head. "Let's play spies! The tourists are the bad guys, and we have to stalk their every move...but we can't let them see us! If they do, they'll shoot us with their water guns! Let's follow them, and be super, super quiet."

Willie's eyes lit up, "Yeah!"

"*Shhhh!*" she hushed. "We have to be like mice..." She tiptoed carefully forward, and Willie followed.

All at once, before Millie was ready, the group re-entered the Main Hall. The children ducked behind another plant and hugged each other tightly, attempting to cover up their giggles of excitement.

The perky tour guide then led the group into The Royal Gift Shop, and Millie and Willie followed close behind. They continued their game of spying as they made mad dashes toward the indoor garden, peeking out from behind the wishing well, then popping their excited heads back in. They followed the train of visitors into The Royal Hall of Fame, through The Queen's Library, and into The Secret Passageway (which wasn't really a secret; it had been built exclusively for tourist enjoyment). After a full, sixty-minute excursion, the tired guests returned to the Main Hall, and concluded the tour.

Millie and Willie came out of hiding as soon as the crowd left. "That was soooo fun! And they didn't even see us!" Millie laughed. "We're such good spies!"

Several families aimlessly wandered around The Gift Shop, and others had stepped inside the restaurant because the dinner hour was approaching. "Mom, look!" a strange voice suddenly called out. "It's the Prince and Princess!" A little girl stepped out of The Royal Gift Shop with a Princess Bridget plush doll in hand, and pointed as her voice trembled with excitement. Her parents rushed out to see what her commotion was about.

They laughed loudly, and others came quickly to evaluate the scene. It was a sight to behold—little Prince Willie standing in his boxers, a cape wrapped around his shoulders; and Princess Millie wearing an aviator hat and goggles that were three sizes too big for her, with Mr. Pork Chops strapped to her head. Someone snapped a picture, and other flashes followed. The Prince and Princess suddenly dashed out of the room. Willie darted up the stairs, and Millie down the long hall. She reached a steel door, which opened with a button, and ran down the stairs into the basement. There was only one person she could talk to during a time such as this.

Racing into the kitchen, her nose was greeted by various smells. The enormous kitchen was Millie's favorite room in The Palace. It was always buzzing with activity, as workers decorated cakes, fried foods, mixed sauces, created new recipes, diced vegetables, arranged fruit platters, baked loaves of fresh bread in large steel ovens, butchered slabs of meat, and washed dirty dishes. Beepers, timers, whistles, and bells went off as the duration of cooking times were over, and one batch was asking to be pulled from the oven so that another could take its place. Excited chatter filled the air Hired chefs wearing white hats went about their work. Dozens of maids, dressed in the proper décor of a sky blue apron and nametag, scurried in and out of the chaos, carrying forth dishes of delicacies during the dinner hour, and returning with empty plates in hand. The kitchen was now preparing for the Royal Restaurant's most hectic time of day. It was also Millie's favorite time to talk to Clark, the Head Cook.

Millie raced past the cake decorating station, where a chocolate fantasy cake was becoming a reality. She paused, stopping in her tracks to admire the delicious treat. The cake which looked like the Royal Castle itself caused Millie's eyes to grow wide. She desired to lick the sweet icing. Millie resisted the urge, as she knew the test cake was being prepared as a possible option for Addison's Coronation. Even though they were weeks away from the grand event, just the right cake had to be chosen, which meant that many test cakes would be baked, decorated and scrutinized. Millie hoped that if she was in the right place at the right time, she might be lucky enough to have some of the leftovers.

Millie continued past the frying station, the soup station, and the meat station. She found Clark dicing carrots.

"Amelia Earhart, reporting her landing!" Millie ran up to him.

The middle-aged man who had trouble hiding his grey hairs, paused from his work and greeted Millie with a warm smile. She ran into his arms, and he lifted her up and plopped her onto the counter. "Well if it isn't Miss Amelia! Long time, no see! Where have you been traveling to?"

Millie watched his strong, careful hands, as he handled his knife on the cutting board with great speed. "Everywhere!" she exclaimed. "But Pork Chops was getting jet-lagged so we decided to come see you."

"Well, I'm mighty glad you did," he grinned. "How are Princess Lessons going?"

She frowned, making a perturbed face, "Awful! I'd rather be down in the kitchen with you, cooking."

Clark laughed, understanding Millie's feelings on the matter. He had heard about her great disdain for Princess Lessons, which included painful dance classes, and instructions on how to conduct herself as a young woman. Millie had filled Clark in on the fact that she planned on *never* growing up. Most adults would try to speak some common sense into the girl, but Clark never did. He simply let her be and allowed the young Princess to vent her feelings. He always looked forward to Millie's visits, as the sight of her electric smile and eager eyes always cheered him up.

For Millie, Clark was perfect to talk to. He never tried to change her mind on a subject. He simply listened, and smiled, and nodded. Millie was sure he was even a much better listener than Pork Chops.

"Guess what!" Millie suddenly cried out, remembering her exciting news. "Addison promised that he's going to take me camping! In a real tent and everything!"

"Well," Clark beamed, "don't that beat all? You're one lucky girl!"

"We're going to build a fire and roast marshmallows, and look at the stars, and... hey, maybe you can come with us!"

Clark smiled, "That's thoughtful of you, but my place is here in the kitchen, remember? Your place is upstairs learning all there is to know about being a Princess."

Clark found it a challenge to explain to Millie the difference in their social statuses. Royal blood really had no place speaking and pursuing friendship with the servants. But she didn't quite yet understand her place in society, nor the great disadvantage of his.

Millie sighed, "I still wish I could work down here in the kitchen with you."

Clark smiled, "Little girl, you're a *whole* lot luckier than you know. Just be thankful to God for who you are and the family you have, and the special life He's given you."

Chapter 6 – Awkward Interview

The cameras were rolling, and Bridget put on her very best smile. Sitting in The Royal Conference Room with Gretchen Stanwood, editor of *Totally Teen*, Bridget's cascading blonde curls had been retouched, as well as the light dashes of pink blush on her pale cheeks. Her blue eyes sparkled as she smiled at her younger sister, Hope. The seventeen-year-old brunette looked nothing like Bridget. With long, straight, brown hair and hazel eyes, she possessed a different kind of beauty than her supermodel big-sis. Even though Hope didn't feel like she was pretty enough for her face be plastered on a magazine cover, the world seemed to differ. Tarsurella was obsessed with the Royal teen fashion icons, and embraced what made their polar-opposite images unique. Although Hope preferred sweat pants and Captain Crunch over designer dresses and fancy sushi parties, she was expected to follow in the footsteps of her glamorous older sister.

Gretchen held a sparkly-silver microphone in her hand, ready to interview the Royal starlets. Just seconds earlier, Patricia, their publicist, drilled them with possible questions, reminding the girls about the diplomatic way to avoid any politically- ill-flavored inquiries. Although most interviews only consisted of talk about their clothes, events, and daily life in The Palace, occasionally someone dropped a bomb that they graciously defused. The real interview had now arrived, and the girls were ready for it.

"Hello, *Totally Teen!*" the excited anchor spoke into the camera. "I'm here at The Royal Palace in Tarsurella, with two of our favorite fab icons: Princess Bridget and Princess Hope! It's such a pleasure to be chatting with you two today." She smiled at the Princesses, "You are viewed as positive role models by young girls in Tarsurella, as well as all around the world! So tell us, Bridget, how would you describe the responsibilities of your position?" Gretchen asked.

Patricia, Deborah, Shay, and a slew of makeup artists stood behind the camera, watching.

Bridget took a breath before responding, "I would describe my responsibilities like that of any other citizen in the world. To stay true to ourselves, our families and friends, and reach out to others in hopes of making a positive impact. My job is just as important as any other teen. The only difference between me and other young people my age is that I'm living in a bit of a fishbowl."

Patricia gave her thumbs up, as if to say, "Nice answer!"

"How would you describe a typical day in The Palace?" Gretchen questioned eagerly.

"The word 'typical' does not really apply to us," Bridget laughed. "Lately our schedule has been crazy. Every day it's different. I wake up and say, 'Oh, I'm flying to Paris today? Okay!' When I was younger, I had a very set schedule and routine I followed every day, which I think was very important for me. But lately, with preparation for Addison's Coronation, as well as my college studies, my schedule has been a lot more spontaneous."

"Your fashion is always on point!" She looked at Hope, "Can you tell us about the gown you're wearing to Prince Addison's Coronation Ball?"

"I cannot," she grinned mischievously, "Its top secret. You'll have to wait until then for the grand unveiling."

"Several days ago, you both made an appearance at the *Gold Rush* movie premier in France. The red carpet was absolutely star-studded! With the presence of Jamie Drift, Dustin Cleaver and Molina Topez, it was quite the event! A hot new band, *Kennetic Energy*, made an appearance, as well. Their hit single, "Outta This World" has sky rocketed on the charts! *Kennetic Energy* has become an overnight sensation, and I know we all have their song stuck in our heads! So tell us, Hope, did you get to meet the hunky heart-throb and lead singer, David Carter?"

Hope felt her cheeks flush red. She was not expecting a question like that one! "Uh..."

Yes, she had met him. The pop singer accidentally splashed his punch on her evening gown. The red liquid left a nasty stain, and he stuttered in complete embarrassment.

The awkward flashback flooded into her mind...

"I'm–I'm–so sorry!" he had fumbled, grabbing a handful of napkins and pressing them onto her dress, frantically trying to sop up the mess. All at once he realized the enormity of what had happened. He hadn't just spilled his punch on any girl. No, it was the *Princess* of Tarsurella.

David Carter, the young American popstar, didn't know much about Tarsurella. David had never learned about it in school, but heard enough about the rich heiress and her family who were thought of as mega-superstars in the states. The sisters graced magazine covers, appeared on talk shows, and even had their own line of fashion dolls. He dropped the napkins, realizing in horror that he had just touched Royalty. What was he thinking?! Couldn't he get in massive trouble for that? The girl had a Royal security swat team attending the event with her. The intimidation was real.

"I–I–" he cringed, suddenly dropping down on his knees, "Forgive me, Your Highness!"

Hope starred at the boy who was awkwardly kneeling before

her. "Stand up!" she hissed. "Someone will see you!" She didn't want to make a scene out of what was happening. She had never seen *anyone* bow down to her before, and it was extremely freaky.

"I am so, so, *so* sorry!" The expression on David's face looked as though he was headed to a sure death.

Hope raised her eyebrow. What was he thinking, she was going to chop off his head or something? The guy was acting like a total fruit loop. "It's okay," she reassured him in an irritated tone, "Just don't let anyone see you. The press will make a huge story out of this if they see us together. The best thing you can do right now is walk away *casually*."

"But, but I, um…" he stuttered, wishing he could at the very least get her autograph. It's not every day you bumped into Royalty! But he knew now that any chances of getting on this Princess's good side were completely shattered. After ruining her dress, as well as her evening, he figured the best thing to do would be to leave. He inched away from her, and after he had left her presence, Hope sighed with relief. Shay was able to pull out a handy-dandy stain-remover pen, and magically make the boo-boo disappear.

Until now, Hope had been able to keep the immensely awkward scene under wraps. But the pretty, little band aid that hid what happened, was being slowly ripped off in front of the rolling cameras.

"Well, I…" she glanced at her hands, wringing them uncomfortably. She wisped a stray strand of hair that had come loose from behind her ear. She glanced up, knowing she couldn't lie. "Yes. He seemed uh…very nice. I only spoke with him briefly."

Just then, doors to The Royal Conference Room flew open

and a crew of people walked inside. "Yes, yes," the loud voice led, "right this way!"

The interruption brought a sudden halt to their interview. Following the man was a parade of people with guitar cases, speakers, microphones, and–*Kennetic Energy*! Hope immediately recognized David, and the pixie-faced blonde named Laney who sang with him. A drummer, bass player, and keyboardist followed.

Hope's eyes shot to Deborah whose surprised expression appeared as though something had gone terribly wrong. Her high heels clicked across the floor, quickly confronting the man who walked in. Although their voices were low, the quiet room had fantastic acoustics and they were heard clearly.

"Sir, I don't have you scheduled to practice here until seven o'clock," she told the band manager. "I'm afraid you're early, we're going to have to ask you to leave. We're in the middle of an interview."

"Why, if it isn't David Carter himself!" an excited Gretchen exclaimed. She stood up and bounded across the room, and her camera men followed her to the action. "My name is Gretchen, editor of *Totally Teen Magazine*, may I ask you a few questions?"

David's frightful brown eyes were not expecting this intrusion. In fact, he was still getting used to the idea of people asking for interviews. It was just too weird.

For David, everything had happened so quickly. Just a few months ago they were writing songs and rocking out in his basement. But after their single went viral, the momentum hadn't stopped, and a whirlwind of unexpected opportunities unfolded. But now, as a microphone was shoved up near his mouth, he couldn't hide the surprise from his face. The bands original plan for today was to come in, set up, and do a sound check. He had no idea that the paparazzi would be waiting for them inside.

"Sure," he eyed his manager cautiously, as if to ask for permission.

"I was told to be here at five o'clock," the gruff manager stood his ground.

"Sir, we must ask you to leave," Deborah spoke in a firm voice. "There was obviously a mistake in scheduling. I apologize for the inconvenience, but Princess Hope is in the middle of an interview."

David felt himself begin to sweat at the mention of her name. His mind raced frantically. Was she here?!

The Palace was *huge*, much larger and more magnificent than he had thought it would be, and he never considered the idea that he might end up in the same room with Princess Hope again. At least, not until the Coronation. But even then, they would be busy backstage, and with their conflicting schedules, she could easily be avoided. But now what? What would she say to him? Would she command him to leave? First he spilled punch on her dress, and now this?! He spotted her sitting in a chair on the other side of the room. He quickly looked away.

Hope could scarcely believe that he was here, as well. What were the chances of that happening? And just after she stuttered in front of the camera about him! But neither Hope nor David had a thing to worry about, as Deborah shooed *Kennetic Energy* out of the room until further notice. After being evicted, the band wandered into The Royal Gift Shop to have a look around until it was their new time set for practice. David was beyond relived. He had been rescued from any further interactions with the Princess.

The busy day was finally winding down to an end as the Royal Family joined together for dinner, with the exception of Bridget and Hope, who would join them shortly due to the fact that their interview ran late.

They all sat in the formal family dining room, at the long banquet table spread out before them. The children's father sat at the head of the table, with Addison on his right and fourteen-year-old Asher on his left. Following was Chasity and Jillian on the left, and across from them on the right were Bridget and Hope's empty chairs, then Millie and little Willie at the end.

The King smiled with love as he gazed at each of his children. They were perfectly silent as he bowed his head and began the prayer:

"Heavenly Father," the King's voice resounded, "I bless You this evening, thanking You for the wonderful gift You have bestowed upon me. It is an honor to have so many beautiful, smiling faces at my table tonight. We ask You to bless this food we are about to receive, and bless those who prepared it. Amen."

Everyone echoed with their own "Amen."

All at once, the loud chatter of their large family filled the room. They each buzzed about the happenings their day, everyone talking at once. Their boisterous family was what brought this quiet room to life. Without them, it was only an empty space with an ancient table, fancy chairs, and expensive dishes. But when the family spoke and laughed with one another, the formal dining room became a beautiful atmosphere of joy and love.

Monsieur Michael placed a roast on the table to accompany their various dishes of mashed potatoes, corn, and green beans.

"Thank you, Michael," the King's voice boomed above the noise, "it looks splendid."

The King was accustomed to this level of noise, but after the stress and challenges of the day, he found an unwelcome headache pressing into his forehead.

"Daddy, Daddy, guess what!?" Millie called from her end of the table, "Addison said he's gonna take me camping! Like a real adventurer!"

"Millie, don't use your fingers!" Jillian scolded. "That's what your fork is for! Dad, when can we play backyard football again?" Jillian asked amidst the noise. "It's been nearly forever. You need to take a day off, so we can just hang out."

"Jillian, don't be stupid. Dad can't take a vacation from running the country." Asher lowered his voice to a haunting tone, "Danger *never* sleeps." The slightly-tanned boy had a thick head of black hair. His brown eyes teased his little sister.

Jillian laughed, "Ha! That's what they must have taught my new security guard. Have you met him, Dad? Seriously, he's constantly worried that I'm gonna trip and fall on my head, or something! He freaked out when my left shoe was untied. And then I was reaching for a book in the library, and he jumped out ahead of me and said, 'Princess, I'll get it for you! You might break something!' "

Millie perked up, "He sounds more protective than Chasity's new guard. He let her trample through the gardens on Nicholas in a dead gallop!"

Chasity tossed her sister a warning look, as if to say *"shhhh!"*
Hanson hadn't *let* her do that. In fact, the horrified look on
his face when she came barreling past him was quite comical.
She had been trying to work with Nic in the polo pasture, but
the animal was far too feisty. He had decided to bolt, and
when he neared the fence, he soared right over it. Thankfully,
Chasity was still attached to his back. Despite Nic's
disobedient behavior, it had given her quite the adrenaline
rush.

The King opened his mouth to respond to his children, but
he could scarcely keep up.

Suddenly Hope entered in a flustered manner. Bridget
followed.

"Dad?" Hope asked before sitting down, "Did you invite
Kennetic Energy to Addison's ball? How could you *do* that?! You
should've checked with me first. I didn't know you were
hiring entertainment like–"

"Whoa, whoa, whoa," he held up a hand. His daughter was
about to burst into a flurry of words, babbling on about
something that he knew nothing about. "If you have
concerns about our entertainment choices for Addison's ball,
please speak with our event coordinator about that. I had no
say in who would be performing."

"But, didn't they show you the list before hiring the
performers?"

"Yes, they did, and I approved. I thought *Kennetic Energy* was
some kind of illusionist magic act. I thought perhaps it might
be interesting."

Jillian's mouth hung open in shock, "Magic act? Dad, *Kennetic*

Energy is like the *biggest* thing in music right now! Their lead singer, David Carter, wrote a love ballad and it's smashing records on all the charts. They hit number one on iTunes the *day* it released."

The King laughed turning to his son, "Wow, Addison, sounds as though you got lucky with these guys. I had no idea that the 'newest big thing' in music would be performing at your Coronation, did you?"

Addison only shrugged, never having heard of the band.

"Speaking of the Coronation," the King continued with a twinkle in his eye, "how did your afternoon with the young ladies go?"

Addison bit his lip. "Um, actually, I wanted to talk to you about that. I—"

Asher suddenly pushed his chair away from the table and stood up. "Can I be excused?"

"Why Asher, you've barely touched your food. Sit back down and finish your meal."

"I'm not hungry," he responded, crossing his arms.

"Asher, I told you to *sit*. You know the rule, no leaving the table until everyone has finished."

"Why?" he spoke angrily as his eyes flashed at him, "So that we can carry on about Addison's stupid ball?"

"Asher!" the King scolded. "Apologize to your brother."

"Sorry," Asher spoke sarcastically as he rolled his eyes. Then he mumbled under his breath, "I'm sorry that you were born."

The King's eyebrows shot up. "Asher!" his voice boomed. "How dare you use such a disrespectful tone! Not only is Addison your brother, he is your future King! Go to your room, right now."

Asher tossed his napkin into the middle of the table before getting up, "Thank you." His dark attitude was a complete mismatch to his words.

The King opened his mouth, ready to reprimand him again, but wasn't sure what to say.

What *could* he say? Asher was drifting further and further away from him. It was as if the boy had built a un-scalable tower wall around his soul, and nothing could reach him. Vile words were always coming from his tongue, as he verbally attacked his siblings. He spent every ounce of free time on his own, refusing to participate in family activities. The King's heart burned with frustration toward his wayward son. The past few years had been getting worse. Punishments meant nothing to him. His grades were slipping; his attitude was terrible and unfeeling. It was like he didn't care about anyone but himself. Nobody could get through to him.

"Maybe you should take his video games away," Bridget suggested. "I think he's addicted. That might knock some sense into him."

The King sighed. It was times like these that he longed for his wife's wisdom and comforting presence. She would've known what to do. *Lord, help me*, He prayed quietly. *Managing my family is far more complicated than running the country.*

Willie's contagious laughter swept through the Family Room. Millie joined in the chorus of laughter with giggles of her own, as the joyful brother/sister duo sat gleefully on the couch. The familiar animated characters of *Phineas and Ferb* flashed on their TV screen. The brilliant cartoon brothers carried out plans for their latest invention, giving Millie many ideas for tomorrow's adventures.

"Son," the King addressed Addison as he entered the room, "I know I promised that we'd talk at seven, but I think I'd better go check on Asher first."

"Yeah, good idea," Addison replied. "He seemed pretty upset."

"Daddy, Daddy!" Millie called, "Come watch!"

The King smiled compassionately at his daughter, "Not this time, sweetie. I need to go talk with your brother. Maybe later." He left the room to go confront Asher.

"Princess Millie and Prince Willie," a young maid addressed the Royals, "it's time for your baths."

Willie groaned. Millie grabbed an armful of Barbie's to bring into the tub with her. "Tonight," Millie's excited voice trailed out of the room as she followed the maid, "there's going to be a huge shark attack! And the shipwrecked pirates will have to ask the mermaids for help because of their mystical powers, and then..." Millie's voice trailed off through the hallway, until she was no longer audible.

The King entered a second time. Addison was surprised.

"He wouldn't talk to me," His Majesty sighed as he released the tie from around his neck. "The door to his bedroom was locked, and he refused to open it. I don't want to make this whole ordeal worse than it already is, so I guess I'll have to wait until morning. Addison, let's head down to The Guest Hall; it's nice and quiet there. We can talk about whatever it was that you wanted to speak with me about this morning."

The King found certain strength in the quietness. Finally able to hear himself think clearly, he breathed deeply. The area was completely still, and the empty room was greatly appealing to his Majesty. Addison, on the other hand, found the silence between them to be uncomfortable, as his mind raced for words.

"So, tell me son," the King sat, and poured himself a cup of hot tea, "how did your meeting go with some of the young ladies on our guest list?"

Addison poured himself a cup of tea as well, but did not allow himself to be at ease. "Um, yeah. They were all beautiful Dad, but–"

"Did you happen to take a particular liking to any of the young women?"

Addison sighed, "Um, no. I mean, I'm sure they're all nice, and they have interesting backgrounds, and pretty faces, but I know next to nothing about any of them. At this point they all feel like clapboard buildings in the Wild West. They have some nice paint on the outside, but that doesn't say much for what's inside. "

"I completely understand," the King nodded. "You can't get to know who they truly are unless you spend more time with them. So this means you wouldn't be opposed to getting to know a few of them better?" The King asked.

"Of course not," Addison sighed, "but I would prefer to go

about this in my own way. Lining them all up in a stuffy little room makes me feel like I'm at a horse auction, or on a freaky dating game show. It's just not natural, Dad."

The King laughed. "I hear you. I'll tell Deborah to set up some more comfortable habitats. What about a friendly game of tennis? Or a polo match?"

Addison continued talking, but felt like his father wasn't hearing him. "How is that any different? Asking Deborah to set up meetings with them makes it all feel completely staged. It's just not normal."

"Addison," the King spoke slowly, "your life isn't normal. You have been raised in a greenhouse, of sorts. The temperature, your surroundings, have been masterfully controlled and carefully chosen, with the purpose of nurturing you. You've been preparing your entire life for the job that is quickly approaching. Your mother was a master gardener. She knew that if you tossed certain plants outside before they were ready for the wild elements, the sun might scorch them, or a torrential downpour could kill them. The Palace has been your greenhouse. And the reality of this situation is that you're not attending University like other young men in Tarsurella. You're not meeting young ladies at church, or mingling with them on some newfangled dating site. So how else are you expected to meet anyone with queenly potential? The ladies whom we have selected to meet with you are only those who we believe may help nurture your life in the greenhouse."

Addison sighed. What his father was saying was true. But still, couldn't they go about this in a slightly different way? He didn't want his relationships to feel fake and contrived.

"Trust me, my dear boy," the King continued, "arranged courtships might feel a bit old-fashioned, but they can be a beautiful thing. That's how I met your mother, you know. And my, what a gem she was. Choosing to go about things in a noble, respectable manner, will also help set an example for your siblings who come after you. They look up to you Addison, and if you set the example for healthy, honorable relationships, I believe they will follow in your footsteps. We've already seen the damage that can happen when one tries to escape the greenhouse and be like a wildflower. Bridget was hurt so very deeply. I never want that to happen again, for you, or any of the kids." The King rubbed a weary hand through his receding hairline, "Is that all you wanted to discuss tonight, Addison? I'm about beat."

Addison bit his lower lip. He could see that his father was tired, struggling to keep his eyes open. "No, that's all." He headed for the door, "Goodnight, Dad."

Addison woke up drenched in a cold sweat. Panic coursed through his veins as he awoke from the vivid dream. The red numbers from his digital clock flashed at him: 3:05 a.m.

Addison rolled over on his pillow, facing the darkness, and took a deep breath. He realized he had been nearly hyperventilating. Though the nightmare was over and had vanished into the darkness of the night, every time he closed his eyes the familiar scenes would reappear.

It was the third night he had experienced the same dream. Appearing to take place on the night of his Coronation, the Royal Crown was lowered onto his head, as faces of family and friends surrounded him with proud cheers and teary eyes. But the moment Addison was crowned, sudden havoc broke out. Screams of horror filled The Ball Room, as enemies with machine guns invaded The Palace. The sounds of echoing gun shots and blood-curdling screams caused Addison to take off running, running, running....Until he woke up in a sudden panic. Breathless.

He sat up and turned on his bedside light, hoping to drive those shadowy images away. He rubbed his eyes and pinched the bridge of his nose. He needed to think about something else. He knew better than to let a silly dream upset him so deeply.

It was ludicrous to entertain the thought that enemies would invade on the night of his coronation. Their security team was one of the finest in the world, as well as their automated security system. He had often heard his father refer to the system as "The Wall of Fire." He knew that they were protected 24/7, with the careful, eagle eyes watching every member of his family. He had no need to fear any harm. Yet, he had a terrible feeling that the dream wasn't about what might come from the outside—but instead, something that would come from within. The only person who had the power to fail this country and bring utter ruin to everyone, was him.

The idea of falling short of his father's expectations terrified him. Dad had reigned so flawlessly, and his faithful citizens stood by his side, even when there were rebellious rumblings coming from the streets. Addison knew that some riled-up rebels desired change. They wanted a democracy. And even though a huge percentage of Tarsurella would be eternally faithful to the crown, Addison dreaded what might happen when a change of leadership happened. Would the people be upset? Would they love him as much as they did his father? Or would he be the first to mess up their nearly-perfect track record of peace and harmony?

Addison reached for his Bible, and flipped to several verses which warned him against worrying. "Don't worry about anything, but instead pray about everything," he spoke out loud, reminding himself of these simple truths. "Trust in the

Lord with all your heart, all your soul, all your mind, and all your strength."

Addison tried to pray, but found his thoughts drifting to the possible worst case scenarios. Addison glanced at his clock again. If he continued thinking like this, it was going to be a long night…

Chapter 7 –Palace Popstars

It wasn't often that Bridget paid any mind to what the media had to say about her family. But as she saw the magazine lying on their kitchen counter that morning, she couldn't help but pick it up. Staring at her on the front page were the wide eyes of her little brother, Willie. And beside him stood Millie with an astonished look on her face. The photograph had been taken in The Palace's Main Hall, Bridget could be sure. Because where else would Willie have been running around freely in his underwear? She laughed out loud, reading the headline, "Royal Munchkins on the Run!"

Bridget shook her head carelessly, wondering what Mother would have thought about Willie and Millie's wild *adventurer* escapades. The Queen likely would have laughed, and encouraged them in their imaginary games. "We grow up far too quickly," Bridget recalled her saying many times. "It's best we stay young-at-heart for as long as we possibly can."

Bridget carried the magazine across the kitchen and into the living room, her fuzzy pink slippers sliding across the hardwood floors. She pulled her pink bathrobe over her shoulder and embraced herself, relishing in the warmth of her robe.

The room was completely empty, as she had awoken long after everyone else in her family. She was fully immersed in the usual college-life schedule of staying up *way* too late, then waking up half past noon. With the freedom of taking her college classes online, her life wasn't enslaved to an alarm clock. And for that, she was thankful.

Just then Hope entered the room, making a beeline for the kitchen. She searched the pantry for a chocolate bar. The craving had come upon her quite suddenly, causing her to be aroused from quiet studies in her bedroom, and sent her raging into the kitchen, opening and closing cupboard doors frantically.

"Morning, Hope," Bridget called from where she lay on the couch, leafing through the magazine.

"Do we not have *any* chocolate in this house?" Hope asked.

"You know Dad doesn't want us eating that junk," Bridget replied. "Besides, it's bad for your skin. Chocolate and pimples are besties."

Hope paused from rummaging through the kitchen to consider her sister's words. Oh well, she could suffer through a few pimples. If only she could experience that sweet explosion of flavor melting inside her mouth. Yes, it would *totally* be worth it. She picked up a phone hanging on the wall, "I'm calling for room service."

Bridget popped up from the couch and slid the magazine across the counter, "Look, our sibs made the headlines."

Hope burst out laughing, "They are too cute!" Then she told the kitchen service, "Hi! May I get two peppermint dark chocolate bars sent to my room? Thanks, Clark!"

"Whoa," Bridget suddenly stopped flipping through the glossy pages. "Hope, since when are you in a relationship with David Carter?"

"What?!" Hope slammed the phone down and darted across the room. "You've got to be kidding me!" She leaned over her sister's shoulder to read the print for herself.

Adorable New Couple Alert!
Inside sources tell us that Princess Hope has finally found her dream boy! Be jealous girls, be very jealous. It's none other than teen sensation,

David Carter! Rumored to be performing at Prince Addison's
Coronation Ball, the Kennetic Energy star has been seen cozying up with
this Royal—

"What!?" Hope cried again. "That's insane! Who would write that?"

"It's the stupid paparazzi," Bridget sighed, throwing the magazine into a nearby garbage can. "They get paid to come up with stories like that. It's none of their business, yet they turn it into a highly lucrative one. The juicer the stories they come up with, the more magazines they can sell, and the more money they make. Even if it's fabricated nonsense."

"That is outrageous!" Hope seethed, feeling hurt from the lies that tainted her reputation. "Who would even dream up a story like that?"

Bridget placed both hands on her sister's shoulders to calm her, "I'm sorry, Hope. But try not to let it get to you. The media is always writing crazy stories about me, too. The best thing to do is just ignore them. I've got a one o'clock nail appointment with Shay. Do you wanna come get yours does as well? We can talk more about this if you want."

Hope shook her head, still cooling off from the heat of anger induced by the sudden blow, "No thanks." She placed determined hands on her hips, "I've got something better to do."

"What's that?"

"I'm gonna go have a talk with our event coordinator," Hope bit her lip determinedly, "and see if we can't remove *Kennetic Energy* from the performance line up."

"Hope, you can't fire them, just because of this silly little rumor! If you do that, the media will come up with *another* story, even more dramatic than the first one. I can see the headline now," Bridget framed the words with her hands, like she was reading a billboard, "David and Hope: The Crushing Breakup."

"Good," Hope was pleased with the fantasized outcome, "I can't have people thinking I'm dating someone that I'm not."

"I know you want to protect your integrity and your reputation," Bridget counseled her quietly, "but think about it from David's perspective. Here he is, a young artist who just experienced the biggest break of a lifetime for his band. He was asked to perform at a mind-blowing venue, The Palace in Tarsurella! Can you imagine how disappointing that would be for him, if he suddenly got fired?"

Hope shrugged casually, "There will be other performances– The Super Bowl, The United States Presidential Inauguration…"

Bridget held up a hand to silence her sister, "Opportunities for people like David Carter are few and far between. It's really selfish of you to take this away from him, just because you want to protect your name."

"I'm not being selfish!" Hope argued, before heading for the door, her eyes flashing mischievously. "Besides, we can always call everyone's favorite popstar, Jamie Drift. I'm *sure* she could make it up to him."

It took Hope longer than she had anticipated to track down Eva, their event coordinator. She finally found the flustered woman in the Main Hall, barking commands at everyone within a five-foot radius of herself. At the sight of Princess Hope, Eva imminently sweetened up, and turned off her

Army drill sergeant voice.

"Princess Hope," she greeted with a smile, "may I help you, dear?"

"Yes, actually. I wish to discuss the performance guest list with you. There are a few changes I'd like to make."

Ava's smile flipped upside down, "I'm afraid it's much too late for that. I've immensely enjoyed talking with you, and I'm mournfully sorry that I cannot grant your request, but I must be moving on to my next task; I have a million and one things to do." Ava excused herself and marched into The Queen's Ballroom, turning her drill sergeant voice on again, commanding her workers to follow.

Hope followed as well, not quite ready to give up.

The Queen's Ball Room was one of Hope's favorite spaces in The Palace. Regal marble pillars, beautiful and strong, sprouting up like majestic oak trees from a foundation of mosaic pavement. The stunning floor sparkled beneath the soft light of hanging chandeliers from the cathedral ceiling. The room was pampered with fresh flowers from The Royal Garden. The Ball Room was generally open to the public during tours, but now it would be roped off, forbidding access as the Royal Staff prepared the room for Addison's Coronation.

As Hope entered, she was greeted by the sight of maids on their hands and knees scrubbing the floors, style coordinators rearranging flowers, maintenance men wiring an indoor fountain and installing a decorative waterfall for the East Wall. Dazzling lanterns and strings of lights were being spread across the ceiling, and down the white linen-draped walls, by men who stood at daring heights on a wobbly scaffold. A string of lights was also being placed upon the front of a second-floor marble balcony which overlooked the entire room.

And that's when she saw him. Standing high on the balcony was David Carter and the rest of *Kennetic Energy.*

The band was doing a sound check, making various noises and unharmonious racket on their instruments. They were half singing, half speaking odd phrases into their microphones.

"Check, check, one-two, one-two!" Laney tested her mic.

Hope examined the scene. The drummer had an intimidating punk-rock look happening. His black hair hung in his face like a shaggy dog, and his sticks beat up on the drum kit like he was going to war. The drummer was pumping out a beat which echoed through the whole room.

Then her eyes moved over to the guitarist. Her fingers picked graciously along the strings. Standing beside her was a guy with a bass guitar strapped around his shoulder and a head of black curls sprouting out the top of his scalp. On the other side of the stage was a small keyboard where a girl with an angelic voice joined in the song. The short, blonde girl was clearly talented.

Finally, she let her eyes rest on David Carter. The brown-eyed boy had one of those stereotypical, overrated, teen-pop-sensation voices–the kind that tend to make girls' knees melt like chocolate in July.

Hope suddenly realized that she had been craning her neck upwards. She glanced around to make sure no one had seen her fawning over the scene, then returned her eyes to Ava who was on the other side of The Ball Room, telling a man that the flower arrangement "just wouldn't do."

"If I went to the Milky Way, I would stop at every star and tell them…." David's voice floated through the room. Hope tried to stay focused as she made her way toward Ava, but the familiar lyrics distracted her. She had to admit that their song *was* really catchy.

"I am feel'n so undone, so outta this world…
'Cause I'm your superman, and you're my damsel in distress,
The day that we first met, I'm Romeo, you're Juliet,
The way you look at me, I can't even breathe,
I just gotta tell someone, gotta tell someone—"

The song was suddenly interrupted as all instruments and voices were cut silent. "Announcing:" a booming voice suddenly overtook the intercom, "Princess Jillian!"

With an amused look, Hope turned toward the main doors as they flew open for an embarrassed Jillian. Her security guard, Lance, had overridden the entire sound system with his announcement. Darcy trotted in at her heel, and Lance followed closely behind, closing the doors behind her.

The interruption threw the band off a bit, and they weren't sure if they should keep playing, or wait until she left the room. Their manager gave them the instruction to go ahead, so they picked up on the second verse.

"If I could go back in time, and set the planets all in line, I would show them…
That baby this is destiny, 'cause now we're making history.
'Cause I'm your superman…"

Jillian immediately recognized the song. It had been on repeat in her iPod during her morning jog. She wondered why the workers were listening to this song, but then she realized it was a live performance! She glanced at the stage where

Kennetic Energy sang their hit single, and grinned. She wondered if she might have the opportunity to meet them and let them know that she immensely enjoyed their music.

"Be careful, Princess," Lance's cautious voice warned, "the wet floors are a safety hazard. Should I tell the maids to cease from their scrubbing?"

"No, Lance," Jillian sighed, rapidly growing tired of his foolish antics, "that isn't necessary."

"Princess," Lance continued, "the loud music coming from the balcony is a proven hazard for early deafness. Should I ask them to quit playing until you finish your business here?"

Hope covered up a laugh. She had not seen Jillian's new security guard, but had heard a great deal about him. She concluded that Jillian's description of him was generous, and could see now why she wished to get rid of him.

Jillian took a deep breath, counted to three, and grasped the frail fringes of what remained from her patience. "How would you like to tell the band that if it's at all possible, I would wish to meet them after their practice?" Jillian asked kindly.

Lance nodded right away, pleased to offer his services, "Yes, straightaway, Your Highness." He turned on his heel, and left.

Jillian shook her head, explaining to Hope, "I have to send him on errands if I ever want a free moment away from him. I don't think we've ever had a guard like this, in all of Palace history!"

Hope laughed out loud this time. Jillian said nothing, but her exasperated expression confirmed her sister's amused laugh, and decided to change the subject.

"They're really good, aren't they?" Jillian asked, referring to the band.

"Yeah," Hope replied, "it's really too bad that I have to remove them from our list."

"What? Why? Hope, you can't! They're so good!"

"Wait until you hear what happened, then you'll understand!" Hope raised her voice to be heard over the noise, "You'll never guess what Bridget found published about us—"

The song suddenly stopped, and Hope realized that she had been talking way too loud. She clamped her mouth shut. David and the band could probably hear her now!

Lance summoned the band to come down from the balcony, and much sooner than Jillian had expected, the band stood ready to meet her. Hope spotted them descending from the stairway, and pointed a subtle finger. Jillian twirled around, and all five band members approached.

"Presenting, Princess Jillian and Princess Hope," Lance formally introduced them, as if they didn't know who they were already.

"Hey, what's up?" Jillian smiled.

The shaggy-haired drummer did a double take, shaking his head like an animated cartoon character. His long locks bounced all over the place, until finally his head stopped moving, and his jaw hung open several inches. Then he gave the Royal sisters a rock and roll sign. "I'm a huge fan of this whole monarchy thing! You girls *rock*! And your Palace is like the bomb!"

The sisters laughed. The young bass player had an equally surprised and starry-eyed expression plastered upon his face. He was too stunned to speak.

David was quiet as well, but it wasn't from being star struck. He found himself growing increasingly uncomfortable being in the same room as Hope, as the events from their first meeting replayed in his mind like a broken record.

"We are *so* honored to be meeting you," the shortest band member standing in the middle of them spoke, making eye contact with each of them. "It's kind of surreal. I'm Laney by the way, and this is Zac," referring to the shaggy-haired boy; "Justin," the bass player; "David, and my best friend, Sarah." Sarah offered a shy wave, but no one else spoke. So Laney continued, "We just can't believe we're here! We were totally stoked when we were asked play for Addison's Coronation. It's taking a while to sink in. It seems like just last week that our audience was my Jack Russell terrier, and David's Westie. So, as you can imagine, this is totally crazy for us!"

Jillian smiled, "Well, I cannot speak for my sister, but I am just as honored to meet you all, as well. I was *just* listening to your song this morning, and it's been on repeat for pretty much all my jogs! The song is really excellent, and you've all been blessed with an amazing, God-given talent. I'm really looking forward to hearing your new songs as they come out. I've already preordered your CD!"

Now it was Laney's turn to be surprised, "Are you for real? You are actually listening to our music? Cool beans! That means so much to us, like you wouldn't believe! Hey, how would you two like to be the first pair of ears that hear some of our brand new music?" Laney excitedly suggested. "David's been writing some amazing stuff, and it would be great to hear feedback from fans who won't go and post it on the internet."

David looked at Laney. Huh? What was she thinking?!

"Of course!" Jillian's voice rose with excitement, "That would be wonderful! We would love that, wouldn't we Hope?"

"Um, actually," Hope shifted her weight uncomfortably. How could she state this tactfully? Were there any words to graciously sugar-coat the fact that she was planning to fire them? How could she express the fact that the made-up stories about her and David were getting completely out of control? "Jillian and I have a scheduling conflict."

"We do?" Jillian cast a leery glance in Hope's direction. What was she speaking of?

Hope nodded, "Mmm, hmm. It's called school."

Chapter 8 – An Old Friend

Hanson shifted in his seat. The hard wooden desk sent a dull ache through his back. It brought back unpleasant memories from Grammar School. He resisted the urge to let out a frustrated huff of air from between his lips. *I did not go to school*, he thought angrily, *just so I could end up back in school.*

The boredom eating away at him was like a slow and vicious cancer. Although the maddening monotony was an invisible force, he was beginning to have trouble masking its effects.

Today, Hanson had been sitting through a three-hour-long lecture about Captain John Smith, which was extremely yawn-enticing. Miss Christy finally excused the class, and Hanson stood up simultaneously with Chasity.

"Where to now, Princess?" he asked, desperately hoping she wasn't going to go sit in her room and read. He *hated* when she did that.

"I believe I'll go to the stables and ride Nicholas for a while."

"Is he that crazy beast you were riding yesterday?" Hanson gathered up an armful of her books without being asked.

Chasity didn't smile, "He's not a beast." She was very defensive about her beloved Nic. "He's merely a colt and still in need of a firm hand, strong boundaries, and some TLC. He's just a little rough around the edges."

"I received a strong reprimand for letting you ride alone yesterday," He replied. "I thought you told me that another staff member would be riding with you. I hope you realize that if you break your leg or something while you're out riding him, I'll probably be fired."

Chasity laughed as they exited the school room, "If such a terrible fate were to befall me, I'm sure they would give you a little bit of grace, being the newbie that you are."

Hanson made a face, pulling his head in slightly and squinting one eye. "Newbie?" His voice was loaded with irritation. "Do you have any idea how many years of preparation and training I've had for this job?"

"Well pardon me," Chasity retorted sarcastically as she rolled her eyes, "I didn't realize that one must go through such a rigorous training process in order to learn how to follow me around, twist off any jar lids I can't manage to open, and kill The Palace spiders."

"Trust me, Princess," Hanson bantered back, "if I would've known that your life was *this* boring, I might've waited a few more years to apply for the job. Like, maybe when I turned 80."

Chasity snorted disgustedly. "Oh, come on, my life isn't *that* dull. Just seconds ago you were complaining about the possibility of me breaking my arm, and now I'm blamed for not being exciting enough?"

"Forgive me, Princess," Hanson continued, "for being so blunt, but have you ever even been outside? I mean, in the *real* word?"

"Of course!" Chasity was miffed by the way that Hanson was belittling her. "My sisters and I attend premiere parties, vacation in the Swiss Alps, and visit other monarchies around the world. Believe it or not, I actually have a really exciting life."

"No," Hanson cut her off, making the conversation steer in a much more personal direction than what his job description advised him to, "I mean the *real* world. Have you ever roamed the halls of a public school, gotten a wand of cotton candy at the fair, or gone out to the midnight movies with your friends? You're a senior, right? I'm talking typical Tarsurellian, growing up, rite-of-passage sort of stuff. It's like you live in this sheltered little bubble, and the only adventures you're allowed to have are the ones in your books."

Chasity couldn't find words to reply, and Hanson knew he had stepped too far over the line. He fixed his brown eyes forward on the steps they were about to descend. He cleared his throat, deciding it would be best to change the subject. "From now on, I'll be horseback riding with you. Headquarters said it isn't safe to be riding alone."

"What?" Chasity's blue eyes darted toward him as her mouth hung open in shock, "That's never been a rule before!"

"I don't make the rules," Hanson shrugged. "I only enforce them."

"But riding is the only time that I ever get to be truly alone!" she vented. "There's not much opportunity for fresh air and personal space around here." Chasity felt like the walls of her alone-time were caving in. She was *not* fond of the idea of having Hanson ride with her.

Hanson pressed the automatic door button that led to the gardens, which was the head of the trail that would eventually bring them to the paddock, stables, and riding arena.

"Hey, I'm not crazy about the idea either," Hanson groaned. "Horses stink."

Chasity's eyebrows popped up. "Looks like someone had a spoonful of bad attitude for breakfast this morning. Goodness, I've never met a staff member who complained this much!"

And I've never met a Princess who was such a Royal pain. Hanson bit his tongue. He wouldn't dare speak such a thing. But oh, was he thinking it. He knew that working for the Royal Family would be an experience, but he didn't know that he would be babysitting such a self-absorbed, bossy, immature girl. She seemed unbelievably moody, and Hanson knew that he'd better watch his step, or else Chasity might pull out the Royal scepter and smash apart his career.

They walked in silence until they entered the stables. "Would you care for me to fetch your horse, Princess?" It pained Hanson to speak so kindly to her. But his job demanded it.

She wrinkled her nose, as if irritated with his offer. "Thank you, but I think I can handle 'the beast'."

Hanson was quite relieved, because he hadn't a clue how to tack up one of those ginormous creatures towering in the stalls. He wasn't exactly *afraid* of horses. Hanson had been taught in the Academy that fear wasn't allowed to be in his DNA. He would never admit it, but horses were daunting. Hanson had dodged bullets, fought ninja warriors, and landed planes in his Secret Service training. Yet, despite mastering all of those tasks, it still made him nervous to think about riding horseback.

It took Hanson's eyes a moment to adjust to the change of lighting. The barn was well lit, but dim in comparison to the glaring sunlight seen just seconds before. As his eyes slowly shifted, he was able to make out the scene before him. The horseshoe-shaped tunnel wrapped around an indoor arena, with stalls lining each long hall. Several workers wheeled past them with loads full of horse manure. In that instant, Hanson was thankful for his job. At least Princess Chastity didn't smell as nasty as the horses did. Hanson followed Chastity as she seemed to know where she was going. Quickly enough she approached the stall where her beloved Nicholas was lodging, his large jaws munching on a mouthful of oats.

"Good afternoon, handsome!" Chasity greeted him with an eager hug on his broad neck and a kiss on his furry cheek. She unlatched the stall door and stepped inside. "You can wait out here," she told Hanson. "It'll take a few minutes to tack-up."

Hanson nodded, and wondered if she expected him to do the same. His eyes scanned the area for someone who might assist him. He spotted a tall, dark man wearing faded blue jeans and a colorful plaid shirt, a worn out cowboy hat, and boots that had seen better days.

"Sir," Hanson spoke to the man, "I'd like a horse. With the saddle and stuff already on it."

Instead of rushing off to do his bidding, the man only laughed, "My, my, aren't we bossy! You must be new."

Chasity popped her head out from Nic's stall, and smiled at the familiar cowboy, "You'll have to excuse him; he doesn't have much experience with horses." She directed her conversation toward Hanson, "Moss has a rule: you ride, you tack up. It's part of being a responsible horseman or horsewoman." She turned back to Moss, "I'll teach him all the basics later, but would you mind assisting him just this once? I'm in a hurry to get Nic out before sunset."

Moss nodded, "Sure thing, Your Highness. I'll be right back with your horse, sir."

Hanson let out a puff of frustrated air from between his lips. He anxiously patted his hands on his pants, feeling nervous about the upcoming ride. He really was not looking forward to it. He leaned against a thick wooden pillar and took a deep breath. He needed to compose himself before Princess Chasity picked up on the fact that he was nervous. That would only bring on more insults. She seemed to disrespect him enough as it was already.

Hanson heard the sound of female laughter burst out. He turned his head down the long hall where a small group of young women around his age entered the scene. Their excited chatter was loud and high pitched – just like the way all females were on their way to the bathroom, traveling in their giggly little packs. Two beautiful looking ladies made their way down the aisle, leading horses on either side. Another spout of laughter poured out of the one with the mane of red hair. Hanson immediately recognized her. It was Lilly Chesterfield. She was dressed in tall, black English riding boots, tan pants, and a red riding coat; the usual attire for English Dressage. As they approached, Hanson tried to look away, knowing that work wouldn't be the proper place to reconnect with this old friend. He tried to distract himself, but was completely taken by that familiar, freckled face.

Lilly stopped in her tracks as soon as she saw him. "Hanson? Hanson *Fletcher*?"

This caught Chasity's attention from where she put Nic's saddle blanket in place. Her ears perked up, along with Nic's, and followed the conversation.

"Hey!" Hanson greeted awkwardly, unsure of whether or not it was okay to be talking with her. But he couldn't hide the excitement in his voice. "Wow. Yeah, it's me! How are you? How have you been?"

"I can't believe it!" Lilly's fair face was lit up with joy, "I'm absolutely great, what about you?" Lilly shook her head as if she was staring at a daydream, "Everyone thought you completely vanished after Middle School! This is crazy! Um, like what are you doing here?"

"What am I doing here?" Hanson laughed, "What are you doing here? Honestly, this is the last place in the world I would've ever imagined bumping into you!"

"Well, I've been invited to The Palace by Prince Addison, to stay here for a few days," Lilly started to explain. "Our families became pretty close friends over the years, and–"

Chastity stepped out from her hiding place in the stall, with her head cocked slightly. She hated to interrupt their little reunion, but she was much too curious not to.

Lilly saw Chasity emerge from the shadows, "Oh, hello!"

"Hi," Chasity offered a smile. Before stepping out to see who the mysterious stranger was, Chasity had recognized the name Chesterfield. The Chesterfields owned a beautiful thoroughbred farm, and often hosted races and polo matches that she attended. Although she had never spoken to Lilly personally, she recognized the spunky redhead from past functions. "So, I couldn't help but notice that it seems like you two know each other?"

"Yes!" Lilly replied, completely enthusiastic. "We used to be really close. I'm still in awe that he's here! How in the world did you get connected with the Royal Family?" Lilly's gelding huffed impatiently as he lifted his hoof and stomped it down again. He was eager to return to his food source, and standing in the center of the stable chatting with old friends wasn't exactly on his agenda, as his stomach suggested otherwise.

"I was recruited by the Secret Service," Hanson glowed as he spoke to her. "So after Middle I started training and, well, here I am."

Lilly's mouth hung open, "No way! That's amazing! So, like, what do you do here? Or is it a big secret mission and you can't tell me?" She laughed at her very un-original joke.

"Actually," Hanson shot a weary glance toward the Princess, "I babysit her."

Chasity's face twisted, shocked that he would speak so shamefully of her in front of his friends.

Lilly laughed, "Aw, how cute. I've really got to get Stormy taken care of, but when can we talk? We have like a million and one things to catch up on!"

"I get off work at seven," Hanson replied without skipping a beat. "I'll meet you at the front desk, 'kay? We can grab dinner and go to some of our favorite old spots."

Lilly was more than pleased with his answer. She squealed, "Perfect! Sounds like a date. I can't wait!"

"Define *manifest content*," Bailee read the flashcard with confidence. "Don't worry, it's an easy one," she reassured her sister.

"Says the girl who's holding the answer in her hand! Uggh, let me think." Kitty covered her eyes as if it would help her concentrate. When that didn't work, she tapped her fingers on the table like a mini drum. "Um, um, um, um...." The stressful gesture didn't help relieve any tension.

"I'll give you a hint," Bailee tried to help her distressed sister, "It has to do with dreams."

"Gah!" Kitty exploded, "I give up!"

Bailee read the card, "manifest content– in Freudian dream analysis, the surface content of a dream, which is assumed to mask the dream's actual meaning."

"That's it, I need a coffee break," Kitty peered into her empty mug. "I'm telling you, these psych terms are going to be the death of me!"

Bailee frowned, "Don't be so hard on yourself. You're going to get this. It's only the first semester."

"I don't get why Bridget is so envious of us," Kitty stood up, stretching her weary bones and heading to the counter for a refill. "When I told her we were coming to Starbucks to study for our psychology test, she practically started drooling. Meanwhile, she's going to school online via the comforts of her own couch, because she can. For us, passing or failing school isn't an option. It's a matter of survival."

"I guess it's all about perspective," Bailee reasoned as she followed her sister to the counter. "Everyone seems to want something they don't have. Hey, I could probably write my next paper about that!" she giggled.

After refilling their mugs with creamy goodness, Bailee nudged her sister, "Hey look, it's Sapphire!" Kitty waved to her fellow classmate, and Sapphire motioned them to come toward her table, "Hello girls!"

They made a beeline for her booth in the back and plopped down. "Studying for the exam?" Kitty asked.

"Not at all, actually," Sapphire giggled, her adorable English accent drawing out every word. "I'm here with my new friend, Vanessa, and we're a bit too giddy to think about school affairs."

Vanessa tried to control the urge to raise her eyebrows. *Friend?* She wanted to choke. *More like frenemy.* Ever since she arrived at The Palace, Sapphire hadn't been kind to her. Her little insults covered with sugar and smiles didn't fool Vanessa. She saw straight through her candy-coated poison. She wanted to shake her head.

What a strange day it had been, very similar to the previous one. Vanessa had packed her bags to fly home, rode the elevator down to the lobby to check out, then got word that Prince Addison wanted to see her and a few of the other girls. Again.

At first, she wasn't sure what to think of it. She needed to get home. She had a life to attend to!

Then, when Sapphire discovered that it was only Lilly, Vanessa, and she who had been invited to return, she immediately contacted Vanessa and asked if they could hang out. Vanessa was hesitant, but what else was she going to do while hanging around in Tarsurella for another day? She had already explored the castle, seen the tourist sights, and done everything their quaint little town offered.

Sapphire was elated by the fact that she was in such good graces with the Prince. She quickly filled Kitty and Bailee in on the exciting news.

"And so, tomorrow morning we shall be playing tennis with His Royal Highness," Sapphire gushed. "I asked Mother and she contacted the college to get me excused from class in the morning. She said that if I can capture the heart of our dear Prince, what need is a formal education?" Sapphire laughed.

"Seriously?" Vanessa was disgusted with the statement. "You

think marrying a Prince is more important than furthering your own personal achievements and education, preparing yourself for the possibilities of your future?"

"Oh, my dear, naïve, little American friend," Sapphire reached across the table and patted her daintily on the hand, "do you have the faintest idea what Prince Addison's net-worth is? Not to mention, the net-worth of the entire Royal Family?"

Bailee and Kitty exchanged glances. Sapphire was not aware of the fact that they were so close to Princess Bridget. They felt like spies collecting important information.

"Perhaps the greater question to be asking is, are you aware of how many Tarsurellian citizens are growing unhappy with the rule of this monarchy?" Vanessa boldly asserted her opinion, "In my time here, I've been doing research about the governmental structure of this Kingdom, and from the data I've been collecting, it appears as though this monarchy isn't going to last forever. People want change. Real change. They want freedom, and democracy, and as charming as this whole fairytale nation appears to be, the sustainability of it just isn't realistic."

Sapphire gasped, "Blasphemy! How dare you speak such ill words against the Crown! Ugh, Americans. They have no appreciation for true beauty and history when they see it. Prince Addison would never choose you to be his wife, as rebellious and gutsy as you are."

"His wife?!" Vanessa laughed, "Well, I would hope not! Palace life is *not* my cup of tea."

Sapphire appeared pleased. "Well, with you out of the running it appears as though my only true competition is that flirty, air-headed Lilly Chesterfield. She would never be faithful to the Prince. She's always seen running about town with this young lad or that–" Sapphire grinned as she looked toward the door. "Don't look now girls, but you won't believe who just walked in the door. With company, nonetheless."

Naturally, all three of them craned their necks in the opposite direction, to see who Sapphire was speaking of. Strangely enough, a smiling Lilly Chesterfield with a male escort entered as if perfectly on que.

"Yoo-hoo! Miss Chesterfield!" Sapphire called across the Starbucks lounge. Lilly spun around and grinned when she saw the familiar faces. She confidently walked toward them, hanging on Hanson's arm.

Chapter 9 – Don't Mess with Bridget

Early morning sunshine radiated from the tennis court, where Addison reached into his pocket for a lime-green tennis ball. "Are you ready?" he asked cautiously, feeling out his competitor's current status.

The spunky redhead, whom Addison was aiming for, replied with a cheery, "Yep!"

Addison glanced at Vanessa, his teammate, who offered him a confident nod.

He bounced the ball off the court and it flew into the air, where his racket made contact and sent the little object flying across the net. Lilly Chesterfield made a swift attempt to kiss the ball with her racket, but it was to no avail.

Addison tossed Vanessa an exhausted glance. This was the *ninth* time Addison served the ball and Lilly missed. Lilly was a beautiful girl, but had no sense of hand-eye coordination whatsoever. Sadly, her team-mate was just as untalented.

"Sports-challenged" was how Bridget described herself. The original plan, which Addison was surprisedly informed of as soon as he woke up, was to play several tennis matches with Sapphire, Lilly and Vanessa. He shouldn't have been shocked that his father and The Palace staff had set up another meeting so quickly, but he was. By the time he changed into a comfortable pair of shorts and casual tennis shoes, he received word that Sapphire had come down with the flu during the night and wouldn't be joining them. So Addison decided to ask his sister, Bridget, to take Sapphire's place.

Under different circumstances, Bridget would've turned down his offer, but late last night she'd received a call from her besties, informing her about the airheads who were trying to steal Addison's heart.

"You should've heard their conversation!" Kitty spoke, short of breath because she was trying to relay the information so quickly. "All they care about is your brother's Royal title. If he even considers dating one of these ditsy girls, the Kingdom is going to be doomed!"

Bridget laughed. Kitty could be so melodramatic. But when Bailee joined in and gave her two cents' worth, Bridget started to seriously listen. "Addison might not be able to see what's going on here because the girls are so charming. But you need to keep an eye out for him, Bridg. Especially the American girl. She was listing off everything wrong with our monarchy, and how we're going to turn into a democracy."

Bridget gasped. "That's terrible! Wow, this sounds serious. If you hear or see anything else suspicious, let me know, okay? I'm not going to stand by and watch my brother get trapped in a web of deception."

Bridget was a terrible tennis player. But at this particular point in time, she cared more about her brother's safety and emotional wellbeing, than how foolish her backhand swing looked.

Bridget studied Vanessa intensely. She had known the Chesterfield family for quite some time, and had already pegged their family as gold-diggers. They possessed a huge family fortune, and it was no secret that they wanted their daughter Lilly to marry well. But Vanessa was like an unworked jigsaw puzzle that Bridget was determined to figure out. *An American, huh?* Bridget twisted her lip thoughtfully. Vanessa's short brown hair was cut in a cute, chin-length bob. She was tall and slender, but didn't show up to the tennis match wearing anything ultra-adorable. Jeans and an aqua blue *Save the Whales* T told her that she hadn't put much effort into trying to impress her brother.

Lilly, on the other hand, was all dolled up in a baby-pink, designer knee-length tennis dress. She wore her signature hair in a fun up-do. With a matching pink tennis racket, Bridget almost thought she resembled the animated Princess Peach character on *Mario Tennis*. She made the same high pitched, girlish noises every time she attempted to smack the air.

"Sorry!" Lilly apologized, glancing at her racket sheepishly, "I've never been very good at tennis."

"It's okay," Addison sighed, feeling no desire to finish the game. "Why don't we take a break?"

"Sounds great!" Bridget volunteered, happy to be done with the embarrassment. "I think Deborah is setting up tea on the Garden Terrace."

Addison bent over to collect his tennis bag. He stood up, noticing Vanessa's shirt. "So, are you just as passionate about saving the whales as you are about helping the homeless?"

Vanessa detected a hidden smirk in his voice. Was he making fun of her? Her eyes narrowed cautiously. "What do you have against my passion for endangered whales who are mercilessly being held captive in heartless amusement parks? Don't they have a right to freedom just as much as the rest of us?"

Addison laughed as he hopped into the driver's seat of his golf cart. "Oh, I have nothing against whales and their freedom. I just wanted to check and see if the whale thing was simply a trend, or if animal life preservation is something you're truly into. If so, I should warn you that there will be meat served at The Ball." He winked.

Vanessa laughed, also moving toward the cart, not feeling at all offended by his light-hearted jab.

Lilly suddenly cut in front of her and slipped into the empty seat on his cart. "It is such a lovely day!" she burst out toward Addison, "And I am so flattered that you would take time off in the midst of your busy schedule to spend it with a common girl like myself. I can only imagine how busy you must be preparing for the big Coronation! Nevertheless, I am *so* looking forward to the rest of our day together! Tea on the terrace, late-afternoon golf, followed by a beautiful horseback ride into the Tarsurellian sunset—"

Vanessa raised an eyebrow. "Nobody said anything about an evening horseback ride. My flight leaves at three."

"Oh, what a pity." Lilly smiled triumphantly at Addison and shrugged, "I guess it will just be the two of us, then."

Vanessa got the message, and retreated to Bridget's golf cart. She said nothing as Bridget hit the gas pedal and whipped around a corner. Vanessa gripped her fingers tightly to the seat. Bridget was not the most cautious driver!

"So, are you interested in my brother?" Bridget wasn't going to play coy. She wanted everything out in the open, all cards on the table.

"What?" Vanessa could scarcely believe her ears. "Interested? Like, romantically? Absolutely not! I don't know what kinds of games these other girls are playing, but I bought a ticket to the Prince's Coronation Ball so I could help the homeless, not snake my way into the Royal Family."

Bridget laughed, "Forgive me, darling, but I find that slice of bologna hard to stomach. Are you attempting to sell me on the fabricated idea that you care about the homeless more than you do about Addison's fortune? That's not very believable."

Vanessa crossed her arms, "I am quite offended that you're assuming I would lie to you. As if I have some kind of alternative motives for being here. I'm not entirely sure why all the ladies around here are fangirling over your brother, but I can strongly reassure you that I am *not* one of them."

"So you're honestly telling me," Bridget continued, "that you have no desire whatsoever to wear the Crown, share his bank account, and assist him in ruling the country?"

"Of course not!" Vanessa spat. "I would never want to be part of a monarchy. I don't think it's right for one man, or woman, to have all the power over a nation. It's like a borderline dictatorship! People should be free to choose and elect their leaders. Every nation should have the opportunity to govern themselves."

"Please," Bridget held up a hand, "don't talk politics with me. Just because you're mad about what I said, don't go slamming the Crown. I could say one or two choice words about your country, and that dream-come-true democracy of yours, but I shall refrain myself from doing so. Forgive me if I've offended you by being so quick to assume you had a pre-planned agenda in coming here, but he's my brother and I love him; and you cannot blame me for being protective of him."

Vanessa frowned and didn't bother to respond. They had already made it back to the Garden, and it was time to get off the carts. Bridget bounced out of the driver's seat and strutted over to the tea-table as though nothing had happened. Vanessa seethed with anger inside. *Whoever the poor soul is that actually ends up marrying Prince Addison,* Vanessa thought while shaking her head, *had better be warned about that lovely sister of his.*

The Queen's Ball Room was lit up with a warm and magical glow as darkness settled upon the castle. Hanging twinkle lights made the room feel as though something spectacular was about to happen. Bridget was genuinely impressed by what the decorating team had done. Even though she had grown up in the folds of such luxury and extravagance, it never ceased to amaze her. The mood lighting made everything feel so much more real; Addison's Coronation was right around the corner.

A small assembly of privileged palace workers gathered together to witness the first rehearsal for the coming Coronation. This was only the first of several to follow, as everyone knew that the ostentatious event would be nearly impossible to master without much trial and error beforehand.

Mrs. Gram addressed her crowd: The Royal Family. Everyone was present. Addison, Bridget, Chasity, Hope, Asher, Jillian, Millie and Willie.

Bridget knew that the rehearsal was vital, but it was late into the evening, and they all had places they would rather be. She surpassed a yawn. Bridget glanced at Addison, who scratched an imaginary bug bite on the back of his head. She could tell that his mind was somewhere far away. She couldn't help but wonder if he was thinking about either of the ladies whom he had just spent his day with. Bridget desperately hoped he wasn't.

Vanessa had flown back to the states, and was out of the picture now. She wouldn't return until the eve of The Ball.

But even then, the chances of Addison even having an opportunity to chat with her would be slim. Bridget knew that her words to Vanessa were harsh. Perhaps even cruel. But Bridget didn't care. She felt that her verbal assault was necessary to protect what mattered to her the most. She felt a lion-like spirit arise inside. There was no way that she would let Addison suffer the same things she had. Girls like that, had no business playing games with Addison's heart.

Flirty Sapphire was knocked out with the flu. Now, the only remaining contestant she had to be concerned with in Addison's love life was Lilly.

"The Royal ceremony shall begin as the brass trumpets sound, calling all guests to attention in The Main Hall." Mrs. Gram mentally walked them through each step of the evening. "Then, as the Tarsurellian Orchestra begins to play, Addison shall descend from The Grand Staircase, and parade into The Ball Room. The rest of you shall follow, one by one, allowing our guests adequate time to stare in wonder and take as many pictures as they please, as each Prince and Princess floats down the corridor. After last in line, Prince William, arrives, the King shall descend and present his speech.

"Then, Prince Addison will waltz with the dance partner of his choosing. For the second dance, each will be assigned with a partner of their own to dance the Minuet. Following these two very special dances, the guests will then be offered a gracious hand of invitation to dance to their heart's content! No member of the Royal Family shall be required to continue dancing, following the first two numbers.

"When you're through dancing, you are to mingle with our guests, then move into The Royal Conference Room where the press will be waiting for Prince Addison's speech. This event shall be followed by a photoshoot, and the floor will be open to the press to ask questions and pursue interviews.

"Following Addison's speech, you are to gather outdoors for the Horseback Ceremony. Then, the grand finale, Addison's historical crowning will take place in The Throne Room. We will, of course, rehearse every element required, to see to it our evening goes flawlessly. But as of yet, are there any questions?"

Millie raised an eager hand, "When do get to eat the chocolate cake?"

Mrs. Gram shook her head, "The cake is for our guests, Princess Millie. You shall gracefully refrain from doing so. We must be on our best behavior, as the eyes of the entire world will be upon us that night! Photographs with Royals, as the American's would say 'stuffing their faces', are terribly ungraceful."

Millie felt her heart fall in disappointment. She had been watching Clark construct her dream cake for so long, and now she would not even get to taste the tiniest lick of frosting? A sudden, reassuring thought came to her, and it revived her spirits. Millie could feel her heart beating again, with a fresh hope, knowing that chocolate was on the horizon! Millie smiled to herself, *I will ask Clark to secretly save me a slice.*

♔

Following dance rehearsal, each child bid Mrs. Gram goodnight, and promptly exited The Ball Room. In the Lobby, ceiling lights were dimmed, and the front desk was now closed to any tourist activity. Bridget knew in full confidence that the front doors were bolted, and the security systems had been engaged. Though their security guards were nowhere to be seen, she knew their careful watch continued from the Main Security Tower all through the night.

Bridget's feet ached from the pair of three-inch high heels that she was to wear for the event, and as she began to tiptoe up the staircase she could think of nothing more fulfilling than soaking her tired toes in a hot bath. Little Millie had something quite different in mind.

"Where are you going sweetie?" Bridget asked Millie, who wasn't following the group up the staircase. She was headed down the hall.

"I'm a Marine Sci-chologist and ocean adventurer!" Millie explained all in one breath. "And the Little Mermaid just swam to me, and told me that Captain Clark has sunk his ship in the deep! I must go rescue him before it's too late!"

Jillian had little patience for Millie's whimsical ideas. "It's a Marine *Biologist*," Jillian corrected her, "And no, you're not, it's nearly bedtime."

"But Clark needs me!" Millie pleaded.

"Our cook is *not* drowning," Jillian snapped back. "It's all in that silly head of yours."

"No, it's not!" Millie raised her voice, echoing through the empty hall. "Arielle the Mermaid *told* me so!"

Overhearing the squabble, Addison stepped in. "Millie, you have fifteen minutes until bedtime. Think you can save Captain Clark before then?"

Millie grinned, revealing a mouthful of teeth and gratefully saluted him, "Aye, aye, Captain Addison!" Then she took off in a sudden bolt down the hallway.

Jillian shook her head in disappointment, "I don't know why you always do that, Addison. You shouldn't encourage her in those ridiculous games she plays. She's going to have to grow up sooner or later."

"Yeah," Addison placed a gentle hand on his sister's shoulder, "but Millie should have her fair share of time spent in Never-Never Land. Adulthood will be here before she knows it."

"Hey, is anyone else hungry?" Hope asked, suddenly changing the subject.

"I could certainly eat something," Chasity replied. "All that rehearsal for entering and exiting and curtsying can really wear a girl out."

Bridget nodded, "I totally agree." As much as her feet hurt, she wanted food more. "I vote we head to the kitchen."

Her suggestion was favored by all, with the exception of Addison who admitted to being overtired. Asher had already escaped from the pack and locked himself up in his bedroom. Addison headed upstairs, while the rest turned down the long hall to the basement kitchen.

The vast expanse of kitchen space was quiet and still. The Royal siblings walked through the main isle, passing several cake decorators who worked late hours in order to perfect their masterpieces, and by a row of dishwashers where several maids were unloading and stacking the clean dishes in their assigned cupboards.

"Look, there's Millie!" Willie announced, his feet picking up speed as soon as he spotted her.

The girls couldn't help but laugh. Willie was right. There sat Millie on top of the counter, excitedly chatting with her favorite person, between enormous bites of a rich slice of chocolate cake.

"You said you were rescuing Captain Clark from drowning," Bridget teased her with a laugh. "It looks like he needs to rescue *you* from this piece of cake! Millie, it's almost bigger than your head!"

"I did too rescue him!" Millie argued, obviously missing the joke. "This was the reward he gave me!"

"She speaks the truth," Clark winked. "Would anyone else care for a piece?"

They could not turn down such a mouth-watering offer, and soon were each situated with a fork, spoon, and glass of milk.

"Mmmm…" Bridget raved, "this is delicious. Clark, your cakes are always superb. As the French say, '*Je suis fabuleuse!*' Are you sure we should be eating this, though?"

"Sure!" he smiled, "It was only a practice cake."

"Well, I don't find anything wrong with it!" Willie grinned, chocolate frosting smudged across his nose.

Bridget glanced at her watch, then made the announcement, "Millie it's been fifteen minutes. Remember what Addison said? You and Willie need to head upstairs and go to bed."

"Aww man," Millie slid off the counter regretfully, "thanks for the cake, Clark!"

"Yeah, thanks!" Willie attempted to lick his nose as he stretched out his long pink tongue, eyes crossing. He tried with all his might but couldn't quite reach it.

"Anytime," Clark laughed at Willie's antics, handing him a napkin. "I'd better be headed home, too. It's getting late." He turned to Hope, "Feel free to help yourselves to anything else."

"Will do," Hope's eyes sparkled, always pleased by Clark's genuine kindness and fatherly heart toward Millie and Willie. "Thanks again."

"Now *this* is chocolate," Hope sighed dreamily, licking her fork, careful to collect the last crumb, savoring the lasting flavor. "Why couldn't I find any upstairs in our kitchen?"

"Because Dad knows better than to have junk like this lying around where we can get to it," Bridget replied, "Or else we might be tempted to eat chocolate cake *every* night before bed. And that would be horrible for my complexion."

"Bridget," Jillian rolled her eyes, "Dad doesn't want us eating healthy just so we don't get pimples. He wants our bodies in good working condition. I think it's much more important what we can *do* than how we look. If I ate cake and sweets all the time, I wouldn't be able to jog the three miles I do every morning."

"Are you really up to three miles now?" Hope asked in surprise. She remembered the day Jillian first starting running with her new puppy dog. It had only been a few months, eight maybe, and Hope was quite amazed. "How is your security guard at keeping up with you?"

Jillian smiled, "He tries."

"Maybe we should switch guards," Chasity spoke slowly, the new thought forming on her lips sounded strange to her. "Hanson appears to be bored out of his mind with me. I've tried to encourage him to read or something to help pass the time, but he refuses. He might enjoy jogging in the morning. It may give some of his cooped-up energy an escape route."

"Chasity," said Bridget, "You know it isn't our place to meddle with our employees' personal preferences. If your guard has a problem with you or your daily routine, he'll have to speak to Jackson about it."

"Or, you could come jogging too," Jillian suggested what Chasity viewed as the impossible. Waking up before dawn to exercise was *not* her idea of fun.

"Who came up with that rule anyway?" Chasity dug a little deeper.

"What rule?" Jillian echoed.

"The rule that we're not supposed to concern ourselves with our employees on anything more than a strictly business level?" Chastity questioned. "We're not allowed to ask them about their pasts or their favorite movies, or what they do after they clock out. It's like they know everything about us, but we never even learn their middle names."

"That rule," Bridget explained, "has been in place since the birth of our nation, really. It's a separation of birth rights that nobody can do anything about. We are to treat all our employees with grace and kindness, but never engage with them on a deeply personal level. I'm sure there are many reasons why this rule is in place, but I believe the most important one would be a security issue. We never know who our enemies might be, and sharing the secrets of the Kingdom with an outsider is like what the Bible says, tossing your pearls before swine. They could totally turn and tear you into pieces. I know from personal experience." Bridget paused before finishing in a quiet voice, "There are too many people in this world- *boys,* to be specific- that want to get close to us, simply to steal something. Trust me girls, it's not worth the risk of having your heart broken. "

A blanket of silence fell over their discussion like a heavy fog, as everyone reflected on Bridget's past pain. They were all sensitive to their sister's wounds, and everyone tried to be as gentle as possible when talking about it.

"I understand entirely what you're saying," Chasity replied, "but I wasn't asking why I couldn't get *romantically* involved with Hanson. I was merely saying that I thought it might be nice if we could at least be friends. You know, if he could open up a little bit. There are so many things I'm curious about. Like where is he from? Why did he desire to become a security guard? And why was he so thrilled to reunite with his lady friend in the barn?"

Hope's ears suddenly perked up, "Lady friend?" She laughed, "Chasity this is so unlike you. I've never seen you so interested in an employee's *love* life before."

"It's not his love life," Chasity was quick to reply, "at least, I don't *think* it is. But they were definitely old friends with a colorful history. It seems odd that he would be connected with the Chesterfield family. Lilly said she was here to see Addison, so how can I not be at least a little bit curious about their past?"

"Wait. Lilly Chesterfield was flirting with your security guard?" Bridget scrambled to put the puzzle pieces together in her mind. "I wonder if that's the same guy Kitty and Bailee saw her with in Starbucks. The girls said that they definitely looked like an item." Bridget shook her head, "I have such a bad feeling about that girl. Addison should not be wasting his time with her. Chas, keep an eye on your security guard, okay? I'll ask the girls to be on the lookout as well. If Lilly *is* dating someone, we need to tell Addison."

"Are you sure Addi would want us *that* involved with his

personal life?" Hope asked, "You know what they say about people who meddle. It never ends well."

"Trust me, girls," Bridget spoke confidently, "love is blind. Addison won't be able to see the flaws in these ladies unless we expose them."

Chasity and Jillian tossed one another uneasy glances. Bridget could be a little bit over-zealous in her judgement of the character of others. They didn't have any facts about the situation, and so far everything was based on "hearsay." They knew better than to be hasty and jump to conclusions.

"Dude!" A surprised voice rang through the kitchen. All of the girls turned their heads toward the double swinging doors, where two male figures stood. "Oh man, it's them!" the young man exclaimed. He excitedly grabbed the shoulders of his buddy and started shaking him.

Jillian and Hope immediately recognized the duo. David, the lead singer of *Kennetic Energy* slid out of his friends' excessive shoulder-shaking, and shifted his eyes to where Princess Hope stood. He tensed up, as if he had just intruded upon a very important meeting.

"Hey, what's up?!" the shaggy-haired drummer waved at them as he quickly moved to where they stood.

David opened his mouth to apologize and exit, but it was already too late. His crazy friend had joined their circle, and David had no choice but to go rescue Zac before he made an even bigger fool out of himself.

"Dude! Who would'a thought we'd meet you all down here!" Zac was truly taken aback by this happenchance, "I mean, when we checked in, they said we would never see you guys downstairs. This is crazy!"

Jillian laughed, "Well, we *do* live here. And we're allowed to leave our rooms every once in a while." She giggled.

Chasity was confused as her sister chatted easily with the strangers. She felt like she was missing something. Who were these guys? The first male sported greasy hair which flopped like a thin mop all over his forehead. His neon green shirt had the letters, TEAM USA, and he wore a pair of skinny, skater-boy jeans, which looked as though they had been through a paper shredder.

The second was taller than his friend, and more muscular. He, unlike the first, looked as though he might be able to withstand a strong windstorm without being swept away with stray newspapers. His defined face was fastened shut with a frown, and the way he clasped and unclasped his hands together, he appeared to be very nervous. He wore black dress pants with a white shirt and red tie. As Chastity observed them, they appeared to be extreme opposites. The first was over-confident and talkative, giving much preference to the word *dude*, and riding on the thin line of nearly being obnoxious. The second was quiet, reserved, and handsome.

"We're staying in one of the Suites upstairs, and dude, now I know why they call it a Suite!" Zac monologued. "It's totally sweet! Did you know it's got a video arcade, a bathtub made of gold, and 24/7 room service? Oh, and they don't leave those pathetic little mints on your pillow, dude, they leave like massive hunks of chocolate! It's totally epic! So we ordered room service, and dude, I saw the lobster on the menu, and totally had to have it. Because, I mean, we're rock-stars now, staying in a legit castle, and it's not every day you can order lobster in a castle! So then David and I were talking, and I was like 'Dude, let's go down to the kitchen and watch them make it'! 'Cause I was like, how do they make it without getting their hands cut off by the vicious lobsters? I mean, lobsters are huge, man! But then I saw the Baked Alaska, and I thought it would be pretty supendipulous to see them bake Alaska. Like, how do you do that? Alaska is so honkin' big. Can you really bake it? But man, then I saw the snails and was totally gonna get those as appetizers, because you can't order grub like that in the States. I mean, I guess you could, but hello, castle in Europe! Time to live large or go home, right? But it grossed the girls out, and then Laney threatened to quit the band, and so I was like, whatever dude, I'll just go with the lobster."

"Um, I'm sorry; he's never been out of Kentucky," David laughed uncomfortably, trying to offer an excuse for Zac's psychotic rambling. Zac had no grip on the concept of social manners or a basic idea of class. He sounded like he was talking to the girls at high school back in Cross Creek, and was completely unaware of the fact that they had changed time zones, continents, and company. These were *Princesses*. David wanted to slap his friend in the forehead with something much harder than a V8 bottle. These girls were far too important to suffer through Zac's display of his pathetic usage of the English language. Why didn't Zac *get* that?

"Yeah dude, and I've never seen a chocolate fountain either. Is there one here?"

Jillian laughed, "No chocolate fountain. But we do have a room of mirrors that was built under The Palace back in the Eighteen-hundreds. You might want to check that out tomorrow, it's pretty cool. How long are you all staying?"

"Three days," David spoke this time, trying to spare the Princesses of Zac's unnecessary details, "Well two, actually. We're just here for rehearsal, but thank you, Your Highness, for your recommendation. We will have to check that out."

"Oh please, none of that 'Your Highness' stuff," Jillian

wrinkled her nose, "It's extremely awkward. Just call me Jillian. I'm sorry that you all have such a short visit, but I'm very much looking forward to your return, and to your performance at the Coronation!"

"Yeah, it's a real bummer we've gotta go back to the States," Zac grumbled. He gave a thumbs down and made a deflating noise with his mouth. David wanted to slam his face into the counter. It sounded like Zac had sat on a whoopee cushion. You do *not* make noises like that around Royalty.

"I would still like to hear that new song before you leave though." Jillian said, "Like Hope mentioned, we have school and our schedules are a little crazy, but I'm sure we can squeeze in an appointment. Why not go to the front desk tomorrow morning, and ask to coordinate something with Deborah? I'm sure she can fit you in. Let her know that I sent you."

"Okay," David glanced at Hope, then quickly looked away, surprised again by how beautiful she was. "Yeah, we'll do that."

The King tossed a quick prayer up to Heaven before knocking on his son's door. The final thing on his "to-do" list for the day was to have a heart-to-heart conversation with Asher. It promised to be a challenge. As the King stood outside the door of Asher's 'Man Cave', he prayed for help. *Tear down the walls that he's been building up, Lord.*

After several more knocks, Asher appeared at the door.

Asher's bored face greeted him. The visit was unexpected, so he didn't say anything.

"May I come in, Son?" The King asked, trying to be respectful of Asher's personal space.

Asher shrugged, and the King took that as his permission to enter. It had been several months since the King last stepped foot in his son's room, and he had nearly forgotten how impressive the layout was.

Asher's sporty suite was complete with a miniature arcade, half a basketball court, and expensive workout equipment. With a room like this, Asher never had much reason to leave. The King scooped up a ball from the court and dribbled a few times, "So, how's life in Asher's world?"

An irritated expression played across Asher's young face as he huffed. "Dad, don't try and beat around the bush. I know you came here to talk to me about my bad grades and my bad attitude, so let's just get this over with, okay?"

The King dribbled a couple more times, attempted to shoot from the free throw line, and missed. Asher rebounded the ball and tossed it back to his dad.

"Miss Christy tells me that you're not applying yourself in your studies. She really believes in you, Asher. She says you're a bright kid who has magnificent potential." He attempted another shot.

Asher grabbed the ball and took a lay-up. He was angry, but never too mad to play sports.

"Why aren't you trying?" The King pursued the matter further.

Asher threw the ball at him, and even though he was only trying to pass it, the King could feel resentment in his throw.

"Maybe I am trying."

"Are you?" The King raised an eyebrow.

"What's the point, Dad?" Asher huffed. "Addison's getting the whole Kingdom, and-"

"Oh, so is *that's* what this is about." He shook his head with disappointment. They had been over this several times before. "Asher, you are not Addison, and just because he was firstborn doesn't mean-"

"Dad!" The volume in his voice raised several notches higher, "Yes it does! He being firstborn means everything! He inherits it all. The Crown, the Kingdom, the country, The Palace... and what do I get? Absolutely nothing."

The King found himself growing impatient, but worked to keep his voice calm, "Asher, that's not true-"

"Yes it is, Dad. And you know it."

The King sighed, "Your brother has been nothing but gracious to you about this situation. He's told you over and over again that he wants your assistance in running the Kingdom! And if you chose to buckle down and apply yourself to your studies, once you graduate, he would be happy to give you a great position in Parliament."

"Oh yeah," Asher forced a fake laugh, "because that's what every guy dreams of. Being a washed-up politician working in a cubical funded by his fat-headed brother."

"Asher!" The King raised his voice, "You have no right to speak about your brother like that. My goodness, young man, I don't know where this nasty attitude toward your siblings has been coming from, but it needs to end!"

Asher rolled his eyes, crossed his arms, and plopped down on the basketball, ready for the angry lecture coming his way.

"This snobbish air of disrespect pouring out of your heart is like a smelly garbage dump!" The King continued, "I don't know what has gotten a hold of you lately, but you need to check yourself, young man."

Asher counted on his fingers as if he was taking mental notes, "Smelly heart, garbage dump, toss out the trash. Got it. Now are we done?"

The King could feel invisible smoke pouring out of his ears. "No, we are *not* done," He snapped. "And this conversation is not going to be finished until I say it is! These past few months you have been severely testing my patience. And if you don't straighten up soon, I'm going to have to take serious steps of discipline and punishment. If you're not willing to follow the rules of love, respect and obedience in our household, then you will bear the iron fist of consequences!"

Asher raised his eyebrows, surprised to hear that his father was considering taking action. Usually he was such a softie.

The King could tell that he finally had his son's attention. "On the day you were born, your mother and I dedicated your life to the Lord, both purposing in our hearts and promising to raise you in a strong Christian home. We made the commitment to pour the Word of God into you at a young age, give you love, structure, and encouragement. Asher, you've been given all the materials and spiritual benefits that a young man could ever ask for! And to be quite honest, this ugly rebellious streak that I see rising up in you is shameful. Continue down this path, and I foresee enrollment into military school in your near future. It's your choice, son. Either you shape up, or ship out."

Chapter 10 – Sparkly Prison Cell

Bridget glared hatefully at her sparkly wall. "*You,*" she hissed, "are nothing more than a couture' prison cell."

Bridget flopped onto the fluffy cream comforter spread across her queen-sized bed. She let out a frustrated huff, then ran irritated fingers through her hair. She quickly grabbed her phone and speed-dialed Kitty.

"I'm trapped." She vented, "I'm locked in a pretty jail, where everyone dresses way cuter than in those ugly orange jumpsuits. But it doesn't matter because I'm still stuck."

Kitty resisted the urge to laugh, "Oh dear! It sounds like you put on your pair of drama-queen pants this morning!"

"Kitty, I'm serious." Bridget sat up and crossed her legs. She glanced at her laptop, where a pink mug of steaming hot-chocolate sat beside it on her computer tray. "I have no life. While everyone else is out having fun and going to college and shopping at cute little vintage stores, I'm stuck here, doing school in my room. End of story."

"Bridget, you were in Paris just a few days ago!" Kitty reminded her friend, "You have your own private jet! You, my dear, are *anything* but stuck."

"Maybe not in the obvious, most literal sense of the word," Bridget replied, "but in the place where it matters most, I am. It's like my soul isn't allowed to grow any wings. I would give *anything* to leave this palace, blend in with the crowd, and just explore!"

"Then why don't you?" Kitty asked, "What's holding you back?"

"My security guards," her answer was simple but true.

"Have you ever considered studying abroad?" She planted a new idea, "What about London, France, or Australia even!? Go somewhere romantic and exotic; get a little apartment and live out your goofy little dream. Surely your dad would be okay with that."

Bridget sighed, "He would never let me do that."

"Well, have you asked him?"

The phone fell silent. Bridget realized that she hadn't.

"Listen girl, you know I love you," Kitty spoke frankly, "but maybe it's time you stopped complaining about your situation and actually did something about it! Let your dad know how much this means to you. You need space to grow. Room to adventure! And yeah, it might be a little complicated with security details, but if anyone can handle it, you guys can. You have the best security team in the world."

Bridget felt herself growing excited about the idea, "Wow, I think you're right." She giggled, "Wouldn't it be crazy if my dad actually agreed to this? Can't you see me working on school papers at a little coffee shop in London, or riding to work on a moped in Paris?!"

"Yaass!" Kitty shared in her excitement, "Your wings of independence will be sprouting like nobody's business!"

Bridget laughed, resituating herself on the bed, barley able to sit still. The thought of such freedom sent bolts of excited electricity through her heart, "I would finally have the opportunity to live a normal life! No more curtsying, or fancy dinners with the Prime Minister. Just the freedom to live!" Bridget's beautiful daydream came to a screeching halt as she faced the difficult reality of the situation. "Now let's hope that I actually have the guts to take the first step - asking my dad."

"Come in!" The King responded to the knock on his Sitting Room door. He glanced up from his Bible and cup of tea, and smiled at his beautiful daughter standing in the wings. Bridget floated into the room, wearing a casual pair of blue jeans, and her over-sized, mocha-colored sweater. Her long locks were tied in trendy side braids, with several spirals of curl winding out here and there. His daughter wasn't wearing a crown, heavy makeup, or a pair of high-heels, but she was perfectly lovely in his eyes.

"Oh, I'm sorry, are you busy?" She stopped halfway to his easy chair, her bare toes pausing to rest on the argyle carpet. She had thought perhaps she could catch him between meetings, for his scheduled 'tea time', but it appeared as though he was in the middle of an important meeting with God.

"I'm never too busy for you, darling." He set his Bible aside and took a sip of tea, "I was just talking with the Lord about some things, casting my cares upon Him, trying to get His perspective on life. What's on your mind, my dear? Anything I can add to my prayer list?"

"Actually," she lowered herself onto the footstool near his chair, "yes." She inhaled deeply before revealing the news, "I would like your permission to study abroad."

The King's eyebrows popped up, having no control over the automatic reflex that appeared on his face in the wake of surprise. He gently lowered his tea cup to its saucer and clasped his hands together, "Are you having trouble with your studies? I thought you were enjoying your online courses?"

"But see, Dad, that's part of the problem," she continued. "They're online. I'm completely missing out on the college experience. No crabby professors or lively classroom debates, or long walks on campus property as the leaves are falling. There's so much more that I want to do and experience! And an internet classroom just won't let me."

"Bridget, we've discussed this previously," he explained, "and the reason we chose for you to attend University online is because of the safety issue. You're much, much more protected here at The Palace than you would be living on a wild campus somewhere. Besides," he added a smile, "I quite enjoy having you at home."

"But what if I went to school in another country?" Bridget wasn't about to let her dream die so quickly. "We could choose a really chill place, where other Royals and celebrities attend, and it wouldn't be a huge deal. You can send a security team with me and I can get an adorable little apartment and-"

"No," the King shook his head, "that's not possible. Far too risky."

"But Dad!" Bridget couldn't hide the whine and displeasure in her voice, "I've already thought through all the details and it's totally doable! It's not like everyone out in the real world is set on kidnapping or murdering me! And how could they, with like ten-trillion Royal security guards around? I'd be perfectly safe!"

The King knew this was a hot topic with his daughter. He tiptoed forward carefully, yet firmly stood on his previous statement. "I'm sorry Bridget, but my answer is 'no'. Of all the insecure locations for our family to be, a college campus would be one of the worst! Even if you weren't an heiress with Royal blood, I'd *still* be concerned about letting you run around in a place like that. My goodness, the majority of young people these days have gone absolutely mad; partying, drinking, as well as things much worse which are not even worth our time mentioning." He shook his head again, "The Lord only knows what kind of danger could befall you there. Far more drama than what we want to get ourselves into, I am sure."

Bridget could feel herself losing. If she couldn't change his mind, these palace walls would close in and suffocate her! "You're being completely unfair!" She struggled to make herself heard, "Don't you trust me? Don't you think I could handle myself out there? I'm not like those other girls!"

The King kept his voice steady, "Of course I trust you. But there are many crooked, vile, messed up people in this world, and it is them I do not trust. And, my dear, I know you're not like the other girls. You are unique, called by God to have such a powerful and purposeful destiny! You've been chosen and set apart, and extremely blessed. You live differently than the rest of the world does. Rest in that reality my daughter, and don't desire to be like the rest of them."

Bridget clenched her fist, struggling to keep her cool. Great, now he was bringing God into the argument! As if God were the one forcing her to be here. Angry thoughts zipped through her mind. *This isn't God's fault!* She wanted to snap,

It's your fault! You're way too over-protective! And how in the world am I ever going to discover His plan and purpose if I'm trapped here for the rest of my life?!

Bridget kept her lips locked tight, knowing that if she allowed a crack in the dam, it would all come rushing out. She forced a smile onto her face, "Glad we talked." She stood up and headed for the door.

"Honey, wait!" The King called after her, "You're obviously still upset with me. We can talk out whatever you need to."

"No, it's fine." She twirled around, "Enjoy your tea." She closed the door behind her.

The King let his discouraged head fall into his hands. "Oh Lord," he prayed, "what am I doing wrong?" He sighed, knowing that his wife would've known exactly what to say. She was such a natural at connecting with each of her children's hearts, talking them through disagreements, and making sure that they felt loved, understood, appreciated, and cherished. The King felt as though he had been failing deeply in that department. "Only a few more weeks. Then I'll be released of my Kingdom duties and be able to focus my heart and attention completely on being a father. That is a full-time job in and of itself! I don't know how You do it, Lord! You have billions of kids to keep track of!" He chuckled, "I'm pretty sure a large handful of them have some bad attitudes."

Chapter 11 – The Royal Library

"…and *this* is The Library." The emphasis placed on those five words were quite extraordinary, but didn't nearly do the room justice. Every wide-eyed tourist who entered the mind-blowing room wore the same expression on their face. And though thousands of visitors had passed through this common attraction in The Palace, their dramatic reactions never faded.

Today, only five lucky people were led on the usual trek through The Palace. But this time they were led by three of the Princesses themselves. This special VIP treatment was something tourists would pay out of their eyeballs for if offered such an opportunity. But this personalized Royal tour was being paid for with nothing less than the promise of a song from *Kennetic Energy*.

Books. Towering shelves of countless books adorned the walls, filling a room that measured at half the size of a collage basketball stadium. Scaling three floors high, a reader could only reach the top shelf with a scaffold.

David Carter was sure that every book he could ever imagine was hidden amongst them all, like buried treasure. His heart ached to run his fingers over the titles, search for one that intrigued him, and sneak away to a reading tower. The world might have thought that the young lad was a rock-star, but his closest friends knew his true nerdish character. David didn't shy away from the "nerd" title. Instead, he embraced it. A passionate love for books pumped through his veins, and he would never abandon it in an effort to become "cooler."

As a young boy, the highly-esteemed title of "rock star" was never one he envisioned being attached to his nametag. He was a poet at heart. He was entirely fascinated with the power of stories, the magic of lyrics, and what could happen when music and words came together as one. Songwriting was something that naturally flowed out of him. He never could have known that his passion for words would open up so many once-in-a-lifetime opportunities.

Opportunities just like this one. Exploring an ancient castle flooded with books. David's soul panted inwardly, like a thirsty dog, and he was pretty sure that he could spend his entire lifetime just in this room. Perhaps two lifetimes. He tried his very best to guard his great astonishment, but his eyes did not know how to lie.

"Dude, this is sick!" Zac was the first to speak.

"I know," Chasity smiled softly and continued walking, silently hinting to the crew that they must keep moving. The group was only promised an hour alone before the regular flow of tourists returned. "This room has enchanted me ever since I was a little girl. Although I grew up here, I still have to pinch myself every time I step inside."

Zac made a disgusted face at Chasity's reverent words, "Uh, no offence, but I didn't mean sick like that. I mean sick like, dude, if I have to read all these books I'm gonna *be* sick."

Chasity tried not to take offence at his ignorant words. How could one not treasure the great value of a book, and all of its irreplaceable adventures? *American boys,* she thought disgustedly, *they've been brainwashed by video games and MTV, and have no heart to discern true beauty in a book when they find it.*

"I'm having *Beauty and the Beast* flashbacks!" Laney laughed. "This is totally a remake of Belle's library!"

Chasity glanced at David, who wore a peculiar expression. The boy looked as though he had died and was walking through the glories of eternal life.

"Do you like to read, Mr. Carter?" Chasity presented the question with a smile.

"Um, yes." He appeared eager to dive into the great intellectual feast set before him.

"Feel free to check out a book as long as you're staying." She smiled, happy that someone found as much joy in her mother's library as she did.

"A book nerd I am not," Laney interjected, "but I've gotta admit this is pretty legit. Glass elevators, book ladders, Wi-Fi-whoa! Is that a coffee stand? Sweet!"

"Built in the nineteen-seventies," Chasity carried on with her 'tour guide' spiel, "this was our mother's first major renovation to The Palace when she became Queen. After the changes she made to the garden, of course. It took six years to build, furnish, and fill the shelves. She knew *exactly* what she wanted in here. She was such a visionary."

"Chas, you forgot to mention that it's eco-friendly," Hope added playfully. "The bamboo ceiling fans run on wind power, and the entire room is lit by solar panels on top of the roof."

"I was getting to that," Chasity smiled, not minding her sister's interruption. She glanced at Jillian who stood beside her with a shy smile. Jillian had been uncharacteristically quiet on their expedition. Jillian was usually a chatterbox. What was up with that? Perhaps she was just enjoying an afternoon of peace and quiet without her security guard following her every move. Lance and Hanson had to attend a meeting with Royal Security, and the alone time was refreshing. Chasity clasped her hands together, "Any questions so far?"

Zac pointed an eager hand into the air, "Um, if the library is run on solar power, does that mean the toilets all flush in the opposite direction?"

Zac's dense question was greeted by a hard smack in the back of the head.

"You dope!" Laney's harsh voice corrected him, "What kind of a question is that?!"

"Okay, moving on," Chasity chuckled despite the stupidity of such a thing. "Down this hall we have a secret passageway."

"Ohhh…" Laney's eyes lit up, "What's the story behind that?"

"This passageway was built for nothing less than tourist amusement," Hope interjected.

Laney frowned, "Really? Bummer. I was hoping maybe some medieval knights used to travel through here transporting top secret cargo, weapons, prisoners, or something."

Chasity pulled the lever which rotated the "hidden" bookshelf, revealing a dark and dusty room with faux cobwebs and plastic spiders lurking inside. The passageway was obviously designed for tourist pleasure. Anyone who truly wanted to create a secret tunnel wouldn't have made the entrance this obvious. What the tourists didn't know, was that there were secret passageways, tunnels, and underground rooms in The Palace, but they were only used by the security guards, and Chasity didn't know where they were located.

"After you," Chasity stretched out her hand, pointing to the obvious path of travel.

Zac pulled in his head slightly then responded, "Oh no, no,

of course not, ladies first."

"What, are you scared?" Justin the bass player shook his head shamefully, and paraded in before them.

Laney followed, then David, and Zac. It was Jillian's turn to enter, when a sudden ear-piercing scream arose from inside. "A spider!" Laney shouted.

A second scream followed, much more ear-damaging than the first. A body shot out of the dark tunnel, and the Princesses couldn't help their laughter. Zac's already-pale face had turned white as a ghost, as he recovered from the sudden fear.

Laney's contagious laughter was arising from inside, where she called out, "Zac, it was just a fake one! Geesh boy, take a joke!"

After regaining his composure, and capturing his "essence of cool," Zac flipped his hair back and entered again with a deep breath. "Dude, I knew that."

The Princesses followed, knowing that there was no danger in the dark passageway. Hidden security cameras were mounted on every wall, and though they couldn't see anything in the dark, they knew that watchful eyes were always upon them.

Soon a light appeared at the end of the tunnel, and they tumbled into a room with mirrors on every side.

"Cool beans!" Zac spoke, examining himself in one of the many mirrors. "It's like the fair!"

"We apologize for this area being so cheesy," Hope spoke "The Palace is actually a pretty cool place to live. But the tourist section has been designed to be marketed toward five-year-old girls who dream of being Princesses, and want to go home with a Royal goodie bag and plastic tiara."

"No, this is cool," Laney smiled. "It may seem dull to you guys 'cause you've been here your whole life, but in case you've forgotten, we *are* tourists. This stuff totally entertains us. It's been a blast, and my friends are gonna be *so* jealous when I tell them that Princess Chasity was our tour guide."

"I imagine they already are quite jealous," Jillian spoke for the first time as she sat on a bench made of mirrors. "I mean you all are superstars. That's gotta be pretty fun."

"Dude!" Zac suddenly exclaimed, his overly-loud voice bouncing off every wall, "There's an echo in here!"

Zac acted more like a little child with each passing second. After shouting various phrases only to hear them three times over, he began to belt out (in an extremely aggravating and off-pitch key) "Doe-Re-Me" from *The Sound of Music*. Chasity decided she had better put a stop to the second half of the song.

"Okay, does anyone want to see the Hall of History?" Chasity asked. "It holds all of The Palace records including every Royal birth, marriage, coronation, and death."

"I do!" Justin eagerly replied, more than ready to escape the song coming from Zac's mouth.

Laney exuberantly agreed, "Totally! Come on, Zac, let's go read about angry Queens who chopped off the court jesters' heads when they were acting *stupid*!" Zac wanted to stay, but was dragged away by Laney's hand, which was armed with a set of sharp red nails.

"He's right you know, the acoustics in this room are really nice." Jillian smiled at David, "Maybe you could sing us that

[169]

new song you guys talked about."

David glanced at the six-string strapped to his back. He had brought the guitar along on their little tour, knowing that the Princesses wanted him to play at the end. "Uh, sure.' David took a deep breath, "But shouldn't we wait for the others?"

Jillian hopped up from her seat, and just like a teeter-totter, Hope lowered herself to sit as her sister arose.

"Of course! I'll go get them." Jillian didn't have to be asked twice.

It took several seconds for David to realize that he was alone with Princess Hope, and his palms started sweating all over again. He casually wiped them on his jeans, hoping she wouldn't notice.

"Um, this is kind of," David started spewing out awkward words, "well, not kind of, it's actually extremely embarrassing, but I sort of have a confession to make. You see, aw man, I don't really know how to say this. And I made myself a promise, I mean if I were ever to get the chance to talk to you again that I... oh great, now I'm rambling. Ah." He scratched the back of his head, "I'm just gonna come right out and say this. The song I'm about to play is for you. I mean, like I wrote it. Like right after I met you. And um..."

David's courage slowly drained from his voice, and as soon as the words fell, he wanted to shove them all back inside. What in the world was he thinking?! Expressing interest toward a Royal Princess? Was he nuts?! Why hadn't he just kept his mouth shut? Aw man, he was just as bad as Zac.

David always had a deep desire to express his feelings, and that's where song writing came in handy. But now, he was in much too deep over his head.

He tried to quickly recover, "I know, you'll probably think it's stupid and incredibly cheesy, but I never thought I'd actually get the chance to play it for you, and I swore to myself that if I did, I would. So I just thought you should know."

Hope was speechless. She couldn't wipe the astonished look off her face. She was sure that she probably looked pretty goofy, her mouth hanging half-open with her eyes wide as Texas. But what was she supposed to say? What was she supposed to think? She struggled to process and sort through the weight of his words. Was this guy for real? Had he actually taken the time to carefully choose a collection of original words and skillfully weave them into a poetic declaration? Her heartbeat sped up, as she internally panicked. Nobody had *ever* ventured to do something so sweet and thoughtful for her. And it wasn't just someone. It was a *guy*. Unlike Bridget who had a long line of anxious courters piling up in the parlor, nobody had ever expressed any kind of romantic interest toward Hope.

Hope tried not to cringe as she thought about how terrible her attitude had been toward him. Just a few days ago she had considered firing him and shipping his puny little garage band back to the U.S., all because of a pathetic tabloid rumor that made her look bad?

Bridget was right, Hope thought shamefully, *I am so selfish! I was completely consumed and totally worked-up over my own stupid self-image, more so than this guy's musical career. And meanwhile, here he is, writing me sappy love songs, while I'm premeditating the cold-blooded murder of all his hopes and dreams!*

"David, I think that's amazing," Hope courageously replied, "I mean, I'm beyond flattered that you would take the time out of your crazy schedule to sit down and write something for me. But unless that song is about an obscure breakout of

[171]

zits on my face, or how my left foot is larger than my right one, then I totally don't deserve this song. As long as we're being honest, you deserve to know that just a few days ago I-"

Just then, Jillian joined her sister on the bench, followed by the others. Hope fastened her mouth shut, and David didn't want to embarrass her in front of the others, so he decided to carry on with the show.

David cleared his throat and nervously wrapped the guitar strap around his back, fidgeting with the strap until the guitar fit comfortably in front of him. His left hand fumbled with the black capo he placed on the third fret of strings, and turned the pegs, adjusting his strings, doing a quick tune-up.

Laney was suspicious. The boy was a ball of nerves. She had known David Carter for the majority of his life, and had never seen him freeze up on stage. What was his problem? "What song are you doing?" she asked.

"Um, actually," he sounded nervous, "it's new."

He cleared his throat a second time.

His nervous hands begin to pick the strings, and slowly moved into a gentle rhythm which sounded something like a soft lullaby. Jillian sighed contently, and Hope felt her breath catching in her chest. She had no idea what was coming, but she wasn't ready for it.

David opened his mouth,

"Just a small town boy who's been on a ride,
midnight dreams flash before my eyes,
blinded by the bright lights of a Hollywood party at twilight,

I blink twice to make sure that she's real,
'Cause the vision before me is so surreal,
Now I've never seen an angel before,
Until she stepped through that open door."

The song sped up, and David courageously sang the chorus,

"Now I'm hovering, I'm stuttering, butterflies are fluttering,
I'm trying to act smooth as glass, but I know this act ain't gonna last,
I'm covering, discovering, that I'm a fool whose chokin' on his words"

David's brown eyes fearlessly met Hope's as he belted out the last line,

"She'll think that I'm absurd, but I've gotta say these words,
Baby, you have to know I've lost all hope.
I've lost all hope, I've lost all hope."

Hope blushed, completely melting beneath his gaze and the power of his melody. She tried to cover up her smile, but she couldn't stop it from eating up her entire face. It was ridiculously cheesy, yet undeniably adorable.

"I count to ten, and the party ends,
the dream all comes to a sudden end,
And I'm back in my room, staring at the ceiling,
But as hard as I try, counting sheep,
sleep has vanished along with my dream,
Baby you've got know, I've lost all hope."

Hope squirmed on the bench, wondering if anyone else in the room was picking up on the massive hints being dropped. Her name was etched into the very chorus! What was happening?! Surely nobody else could tell that he was singing directly to her, right?

"And my mind travels back to the moment, when I couldn't say a word;

How I regret choking on my nerves!"

David swung the song back around to his chorus, and finished after allowing his guitar a ten second solo. *"Cause baby!"* He crooned, *"I've lost all hope!"*

Applause erupted from around him and now his face matched the same shade as Hope's. He took a deep breath, aware that now he must live with the aftermath of what he had done. What was Hope thinking? Was she completely creeped out? Was she going to call Palace Security and have them all kicked out?

"David, you nailed it!" Laney congratulated him. "That's our boy! Cranking out the hits. Once we add some bass and drums to it, that tune is gonna be electric."

David glanced at Hope, and she bit her bottom lip. What was she supposed to say?!

"Yeah man," Zac offered his two cents worth, "and it's something we can all relate with. Acting like morons in front of cute girls!"

"Well *some* of us can relate." Justin chuckled.

"I agree," Jillian beamed with pure joy, "it was so brilliantly written, and completely relatable. I almost feel like I was there, experiencing every lyric. You should totally put it on the next record!"

"Well," David's smiled back, careful not to look at Hope, "I don't know about that. But I'm glad you guys liked it."

Chapter 12 – Affairs of the Heart

"Guard your heart, above all else, for it determines the course of your life." The King's deep voice broadcasted over breakfast that morning, "Proverbs 4:23. Does anyone know what that passage means?"

Buzzing activity around the family table didn't pause. "Pass the bacon!" Willie told his big sister.

"Where's the syrup?" Millie asked. "I want to build a syrup swimming pool in my pancakes!"

"*Shhh*, Daddy is speaking," Jillian tried to hush Millie.

"Does anyone know what that Proverb means?" The King asked again.

Chasity smiled, slowly answering when she realized that nobody else was going to offer an answer, "That was one of Mom's favorite Proverbs. She always used to tell us as little girls, that our hearts are the most valuable asset we have. More important than Royal jewels, riches, or even the biggest banks, our hearts are worth so much more. She said that if we guard treasuries with guns, and this palace with an impenetrable security system, then how much more should we protect our hearts?"

The King smiled proudly. "Your Mother was a wise woman. Now," he cleared his throat, "I understand that there are times when you children feel like our family's rules and regulations are, oh, how should I say this, entrapping?" He glanced at Bridget, "You may feel as though I'm being over-protective, and not allowing you children to experience the world and all its so-called 'glories'. But every rule that our family has comes from the root of love. Our standards are never given with the purpose of strangling and constricting you, but rather with the purpose of giving you the freedom of having protected hearts."

Bridget looked down at her plate.

"I love your rules." Hope reached across the table and kissed her dad on the cheek, "It proves that you truly care about us, and don't let us run around like crazies doing whatever we want."

Asher snorted, "Yeah, the 'no dating until you're married' rule might seem nice now, but wait until you're a senile old cat lady, living at The Palace, trapped here like Rapunzel with no Flynn Rider to come rescue you."

"Oooo I love Rapunzel!" Millie perked up, "And cats! I want to be an old cat lady. I'm never getting married! Boys are so yucky!"

"Just wait until you get older," Jillian smiled. "Trust me, you're going to change your mind. Especially when you discover boy bands."

Millie curled her lip up, completely disgusted by the idea.

"Guarding your heart," the King continued his morning speech, "is not just something we must do in the area of relationships. It goes so much deeper than that. Guarding our hearts means guarding our minds, and keeping our peace. One of the quickest ways to lose our peace is by worrying." He glanced at Addison.

Addison felt as though his father was looking right through him, and straight into his anxious heart. He didn't know how the man did it, but somehow he knew what was going on in the hearts of each of his children. And he always had just the right words of wisdom to share.

"Corrie Ten Boom said, 'Worry is like a rocking chair. It keeps you moving but doesn't get you anywhere'." the King quoted. "Choosing to worry about situations outside of our control quietly tells God that we do not trust Him as King and CEO of the Universe. Worry tells God that we're agreeing with fear, rather than having faith. So what are some ways that we can keep worry and fear far from our hearts?"

"By knowing the truth," Hope replied, "reading God's Word, believing His promises and standing on them, no matter how we feel."

"And praying," Jillian added, "because when we pray, it helps take the load and responsibility off our shoulders, and put it back on God's."

The King nodded, truly proud of his children. "Absolutely. God's Word and our prayers are weapons. His Word is like a sword. When we pick up the sword He has given us, it can be used to defeat any and every foe. Never forget that, children. It doesn't matter how dire the situation, or how desperate the hour, God's Word is a sword that will bring justice, deliverance, and peace."

The magnificent waterfall thundered in the distance and Jillian sighed with contentment. She was seated on a grassy plain, next to Chasity, under a towering Oak tree. Their horses were tied to another tree several feet away, where Hanson paced back and forth, keeping a keen eye out for danger.

Chasity tried to ignore his restless pacing, but she found it quite comical. Didn't anyone tell the boy that they hadn't *actually* ventured out into the wild? Though several miles away from The Palace, they were still on palace grounds. *I wonder what he's so worked up about,* she thought quietly with a smile before directing her attention back to her little sister.

Hanson huffed, unsatisfied with this entire ordeal. He was observing the girls and their surroundings from a distance, close enough to smell their delicious food, yet far enough not to improperly eavesdrop on their conversation. Hanson's stomach rolled around and made a quiet roaring noise. It was time for his shift to be over. After such long and boring days, clocking out was his greatest joy.

The past few evenings, however, had been massively satisfying. The glimmering promise of seeing Lilly after work was what pulled him through his dull days. Reconnecting with this childhood friend was like a splash of rainbow colors exploding onto his canvas of grey. Lilly's zesty excitement for life and adventure brought a spark of energy back into his bones. After years of training in The Academy, there were parts of Hanson that had become lifelessly robotic. But Lilly was reminding him what it felt like to be alive again.

He glanced at the girls who were completely immersed in their conversation. A fresh wave of disappointment set in as he determined they would not be ready to leave anytime soon. Hanson's list of reasons as to why he had a right to be grumpy was growing rapidly.

Number one, he immensely disliked horseback riding. His horse, Doctor Phil, seemed to share mutual feelings about the ordeal. On their way down one of the many winding paths leading to their hidden waterfall destination, the strong mustang had been spooked. Something gave his horse the jitters, and Hanson felt every strong muscle in the horse's body go tense. Thankfully, Doctor Phil settled down and didn't bolt. That would have been incredibly damaging to Hanson's bravado. Nothing would be worse for his image than the girls witnessing their security guard bouncing up and down like a jack-in-a-box upon an out-of-control horse.

The second reason he hated this whole situation was because they were out in the middle of *nowhere*. After a six mile ride into the wilderness, Hanson wasn't sure if they'd be able to make it back by dark. That reason in and of itself had an entire branch of subcategories as to why it could be disastrous.

The third reason—Lilly was waiting for him. The plans had been made, and failing to show up on time would be majorly jerk-ish. But Hanson had no way to let her know he was held up. He sighed. As long as the girls continued their childish tea party beside the waterfall in the wilderness, he would be stuck babysitting them.

Suddenly, a stick snapped in the distance, causing Hanson's reflexes to jump slightly. His dark eyes flashed in the direction from which the sound had come, but he saw nothing. The horses grazed beside him easily, not displaying any kind of skittish attitude. *Okay*, he told himself calmly, *if the horses didn't notice anything then it's probably nothing.*

The high-pitched sound of girlish laughter arose from where the girls were seated. He tried not to listen, but every once in a while he caught the tail end of their conversation. Their random words floated in and out of his mind. He did his best to ignore them, but what else was he supposed to do?

"...you really think he's cute?" The voice came from Chasity.

"Duh!" Jillian giggled, hiding her head in her hands. "It's really embarrassing to admit, but I haven't been able to stop thinking about him. I mean, I've always admired their music, but after meeting him in person and seeing his handsome heart and adorable personality, and hearing his touching songs, I'm like a hopeless puddle of sap."

Chasity shook her head. "This is crazy. I mean, coming from any other girl, I could understand. But this is *you* we're talking about, Jillian. My baby sister. The girl who used to think boys were disgusting. Mrs. I'm-Going-To-Be-Single-For-The-Rest-Of-My-Life."

"I know!" Jillian laughed, "It's weird. Completely uncharacteristic. But now I'm all nervous and giddy, and I can't stop smiling. I've got the whole 'can't eat, can't sleep, call the doctor because she's lost on cloud nineteen' thing! I've never felt like this before."

Hanson made a face. A tickle of curiosity poked at him, and his ears were tempted to linger. Their voices were quieted, muffled, lost in the rumble of the thundering falls, and Hanson almost wanted to step closer to hear. He mentally smacked himself for it. *Dude, it's just chick gossip. It's better you don't know this stuff anyway. The less you know, the less you'll be tempted to tell.* He redirected his thoughts toward the plans he had that night, anxious to get home.

"Oh Jilly, you've got it bad." Chasity shook her head, "Maybe I should remind you that David is an American rock-star? Who is way, *way* too old for you? I'm sure this is the last thing you want to hear right now, but after the Coronation, it's not very likely that you're ever going to see him again."

Jillian smiled mischievously, "Unless, of course, we hire *Kennetic Energy* to play at all of our birthdays, festivals, and government holidays."

Chasity threw her head back and laughed, "Oh yeah, that wouldn't be obvious at all."

"I know it sounds looney," Jillian gushed, "but I almost feel as if he could've written that song for me, you know? I mean, when he was singing those words, it felt so real. Like, he was speaking directly to my soul!"

"Um, excuse me," Hanson cleared his throat and stepped closer to the girls, "Your Highnesses, pardon me for interrupting, but I would suggest heading back to The Palace soon. I'm sure your father will want you home before darkness sets in, and we have a long ride ahead of us."

"Oh wow, I guess he's right," Jillian glanced at the sky, realizing that the sun would soon set. "We completely lost track of time." She shrugged at Hanson before gathering their scattered food items and collecting them in the picnic basket, "My bad."

"There's no need to apologize," Chasity spoke up. "We were in the middle of a very important conversation," she explained to Hanson. "Girl talk."

"Trust me," Hanson resisted the urge to roll his eyes, "you two won't be discussing anything that I haven't heard before. You're not the first pair of girly chatterboxes I've been around and had to learn how to tune out."

"Oh yes, I'm sure," Chasity bantered back as she stood up with her sister, helping her fold the large purple picnic blanket. "Seeing how you have so many lady friends, I bet you've got *lots* of experience with that."

Hanson opened his mouth, ready to fire back, but he stopped himself. He needed to remember his place.

The girls finished packing their picnic up, and mounted their horses. Once they were back on the trail, Jillian slipped in her earbuds, allowing herself to be swept into the beautiful dream-world that *Kennetic Energy*'s music created for her.

Chasity tried to enjoy the silence and soak in the glorious views, but a question burned on her tongue. "Your friend, Lilly Chesterfield, are you two like…" She paused before spitting out the word, "Dating?"

Hanson made a strange face, surprised that the Princess would be asking him something like that. "Forgive me, Your Highness, but it's against Palace staff code to discuss such matters."

"What?" Chasity wrinkled her nose, "I've never heard of that rule."

Hanson sighed, realizing that she wasn't going to let this go easily. "Trust me, it's there. It's in section 62-B of the employee handbook."

"What about the rule that says you're not allowed to refuse the request of Royalty?" Chasity asked. "Wait, no, I'm not just requesting, I'm demanding. Yep, kicking it up to a full blown command that you answer my question."

"Wow, okay, nothing like abusing Royal powers," he spoke sarcastically. "No. We're not dating."

"Good," she replied bluntly.

Hanson was stumped, and completely irritated by the fact that she had the power to stomp all over him like this. "Will I be granted the great right of knowing *why* you asked this question, or is that luxury only given to those who tower high above my lowly security guard status?"

"There have been rumors," she replied, "and as I'm sure you must know, my brother has been getting to know several young ladies in the community who he may or may not be interested in. If Miss Chesterfield was in a committed dating relationship, it wouldn't be fair to Addison to—"

Suddenly, Nic reared in a panic.

Chasity clung to his mane, "Whoa, boy! Whoa!" she called out, trying to settle him down.

Jillian ripped her earbuds out, eyes wide with panic.

Hanson felt himself tense up, ready to pounce forward and do something. But what could he do?

"Your Highness!" he called out. "Settle that horse!"

"Something spooked him!" she called back. "Whoa, Nic, whoa!" She remained solid on the back of the rearing animal. Every muscle in her body clung to maintain her balance as she battled the law of gravity. Hanson was amazed that the strong horse hadn't thrown her tiny little frame off.

All at once, a blood-curdling scream was heard. Hanson's eyes darted upward, following the terrible noise, shocked to find a cougar perched in a tree.

The blood-thirsty creature revealed its nasty teeth, hungry for horse flesh. The cat was hunched over, ready to pounce.

In a blink, the cougar stretched out and flung itself from the tree, aiming for Nic and Chasity.

Without thinking, Hanson reached for his hidden gun and aimed. The cat continued to fall toward them.

Chasity screamed and dug her heels into Nic's side, as he took off in a bolting gallop.

Hanson's shot was successful, and the dead cat thundered to the ground.

"Stay here!" Hanson commanded Jillian, aware of the fact that her horse had stayed completely calm amidst the turmoil.

He gave his horse a quick tap on the flank and yelled, "Dr. Phil, go! Go!"

Dr. Phil lurched ahead with a terrifying gallop. *If anything happens to her, I'm gonna be dead!*

The scenery flew by quickly as Hanson focused all his energy on not falling off. *And if I fall off…I'm gonna be dead!*

Dr. Phil quickly gained ground on Nic, who had slipped into the woods. Hanson's throat was tight with fear. His hands shook with adrenaline. He was relieved to see Nic's tail in a clearing just ahead.

"Woah!" Hanson released the traditional command to slow his horse. Hanson jumped off Dr. Phil while he was still moving, and couldn't help but feel like the star of an old western movie. The move hadn't been rehearsed, but Hanson thought the landing was flawless. He almost wished the security cameras would have caught it, so he could watch himself afterword. It had to be pretty impressive.

An electrical pang of panic shot through his body as his eyes suddenly noted the obvious. His heartbeat quickened. Chasity had been thrown from her horse! Nic was oblivious to the entire situation and causally wandered to a green patch to graze.

Chasity lay several feet ahead, sprawled out in an uncomfortable-looking position. He internally cringed as he raced to her side. He anxiously knelt down and checked her vital signs.

"Princess! Princess, can you hear me?"

No response came. He was careful not to move her from the position where she had fallen, as she lay limp on the ground.

He fearfully checked for bleeding, fractures, or broken bones.

The peaceful look on her face was deceiving. Chasity appeared to be sweetly resting in a field of dainty flowers.

Hanson's mind raced, worried that she might have experienced a concussion. It wasn't until Hanson reached her left ankle that he discovered evidence of an injury.

"Red Rover, this is Big Daddy at home base." A sudden voice came into the intercom strapped to his ear, "Do you copy?"

Hanson was surprised to hear the voice. He had nearly forgotten that help was only a call away.

"Yes sir, this is Red Rover. We were confronted by a cougar on the trail. After I killed the cat, Brier Rose Aurora's horse bolted and threw her off. The only bodily injury evident is that of her left ankle. I believe it's a minor fracture. I'm concerned about a possible concussion also, sir; she hasn't responded to the sound of my voice."

"I'm dispatching a medical vehicle now," Jackson replied. "And what is Snow White's status?"

"She is safe and secure, sir," he replied. "Possibly a little freaked out, but no injuries."

"Very well," Jackson sounded more like a concerned grandfather than a man doing his duty, "I knew you would take good care of them. Medical help is on its way. Contact me if there are any changes."

Hanson breathed a sigh of relief before signing off, "Yes sir.

Over and out."

A moan escaped from Chasity's parted lips. Her head cocked slightly to the right, then stopped as though it hurt to move. Hanson gently braced her head with his fingers, making sure that she didn't make any sudden movements.

"Don't move," he commanded. "Are you in pain?"

Her eyes fluttered open, and the crystal ocean of blue met Hanson's concerned stare. Appearing as though she had just awakened from a bad dream; a confused look cast upon her face. She was surprised to see Hanson leaning over her, and his nearness caused her to feel a strange surge of comfort. "What happened?" she mumbled.

"You've been thrown from your horse."

Chasity tried to move, but Hanson rebuked her, "Wait! Medical assistance is on its way. I need you to stay in this position until they arrive."

She took a deep breath. The dull ache in her head temporarily distracted her, until she felt a jolt of throbbing pain pumping through her ankle. "Is Nicholas okay?"

Hanson tossed a weary glance over his shoulder, only to see Nic's tail swishing carelessly as he munched on anything that would fit in that ginormous mouth of his.

"Of course," he replied. "Do you remember your name?"

She looked at Hanson like he suggested she should go back to preschool, "Duh."

Hanson resisted the urge to roll his eyes. Nope, there was nothing wrong with her. She had already gone back to her old bossy, entitled, rude self.

"Just answer the questions." His voice was notably irritated, "Your name? Age? Date of birth? How many fingers am I holding up?"

Chasity willfully spat back her answers. "Can I get up now?"

Hanson released his hands and threw them up in mock surrender.

Chasity sat up and brushed the dirt off her jeans.

"Does anything hurt?" he asked.

"Nothing more than my pride," she replied, ignoring the intense throbbing in her ankle.

"Just so you know, Your Highness, if you weren't my boss this would be the perfect time to say, 'I told you so.' Trail-riding at dusk. Not the best idea."

His offhanded comment brought an immediate scowl to Chasity's face. "Come on, let's get Nic back to the stables before I say something that I'll later regret."

Hanson offered a hand to help her rise, but Chasity refused it. Mustering up her own strength, she struggled to her feet, making a pointed statement that Hanson's help was not welcome. As soon as she rose, the weakness in her left ankle became evident. It buckled with pain, and she lost all of her strength to stand.

Hanson had seen the fall coming, and caught her without blinking. His arms steadied her. Chasity's ankle protested in pain. She winced, covering up the yelp of distress that wished to escape from her mouth.

His assistance was ill-favored, yet unavoidable. Immersed in the bulk of his arms, the closeness of him was disarming, bringing a feeling of weakening that didn't come from her ankle. His handsome features which her heart had secretly admired from afar seemed to be even more impressive up close.

She turned away from his alluring eyes, and steadied herself on the trail ahead. Determined to shake the feeling, she took a bold step forward. His arms carefully caught her, as the step failed. Chasity desired to prove her independence with another step. But her ankle crunched in a torturous way beneath her.

"So, this walking thing isn't working out too well," he spoke the obvious. "Just wait for the medical cart."

"No, I want to ride back."

"Princess, your ankle is sprained! Possibly even broken!" He raised his voice, "I'm not going to let you get back up on that beast!"

"Nic is not a beast!" she shouted back. "And it's not his fault that he got scared and ran! The gun shot completely freaked him out!"

"I had to shoot!" Hanson retorted, feeling completely fed-up with her snobbish attitude. Couldn't she see that he had just saved her life?! "If I wasn't there, that cat would have mauled the both of you!"

"Oh, I'm sorry," Chasity faked a laugh, "is this the part of the story where I'm supposed to pour out my gratitude and high praises upon you, and give you some kind of Royal reward for being so brave and fearless? I thought you were just doing your job? We both know that you don't even want to be here. And if I was just some random girl you met on the street, you wouldn't even be talking to me. I'm sure the company of Miss Lilly Chesterfield is *far* more fascinating for you."

For the first time since Hanson arrived at The Palace, he noticed something hidden beneath Chasity's annoying sarcasm. The traces of it had been so small, and so completely buried beneath all of her insults and snarky remarks. But all at once, Hanson thought he caught a glimpse of what was really going on. The idea surprised him, and he almost scolded himself for even thinking it. He couldn't hide the sly smile that slipped upon his face, as he dug deeper into the possibility. "Wait a minute." He blinked, "Why are you so obsessed with all my interactions concerning Lilly Chesterfield? Or any other young lady for that matter?"

Chasity didn't know how to respond.

"Did I just render you speechless?" Hanson laughed. He crossed his arms, enjoying the fact that for once he was on top of her strange little mind games. He finally had her figured out. He spoke forth the discovered consensus, "Just a note for the future, Princess, jealousy looks *really* bad on you."

Chasity's mouth fell open. She struggled to regain her

composure. "Jealous?!" she spat, "Yeah right! In what universe would I possibly be jealous of–"

Just then, three palace UTV's with flashing lights came onto the scene. Two paramedics leapt off, and Chasity knew that their conversation was over.

"You're dismissed," a doctor told Hanson. "We will take the girls back. Thank you for working the extra hours."

"No problem," Hanson nodded, relived that his job was finally done.

And just like that, he had cracked the shell of masqueraded indifference around Princess Chasity.

So the girl had a crush on him. Who could've seen that one coming? Hanson couldn't remove the smile of victory off his face, as he hopped onto the golf cart offered him, and headed back to The Palace to clock out.

As the paramedics examined Chasity then helped her onto the cart, her face was bright red. Darkness had set in on them, and for that she was thankful. Otherwise, everyone may have seen the turmoil tumbling around in her heart, displayed on her face. *What in the world is happening to me?* she thought angrily. *I'm not jealous of Lilly, or any of those girls. Am I? I mean, Hanson is just my stupid security guard! My ridiculously handsome, incredibly irritating, yet absolutely impossible, security guard.*

The unwelcome emotions she felt concerning him were growing more potent with each passing day. She felt quite helpless to stop them from taking bloom. Like a delicate flower growing in her mother's garden, her emotions toward Hanson were similar to a fragile rose. It was something new, wonderful, and terrible all at the same time. It had highlighted an inner vulnerability she hadn't known existed, and she nearly trembled at the thought. *Am I falling in love with him?*

She had forbidden herself to do so. Like a garden locked up, she kept her heart safe and tight. As a young girl, she had vowed to place the keys in no one's hands but God's. So how had Hanson found his way into it? Was there a back entrance left unguarded that she had not been aware of?

Chasity bit her lip. *Well then,* she thought with a determined and newfound strength, *I'll just have to prohibit him from any further entry. Either that… or build bigger walls.*

Chapter 13 – The Final Threat

After a long week, Hanson was pumped for the evening. Lilly had invited him to a small get-together downtown with a group of her friends. Their time would be free of stress, responsibility, and snooty Princesses. Thankfully, he arrived at the café without being too terribly late.

"You made it!" Lilly popped up from her seat and greeted him with a hug. "Everyone, this is my dear friend, Hanson Fletcher. Hanson, this is everyone! Hanson works in the Royal Security Department at The Palace."

Hanson glanced at Lilly with a raised brow. He laughed nervously, not wishing that his occupation be broadcasted across the entire restaurant, "Not really something everyone needs to know." He lowered himself into a seat beside Lilly as the small crowd laughed.

"That's so cool!" one girl from across the table proclaimed. "It must be a dream come true to work within The Palace's walls!"

"Yeah man, that's a pretty sick occupation." The spikey-haired kid next to him held out his hand, "The name's Doug. So do you get to spend much time with the Royal Family?"

"Yes!" Lilly answered for him. "He's a personal body guard for Princess Chasity."

Hanson tossed a slightly irritated glance at Lilly. Why was she spilling all this info?! It wasn't like his occupation was top secret or anything. But living an existence where his friends didn't know all the nitty-gritty details of his work life sure made things a lot easier.

"Oh, score!" Doug exclaimed, "Those Princesses are hot! Lemme tell ya, if I was Chasity's body guard, we'd be an item faster than you can say–"

"Shut up." Hanson didn't want to hear the end of his sentence. "Show some respect. This is the Royal Family you're talking about."

Hanson was somewhat surprised by the words which flew out of his mouth. But then again, why should he be? Protecting Princess Chasity was his job. And as annoying as that could be sometimes, he took his role very seriously.

Doug threw up his hands, "Whoa, sensitive much?! If I didn't know better, I'd say that it sounds like the two of you already hooked up!"

"She's my boss." Hanson explained through gritted teeth. "My assignment is not only to protect her personal affairs and physical wellbeing, but also her reputation, including what's said behind her back. I know that if she were sitting in this room with us, you wouldn't be saying those things."

"Good luck with that," a young man chuckled from the other end of the table. "The Royal reputation is going downhill fast."

Hanson felt his nostrils flare and his gaze intensify as he stared at the dark-haired guy who wore a red beanie. "What's that supposed to mean?"

"Look, I get that you're a sworn loyalist to the Crown. They give you your paycheck, so your loyalties are fierce. But unless you've been living under a rock somewhere, there's no way you can be oblivious to all of the hate speech and mud-slinging happening toward the Crown. The people want change. And they're not going to rest until Tarsurella has a strong democracy in place."

"That's ridiculous," Lilly shook her head, jumping in on the conversation. "Our nation *loves* the Royal Family. There are like six people in our country who aren't crazy about the Crown. And what does the media do? Report propaganda, trying to make us think that our whole country is up in arms about it. Which we're not. We are a deeply patriotic and loyal people. Addison is going to make an amazing King, and most everyone is thrilled about his rule!"

"And I think he'll make an even more amazing King, if he chooses you as his wife!" a girl from across the table squealed.

Lilly blushed as a giggle escaped, "Oh please, he hasn't even asked me on an official date yet."

"Yet. The keyword is *yet*," the girl encouraged her. "I just know he is going to! I mean, how could he not? You'd make an absolutely perfect Queen!"

Hanson remembered Chasity's words from earlier. Was Lilly truly in the running for possible Queen-ship? Was she on the top of Prince Addison's list of interest? From Chasity's comment, it sure sounded as though something serious may be going on.

"Are you?" Hanson asked, "I mean, would you? Go out with him? That is, if he asked you?"

Lilly's striking blue eyes grinned mischievously. "I would. Unless of course, someone else asked me first."

At that very moment, the bell attached to the door announced the presence of an unwelcome visitor. Their table near the door gave Hanson a clear view of the man who stepped inside. His heart stopped beating for a full second. It was his father.

The deceptive man entered, and appeared to be all smiles as he greeted his son, "Well, hello there!"

A sudden reflex kicked in, and Hanson reached for the small gun hidden beneath his jacket-vest. He allowed his fingers to rest there, nervously ready for whatever may unfold.

"Fancy meeting you here!" he spoke to Hanson with a grin. "What a nice way to spend an evening out, having fun with all of your friends."

Lilly tossed Hanson a concerned glanced, "Do you know this guy?"

Hanson slowly removed his hand from his jacket, without the gun, cautious as to what his father might do. Surely he wouldn't try any funny business out in public. Right?

"I'm his old man!" he explained with a laugh. "Sorry, me being here is probably cramping his style, or whatever you kids say these days."

Lilly laughed, "Oh no, not at all! Forgive me, Mr. Fletcher, I didn't even recognize you! I'm Lilly Chesterfield. I haven't seen you since I was like, five."

"Lilly? Hanson's little friend from primary school?" Mr. Fletcher proclaimed, "My, my, how you've grown! You grew up to be absolutely beautiful; it's a pleasure to remake your acquaintance."

"Aw, thank you," Lilly gushed, falling into the man's crowd-pleasing charms. Hanson hated him for it.

"Well, forgive me for intruding on your little party," Mr. Fletcher was all manners, "but I would like to speak to my son about something for just a moment. Hanson, do you mind stepping outside?"

Hanson could feel the darts of disgust shooting from his eyes, "Anything you need to say to me, you can say in front of my friends."

Mr. Fletcher laughed, "That's not true, Son."

"Go on," Lilly gently touched him on the shoulder, "sounds like your dad has something important for you to talk about. I'll order for you." She gazed at him with such a sweet, angelic glow, Hanson couldn't help but grit his teeth and stand up. He followed his father out the front door, and watched with his arms crossed as Mr. Fletcher lowered onto a bench beneath the front window.

"Take a seat Son," he encouraged him.

Hanson ignored the invitation. "What do you want? I thought I told you to leave town."

"Do you have the chip?" He asked.

Hanson dug into his pocket and handed it to him.

"It's empty, isn't it?" Mr. Fletcher asked.

"I'm not getting your stupid code." Hanson replied. "I told you before. You're gonna have to find someone else to do your dirty family business."

Mr. Fletcher sighed, "That gorgeous red-head sure is a sight for sore eyes. She your girlfriend?"

Hanson felt his muscles tighten up as he struggled to hide the fear in his eyes, "Leave her out of this."

"The basic vibe I'm getting from you is that you're not planning on getting me what I ask. You've got good morals, son. Your conscience just won't let you do it. But that's a simple hurdle to overcome. I believe it's all a matter of simply readjusting your priorities. What's black and white suddenly becomes a bit more grey when there is more at stake." Mr. Fletcher stood up and handed Hanson the chip once more, "Do what I asked of you, or else the morning after the Coronation you will find every single person sitting around that table in there," he gazed through the window, "dead."

Hanson felt a cold shiver vibrate through his spine. The threat was unthinkable. Yet he knew in his heart of hearts that his father would not hesitate to pull the trigger.

"It's a simple task, my boy," he reiterated. "Certainly not worth losing your whole world over. If you want to save your beloved Lilly, get me the code."

Hanson wanted to argue, but he had no words. What could he possibly do? There was nothing he could say to change this man's mind. He knew that his father's threats were not empty. He felt completely helpless beneath the crushing weight of such a decision.

Mr. Fletcher lowered his voice to a harsh whisper, "Any word of this to your buddies at The Palace, and I'll be sure to carry out my earlier promise concerning your mother. But if you do what I've asked, they'll all be left unscathed. You have my word." Mr. Fletcher raised his voice back to the usual talking tone and casually patted him on the shoulder, "Well, I'm glad we had this talk! See you in two weeks!" He turned on his heel, and left Hanson standing outside alone in the cold. His fingers were numb, but so was his heart.

He looked at the warm, happy scene happening inside, where an unsuspecting group of young adults laughed and joked with one another. They were clueless to the fact that their lives were at risk. Hanson felt his stomach drop with dread as he soaked in the beautiful vision of Lilly throwing her head back to laugh. Her red, bouncy curls were the same familiar locks that he remembered as they grew up together. The two of them shared many memories. From the first day of school, their endless adventures on the playground, and awkward first dance in fifth grade; Lilly was a treasure that Hanson wasn't willing to risk letting go of.

Chapter 14 – The Coronation Eve

TWO WEEKS LATER...

Vanessa Bennett rolled her luggage away from the front desk, relieved to finally possess her hotel room key after half an hour of standing in line. The front desk was swamped with visitors from all over the world. It was the eve of Prince Addison's Coronation, and everyone present could feel the excitement mounting.

Young, hopeful Princesses-to-be stood in line with their hot-pink, zebra-striped makeup totes, and their matching overnight bags. Some of the wealthier girls, whose parents had spent a small fortune on this "opportunity of a lifetime", were escorted by hired hair and makeup artists who would work their wizardry early the following morning.

Zac and Justin hurried back to their room to report to David their findings; an over-abundance of single ladies congregated in the lobby. The two wished to venture back and collect phone numbers, but David chided them for it and thwapped them on the head, reminding them that they were professionals now and couldn't act like such morons all the time. Their final rehearsal was in an hour, and with the big performance looming tomorrow, they couldn't get distracted. The guys weren't thrilled about his response, but as usual, they submitted to their leader.

The entire palace was electrified with an invisible charge of energy and anticipation. Though the feeling was invisible, the effects of this force were obvious. From the bustling kitchen in the basement, to the Royal security leaders congregating in the Watch Tower, everyone was chipper and alert. The maids, wardrobe coordinators, dance instructors, and entertainment committee, all the way down to the napkin-folding committee, had been roused to perform at accelerated speeds.

It had been many years since an event so excessively monumental took center stage at The Palace. Camera crews, news teams, and magazine anchors were already making camp just outside the perimeters of The Palace. The red carpets were being unfurled, and roses scattered the paths where Royal feet would soon tread. Die-hard Prince Addison fans pitched their tents just outside the palace gates and put on quite a stubborn protest when the security guards attempted to move them from their makeshift camp sites.

In the Watch Tower, Jackson gave the new recruits a briefing on how the weekend would increase security risks. Jackson's speech to sixty, armed security guards was sobering, as he urged all of the men to be on high alert. He mentally walked them through the details of the weekend, and warned them of things to keep an eye out for.

Hanson was seated near the back of the small auditorium, but his ears were not soaking up any of the information. He was dressed to match the rest of the Royal Security Team, but his heart didn't match Royal protocol. Hanson's blood-shot eyes stared off into the distance. He hadn't been able to sleep again last night, tossing and turning, completely ripped up inside about what the following day would bring. His sleep patterns had been deteriorating as he regretfully meditated on the task at hand. He *had* to get the code for his dad.

It was a choice that brought him an unbearable amount of inner turmoil. Never in his entire life had he imagined to find himself in this situation. It was as if a gun was placed to his heart, forcing him to take actions that he would regret for all of eternity. Yet, if he chose not to follow through, he would lose everything. Lilly, his mother, and even the innocent souls seated around their table at the café.

If he didn't do this, Lilly's young, beautiful life full of promise would be aborted. The days of her destiny would never be fulfilled. She would never have the opportunity to fall in love, pursue a career, start a family, or live out her most wild and wonderful dreams. And Hanson just couldn't do it. He couldn't pull the trigger on her life. Nor could he endure the torture of whatever evil thing his father planned to do to his mother. He had to protect them.

With a sick, regretful feeling, Hanson realized that his father was halfway right. Things were not black and white anymore. Saving the lives of those around him, whom he loved the most, may have to come at the price of betraying the Royal Family.

If anyone found out what Hanson intended on doing, his career, and perhaps even his life, would be over. There was nothing comforting about the thought of spending the rest of his days in prison. But if it was the price that had to be paid, in order to rescue his mother and his childhood best friend, he would be willing to endure it.

Hanson fought the sweat which pressed at his forehead. He had to get his nerves under control. The thought of placing his dad's computer chip in the system tonight made him ill. But it had to be done.

After Jackson's speech, the men were dismissed. Hanson had about twenty-five minutes before he had to clock out of work. It was just enough time to sneak into the Tower.

The Royal Family was commanded to stay upstairs for the remainder of the evening. The main floors were flooded with tourists, and everyone thought it would be best for the Royals to stay out of sight. Everyone would be scouring the main floor, eagerly searching for any signs of their favorite celebrities. So the Royals stayed put, locked in their confines of sorts, as Addison watched all the commotion from his bedroom window upstairs.

He had been rehearsing his speech, but something just wasn't right. His speech writer had helped him compose something flowery, sentimental, and inspiring for the occasion. But something about the words he rehearsed over and over didn't set with his spirit. Oblivious to what the problem could be, Addison tossed the iPad onto his bed and studied the horizon ahead. *Maybe I'm just paranoid.*
The sun was beginning to dunk down, hanging up its hat for the night, giving command to the moon to shine. *Everything is going to work out the way it's supposed to. It always does. God, help me to stop worrying. I know that I need to trust you.*

Suddenly, Addison realized that this was the last evening of his life as a Prince. By this time tomorrow night, he would be The Royal Sovereign and crowned King of Tarsurella.

Addison held his breath as the sun started to sink. The breath-taking colors splashed across the sky, just like every other night. But somehow, Addison knew he was going to remember this sunset. This moment was like none other. For now, the sun was setting on his father's reign as King, and tomorrow, it would rise as his.

The wake-up call wasn't exactly what Addison had been expecting. The gentle "tap" followed by a bigger "TWACK" slowly stirred him to wake. Addison's eyes fluttered open, curious about the noise. Slipping out of bed right before dawn, he turned to the window where the noise was coming from.

Dark, ominous clouds threatened rain in the distance, as a small stone again smacked Addison's window. Standing up, he realized it was a whole string of pebbles, singing a song, one obnoxious note after another. Daring to step closer to the window, he could see a security guard removing someone from the grassy yard below. The small, female figure struggled against the burly man. She looked up to see Addison offering half a smile. The girl screamed out a crazed, "I love you, Addison!" And with that, the guard dragged her off.

Addison shook his head, wondering what was wrong with teen girls these days.

All at once, like a boxer socking his stomach, the wind was knocked out of Addison. The realization of the day hit him straight on - *I'm going to be King.*

He had been preparing for weeks, months even, but with all the busyness it never seemed like this day would actually arrive. But it had. Long before he was ready for it.

A knock came to Addison's door, and he knew that from this moment on his life would radically change.

This is it… Addison took a deep breath before welcoming the inevitable. "Come in."

Deborah entered, and with her the whirlwind of activities that would dictate his day. He tried his best to plaster on a smile, but he couldn't fight the falling feeling in the pit of his stomach.

Deborah gave him the lowdown. The morning would be spent in wardrobe, then they would enjoy a light lunch before one o'clock, when the doors would open to the press. At two o'clock, their honored guests from other nations would strut down the red carpet, and at three there would be a small tea party reception for VIP guests. At four, all the other guests would be admitted, and at five o'clock, the trumpets would sound for Addison to make his grand entrance.

"Here is your coffee, Prince Addison. Oh dear, this is the last time I'll ever call you that." Deborah's face beamed like a proud parent. Her kind eyes caused Addison think of his mother, and then wish that it hadn't. His throat constricted. It caused his heart to ache, thinking about her absence on such a day as this.

Deborah left, giving Addison a few short, sacred moments of silence to shower and shave before he would be needed downstairs. He lingered in front of the mirror, a crazy myriad of thoughts swirling about in his head. He thought of his mother, his siblings, and the fact that this would be his last time shaving in this very bathroom. His father would be moving into the retirement suite, and Addison would have the King's room. It was all happening now.

Half an hour later, Addison met his family in Wardrobe. Their dad was not present, but Addison smiled at the sight of all his baby sisters getting dolled up. They were seated in make-up-chairs, with lights illuminating their faces and make-up artists toiling all around them. Bridget's blonde hair was tied up in large curlers as she sat patiently with a teen magazine in hand, eyes scanning over the pages casually, as if she hadn't a care in the world. On the far end of the line, little Millie had an adorable set of ringlets being twirled onto her head, and a huge frown on her face. She despised having to sit still, and Addison knew it.

"Morning!" he greeted his siblings.

A various mix of "good mornings" rose to him. Some were cheery words powered by coffee, and others were barely mumbled in groggy tones.

"We didn't get any breakfast this morning," Millie announced, obviously grumpy with how things were working out for her.

"That's because we're eating an early lunch," Jillian replied coolly in a sophisticated tone. The eleven-year-old old looked and sounded years older than her age as she lay reclined in a hot pink chair, with some kind of pink rub smeared all over her face, cucumbers covering up her eyes, and a towel wrapped in a tight turban around her wet hair.

"Why can't we eat lunch *and* breakfast?" Millie sounded as though she had woken up on the wrong side of the bed. "A person can't survive without three meals a day! What if we all starve?!"

"Millie," Addison kneeled down beside her chair, and stared at the little face looking back at him in the mirror, "the thing about being a Princess is that stuff doesn't always go your way. It's like we talked about, remember? Being a Princess on the inside? Tonight, after you get on your pretty dress and your fancy shoes, you're gonna look like quite the knock-out. But if you're styling a bad attitude, then all this time spent getting all dressed up is gonna be worthless. A real Princess is gracious and kind and she still has a good attitude, even when things don't go her way. She just kind of... mmm... goes with the flow. Think you can do that today?"

"I can't say it's going to be easy," Millie offered a smile, "but I'll do it for you."

"Thanks," Addison squeezed her shoulder before walking over to Bridget.

"Nervous?" she asked her big brother.

He shrugged, stuffing hands into his pockets, "A little."

"You're going to be amazing tonight, Addi."

"Thanks, Bridget." And he really meant it. It was reassuring to hear those words out loud.
In fact, he hadn't realized how badly he needed to hear them until they were spoken.

"I know *I'm* nervous!" Hope declared.

"Why are you nervous?" Addison laughed.

"The press is going to have a field day with *Kennetic Energy* being here," Hope replied. "The fabricated stories about David and me haven't stopped since they were here two weeks ago! All the gossip sites are buzzing about how my 'boyfriend' is playing at your Coronation. I *know* they're going to be asking me about it."

"Just play it cool, Hope," Bridget offered her advice from across the room. "The press tries to find all sorts of angles, hoping to make us sweat, to say something stupid, or trap us in our words. Don't let them get to you with a silly rumor!

Besides, it's not like you're actually interested in the guy. If you were, now that might be an entirely different story."

Hope felt her face flush red. She quickly started digging through her makeup bag, desperately hoping that Bridget wouldn't notice. How embarrassing! What Bridget didn't know, was that Hope had downloaded *Kennetic Energy*'s new EP, and had been listening to it on repeat. Although Hope hadn't had any further interactions with David after he performed his adorable love song, Hope couldn't help but wonder what might happen at The Ball. For two weeks now, she had been left to her own demise to daydream about it. Was David *actually* interested in her? Would he try to speak to her tonight?

"You're so lucky," Jillian perked up. "I'm not old enough for the press to start making stories up about me yet." She giggled, "but if they did, I wouldn't mind if it included David Carter."

Addison's eyes widened, "Oh no, Jilly, not you, too. Please, you can't possibly be old enough to be interested in boys!" He couldn't believe what he had just heard. Where had the time gone?! It seemed like just yesterday he was holding the little newborn in his arms.

"I'm not a little girl anymore, Addi," Jillian replied in her most sophisticated tone.

"No, say it's not so!" Addison dramatically pretended like she had just shot an arrow through his heart. He clutched his chest and fell to his knees, "Ohhh, the pain!"

Jillian wasn't amused with her big brother's childish antics. She rolled her eyes.

"Jilly, you're hurting him!" Millie scolded her sister, then laughed. "Don't worry, Addi, I'll never want to grow up!"

He crawled over on his knees, then kissed her hand. "Good," he winked. "and let's make sure it stays that way."

Addison spotted Asher, seated across the room on a purple couch where he waited for whatever was to come next. Addison stood to his feet and approached the young man who studied a hand-held game device like it was the Bible.

"Hey, man," Addison lowered onto the sparkly couch beside him, "what's up?"

Asher was irritated with his brother's presence. "Nothing a *king* would be interested in," he spoke in a mocking tone, bashing his brother's soon-to-be supreme status.

"Come on, Ash, don't do this." Addison spoke diplomatically, "I know you're mad at me, but I want to make you an offer. Truth is, I can't run this country without you. There are some really important positions on my board of personal advisors that need to be filled. As soon as you graduate High School, I can get you promoted into Parliament. You'd be like my right hand man!" Addison struggled to reach the young man who remained glued to his gaming system.

Asher didn't reply.

Addison quickly grabbed the device from his hand.

"What the heck!?" Asher cried, "I was right in the middle of conquering the Jade Dragon on level 36!"

"Bro, I'm trying to connect with you here. Have a real conversation. In case you didn't hear me the first time, I said that I need your help. Remember what we talked about in the old days? This is what we dreamed about, when we were just little kids, running around, battling imaginary bad guys and planning to save the world together. Asher, this can be real. You and me, working together again. Like Timon and Pumbaa?" He laughed, nudging his brother playfully in the arm, "Come on. Are you interested in the job?"

Asher's cold eyes locked with Addison's long enough for him to feel the chill. "I'd rather shoot myself in the foot."

Addison couldn't hide the deep displeasure on his face. Nor did he want to. Asher had been sulking around The Palace, acting like a complete jerk for months now. Somebody needed to teach him that it was *not* okay to act like this. Addison firmly placed the device back in Asher's hand. "Glad we had this discussion." His sarcasm was thick, irritation obvious.

Addison would be lying to himself if he said he was surprised by Asher's response. Something seriously disturbing was happening to Asher. After their mother had passed, Asher's heart changed. Due to the pain and turmoil, he distanced himself and had his own way of processing grief through animated video games. Addison could understand and respect the fact that they each had a different way of dealing with the loss. But unlike the rest of the siblings who slowly moved on and healed together, Asher became more and more self-absorbed in his computer world, and less connected to real life. Sometimes, his brother felt like a complete stranger. It was as if Asher had fallen into a deep, dark pit, and it didn't sound like he planned on crawling out of it anytime soon.

Chapter 15 – Fairytale Unfolding

David Cater splashed a handful of water onto his face to make sure he wasn't dreaming. No, he was completely awake. This was real. He slowly dried his hands on a purple towel with the Royal crest embroidered onto it, and couldn't believe how lucky he was. Tonight he would be playing a sold out show at The Palace. Being asked to play at Addison's Coronation was a once-in-a-lifetime opportunity. The night was bound to be spectacular. He and his best friends would play for an adoring audience, then watch in wonder as history is made, as King Addison inherits the Crown. The evening sky would be illuminated with fireworks, and everything in the air would feel wonderstruck. David couldn't help but wonder if he would bump into Hope tonight. He knew that the evening would be jam-packed as the Royal siblings would encounter press outlets and greet their dignified guests. Still, David held onto the smallest sliver of a daydream that perhaps he would see her once more.

If not, he was determined not to leave the country with a heavy heart. The memories made in Tarsurella had been branded into his mind forever. Perhaps he was an absolute fool for sloppily confessing his adoration for Hope, and perhaps she thought he was a total freak and never wanted to see him again. But at least he had done it. A goofy grin slipped onto David's face as he recalled the moment he sang to her in the "secret passage way." It was a moment he would always remember. A moment that he didn't regret. It might even be a tale to share with his grandchildren someday.

"I dunno about you, dude," Zac called from where he lay sprawled out on his bed, "but I'm gonna miss getting chocolate bars on my pillow every day."

"I'm going to miss the maid service." Justin walked into the bathroom and tossed a dirty towel on the floor, "My mom would never let my room get this messy."

"David, what are you gonna miss the most?" Zac asked.

David smiled to himself and the answer came without hesitation, "I'm going to miss everybody's favorite thing about staying at a castle. The Princess."

The pile of gourmet chocolates on Millie's napkin was evidence that she had missed breakfast.

"Whoa!" Jillian commented on the teetering tower of sweets which swayed back and forth as Millie crossed The Tea Party Room. "Careful there, girly! You don't want to get a stomach ache before The Ball tonight. Besides," she winked, "I heard a rumor that there's going to be a chocolate fountain."

Millie regretfully handed a few of the delicacies to Jillian, "Here. I'll share."

Jillian nibbled on a small truffle from where she stood, and observed the entire scene. The room was bursting at the seams with prestigious billionaires, presidents, ambassadors, celebrities, and their families. Bridget and the others swept around the room gracefully, chatting and greeting everyone with elegance and charm. Jillian knew she didn't possess the charismatic flawlessness that her older sisters did, so she chose to hide out by the snack table.

This pre-party was an exclusive invitation-only event which Mrs. Gram told them they only had to attend for twenty minutes or so. They were donned in long formal party dresses, but would soon have to go back to Wardrobe and change into their ball gowns before the main event. Jillian glanced at the vintage cuckoo-clock and wondered if Mrs. Gram might excuse them soon. She was eager to change and get ready for *Kennetic Energy's* concert tonight! It was bound to be spectacular.

A few moments later, the entire Royal Family was herded out of the room and whisked down the hallway, as the rest of the guests were welcomed to relax and enjoy munchies until the main event took place. The thundering waterfall of voices could be heard as they passed closed doors where several press conferences took place. Voices like bees buzzed and hummed in The Main Hall, and Jillian almost wished she could go peek at the crowds. With so much excitement in the air, she wanted to bottle up the memory of it and save it in a mason jar. Events like this just didn't happen every day!

In Wardrobe, the girls' hair and makeup was touched up, then it was time to change into their gowns. The elaborate, breath-taking ball gowns were tailor-made to dazzle and sparkle under the evening lights. As each girl changed into their dresses and donned their tiaras, they felt as though a magical transformation was taking place. Each face glowed brightly with beauty and anticipation, as they each realized what an honored position they were in. They were about to see their brother crowned King.

"I sure hope I don't trip in these high heels as I'm going down the staircase!" Jillian spoke anxiously as she bit her index finger nail.

"Stop chewing your nails, you'll ruin the pedicure!" Bridget scolded, then added with a smile, "And don't worry, you won't trip."

Hope hugged her sister from behind, reassuring Jillian that everything would be okay, "And if you do, I promise to do the same thing!"

That brought laughter to Jillian's stomach, and suddenly she grew calmer. "I'll bet *Kennetic Energy* is way more nervous than we are."

"And I'll bet Addison is more nervous than all of you combined," Addison spoke, and everyone laughed at the light-hearted moment.

Millie embraced her brother's legs with a hug, "You will perform just wondrously, my brother!" Her face shone up at him, "Just don't talk too long so that we can get to that chocolate fountain."

The King's laughter was heard ringing above them all. "Come Addison, I wish to speak with you for a moment."

He beckoned him to a quiet corner in the room, and the King placed a hand on Addison's shoulder. Proud tears formed in his eyes as he spoke.

"I have such joy in my heart today. And yet, it is mingled with pain, when I think about how proud your mother would be to see this. Addison you are, in every way, the man that she hoped, dreamed, prayed for and believed that you could be. You *are* ready to lead this country. I believe in you. Your family believes in you. And this country believes in you."

Addison offered a weak smile, struggling to believe those words, "So I guess that everyone believes in me except myself, huh?"

The King chuckled, "I remember feeling how you feel, Addison. On the day of my Coronation, I was scared out of my mind! I didn't think I could possibly be ready for what lay ahead of me. And even worse off than you are, I had a wedding to think about, happening just one month later! I was a nervous wreck. But your mother, she's what got me through it. She shared a piece of wisdom with me, one that I have carried close to my heart for all of these years, and I shall never forget it. She told me, 'Of course you're not ready! For if you were ready and confident, do you think God would have given you this job? He gave it to you not because you're ready, but because you're weak. For when you're weak, that's the time that God can display His strength. That's the time when he can save the day and gain all the glory through your Kingdom.' Never forget that my son."

Addison smiled, soaking in the weight of the words spoken, "I won't, Dad. And thank you."

The men embraced, and the King quickly regained his composure. Addison tried to follow suit, wearing the same peaceful look as his father, but inside he was shaking.

A large number of staff members huddled into the room like a team before the big game. They took turns giving brief speeches, words of encouragement, and shared goofy memories about Addison as a little boy.

The King read Psalm 20, explaining that it had always been his prayer for Addison, and should be the prayer that they all petition God with concerning their future King. His deep voice traveled throughout the room, as an air of reverence settled upon every soul present. The Holy Scriptures being spoken brought new life to the minds of each one present.

"May the Lord answer you in the day of trouble, may the name of the God of Jacob defend you, may He send you help from the Sanctuary, and strengthen you out of Zion, may He remember all your offerings, and accept all your burnt sacrifices. May He grant you according to your heart's desire, and fulfill all your purpose. We will rejoice in your salvation and in the name of our God we will set up our banners!

"May the Lord fulfill all of your petitions. Now I know that the Lord saves His anointed, He will answer him from His holy heaven with the saving power of His right hand. Some trust in chariots and some in horses, but we will remember the name of the Lord our God. They have bowed down and fallen, but we have risen and stand upright. Save, Lord! May the King answer us when we call."

At the end, they all grabbed hands to pray. As they locked hands, everyone in that room knew that something timeless was taking place. For a brief moment, everything was forgotten. Staff grasped the hands of Royalty, and Royalty the hands of their servants. They knew that they were a team. And whether they played a starring role, or a cameo, none could function without the other. They depended on one another, and in that tender moment they were all reminded of truth. They lifted the entire event up to God in Heaven, and asked that the King of Kings and Lord of Lords would bestow honor upon this earthly King, that he would lead and guide them in peace, justice, and righteousness.

The prayer was finished with a hearty, "Amen!" And then, at Deborah's command, it was time to begin.

They floated out of the room in single file, into the upstairs hall where they were still out of sight from the crowd gathered below.

A great blast of trumpets sounded in honor of their future King. Everyone stood in eager expectation for a glance of the man who would soon be descending The Grand Staircase. Addison took a deep breath, and Deborah nodded that it was time to go.

"Announcing, Prince Addison!" A hearty voice came from below and floated heavenward to where Addison was standing. Next thing he knew, his feet had landed on the first step. A sea of faces greeted him below, as cameras flashed, and live video cameras captured the moment and broadcasted it around the globe. The look etched across Addison's face was one of confidence, strength, and Royalty. He descended down the stairs like a regal lion, speaking silently to his faithful followers that he would guide them the best he knew how. Though he didn't know what lie ahead, he would always walk with faith, keeping his eyes fixed on God above.

After descending The Staircase, cameras continued flashing as he continued his slow, ceremonial steps down the purple carpet. Everyone stood in reverent silence as their Prince walked among them. The purple path led to The Ball Room, where a roomful of people were waiting.

The double doors flung open before him and applause marinated his entrance. He traveled to his assigned position on the floor and waited, as the orchestra began to play. The high pitched, emotional sound of violins, and the deeply-earthy hum from the cellos mingled together sweetly and floated around the room. The grand windows were open, and it was still early enough in the day for daylight to pour inside.

It wasn't long before he saw Bridget gliding into the room, looking like something straight from a fairytale book. She took a proud position beside him, and Addison wondered if she knew just how beautiful she was. One sibling followed another. Simple yet beautiful Chasity, breathtaking Hope, handsome Asher, sophisticated Jillian, adorable Millie, and quirky little William. Soon all the siblings had gathered in The Ball Room and the procession was complete.

It was time for the King to make his highly-anticipated speech. The words of this traditional, beloved King, would be broadcast across the entire world, as every nation savored his wise words. It would be the last speech they ever heard from him as Tarsurella's King.

The King appeared at his podium, which was spilling over with roses and greenery. Faithful citizens were already dabbing their eyes with hankies. The eldest viewers, sitting at home watching on their TV screens, remembered the day when this King was established as their ruler at his Coronation, which felt like only yesterday. Patriotic citizens who loved their country and dearly missed their Queen, were touched by all the roses on display. They knew that roses were Her Majesty's favorite flower.

Millions of ears inclined closer to their televisions, turning up the volume, setting their hearts on the words which poured forth from the King's lips.

" 'I know God will not give me anything I cannot handle'," the King began. " 'I just wish that He didn't trust me so much.' Those words were spoken by Mother Teresa, a woman who astounded the world with the depths of her love for all humanity. A true leader and world changer. Someone who, if we are wise, we would do well to take notes from.

"Perhaps you could say I have been handed my role in life on a silver platter. I had no say as to what family I would be born into, nor did I tell God whether I would like the job to be ruler or not. No unborn fetus tells its Maker what color hair it wishes for, or what color eyes they might like to have. No unborn child can ask to be born into this family or that one. Instead, the Creator does whatever He pleases. He places each child in the exact home, nation, and time in history for which He sees fit. None of us asked for this life, neither did we pre-order the package in which we would like to be delivered! Instead, this precious life was a gift granted so graciously, by the Creator of the Universe.

"For baffling reasons I do not pretend to understand or grasp, God saw it fit to hand me this role of leadership, and I have, by His grace, led this country to the best of my abilities. I can say with a clear conscience before the sight of God and man that I have poured out my life—my blood, sweat and tears, my prayers, and my energy—into caring for, protecting, and upholding this country which I love with my whole heart and soul. There are no words to express how honored I am to be in such a position, and how honored I am to lead a people who care so deeply for their fellow man, who believe and pray for those in authority, and who take a great deal of pride in this country.

"We are a small country, 'insignificant and not worth trifling with', some may say. So small that some maps didn't even bother to put us on them!" He chuckled and the audience joined in quiet laughter, "But let us remember David; a small, seemingly insignificant boy who killed Goliath, the mighty giant. The stones which David used in his sling were common and ordinary, much like us. As we have seen through our country's history, and the history of this world, God uses the weak to shame the strong. He uses the lowly and despised things to shame the proud. For even our Lord Jesus Christ did not come to the earth parading himself like they say a King should, but he came on the back of a young donkey, riding down a dusty road, with dirty, mud-stained feet, coming to be King for the lowest of the low. Humility is this country's greatest weapon. If we were to grow proud and puffed up in our hearts, we would become fools.

"My Father taught me never to despise humility, for when one is humble, that is when one is acting with true honor and nobility in character. There is no human being who I can say displayed a truer heart of Royalty than that of my late wife, your beloved Queen. It was she who always reminded me what was important in life. She reminded me that to possess nothing is to have everything. To be puffed up with pride is to deceive oneself. And the only thing a human being can be truly rich with is love.

"We have raised our children to know that ultimately love is the greatest of all. Faith, hope and love, but the greatest of these is love. Love for your country, love for your family, and even love for the stranger. My son, Addison, has a heart bursting with love. A heart that has been aching to lead this country in an honorable way. He desires to prove to every citizen that you can trust him with your life. He knows that trust is a fragile currency, and that talk may be cheap, but action is the only way to prove that his words are true. He has asked for you to place your hand in his, and to trust him to lead the way.

"By the grace of God, I know that He will write a new chapter of peace, righteousness, and glory in the history of this nation. Though we cannot know what is around the corner—whether disaster, hunger, famine, darkness, or sword—we know that love conquers all of those things. It has been proven again and again throughout the course of history that when humans join in unity, they are indeed unstoppable. I chuckle every time I recall the story of the Tower of Babel. Man desired to build a structure that scraped the clouds. God, from his dwelling place in heaven, said, 'Come let us go down and confuse their languages. For if they set their mind to this, and join hands in unity, whatever they set their minds to will be unstoppable.' What a wonder. Thomas Edison once said, 'If we did the things we are capable of, we would astound ourselves.' Unity makes us unstoppable. Whether we are small or large, this country is unique because it has people who love one another. Together we can weather any storm, ride the tides of life, and always come out as conquerors with a great victory.

"So today, men, women and children of Tarsurella, I stand before you in humility, thanking you for the years of service that you have so graciously allowed me to pour out, knowing that the curtain on my rulership is about to close, and a new season will open. And now, I ask, on behalf of my son, that you show him the same love, adoration, patience, mercy, grace, and oftentimes even forgiveness that you have shown me. He is ready to rule. It is with confidence and faith that I place our beloved nation in his hands. But in order for our nation to continue to prosper with peace, and dwell in security, we must join together as one. The rumblings of rebellion will come to an end, as we lay aside our differences and stand hand-in-hand in unity. Will you do that? Will you humble yourselves and step into this new season with open minds and open hearts?

"Mother Teresa's words ring true. God will never give this country, nor your future King, more than he can handle. So today I stand here, before you all, with the proud heart of a Father beating inside my chest. I am most humbled and overjoyed to present to you, your future King, Addison."

The entire room burst with applause, as tears of happiness streamed down cheeks.

"Long live King Addison!" A lone, young voice shouted from the crowd. Addison turned to see who had lifted the victory cry. His face lit up with a smile as soon as he spotted little Javon. His dark face was illuminated with a grin, as his little voice let out another cry. Echoes began to inforce the cry, soon conjoining in a chant,

"Long live King Addison! Long live King Addison!"

Addison knew what was to come next. They had been rehearsing this moment for months. He was to choose for himself a young maiden to dance with, and perform the waltz. He took confident steps toward the center of The Ball Room, and the room fell quiet as every eligible young girl held her breath.

Who would he choose to dance with?

Sapphire fanned herself nervously, knowing that this may be her last chance to capture the Prince's heart. Whomever he chose for this dance would speak volumes about who he was most interested in. Sapphire stared at him flirtatiously, and attempted to make eye contact. He averted his gaze to where Lilly Chesterfield stood with an alluring look on her face, as her dress hugged all the right places. Addison felt his heart speed up. But he quickly turned his head the other direction.

Massive media camera's zoomed in, and Addison felt his palms sweating. He knew that his mother and father had danced to this very song during his Dad's Coronation, and he wanted to choose a partner that would honor his mother. But who? Who in this room could possibly come close? Who could do justice to such a sacred moment?

It took several long seconds to scope her out, but all at once he saw her. The maiden stood sweetly beside one of the floral fountains, dressed in a dazzling gown. Addison smiled the moment they locked eyes.

Vanessa felt her face flush warm at the sudden attention from Addison. It appeared as though he was looking for someone. Why did he stop to smile in her direction? She wasn't sure what was happening, but obviously this was a very important moment for the young man. She offered a shy smile, encouraging him in whatever came next.

Without warning his feet traveled in her direction. Vanessa quickly glanced over her shoulder, wondering if perhaps he was looking at someone behind her instead. It wouldn't be the first time in her life when she waved to someone who was waving to the person behind her. So embarrassing!

But it wasn't a mistake. Next thing she knew, Addison stood right in front of her. The cameras followed, and Vanessa's eyes grew wide.

"Um, uh, Your Highness," she bowed slightly, feeling off balance and jittery in his presence. She stood unsteady and nervous beneath the large eyes of the news cameras. Like a terrified deer in the headlights, she felt frozen with fear and off her game. "Congratulations," she whispered, lifting her head. She couldn't help but feel like everyone in the room was staring at them. Which they were. "I mean, on, uh, being King and all."

Addison continued smiling, slightly distracted by the rose-gold gown that she wore. It was entirely different from anything he had ever seen her in before. Her closet appeared to be made up of casual attire, and somehow he had expected her to show up in jeans and Converse sneakers. For someone who wasn't interested in flashy clothes and regal events, one would have never known by looking at her. She appeared as though she belonged in this very room, her bodice sparkling with rhinestones, and her floor-length skirt of tulle effortlessly cascading to the floor.

"Thank you," he spoke quietly, all too aware of the cameras that hoped to pick up on his every word. "I know that you traveled a long way to be here this evening, in hopes of spreading awareness and being a voice for the homeless. I believe that a just cause like yours should be rewarded. It's only right that you get several moments in the spotlight. Would you care to dance with me?" He held out a hand, offering his stunning invitation.

Vanessa felt her breath catch. She quizzically stared into his eyes, as if asking the silent question, 'Are you serious?'

This was completely unexpected! Her head started spinning with dozens of reasons as to why she couldn't dance with him. Yet all at once, without thinking, she felt herself reach for his hand and receive the generous offer. His splashy blue eyes were like the gravitational pull between the ocean tide and the midnight moon. Their hands joined like magnets, and despite the arguments shooting off like mini-explosives in her head, she allowed him to lead her to the center of the dance floor.

Hundreds of eyes looked at her. She could feel their venomous stares shooting hateful bullets at the back of her head. Now that Vanessa had left the safety of the sidelines, she wanted to dash away as quickly as possible and hide in the thick crowd. What was she thinking?! What were the *other* girls thinking? What about everyone watching back home; her parents, her family, and her friends?!

Vanessa felt like a fake, trying to fit into some kind of cookie-cutter Disney fantasy Princess role that would never work. She wasn't an actress. Everyone would see right through her.

"I can't dance," she whispered to Addison, her green eyes stricken with fear. Now she was trapped. She couldn't dance with him. But she couldn't run away either. The only choices she had were humiliation, or more humiliation.

"Just follow my lead," he instructed, replying in a whisper so that the cameras wouldn't pick up his words, "and keep my eyes as the focal point so you don't get dizzy from the spinning. Don't look at your feet. I promise not to crush your toes."

A sudden song rose from the orchestra, and Addison reached for her other hand, pulling her closer for the dance. Vanessa took a deep breath, and Addison thought she looked as if she were about to dive into an unknown ocean, and was saving up as much oxygen as she could before taking the plunge.

The music instructed Addison's feet through steps he had rehearsed a thousand times, and he gently led Vanessa through the uncharted waters. Though she had no formal ballroom dance training, she caught on quickly.

It didn't take long for Vanessa to completely forget about the lingering crowds and the jealous stares. As she fixated on Addison's eyes, the dance took on a life all its own. She floated through the steps, allowing him to make whatever gentle corrections were needed.

From the outside looking in, it appeared as though the dancing couple had rehearsed many times. They moved together in flawless unity. Sapphire's jaw dropped, unable to process what was happening. Lilly was just as shocked. Bridget shook her head, deeply displeased with where this was leading. *The little American twerp lied to me!* Bridget thought venomously. *Not interested in my brother, you say? Yeah right!*

The King watched in wonderment as sweet memories flooded his soul. It felt like just yesterday that he was dancing to this song with his beloved bride. He couldn't hold back the tears. Deborah subtly slipped him several tissues.

"Thank you," the King whispered, truly meaning it. "Who is the young lady? I don't recall seeing her before. She is quite lovely."

"Vanessa Bennett," Deborah replied. "And you haven't met her, Your Majesty. She's an American."

"Well, it appears as though Addison has taken quite a liking to her." The King grinned. "I shall like to meet her as soon as possible. Please set up a dinner for which we may get to know her better, in the near future."

"Yes, Your Majesty," Deborah nodded.

As the song ended, the roar of applause filled the room. Addison clutched Vanessa's hand and bowed to the adoring audience. Vanessa quickly caught on and curtsied graciously.

He led her back to the sidelines where she was met with hateful stares by the young women attending. She tried not to be smug, but she couldn't hide the smile which crept onto her face. The girls were furious, and even though she never intended on making them squirm like this, it was quite hilarious to her. She wished to pull Addison aside and ask why in the world he had chosen *her* for the dance, when it was obvious that there were dozens of much prettier faces adorning the room. But now wasn't the time.

A man on the platform above announced, "And now! The Royal siblings will dance the minuet."

The sudden rise of music announced that everyone should take their places. This time, Addison was to dance with his sister Bridget. Vanessa felt a twinge of disappointment, and the emotion was shocking. What was wrong with her? Why was she feeling so off-kilter tonight? Just yesterday she was completely irritated and fed-up with all this palace nonsense, and couldn't wait to get tonight over with. But now that the regal experience was coming to a close, she almost wished it wouldn't end. The disappointing truth of the matter was that after tonight, she would probably never see Prince Addison, or rather, *King* Addison, ever again.

There was still the hope of presenting her request for the homeless at the banquet dinner and offering the petition which had been signed by nearly everyone back at her home town. It had been hard enough to convince her friends, family, and community, that the reason she wished to come to the Coronation was solely for those in need, and not to capture the affections of the rich European Prince. But now, after her unforgettable dance with the Prince, it would be even harder to convince those back home of her true purpose. Vanessa struggled to watch the dance, as she worried about her plan. She had to figure out a way to prove to her friends and family that she had accomplished the purpose for which she came. Otherwise, she would look like a total flake.

After the sibling dance, applause ensued and the Master of Ceremonies instructed the press outlets to begin moving to The Royal Conference Room, where Addison would give his speech. The rest of the guests would have the honor of hearing a handful of Hollywood's hottest bands.

"Ladies and gentlemen, I am proud to present to you a pop band that has swept the world by storm! An unstoppable force who cause an infection of adoration to be spread everywhere they go! Ladies and gentlemen of the Royal Court, put your hands together for, *One Infection!*"

An adequate rumble of applause and cheering rose from the crowds, as several young ladies in ball gowns bounded toward the balcony stage, eager to get front row seats, cheering their favorite band member's name. The pumping bass began pounding through the room as the latest pop sensation crooned their catchy tune.

Vanessa peered toward the lofty golden clock, and realized that she still had a good hour before dinner would be served. She decided to take advantage of the break and visit the restroom. She wasn't a *One Infection* fan.

She slowly cut through the crowds, zig-zagging through the throngs of people. Several young ladies screamed and dashed past Vanessa, freaking out over who was on The Royal Stage.

Vanessa felt a small tug on her gown. She spun around, surprised to see a little girl who appeared about six or seven. "You're the girl who danced with Prince Addison!" she spoke excitedly. "Can we take a selfie!?"

Vanessa laughed, not sure which was more bizarre. The fact that this little one was fangirling over her random dance with Royalty, or the fact that she actually had her own cell phone. "I guess!" she shrugged. The two posed, and Vanessa offered a kind smile.

"My friends are going to be so jealous!" the little girl triumphantly declared. "Especially if you end up marrying him!"

Vanessa opened her mouth to protest, but the girl had already skipped off. *Goodness, this country is obsessed with marriage,* she thought to herself. *Maybe my next project should be helping the girls of Tarsurella focus more on their education, and less on their crazed infatuation with finding husbands.*

Vanessa exited The Ball Room, and smiled at a security guard who opened the door for her. The black-suit-and-tie security guards were everywhere. She headed down the hall to find a bathroom, keeping mental note of where she was, in hopes of not getting lost. The Palace was huge. After walking only several yards, she found a vintage sign for the 'Powder Room'. She prepared to turn, but someone grabbed her attention.

"Excuse me, excuse me!" The perky looking woman in high heels and a lime green, mermaid-style dress awkwardly waddled toward Vanessa. Her dress was so tight that it gave her little room to do something very important–walk. "My name is Mona Vella from *Bonjour* Magazine! We want to get an exclusive interview with the girl who captured Prince Addison's heart!"

"What?" Vanessa laughed, "I think you've got the wrong girl!"

"Aren't you the lucky young woman who danced with Prince Addison?" she insisted.

"Well yes, but you see, that's just a misunderstanding, I mean it's not what it looks like, we're totally just friends, I mean, not really even friends, I hardly know him–" Vanessa tried to explain, but someone else burst onto the scene.

"Mona Vella!" Sapphire exclaimed, "Chow darling! I love your magazine; I'm an absolute fan. The last piece that you did on Felt and Florals was entirely smashing. Oh, I see that you've met my friend Vanessa? She's a doll, you'll love chatting with her!"

Vanessa's eyebrows shot up. The nasty mind-games that these girls played were hard to keep up with.

"Yes!" Mona replied excitedly. "I was just asking her about her relationship with Prince Addison! She claims that they're 'just friends', but we all know that's impossible!" Mona laughed and turned toward Sapphire, "Do you have any details to dish?"

"I know it seems quite unbelievable," Sapphire replied, "that a woman with Vanessa's dashing intellect and alluring charm wouldn't be romantically interested in our beloved Prince. But it's true! She quite detests the man. In fact, she was practically forced to come here against her will. She only attended to help out the homeless. She cares nothing for the Royal Family. She believes that our lovely little nation isn't going to last much longer. You should've heard the vile words that she spat off concerning Tarsurella! Something about terrorists, or democracy, or–"

"That's not what I said!" Vanessa raised her voice, "You're taking everything completely out of context!" She glanced pleadingly at Mona, who was recording the entire conversation on her iPhone, "I would never wish this nation ill harm. Please don't believe her, you haven't even heard the full story."

Another man popped onto the scene, and a large camera followed him. "Criss Briss here, TNN News." He reached out his hand to shake with Vanessa's. "We'd like to do an interview!"

"Yes, and afterwards we're next in line!" another woman spoke. Her microphone clearly spelled out the shocking words, "FOX News".

Vanessa felt her mouth go dry, as Sapphire's mouth sped up. Things were getting completely out of hand!

"So tell us, Miss, when did you and Prince Addison first begin dating?" Chris Briss shoved the microphone in her face.

"D-dating?" she stuttered. "What? No! I, I don't even–"

"Excuse me, Miss Vanessa!" a clear voice called above the noise of the busy hall. Vanessa looked up in a panic, as another woman elbowed her way through the small crowd that was forming, "You're needed in the other room, to prepare for the banquet."

Vanessa was more than relieved. It was Miss Deborah.

"But wait, we're in the middle of an interview!" Chris protested as the camera whirled around and caught a glimpse of Deborah. The microphone was now in her face.

"I believe the Master of Ceremonies instructed all of our press outlets to make their way to The Royal Conference Room. We ask that you do not crowd the hallway." She removed the wireless mic from Chris' hand and placed it in his shirt pocket, "Interview over. Come along, Vanessa."

Vanessa breathed a sigh of relief and quickly escaped with Deborah. "Oh my goodness, I cannot thank you enough." she spoke once they were out of hearing distance of the crowd. "I was dying back there! My mouth went dry, and my brain stopped working, and they were shooting off all sorts of crazy questions!"

"I understand," Deborah spoke compassionately as they continued down the hall, "the Media can be ruthless."

"On the newsstands back home, we see all kinds of published garbage about the 'scandalous Royals of Tarsurella'. Sadly, I used to believe every disgraceful word," Vanessa confessed, "but now I see how easy it would be for the press to take a simple story, blow it out of context, and completely twist the truth."

Deborah nodded as they turned into a quiet room, "Freedom of speech is a right that many abuse. At The Palace, dodging bullets from the press has become a way of life. It sounds as though you have a better understanding of what the Royal Family goes through on a daily basis. Nevertheless, it may be a challenge, but the King always chooses to look on the bright side, and to count his blessings. There are many good media sources who share factual truth. But they are very few, and far between. This is The Green Room; you'll be safe here from any unwanted visitors. Would you care for tea?"

Vanessa smiled gratefully at the woman. "Thank you. You know you really don't have to go through all this extra trouble just to help me. But I do appreciate it."

Deborah smiled back as she walked toward the counter where a black tea pot sat on an electric warmer. "As a mother, I know that if my daughter were off in a strange country, I would feel much better knowing that someone was keeping an eye on her."

"Is there a restroom nearby?" Vanessa asked, regretfully changing the subject. Deborah seemed like such a lovely, confident, and caring woman. She would enjoy chatting with her further.

"Yes, right through the back; that will lead you to The Makeup Room, then there's a small restroom on the left."

Vanessa expressed her thanks once more, then departed. The Makeup Room was just as impressive as every other room in The Palace. Six full-mirror vanities were lined up on the wall, as bright lightbulbs added an extra elegant feel. Vanessa felt like this room might be similar to the backstage area of a big NYC musical production. She wondered if this was where the Royals got ready earlier.

Suddenly, a door opened and Addison walked in. She was surprised to find him alone, without the usual entourage. His cheeks were slightly flushed, and he appeared to be on a mission. "Oh, hey!" He was just as surprised to see her. Then his eyes darted around the room, "I'm looking for a pink and brown cheetah-print makeup bag."

Vanessa tried not to smile, but her eyes gave it away. Those words sounded *so* strange coming out of his mouth.

"For my sister!" he quickly added, realizing how awkward that must have sounded. "She forgot it."

Vanessa allowed her smile to take predominance of her face. "Of course."

She joined him in the hunt, glancing over the vanity counters which appeared to have exploded with makeup and haircare products. Within seconds she eyed the cheetah print, and handed it to him. She was impressed with the fact that he hadn't sent an employee to look for it, especially on such a busy night. Instead, he ran all the way back here for his sister.

"Thank you," he smiled.

She shrugged, "Cheetah print is pretty easy to spot."

"No, I mean for tonight. For the dance," he explained. "I completely put you on the spot."

"Oh, it's no big deal," she waved her hand casually through the air, acting as if she ball-room-danced with Royalty all the time.

"I have to get back," he motioned toward the door, "but I want to make it up to you. I have something for you to consider. I don't know exactly what your future plans are, or how you envision your life-long career playing out, but come January there is going to be a huge employee turn-over.

People who have been working with my dad for decades will be retiring, and there are many positions that need to be filled. There's a full-time opening on our Helping the Homeless Committee, and I honestly can't think of a better person for the job."

Vanessa's eyes widened. "Are you serious? I, I don't even know what to say! I mean, I've always wanted to help the homeless in a real, tangible way, but never in my wildest dreams would I have pictured an opportunity this amazing!"

Addison was pleased with her answer, "I wish we could chat longer, but I really have to go. I'll have Deborah send you all the details."

"Wow. Yes, sure." Vanessa was nearly speechless. "Thank you."

"We'll talk more soon." He smiled one last time and gently touched her on the elbow. It was a friendly gesture, but Vanessa didn't know how to respond. Before she had the chance to form any more words, he was already out the door.

Chapter 16 – Escape

Millie stifled a yawn and struggled against her tired shoulders which wanted to slouch forward. She rolled her eyes upward, studying the sparkly chandeliers. This had been the *longest* day of her life. She stared forward at Addison who stood on a platform, giving a speech to the entire world.

Millie had tried hard to listen to his words. She really had. But it was boring as mud. She allowed her mind to drift off and daydream about if she were crowned King. Or Queen, rather. She knew exactly what she would do! Her party wouldn't be boring at all! She would fill The Ball Room with colorful twisting slides, candy machines, and bubbles! The flowers would be made of Skittles, and they would build a rainforest with real, live animals in the castle. The pool would be purple, her jet plane pink, and she would definitely travel to the moon, and use the sparkles of the stars to make her clothes. No, she would not be a boring Royal! She'd find the end of a rainbow, and capture all its colors to paint the world with. No one would be allowed to wear anything boring, and everything would be bright and colorful. Water would taste like Kool-Aid, Funky Hat Day would be a national holiday, and everyone would ride scooters instead of cars. Millie would proudly announce to the world her new rules, and the room around her would burst with applause. Yes, she could hear their clapping even now!–

Oh, wait, no, they were clapping for Addison. The speech was over! Millie joined her hands together with the rest, knowing she was just one step closer to that chocolate cake.

"What do we do next?" Millie felt like she was just waking up to a tree full of presents on Christmas morning, "Is it cake time yet?" The fact that Addison's speech was over ignited her excitement.

"Photoshoot in The Main Hall," Jillian told her. "The Press is going to ask us questions."

Millie's forehead tightened up, "Oh. Great."

Addison led the way, as everyone crowded behind into The Main Hall. The Royals were greeted with the blinding lights of camera flashes, and people shouting from every direction, "Prince! Princess! Over here!"

Millie squinted under the bright lights, but her older sisters took it all in stride.

Bridget spotted a young interviewer who eagerly pressed towards the front, a teen girl with two crazy piglets spiraling out of each side of her head. Bridget made eye contact and slowly approached.

"Hi!" the young girl was thrilled. "My name is Stacie and I'm with *Tween Weekly Magazine*! Your dress is gorgeous, who made it?!"

"Thank you," Bridget spoke into the recorder which was shoved into her face. She knew the drill. "Victoria Stefan crafted this lovely piece of art, and I am so grateful to her for allowing me to model her creations."

"Princess, Princess Hope!" Somehow the words were clearly delivered among the muffled shouts. Sometimes Hope felt overwhelmed at press interviews. With everyone shouting and waving their hands, the whole scene resembled the bidding process at a horse auction. The woman had gotten her attention, so Hope pasted on a smile.

"Princess, hello, I'm from *Oh Snap!* Teen Magazine. Rumor has it that you and a particular young man from *Kennetic Energy*, David Carter, are in a relationship. Is that true?"

Hope raised a hand to her cheek as she felt them flush red. Thankfully this wasn't being filmed. Her throat went dry and scratchy as she spoke.

"David Carter is a wonderful young man, but a relationship of anything beyond a great friendship remains to be nothing more than a rumor."

The woman appeared satisfied with her answer, and Hope quickly moved on to further questions.

Whew, that was close. She hoped the red shade would soon dissolve from her cheeks.

Addison answered questions about world peace, nuclear power, and the first actions he would take in his new Royal office. The King was asked what he would do with all his free time, and Asher was asked if he was proud of his big brother. The Royals had been trained to handle the press in a tactful manner, and no question caught them off guard.

Deborah slowly directed them outdoors to get ready for the Horseback Ceremony, and one by one, members of the Royal Family trickled away. Chasity was given the okay to take her leave, and she bounded at the opportunity. Grinning a goodbye, she then hitched up her skirts and slowly made her way down the long, empty hallway. Though her sprained foot caused her to hobble slightly, she wouldn't allow that to dampen her spirits. It had been a beautiful night thus far, and her favorite moment was still to come—the Horseback Ceremony.

Her family had already left for the paddock, and Chasity smiled, realizing that Hanson was nowhere to be seen. He had been overly concerned about her foot, completely babying and overprotecting her now that her ankle was injured. The whole situation was freakishly embarrassing, and she was relieved to have the guy out of her hair. He had disappeared sometime during their press interviews, and now she was free to travel through the empty West Wing of The Palace, toward the paddock. She took a deep breath and smiled to herself. *"I wonder if this is what freedom smells like,"* she thought, giggling.

Suddenly, a man jumped out in front of her from behind a large marble pillar, nearly causing Chasity to fall over in fear.

"Princess!" he called to her as though she were not just inches away. The man had an ugly mouth of yellow slimy teeth, a large scar scraped across his nose, and a receding hairline. He was standing so close, she could actually smell his breath. It smelled strong of liquor and smoke. Revolting.

"How do you feel about your brother becoming King?" The man wasted no time in shooting her with questions, "Don't you know that this is the downfall of your Kingdom?! Pretty soon, it's all going to end! Freedom, that's what the people want! And that will only come in the form of a democracy, where the people are free to govern themselves!"

"I beg your pardon, sir!" Chasity fired back, "but that is no way to speak to Royalty. You are completely out of line with your comments!"

He took a daring step closer and suddenly snatched her wrist, "Change! We want real change! That's what the people want! Answers! Not a bunch of stuffy, rich, know-it-alls in this bubble-wrapped castle who sit on their behinds all day and drink tea!"

She struggled to break herself free of his grasp, but his dirty grip tightened. "Let go!" she demanded. Her eyes frantically searched the empty hall, filled with fear by the fact that nobody was present to help. Where were the security guards?

The man's glazed-over eyes burned with hatred and alcohol as he moved in ever closer. His potbelly pushed into Chasity, nearly causing her to tumble over backwards. But his tight grip kept her standing.

"This will be the downfall of the crown!" he spat. "Mark my words! It's all coming to an end! Your precious Kingdom and your pretty palace–it's all gonna fall!"

"Sir, I am warning you," Chasity spoke with all the mustered-up strength and courage she could find. She struggled to keep her voice steady and firm, "You must let go of me at once."

"The pretty palace is coming down," he spoke again, rambling on like a mad-man. Chasity could tell that he was practically insane, and there was no telling what this wild man might do. "But you," he grinned, "you sure are pretty to look at."

All at once, the wind was knocked out of the man as someone rammed into him from the side. The tight grip on

Chasity's red wrist instantly released, as Hanson pushed the man to the floor. He struggled against the young man atop his back, fighting to flop around on the floor.

"I will remind you of your right to remain silent," Hanson slipped a small knife out of the man's pocket with ease. "Sir, you do realize that laying hands on a member of the Royal family is punishable under the federal law?"

Chasity watched with wide eyes. Hanson had taken the man down as quickly as a hunter attacking his prey. She blinked, and the man was suddenly on his face. The roly-poly man yelled out a string of murderous threats and ramblings, but his words were slurred together under the influence of whatever substance was in his body.

Backup quickly appeared, and several men in black "escorted" the man away. Hanson was freed of the burden, and glanced at Chasity as though nothing had happened. Chasity stood frozen in place, and Hanson wondered why she wasn't moving.

"Come on, Princess, let's get you out to the paddock. You're needed for the ceremony."

She took a breath, trying to fight the feelings of great admiration, wonderment, and eternal gratefulness toward this guy. She wanted to hug him, but she knew that would be completely inappropriate. She took a deep breath, and struggled to release the shock and awe of everything that had just taken place. "Yes. Of course."

Paths between The Palace, paddocks, and stables were lit with exotic Tiki lights, as the fiery torches lit the way to where guests gathered for the momentous ceremony. A marvelous parade was about to take place, with many guests anxiously awaiting the event leading to the evening's climax—the Coronation of Prince Addison. Others remained inside The Palace, not willing to give up their front row seats for the Crowning in The Royal Throne Room.

The pompous ceremony began as a small division of Royal security mounted their black and grey horses, leading the way for the trumpet players who followed closely behind. Their horses were dressed in roses, Royal colors, tassels, and perfectly polished silver bells.

The extravagant procession was a display of the King's wealth and majesty. Jugglers, fire throwers, and the Princes and Princesses themselves all made their way on horseback down the lit-up path. The parade struck a match of child-like wonder in every eye that witnessed the extravagance.

The scene took everyone's breath away. The King rode behind his family in a carriage, with grey dappled beauties dancing down the path as they hauled their cargo of utmost importance. The King descended from his carriage and lit his torch from the ring of fire on the lawn, which surrounded a miniature statue of The Palace. He then handed the light to his son.

Addison's face glowed in the light of the flickering flame, and everyone cheered. The moment was unforgettable. The King's Royal reign came to a glorious end, as it was time for a new generation to carry the flame forward. Addison mounted his horse with the torch in hand, and paraded fearlessly ahead.

The procession traveled to the Main Entrance of The Palace. Addison was the last to arrive. An overwhelmed heart basked in the love his people bestowed on him. He dismounted his horse, and slowly placed his torch in a golden bowl which was shaped like a crown. The crown shape blazed with a bright ring of fire. The crowd cheered.

Addison waved to his adoring citizens. A little pair of blue eyes pleaded for his attention from the sidelines. He paused to autograph the book of a little girl. She couldn't have been much older than four. Addison remembered when each of his baby sisters had been this age.

"What's your name?" he asked, carefully taking the book from her hands.

The girl only stared at him. Her mouth remained shut. A teary-eyed mother sniffled as she squeezed her daughter's hand,

"She cannot speak, Your Majesty; she is deaf. Her name is Tabitha."

Addison continued his gaze, studying the face of the girl in front of him, knowing that he would never forget it. The image burned in his mind. Her little face was etched onto the forefront of his heart, like the irremovable ink of a permanent tattoo.

This is why I'm here, he thought humbly. *This is why I am alive. For her. For Javon, Tabitha, Millie, Willie, and every other child who deserves a chance at living their lives to the fullest. Lord, help me. Help me create a safe Kingdom with an everlasting legacy for these kids. A*

place where the next generation can live, and laugh, and dream, and fly.

Addison finished autographing her book, and a smile lit up her already glowing eyes. Her mother choked out a thank you, then Addison shifted his attention forward. He could do it now. He could become King of his country.

Every step forward was taken for what it was—a gift. An opportunity so priceless, a realm of influence so enormous, a destiny so uncommon. He was only several footsteps away from becoming King.

His adoring citizens tossed roses, chocolates, and golden coins upon his path. They believed in him! They wanted him! They trusted him! The realization of those truths caused Addison's heart to soar.

He was no longer walking toward the Throne Room, no, he was flying! His heart was already there. In his heart, the priestly blessing had been spoken. The crown was already upon his head. He could handle whatever came his way, because they believed in him. They really, truly believed in him!

Suddenly, an abrupt gunshot punctured the air. Addison froze.

The shocking sound vibrated through The Palace, terror echoing in its deafening bang. A lone scream cracked through the air like a whip. Tiny hairs on the back of Addison's neck stood at attention. A dreadful fear crept across his skin.

Within a second, another shot was released. More screams erupted.

"Your Highness, get down, get down!" the authoritative voice from behind demanded that Addison get in a safer position. Addison fought past the paralyzing weight of fear which gripped his heart, and obeyed his security guard. Addison dropped to the floor.

Those nearby fell to their knees and covered their heads as well, fearful of the distant gunshots.

"Crawl, crawl! Go, go, go!" Addison's security guard shouted at him.

Addison didn't fight the command. He bounded into action, army-crawling down the carpet. Three fearless body guards hovered over him, using their bodies as a protective covering. "Move, move, move!" the man shouted above all the noise. "Code red, this is a code red! We need backup!"

Addison's mind swam with panic. He raced forward, arms numb and unfeeling to the carpet burns searing his skin. His tunnel vision focused on the most important task at hand, finding an exit.

Despite the screams and chaos all around, Addison continued moving forward. He couldn't allow the panic to sway him.

The gunshots ensued. Within seconds, six more guards ran toward Addison with tall bullet-proof shields. They used them as wings of protection and commanded Addison to stand up and run.

He quickly rose to his feet, surrounded by the swarm of security guards with their ten-foot shields.

"This way, this way!" Addison ran as he was directed. His feet felt like led. Even though he wanted to move faster, it was as if he was trapped inside of a nightmare. The kind of dream where everything happened in slow motion and it was impossible to move as quickly as desired. Addison's heartbeat pounded.

This, he thought, *I've been here before. This was the nightmare...*

The face of the little girl outside flashed into his mind. Then a new thought arrested his heart. His siblings! Where were they? Were they okay?!

"Millie, Willie!" he shouted above the noise. "Where are they!?"

"We'll handle that!" a big man shouted back at him. "Just keep your head down and keep moving!"

The man had a point. Addison couldn't exactly run off and rescue anyone while his life was in danger. Still, his heart crunched with a pain he hadn't felt in years. The thought of losing another family member was paralyzing. He shook his head, feeling his entire body weaken and grow dizzy at the thought. He had to stay focused. He had to get out of the mayhem alive.

Suddenly, they reached a back room where Addison was ordered to travel down a flight of stairs to the basement. His feet pounded down the stairs. Two guards accompanied him. The rest returned with their shields to reemerge in the chaos.

Oh, dear God, my family. My family! Addison's thoughts were a blur. He half prayed and half worried as they arrived in the kitchen. Guards quickly bent down and opened a steal hatch built into the floor. A small opening, just large enough for a man to crawl into, was revealed. Addison had never noticed any kind of hidden get-away like this, but now wasn't the time for figuring out The Palace's secret passageways and hidden enigma's. The guards knew what they were doing, and that was all that mattered.

Addison quickly lowered himself into the floor, legs first. The compartment in which he landed was made of steel. The bulletproof hide-away, no larger than the size of a walk-in-closet, had two rows of bucket seats with thick black seatbelts. Addison was confused. It looked like a vehicle of some sort. But weren't they in the basement?

The two guards were in a heightened state of action. They spoke all sorts of commands and code words which Addison didn't understand. Perhaps he could have, if he really tried, but his mind was still reeling from the shock of it all. He struggled to wrap his brain around what was happening. Addison had never heard his two quiet guards talk so much.

Within seconds, buttons had been pressed, and a colorful dash board with controls was revealed. Addison might have been impressed, if he wasn't so badly shaken. The guards took their place in the front seat. The steel wall which they had been staring at, suddenly parted and a glass windshield appeared. There was a long, empty, underground tunnel ahead. Addison suddenly realized what was happening. They were in an escape pod.

"Buckle up, Your Majesty!" the guard who sat in the co-pilot's seat instructed. "This is going to be a bumpy ride."

"But what about my family? Where are they?" Addison protested, "We can't leave without them!"

"Our priority is to extract you as quickly as possible from the premises. We will offer updates on your family members as soon as we receive word." He then clipped a small headset onto his ear and spoke in an official sounding tone. "Big Daddy this is Milo and Otis, do we have a clearing for takeoff?"

They waited a few seconds. Addison regretfully sat down and fastened his seatbelt. He wanted more than anything to rush back upstairs and find his family.

"Big Daddy, this is Milo and Otis, checking in, do you read me? We have Simba and we're in Anakin's pod. Our destination, Nebu."

The guard tossed a concerned glance at his partner, "I've lost all connection with the Tower. We're going to have to get Simba out of here, whether or not we have a clearing for takeoff."

"What if the other pods are being dispatched at the same time?" the guard expressed his deep concern. Although it wasn't spoken, his fellow guard knew what he was thinking. Getting into a collision with another pod who was gaining speed on the underground track, before bursting outside, could be deadly.

"That's just a chance we're going to have to take." The guard sucked in a deep breath of air.

Addison watched with wide eyes as the two men skillfully activated the machine and prepared to launch. In a few short seconds, the pod was fully charged and gained momentum as they shot through an underground tunnel.

The powerful movement caused Addison to feel pinned to his chair. He squeezed his eyes shut, praying that this would be a successful launch. It was clear that the guards were worried.

Make a clear path, Lord! Addison prayed.

He reopened his eyes, anxious to see what would occur. Within seconds, a portal opened and Addison spotted blue skies ahead. He felt as though they were descending up the track of a crazy-speed roller-coaster. He didn't understand how this was taking them upward, but the next thing Addison knew, they were out of the castle, and in the air!

Their tiny little pod flew forward at a speed that Addison hadn't known was possible.

Chapter 17 - Captive

Chasity had just reached the Throne Room when the first gunshots were heard. The sound gripped her entire being with a fear she had never experienced before. The screams were only faint on the other end of the long hall, but the eerie sounds traveled through like a heart-piercing arrow with the building's harrowing acoustics.

A voice immediately followed on Hanson's intercom, "Code red! I repeat this is a code red! To anyone who can hear me this is a—"

Hanson didn't need to be told twice. He instantly grabbed Chasity's hand and started running. The sudden pull forward caught her off-guard.

"Where are you taking me?!"

"Just trust me!" he shouted back at her.

Normally, Chasity might have struggled against his demands. But the screams were getting louder. She quickened her speed, her ankle shouting at her all the while. But she didn't care. The high heels strapped to her feet made the task of running even more difficult as she strived to match Hanson's long strides.

Asher ran through the hallway, huffing, his chest begging him to stop. But he wouldn't. Somehow he had lost his security guards, and hadn't a clue which direction to go. He bounded up the stairs, headed for his bedroom. Like a scared little boy traumatized by a thunderstorm, he felt completely defenseless. He turned sharply to the left. His thin shoulders suddenly slammed into a man who had just left his bedroom. A creepy grin slipped across the man's face as he reached down,

"Why, Asher, I have been expecting you."

The man pulled back his burly arm and slammed his fist into Asher's head.

"Everyone on the ground, to your knees, put your hands in the air!" The demands came from a dark man of Middle Eastern descent who spoke broken English.

David's heartbeat was so loud he was sure that everyone in the room could hear it. Laney knelt beside him, sniffling, fighting back tears, scared for her life. Every entrance to The Ball Room was guarded by men whose muscles appeared to be made of steel–and if that wasn't sending a loud enough message, their intimidating machine guns were prepared to force everyone into submission. The room grew strangely quiet as each fearful guest raised their hands in fear.

"We are not here to play games!" the man howled. "Anyone who fails to submit to us will be killed immediately. We show no mercy."

Hateful eyes scanned the crowd from every direction, more than ready to enforce their terrifying rules on any foolish man who dared to challenge them. David felt his breath cut short. What was happening?!

One moment they were playing a rock show, and the next

minute their lives were being threatened at gunpoint. David lifted his head subtly enough to look for any sight of Royal security guards. None of them were present. What was this, some kind of lockdown, or fire drill? Usually The Palace was crawling with security agents, where had they all disappeared to?!

The intimidating troop of men with machine guns patrolled the area. Their unwelcome presence had littered the glorious room like garbage on the side of an interstate. The beautiful Ball Room had suddenly become a command center for these terrorists.

The men paced back and forth throughout the room, walking proudly around, as though they had conquered a new territory. Several enemy guards made rounds about the room, collecting the civilians' cellphones. Of course, everyone gave them up. Fighting for the rights to their cellular devices was not worth getting shot over.

But what could they possibly want here? The answers came much too quickly to David's mind. Ancient jewels, trillions of dollars in The Palace's treasury, wealth, power, and the demented satisfaction of seeing Royal blood spilled on the ground...

A darkened image of the possibility of these men assassinating the King flashed to the forefront of his mind. He then thought of Addison, Bridget, Asher, Chasity, Hope–

He nearly withered with dread beneath the weight of the helplessness he felt. The thought made him sick to his stomach. They could all lose their lives!

Then the terrifying thought dawned on him, that he might very well lose his own as well.

Clinging to Jillian's tear-stained ball gown, Millie hid her face within the silky material. Tears were streaming down the little girl's face, as she choked back sobs.

"*Shhh...*" Jillian's voice shook as she stroked Millie's hair, struggling to make her voice sound braver than she felt. "Everything's going to be okay."

Jillian could feel her sister's shaking body as she sat pressed against her. Her own hands quietly trembled as they huddled together in the dark. Waiting.

Tragedy had suddenly crashed upon the carefree shoreline of their lives. Like an unsuspecting tsunami, Jillian felt as though the wave had stolen her footing and swept her out into the deep. Her false sense of adult-like maturity had vanished. Jillian felt like a frightened little girl that needed to be rescued.

The terrifying band of men who had attacked Millie's body guard had snuck up on them like thieves. Millie shrieked in horror as the scene unfolded. Jillian had grabbed her sister's wrist and ran, not allowing the shock of the situation to settle in. Somehow, she had the presence of mind to lead them upstairs to Millie's tower bedroom. Bolting the door shut, she could only hope that these dark enemies would not find them. Now, huddled together in the green slide, this plastic play place had become their stone wall of refuge.

"Someone will come for us soon," Jillian whispered, fighting back tears of her own. "Don't worry, God is here with us."

"But what about Daddy? What if something happened to him? What if he–" Millie's voice cracked, bringing on a whole new wave of tears.

"I don't know if Daddy's okay," Jillian spoke calmly despite the fear she felt, "but God does. Psalm 91 promises that we will always be protected, and that if we call to Him in times of trouble He will save us." She took a deep breath, trying to reassure herself just as much as her baby sister, "All we can do is pray. But I know that God will hear us."

His Royal Majesty felt as though the very floor fell out from beneath his feet. An avalanche of emotions toppled over him, each of them wrestling for his attention. The champion emotion of fear had come out on top. Even though his own life was no longer in danger, he still had much to be distressed about. He had been extracted from The Palace faster than he could blink. His Royal security had done their duty, protecting The Palace's most valuable possession, the King Himself.

Yes, the King should have nothing to fear. He had reached his asylum, his safe destination far from The Palace, an undercover home in Monaco where he would lodge until it was safe to return home. This thought should have comforted him. But the King cared very little for his own self-preservation. Only one thought surfaced in the midst of panic. He feared for the lives of his children. Pinching the bridge of his nose, the dull headache was nothing compared to the choking feeling of dread that had rooted in his heart.

"Deborah," the King looked up from where he had held his head in his hands, "I need a briefing on my children. I have not heard *anything*."

Deborah bit her bottom lip, attempting to stay composed during this un-expected, life-shattering event. Despite a few brown hairs out of place, Deborah still appeared completely in control. That was just one of many things the King admired about his secretary. Despite the danger and chaos, she had remained calm.

"The report is the same as it was five minutes ago, Your Majesty. We've lost all connection with the Main Tower; somehow it's been completely cut off. Give your men time. They are working as efficiently as possible, and will report to you as soon as they hear something."

The King felt his hands clench up, as the left vein on his head enlarged. He felt like punching something! Couldn't anybody give him a piece of information?! He had one of the finest, most secure palace protection systems on the planet! How in the world could they possibly "lose connection"?

"Would you care for a cup of coffee, Your Majesty?"

An angry fist slammed onto the small end table beside him, "Does my staff really just expect me to sit here and wait?! Drink some coffee, and, oh, I don't know, read a magazine maybe, while my children's lives are in danger?!"

Deborah took a deep breath, trying not to be surprised by the King's outburst. She had never seen him so livid.

Her shocked expression was evident to the King, and he instantly regretted his words. Deborah wasn't the enemy. She was just as helpless as he was. The King's expression suddenly softened as he lowered his voice.

"Forgive me," he spoke slowly, his voice cracking as he fought back tears, "I just want to know that my children are alright."

"As you should, Your Majesty," Deborah nodded respectfully, "but I'm afraid there's nothing we can do right now besides pray and trust."

He lowered into his chair, feeling defeated.

The heavy doors suddenly opened, parting way for a posse of men dressed in black. The King recognized them as his own. Feeling a sudden burst of hope, the King rose eagerly. Maybe they would bring him news.

"Your Majesty," Jackson bowed upon his entrance, "we have received word from Simba's guards. Addison, is safe. He was removed successfully and flown to a safe-house in Italy. Briar Rose, Chasity, is reported as secure in her town of refuge in Greece. Cinderella, Bridget, has been safely extracted, as well as Little Bear, young William, whom we've placed with his big sister in the Netherlands."

The King could scarcely breathe, "And what of the others?"

"We have not yet received word," Jackson's tone was subdued as he spoke in a grave voice, "Communication with anyone left inside The Palace has been severed. Somehow the enemy has destroyed our back-up lines, and until we send in spies, we have no way of knowing the extent of the damage this enemy has done, or may threaten to do."

"Dispatch a rescue squad immediately!" the King ordered. "If any of my children are left inside, I want them out *right now.* The King crossed his arms, his tone all business, "Who exactly is our enemy? What are we dealing with here?"

"We're working to uncover details Your Majesty, but it appears as though it is an organized group of warlord terrorists."

"How did they infiltrate?"

"It is still unknown, Your Majesty."

The King frowned, "If you find that there were any underhanded activities going on, any member of the Security Team or our staff who shared codes, passwords or handshakes with the enemy, I need to know any and every detail that you uncover. But discovering whoever plotted this wickedness and prosecuting the traitor will come with time. Tonight, I only want one thing, Jackson: This is my highest priority–that my children to be brought to safety."

Jackson nodded, "I can assure you one thing, Your Highness, this ambush took some lengthy and carefully-calculated planning. Our system is so complex that no one could attack on a whim. Whoever is at the root of this plot has been desiring your demise for years, and I fear they won't settle for anything less than to see the fullness of their plan come to pass. We must act with extreme caution, and do nothing hastily. We're dealing with professional terrorists who desire to see the end of your reign. They have a carefully mapped-out trap, and we must be careful not to step our foot into it. By shutting down our Main Tower, they have both blinded us and made us deaf.
Performing a rescue will not be an easy task. Our allies are

rallying and have promised to come to our aid.

Your Majesty, I say this with the utmost respect: I love your children and care for them as my own, but right now they are the enemy's only source of power. Holding them hostage gives easy access to what they really want. I would advise waiting to send a rescue team, otherwise I believe we'll be walking right into their trap. Keep in mind that we do have citizens trapped inside The Palace as well. This is not a simple rescue mission. One wrong move and we could have hundreds of innocent lives taken."

The King felt his forehead stiffen as his brows lowered. Never had he and Jackson disagreed on anything, until this very moment.

"*Four* of my children are trapped inside," the King spoke, his voice thick and commanding. "I will not rest until I know they have been safely removed."

"But Your Majesty," Jackson tread carefully, "This is an enemy we have never dealt with so intimately before. Their methods of torture and terror are merciless and barbaric. One wrong move, and there are innocent lives to be accounted for. Along with your children, we must remember the civilians trapped inside, who represent many different nations and world powers. This is no longer a Royal Family issue, but rather an attack that concerns the entire world. Our enemy has declared war upon us and we must treat it as such."

The King lowered his head, fighting back words that he might regret later. Deep down, the King knew that Jackson was right. His family could not be the priority, when so many citizens were in danger. He looked up at Jackson's piercing eyes and saw deep wisdom penetrating.

"I trust you, Jackson. Do as you see fit," the King spoke mournfully. "Tarry the rescue if we must, until we have more information, but *please* get them out of there as soon as possible. This is not a request coming from a King on behalf of his nation, but from a father on behalf of his children."

Chapter 18 - Don't Lose Hope

Hope wasn't aware of the hour. Bright, illuminating lights lit up The Royal Boardroom where Hope sat in a chair, handcuffs around her small wrists.

Burly men with ginormous machine guns guarding every entry way mulled around the room, speaking to one another in a foreign language. Their hushed mumbling gave Hope the chills. It was like the eerie chorus to a terrible horror movie. The blinding lights shone in such great contrast to the thick darkness that Hope felt crawling up her legs. Her heart was numb with fear as she wondered why she was in this room.

It had been several hours since a man with a wickedly disgusting smile ordered that she be brought into The Boardroom. The handcuffs were slapped onto their prisoner, for an extra precautionary measure. She had fought the muscular men who took her as their captive, but to no avail. All she could do now was keep her spirits up. Her eyes flickered with determination. She would *not* be intimidated. She didn't know yet just how much these thieves had stolen from her, but they would not steal her hope. Glancing to the window, she imagined that at any second now a security guard would break through the shattered glass and take her away. She was confident in the fact that her rescue was coming soon.

Glancing at the clock above the door, she finally realized the time. Two-twenty-two, AM.

Just then, double doors swung open as the creepy-looking man entered the scene. He was escorted by several more guards as they dragged in another prisoner.

"Asher!" Hope let the name escape from her lips. She wasn't alone after all!

Her black-haired brother looked up and tossed her a defeated look. Several ugly, black-and-blue marks on his face showed that he had been beaten.

She gasped. "Oh, my Lord!" Hope cried, Ash, are you okay?"

The man who appeared to be in charge of this twisted operation cleared his throat. Hacking up some flem, the man let loose a string of saliva which showered onto the Royal Crest engraved in the floor below. Asher didn't respond.

Hope felt her guts tighten with hatred as she witnessed the event, "How dare you show such disrespect to the Crown! If you think you're going to get away with this, my Dad is gonna come in here and whip your–"

"Silence!" the man suddenly shouted at her. Reaching across the table, his iron hand slapped her cheek, leaving a hard sting of his venom behind. Hope felt the burning on her cheek bring tears to her eyes, and that only served to stir up her anger.

She retaliated from the blow, and even though her face stung, she spoke with a determined grit. "I demand that you release me and my brother from these handcuffs. Despite your false attempts at pretending to overthrow my Father's Kingdom, we are still Royalty, and demand that we be treated as such."

The man acted as though he hadn't heard her. Brown, squinty eyes shot darts of hate toward the two, as he spoke on his imaginary platform.

"I believe I failed to introduce myself. My name is Smashman Zero-Zero-Eight." He smiled at Asher, "A friend of your brother's."

Hope slowly turned her head to face him, "That's-that's impossible. You don't know this guy, do you?"

Asher's head only hung as he stared at an invisible spot on the floor. No response came.

"If it wasn't for Asher, none of us would be here."

Hope felt her hands start to tremble. "What?" She couldn't stop starring at Asher. "That's not true, is it? Tell him it's not true!"

The man laughed, "The two of us are great friends! Asher here made a fine online gaming buddy. For years, I was his apprentice, and he taught me how to beat every level. But now, the tables have turned, and it's my turn to win. Asher gave me the cheat codes, and now, it's 'Game Over'."

"You okay, Laney?" David asked quietly. He was pretty sure she was done crying now. Seated on the hard floor along with every other hostage, he placed his arm around her like a friend would.

She sniffled and forced a smile, "Yeah, I guess so. It's just pretty overwhelming, ya know?"

He nodded. There were no words for a time like this. Silence was about the only thing that was happening. It was nearly dawn and long hours of waiting had passed. Nothing had changed, and they had received no update on their fate. The locked room demanded that no one leave, and the couple hundred people crowded into The Ball Room were growing restless.

Especially David. Despite how hard he tried to reign-in his thoughts, he couldn't stop thinking about Hope. Was she okay? Would any of the guards dare hurt her, or even worse—? David stopped. He couldn't let his mind go there. Somehow, she had to be okay.

Sudden commotion in the front of the room drew his attention toward the doors on the left wing. A small army of men paraded in, as a man who appeared to be in charge lead the procession.

David caught sight of a shimmering ball gown, and his breath caught. It was Hope! He allowed his eyes to linger on her as she marched fearlessly behind this band of terrorists. Her brother, Asher, was being led with handcuffs as well. David couldn't believe the courage he saw blazing in her eyes. She was even more beautiful than before. His heart rate quickened as he slowly clenched and then released his fists. If any of those men touched her...he imagined himself knocking several of the hitmen out who surrounded the Princess, then grabbing her hand and providing her escape. But where? How? There were so many guards. David's mind reeled with possibilities.

One man took the King's platform where His Majesty had just stood several long hours earlier making his speech. Had that really been such a short time ago? To David, it felt like an eternity had passed since then.

Several camera men surrounded him, as if they were going to broadcast what he was saying. The terrified news anchors were not up for the job, but the guns held up to their heads demanded that they follow through and surrender their cameras. The man who appeared to be in charge of conducting this nightmare raised his voice. His words were smothered with a thick, foreign accent.

"I demand silence from the crowd as I send this message to your ex-King. Anyone who speaks will be killed!"

The threatening sting of the man's words were enough to make everyone fasten their jaws tightly.

"Greetings," he suddenly began in a booming voice, his attention pointed toward one of the three cameras. "This message is to declare my victory and your defeat. As you can see, I have your palace and everyone in it held hostage. They will be my prisoners and pawns in this game until I have received what I demand. What I ask is simple; three things. First, give me the wealth of your Kingdom. Wait–I do not ask, I take. See, your Princess Hope will take me there." The cameras shifted to Hope and Asher as if to flaunt the fact that he did indeed hold both the Prince and Princess hostage. "Second, I take the Princess in marriage. She is very beautiful and will serve as my wife."

David's gut twisted in his stomach. It took every bit of self-control to keep from running toward the man and knocking him to the floor. But he knew that would not accomplish nothing. If he ended up dead, he would not be able to help Hope escape.

"Third," the man was not finished. It made David nauseous to hear his toxic words. "I take your throne. I will rule. I am King. All will serve me, and all will serve Allah! Allah will reign!" The man's words were as hard as lead, as they settled like a heavy rainstorm over the mute crowd.

Turning toward Hope he made his first demand, "Take me to the Jewel Room! I will take your bank, and your Royal treasury!"

Hope's jaw tightened with defiance as her eyes squinted, flames of hatred burning behind them. "Never will I—"

The man reached back and struck the Princess on her face, causing her to topple over and nearly collapse on the floor.

The crowd gasped as they witnessed the cruel disgrace. Who dare touch the Princess in such a way?!

David felt all the blood rush to his head, as the adrenaline pumping through his veins increased. He started to rush toward the man, but Laney's firm hands grabbed him.

"Don't!" she whispered fiercely, "He will kill you!"

David's heart felt weak and paralyzed as rough-handed men shoved Hope out of the room, pushing her to lead them to the Royal jewels.

David *had* to get her out of here.

Chapter 19 – Desperation

Sweet sunshine streaming through the window kissed Chasity's face. Eyes shut tight, a soft smile slid across her lips. She could hear ocean waves churning outside her window as the morning birds sang a lovely wake-up song. Her arms stretched and flung out every which way, reaching for a yawn. She found it and flopped the opposite direction on her pillow. Her eyes fluttered opened, and suddenly the peace that had been so near jolted from her spirit.

She did not recognize her surroundings. A fine layer of dust covered a wooden cabinet filled with antique dishes, and a small wash basin sat on the bedside table. She sat up abruptly, struggling to get her bearings. This was not her room. A cracked mirror on the wall showed a tired reflection.

Suddenly she remembered. The horror of the moment flooded through her being. Throwing herself out of bed, not even bothering to change out the clothes she had fallen asleep in the long night before, Chasity crossed the small room and opened the door. She could hear voices downstairs. The final two steps of the creaky stairway announced her entrance.

A small kitchen of people glanced up. Hanson and Lance turned to look, as well as the unfamiliar faces of a stout man and kind-looking woman. She remembered them only vaguely from the previous night. They were the kind souls who welcomed them into their humble dwelling.

"Good morning, Princess!" the woman's face lit up, her Greek accent heavy on every word as she curtsied respectfully. "We are so honored to have you in our home. We hope you slept well."

Chasity nodded graciously, "I was very comfortable, thank you. I appreciate your hospitality."

"Breakfast is hot on the deck out back. You have a glorious view of the ocean with nothing but the breeze to disturb your meal."

Chasity's stomach churned at the thought of food. She couldn't eat until she knew one thing was for certain, "Are they okay?"

The quiet pause which draped over the room was too long. She studied Hanson's tanned face. Worry glazed over his eyes. Why was Hanson taking so long to answer?

"Your Father is safe. As are Addison, Bridget, and William. But the rest are still in The Palace...the last we heard."

Chasity lowered into a chair, feeling herself go faint. Her head started to spin. This wasn't supposed to happen. No, *none* of this was supposed to be happening! She shouldn't even be asking that question! She should be waking up in her own bed, with her very familiar maids scurrying around. She should be waking up to a big breakfast, sitting next to Addison. They'd talk cheerfully about The Ball and–

She felt a small cry trying to escape from the deepest chambers inside. She sniffed and pulled back. She wouldn't do it. Not now. Not with everyone watching her.

"What are you doing here?" Chasity harshly asked Lance, suddenly realizing that he was out of place, "Aren't you supposed to be with Jillian?! Your job is to protect her!"

"We got separated in the middle of all the chaos," Lance quickly explained. "Next thing I knew, the little girls were gone, and Headquarters asked me to come here."

"You had one job!" Chasity bashed, raising her voice to a very ungraceful tone, "One simple task! To protect my sister! And you failed? What kind of lame security guard are you, that you would just 'lose track' of the person you swore to devote your entire life to protect?!"

"Princess!" Hanson's voice was firm, "He did his job to the best of his ability. It could have happened to anyone. Leave him alone."

Chasity glared at him.

"Um, would you like some breakfast, Your Highness?" Mrs. Drakos rose to her feet, attempting to cut the dramatic tension. "Come, dear, I'll show you the way."

Chasity took a deep breath and quietly followed her out the back door and onto the porch. A quaint set of table and chairs were the only decor, with the exception of a bird feeder. Chasity wondered if the Mediterranean ocean waves were always that blue.

Chasity felt Hanson's shadow come up behind her.

"Enjoy your meal, Princess. I hope it's somewhat satisfactory," Mrs. Drakos's red cheeks shone in the sunshine. "Just ring this bell if you need anything." She scurried back inside.

Chasity sat down slowly, glancing at the sea-shore. Wild

waves covered in white bubbly seafoam crashed upon the rocks.

Hanson sat across from her. "Princess, it's important that you know how paramount this situation is. I won't down-play the facts or sugar-coat it. Your entire Kingdom is in danger."

Chasity tore her eyes from the ocean and studied Hanson. His handsome face held all seriousness. He had her full attention now and he continued, "The castle is in lockdown. Hundreds of civilians are trapped inside, being held hostage by the enemy. We've been sent here to Greece and will stay until we have further word. You will be safe here. For now. Lance and I are on continual alert and we may be called to get up and move at any second. You must be prepared to leave at a moment's notice."

"Where would we go next?" she tried to hide the fear in her voice.

"Wherever they send us. It's vital that no one outside of the Security Team knows where any of you are. Your safety could still be in jeopardy."

She glanced down at the hard-boiled eggs on her plate and found no appetite.

As she studied his eyes, she felt as though they held a secret. He appeared deeply troubled. The stress of it all must've been weighing on him. Chasity tried to lighten the mood, "I never thanked you, you know."

"For what?"

"Um, you know," she struggled to find the words, "for saving my life, a couple times."

"Your Highness, that's my job."

Chasity didn't miss the undertones of harshness in his voice. He sounded tired and irritable.

"This may sound a little morbid, but aren't you enjoying this?" Chasity tried to crack the shell of indifference surrounding Hanson's soul, "I mean, at least a little bit? Back home you did nothing but complain about the lack of excitement in my life. This has gotta be better than sitting around The Palace watching me reading a book, right?"

"This is not a game, Your Highness," Hanson eyes fired back. "With all due respect, I don't think you understand the life-altering weight of this situation. It must be too much for your frail little mind to handle. Forgive me for thinking I should entrust you with the details. It was my mistake."

With that, Hanson shoved the chair back, sending it scraping across the deck as he left the Princess to her breakfast in silence.

The shooting pain in Jillian's neck from being curled up inside Millie's tube slide was nothing compared to the pain that clutched her heart. She had been wide awake, praying all night long, begging God to send a security guard to rescue them. But all night long she had endured the silence. No one came.

Last night, she had nearly nodded off to sleep when suddenly the trap door below was heard opening.

Millie's eyes popped open and she wanted to shout, "They found us! We're up here!" But Jillian whipped her hand over Millie's mouth, just in the nick of time.

Two men speaking in an Arabic dialect were heard calling out to one another, then kicking things around in the room below. They looked under Millie's bed, and looked in the laundry hamper. After several suspenseful minutes, the men finally left.

Jillian relaxed her grip on her little sister. Millie couldn't believe what had just happened. "The bad guys are still here! Where are the good guys? Why haven't they come for us? Where's Daddy? Where's Addison, and Bridget, and Hope, and Asher and Chasity, and Willie? Has something happened to them? Are we the only ones left?"

Jillian didn't know what to say. She simply drew Millie's head to her chest, and patted her head in a comforting way, using a motherly tone in hopes of keeping her baby sister calm. "Everything is going to be okay. We're going to stay in this slide tonight. When you wake up tomorrow morning, everything will be fine."

Jillian sighed. Hours had passed since that fearful moment. Now, she didn't know what time it was, but she knew they had been trapped in this slide all night long. Every muscle ached from trying to keep her and her sleeping sister from sliding down.

Lord, she prayed again quietly, *you have to send someone for us! Please. We can't stay up here forever.*

Almost immediately, the door opened below.

"Millie?" a voice called.

Jillian gasped. "Millie, Millie, wake up! It's Clark! Clark, we're up here!"

Jillian shook her sleepy sister awake, and the two of them tumbled down the slide.

Clark caught them in a strong embrace below.

"Clark!" Millie called out, "Oh, finally, you came for us! You're our hero!"

"*Shhhh!*" he hushed them, placing them carefully on the floor. "Now girls, I need you to listen to me carefully. I don't want you to be afraid, but things are not okay yet. The enemy has infiltrated, and we can't let them know that you girls are up here. So you have to be quiet, and do everything that I tell you to, do you understand?"

Jillian slowly nodded, but Millie didn't grasp the concept of being quiet.

"Where's Daddy?! Have you seen him? Is he okay?!"

"Millie," he placed gentle hands on her shoulders, and came down to her level, "I don't know where your Father is. But no matter what, I know that he would want you to know that he loves you very much, and he wants you to be brave. Can you do that for him?"

"I, I don't know Clark," Millie stuttered, fighting back tears, terrified by the thought that he might not be okay, "I don't feel brave."

"Millie, you are one of the bravest girls I know! Why, every day you buzz around this castle going on grand adventures! You've traveled to outer space, fought dangerous aliens, and dived in a submarine down to the depths of the seas. You've swam with mermaids, fought against evil sharks, and slayed every dragon that has ever tried to invade your castle. Right now, there are real men like dragons in the castle. They're not pretend. These men are very evil, and they will not be kind to you simply because you are a child. But I know that you can be brave and overcome these challenges, because you've done it before in your imagination, and now you can do it in real life!" Clark paused to glance up at Jillian, who was desperately sucking strength from his words. "Both of you are. You are Royalty. The blood of your mother is coursing through your veins, and she would be very proud of the warrior-Princesses that you are today."

"Really?" Millie asked, "You think so?"

"I know so," Clark grinned, his fatherly expression of love eating up his entire face. Jillian almost smiled. Clark cared for them so deeply, and wouldn't dare let anything happen to them. He might not be a trained security guard, but he was here for them, and they could count on him.

"Thank you," Jillian whispered, feeling pounds of pressure releasing from her soul.

"Of course, Your Highness," Clark bowed slightly, which caused Millie to giggle.

"So, what's the plan, Stan?" Millie asked, crossing her arms, getting a little bit of her spunk back. "Can we sneak down to the kitchen, past the dragons, and into a pool of waffles with whipped cream? I'm ready for breakfast!"

"Eh, that would be a negative." Clark scratched the back of his neck, hating to disappoint the girls, "Enemy guards are roaming the halls. It's not exactly an ideal time for a buffet."

"So how did you get up here?" Jillian asked with a quizzical look on her face.

"There are secret corridors and underground passageways throughout The Palace that only the staff use. In our jobs, sometimes we need to get from place to place, but are not supposed be seen getting there. The guards have not discovered these passageways yet, and we want to keep it that way. The kitchen staff is working on conducting a plan to get out of here, but we're still working out the kinks. As far as we can tell, all of the power in the Security Tower is down, so none of the security cameras are working, which gives us much more freedom for sneaking around."

"Sooo, this means no waffles?" Millie frowned.

Clark reached into his large pockets, and pulled out two granola bars. "These will have to do for now."

"I've got two Altoids, a pack of gum, and a guitar pick." Zac emptied out his pockets and dumped the treasures of his findings into the mutual pot of his shared friends.

"We are *not* going to eat your guitar pick," Laney chided him.

The band was huddled together in a corner of The Ball

Room, sitting with their legs criss-crossed, forming a tight circle. The entire contents of Laney's purse had been dumped out onto the floor, and her friends were now tossing whatever scraps they could offer into the pile. Their circle doubled as a protective wall from anyone who might try to break in and ask for handouts. Everyone was just as hungry as they were.

"Yeah, well I'm not going to eat your lipstick." Zac huffed.

"Okay, so our grand total is half a blueberry muffin, a Cliff Bar, a protein shake powder packet with no water, two Altiods, and a pack of gum." Laney took inventory. "How are we going to split this up between the six of us?"

"Man, I'm totally craving a breakfast burrito right now," Justin sighed, daydreaming about everything he couldn't have.

"Dude. Word association!" Zac spouted out, "Waffle House."

"Pancake Pantry!"

"International House of Pancakes!"

"Stop!" Laney groaned, "We're hungry enough as it is, without listing off every breakfast joint known to man!"

"How can you guys think about food at a time like this?" David spoke up, reprimanding his friends. "The Royal Family, Tarsurella, and the entire world as we know it, is being threatened! Princess Hope's *life* is hanging in the balance! We can't just sit here and argue about breath mints!"

"David," Laney placed a gentle hand on David's knee, in an effort to calm him down, "I know you care a lot about the Princess, and the Royal Family. We all do. But right now we are completely helpless. It's not like we are in a position to do anything about this! There are armed guards covering every entrance. We're locked in here with no food, no water, and no bathroom facilities. We're hostages. We need to be smart and make a plan for ourselves. We're completely in survival mode."

David tightened his jaw, dissatisfied with Laney's response. He glanced around at his band members who quietly argued about who was going to eat what. They didn't get it. Yes, their lives were at risk, but Princess Hope's was like a time bomb. Chained in the hands of her enemy, every second that passed without rescue could be detrimental. The evil declaration that was made just several hours ago told David that Hope was a powerless pawn in the hand of that man. He was ravenous and cruel, and would use Hope to get everything he wanted. Terror and fear tactics were only the beginning. David knew that. This army of warlords that had hijacked The Palace wouldn't stop until their vile plans were accomplished. He couldn't bear to think what might happen to Hope. It made his stomach lurch, his face grow hot with hatred, and his muscles stiffen up with anger. He couldn't just sit here and wait. He felt like he was going to explode. David suddenly bounced to his feet.

Laney gasped and loudly whispered, "Sit down! They'll shoot you!"

Sure enough, two guards near the eastern entrance pointed their guns at him, "Make another move and we shoot!" one barked.

David threw his hands up over his head as in surrender, "Please sir, I have a question."

"No questions!" the man shouted back. "Sit down, be quiet!"

"I really, *really* have to go to the bathroom."

The two guards looked at one another, unsure of what to do. The whole Ball Room had been on lockdown for the entire night. The sun was now up, and it was the first time someone had requested to relieve themselves. What should they do? If they let this guy go, they would be escorting an endless stream of people to the bathroom. The men conversed in their native language, and then one left the room, and David wondered if he was going to ask the boss.

A few minutes later, the man reappeared and beckoned David with the gun, as if to say, "Come here."

David gulped, beads of sweat running down his forehead as he stepped forward.

"Wait!" Zac suddenly popped up, "I have to tinkle too!"

The room burst out in suppressed laughter, bringing some strangely found comedy in the midst of the nightmare.

The biggest man by the door sighed, and then shouted out loudly enough to be heard across the entire room, "Bathroom line begins here! But no talking!"

Many frazzled and exhausted guests, still dressed in their expensive ball gowns and stiff black tuxes, slowly stood up and made their way toward the door, grateful that they would finally be given this opportunity.

David and Zac were the first to leave, with the smaller of the two guards walking alongside them. They stepped into the empty hallway, and David quickly formulated a plan. He glanced at Zac to his left, and then at the gun resting on the guards shoulder at his right. A shudder of fear vibrated down his spine. How was he going to pull this off?

They entered the men's room, and David slipped into the stall. Frantically, he looked around, desperate to find a way of escape. *There has to be something around here…* he glanced upward at the air vent, and wondered if there was any chance of that leading somewhere. Or if there was any possibility of successfully launching himself up there without the guard realizing. One wrong move, and he could be dead.

Apparently he was already taking too long, because suddenly the door flew open, and the guard stood there with an angry scowl on his face.

David felt his face flush red. Was it that obvious? Did the guard know he was looking for a way to escape? He slowly walked out of the stall, feeling like he had completely missed his opportunity.

Zac dunked his face in the sink, gulping as much water as he could, "Drink, dude, drink! We might never get water again!"

David knew Zac had a point, but his mind was in other places. David turned on the golden faucet, washed his hands, then cupped his hands to bring water up to his face. *There's got to be a way out of here,* he thought quietly, afraid that somehow the guard might be able to read his thoughts, *and I'm going to find it. I might die trying. But I'm going to find it.*

"I'm going to say this one more time," Smashman growled. "Lead me to the ancient treasury *now!*"

"The treasury does not belong to you," Hope spoke firmly, even though she was deeply shaken. Her frail body had been bruised with the beatings of this man. Every inch of her hurt, but she braced herself for yet another blow from the fist of this wicked bully. "It belongs to the Kingdom of Tarsurella, and you are a thief who is not fit to have it."

This brought another blow to her ribs, as he knocked her onto the floor.

"Foolish!" he hissed at her, "If you are to be my wife, you will learn to obey me. But, I suppose, you must learn the hard way." He swiftly turned away from her, and called to another ally "Arvon! Bring him in!"

The doors swung open, and Asher staggered in. He could barely walk, and was being dragged by the burly guard. His body also ached from blows and punches. His head was blurry, suffering a likely concussion from a beating just moments before. The warlords were ruthless and brutal, and had already proved that they would show no mercy until they got their way. "He won't speak!" the guard reported.

Smashman laughed, "Asher, it is time to give up." He grabbed Asher's chin, and held him in a standing position by his black wispy hair, "You lost! If you refuse to tell me where the Kingdom treasury is, then I know how to get your sister to tell me! She is already growing weak." Asher's entire body tensed up, as he fought to wiggle out of his grip. Smashman stepped out of the way, and all at once Asher saw her there on the floor.

The disturbing sight of his sister in such pain knocked the wind out of his chest, and he fell to his knees, feeling a pain far greater than anything he had previously endured. "Hope!" he cried, reeling from the sight. He couldn't believe that this man had hurt her so deeply, "Aggg! How could you?! Don't you dare touch her again!" he shouted at Smashman. "I'll tell you, I'll tell you! Just stop, let her go, please!"

"No!" Hope called back, slightly lifting her head to look at her brother who appeared just as pathetic as she did. "Asher, don't do it! Don't let him have the treasury! We would be selling out the entire Kingdom! We must stand strong. For our inheritance, for our people," she huffed, feeling her head grow dizzy from being lifted up for that brief moment, "everything!" Her voice lowered to a quiet whisper as she let her head down, "If we perish, we perish."

"You, my dear, are like a wild stallion," Smashman glared at her. "You think you are untamable, but I know you have a breaking point. And I will push you until I reach it! Asher, go turn on the bathtub. Perhaps a fresh dunk beneath the water will help change her mind."

"The map!" he cried out frantically, unable to bear another moment of injustice toward his sister, "The map is buried in the barn! Take me out to the barn, I'll help you find it. It will take you straight to the treasury, the bank, the gold, everything–I promise!"

[281]

"Ahh, good choice," Smashman grinned. "You make such a great little gaming partner. Always giving me the cheat sheets. Arvon, get this girl off the floor!" he barked, "And give her something to eat. I am going on a treasure hunt."

Bridget felt her knees go out from beneath her as she tumbled backward onto the couch, "This is impossible," she gasped. "There's no way this can be happening. That's my baby sister!" She fought back tears, "Sir, you have to do something!"

For the first time in his life, the strong security guard felt utterly debilitated. What could he do? He had his orders to protect Bridget and Willie. Now that they were out of The Palace, he couldn't go back and rescue Hope and the others. But, oh, how he wished he could. The man didn't know what to say. A moment of eerie silence settled over the room. What could be said? The scene that played in a continuous loop on the news was hellish. As the citizens in Tarsurella watched their beloved Kingdom fall apart, the entire world looked on.

"Everyone in Tarsuerlla is frozen with fear," the solemn news anchor spoke. The camera flashed away from the image of Hope being knocked to the ground by the fist of an evil bully, and back to where the news anchor was tucked away in the safety of her studio. "The United Nations has declared this a global emergency, and is discussing the possibility of dispatching allies from the United States and Europe to assist in the rescue. There is an estimated number of three-hundred civilians trapped inside, as well as the Royal Highnesses; Prince Asher, Princess Hope, Princess Jillian, and Princess Millie. We are told by Palace Security that the rest of the

Royal Family was safely extracted just moments after the terror attack, and are in cities of refuge. I video-conferenced with the Head of Royal Security earlier today..."

The scene flashed to the familiar face of Jackson. He spoke in a grave tone, "This is a very delicate situation. Not only do we have the lives of innocent hostages at risk, but we also have four of the most valuable people in our nation trapped inside. Our rescue must be strategic and perfectly timed, or else we risk imploding disaster."

"Sir, I know this has been the question on everyone's mind, since the reports from last night's events first erupted along with the disturbing video released on live broadcast by the terrorists—how did this happen?" the news anchor prodded him. "Tarsurella has always been praised for its high levels of security, and we've been told that The Palace is like an impenetrable 'wall of fire'. No one from the outside could get into The Palace without shutting down your entire system. Does that mean that the attack came from somewhere within your own walls?"

"We will not have further information until we do a complete investigation," Jackson stated. "Our main concern right now is working with the UN on a rescue plan. After we ensure that everyone is safe, and Tarsurella is no longer threatened, we will get to the bottom of this vile plot and see that judgement comes to whoever was behind it."

Bridget suddenly shut off the TV. "I can't watch this. There's no way this can be happening. This isn't real life! I need to talk to Dad." Uncontrollable tears welled up in her eyes, causing her mascara to smudge all over her face, "I need to hear his voice, I have to know that he is okay!"

"Your Highness," her guard sighed, "I have my orders. We cannot allow any communication between you all at this point. You have to trust us. Your father is perfectly safe."

"This is insane!" she shouted back at him. "You're telling me that I can't even talk to my own dad?! What about my siblings? There has to be a way to communicate with them!" She choked, fighting back hard sobs, "I can't do this without them!"

She couldn't hold it back any longer, and suddenly the sobs came, shaking her whole body.

The guard attempted to comfort her, "Your Highness, everything is going to be okay. You can do this. You are capable of trusting God in the midst of your weakness. Just rely on Him. Let Him fight this battle for you."

Bridget collapsed to her knees, crying out in prayer. She wanted to find words to lift up to the God of Heaven, but the only thing that came was tears.

"Help them!" she whispered, "Help us, God! Oh Lord, we need you!" She managed to choke out several phrases, but the majority of her prayer was spoken in the language of tears.

The pain in Addison's head felt as though giant hands were squeezing it to the point of explosion. It was as if every nightmare he had ever dreamed had come true in a single moment.

"Barack," he popped out of his char for what felt like the

hundredth time in fifteen minutes, "I can't just sit here. If I don't do something, I'm going to go crazy."

The buff security guard let out a sigh. "Your Highness, that is how we all feel right now. But we have our commands to sit still. We cannot do anything until we get word from Headquarters."

This was utter madness. Addison couldn't believe that he wasn't able to simply call his siblings or his father.

He collapsed into a chair and sighed. "This is torture. I've never felt so completely handcuffed in my entire life."

"In times like these, there is only one thing that we can do," Barack replied.

Addison looked up.

Barack spoke the answer, "Pray. Long before I joined the Royal Security Team, my mother taught me that prayer is the most powerful weapon on the planet. Greater than fear, or terrorists, or any other impossible situation. When things appear to be hopeless, that merely gives God room to take over, and take control."

"Control." Addison sighed, halfway to himself, halfway to Barack. "It's so hard to let go. Sir, will you pray with me?"

Barack nodded. The two bended their knees and lifted up their prayers to the only One who was truly in control of the situation.

"Father God, we come to you with empty hands and broken

hearts," Addison spoke. "We are at the end of our line. There is nothing we can do. There's nothing *I* can do. I have been so afraid of this moment. So afraid of everything spiraling out of my hands, and now that it has… I give it to You."

"Lord, we need You to raise up a deliverer," Barack added. "We need answers, and we need them quickly. We ask that You would stir up hearts from within The Palace walls, to make brave and honorable choices. Choices that will help keep the Royal Family, as well as the rest of the citizens inside, safe. God, we need You to bind the hand of the enemy, and defeat this wicked foe. All of our trust and hope is in You! Bring about a rescue, as swiftly as possible. In Jesus's name, amen."

"Amen," Addison echoed.

Chapter 20 - The Ancient Sword

After every guest in The Ball Room had been given the chance to go to the bathroom, it was almost noon. David anxiously waited for an open opportunity to put his plan into action. He only had one shot, so it had to be perfect. There was no room for mistakes. He had been quietly conversing with Bridget and Hope's friends, Bailee and Kitty, secretly brainstorming a plan.

"Okay," he took a deep gulp of air, "we can do this."

"All of the palace staff, as well as the handmaidens, know the secret code to access the underground tunnels. As handmaidens, we were trained for emergencies such as this," Bailee spoke in a steady tone. "If you can safely get this message to the kitchen staff, you'll be halfway there."

"Our biggest prayer is that the kitchen staff is still here, and that they didn't escape last night," Kitty added, "or else this might not work."

"Are you sure you can pull this off?" David's voice was steady.

"Oh please, I've been studying theater my whole life," Kitty sounded overly confident for the situation. "My parents have always called me a drama queen. Besides," her tone suddenly went dead, "Hope needs us."

David sighed, "Give me a few minutes to get as close as I can to the West Wing doors without looking suspicious. When I look at you, let the drama begin. Act one, Scene one, Action."

After a few moments of David nonchalantly inching his way across the room, he gave her a glance. Kitty suddenly started coughing and gasping violently. Her face went red, and for a moment David grew concerned. Yikes, the girl was really good!

"Oh my gosh, are you okay?!" Laney burst out.

"I-I- can't breathe!" she choked, stuttering out each word dramatically.

"Help her!" Laney screamed. "Somebody help her!"

This caught the attention of everyone in the room, including the guards.

"She needs her inhaler!" Zac called out. He started rummaging through her purse, "She can't breathe!"

"Quiet!" one of the guards shouted as they all drew near, lifting their guns. "No talking!"

"She needs air!" Zac yelled back, "Dude, give her a break, she's like dying here!"

The commotion was enough to distract every guard, and David took his opportunity. He slipped out the doors on the far side of the room, and let the door quietly click behind him.

As soon as it did, he took another breath, and started running down the hallway, desperately hoping that they wouldn't notice his absence. As soon as he arrived at the stairs, he darted down them, praying he would not run into the enemy.

If he did, his life would be over in an instant.

As he turned the corner to the basement kitchen, he suddenly slammed into a thick body with a loud thud. It caused him to fly back several feet.

"Son!" Clark exclaimed, shocked to see him, "How did you get down here? Never mind that, come on, get in the tunnel before someone sees you."

Clark grabbed his shoulders and guided David toward a row of stainless steel refrigerators. Clark opened the door of the faux fridge on the left. David was surprised to find it was the entrance of a secret passageway. Clark moved him forward, and the two stepped inside. Clark quickly shut the door behind them.

"How in the world did you get out of The Ball Room? Didn't the guards see you?" Clark looked gravely concerned as he bolted the door behind them.

David huffed, still pumping with adrenaline from the escape. "We created a diversion. Oh! I'm supposed to tell you... 'the Lion of Judah roars at midnight'."

Clark nodded, as if he understood. "The Palace code to the underground. Keep that in mind, son, you may need it later if we get split up." He shook his head in awe, "I'm still amazed that you got down here. Did they do a headcount? If they realize you're missing, it could be disastrous."

"No," David shook his head, "I mean, I don't think so. Unless they were counting in their minds. I didn't think about that. Either way, we have to move quickly. I have to find

Princess Hope! Do you know where she is?"

Clark wore a grave expression as he spoke, sorrow coming from his eyes, "It's not good. She's in The Queen's Suite. The head honcho, whoever this evil mastermind is, has both her and Asher in his clutches. From what I can tell, everyone else in the family escaped, besides Millie and Jillian. I have them hidden. Are you hungry?"

"No. I can't even think about food until I know that Princess Hope is okay. Do you have directions to The Queen's Suite?"

"Son, you can't just go in there. Trust me, I would if I could but—"

"Stop telling me I can't, okay?" David vented, raising his voice much louder than he should, "The Princess is in danger! Why don't people get that?!"

"Son, I admire your passion to defend the Princess, but there is truly nothing we can do right now."

David continued, refusing to miss a beat, "Do you know how to get to The Queen's Suite?"

"Yes, but like I said—"

"I'm not going to take no for an answer," David replied, having no clue where this fierce boldness was coming from. Under normal circumstances, he would never talk to an adult like that.

Now it was Clark's turn to sigh. "I'll tell you. But we're going to think of a plan first. We're not going to march in there like hot-heads and get ourselves killed! Calmly, and rationally, we'll think of something to outwit them. But let me warn you, son, these men are not messing around. Are you willing to risk your life on this mission?"

"Sir, I would take a bullet through my brain. Anything to keep Hope from enduring the living hell she is in right now."

"Okay," Clark nodded, finally satisfied with the boy's response. For the first time in their conversation, Clark felt like he was talking to a man, and not a hormonal teenage boy. "Here's the scoop. Walk with me…"

With the fire from her eyes, Hope drilled holes of hatred into the gourmet steak set before her. There was no way that she would eat food provided by the enemy. Smashman had prepared a banquet for her. He poured the Royal wine, and used her mother's favorite wine glasses. Of course, she was starving. But the banquet spread before her was tainted with the fingerprints of evil. She would rather die than eat this man's food.

Suddenly, the doors to the Queen's Suite flew open, and Hope looked up. Smashman stood in the hallway, grinning with wicked pleasure. His arms were loaded with ancient, priceless treasures.

"You're a thief," Hope growled at him. "The Royal Treasury of Tarsurella does not belong to you, and as soon as my father finds out what you have done, you will be sorry!"

"Oh," Smashman flashed a fake look of fear, then laughed. He dumped his findings on the table. Gold coins, a silver watch, emerald necklaces, diamond rings, a belt studded with rubies, and a small pocket knife with a sapphire handle, all crashed onto the table. "Those are tough words for a weak and powerless woman like yourself."

"I am not weak!" she fought back. "I have the Crown, and the entire Kingdom of Tarsurella on my side. And you? You have nothing but fear tactics and merciless bullying. That's not real power."

"Really?" he chuckled. "It seems to be working out quite nicely! Thus far, I have high-jacked the Kingdom, shut down the communication center, and taken dominion over The Palace. There are only two things left on my list…" He shouted something in Arabic, and several men came running in.

Hope gasped. One of them carried her Father's—which was supposed to be Addison's—Royal Crown.

"Tonight, I shall wear this crown I shall sit on the throne, and become King. We will broadcast it to all nations, and they will know that Allah is God!"

Hope shook her head slowly in disgust. Her body felt weak, but her spirit was strong. "It isn't going to work. Your wicked plot will be foiled. You're not as great as you think you are, and neither is your so-called god."

Smashman's wild fist crashed into Hope's jaw once more. "How dare you disrespect Allah!"

She whimpered and held her face, but before she could move, another blow came from the other direction, "And you will respect your husband!"

Hope bit her lip. She knew that speaking more would only get her in deeper trouble. But she didn't care. She had to speak.

Her voice trembled as she spoke barely above a whisper, "You are not my husband. And you never will be."

"Eat," he demanded. "This is a wedding feast. After, you will undress and put on the Queen's wedding gown. We will go downstairs, speak our vows before Allah, and send the message to all of Tarsurella that I have conquered!"

Hope's heart raced with fear. Her chest rose and fell, and she breathed heavily as a paralyzing dread washed over her.

This was real. This man would devour her. If help didn't come quickly, it would all be over. Desperation clung to her soul. She did the only thing that she knew to do.

"I lift my eyes up to the hills, where does my help come from, my help comes from the Lord the Maker of Heaven and earth. Some trust in chariots, and some in horses, but I trust in the name of the Lord my God. He who dwells in the Secret Place of the Most High, shall abide under the shadow of the Almighty. I will say of the Lord, He is my refuge, my fortress—"

"Stop!" Smashman yelled, "What are those words you speak? If you are calling down to your gods, they will not help you!"

She closed her eyes. She couldn't give in to fear. *Lord, help me,* she screamed inside. *Be my rescuer!*

"The Lord your God is with you, He is mighty to save you, He will quiet you with His love, He will rejoice over you with singing. Greater is He that is in you, than He that is in the world. Those who trust in the Lord will never be put to shame. God has not given me a spirit of fear, but a spirit of love, power, and a sound mind—"

Smashman's fists pounded onto the table so violently it made

Hope jump. Her eyes popped open, and she saw the face of this man seething with anger. "Fine. Do not eat. Be foolish! I'm going to the King's Wardrobe. When I get back, you had better be wearing the wedding dress of the Queen."

He quickly stormed out of the room, locking the heavy doors behind him. As soon as he was gone, Hope raised herself up from the table, attempting to find a way of escape.

But as soon as she moved, her ribs seared with pain. She collapsed onto the floor and cried out, "Jesus!"

David ran his callused guitar fingers along textured engraving in the wall. Even in the midst of utter darkness, the flashlight app on Clark's cell phone shone brightly. The spotlight pierced through the dark. An ancient mural was spread out before him, with a magnificent map of the underground tunnels leading throughout The Palace. "This is amazing," he breathed. "It's all so complex."

Clark pointed with his finger to the exact location where they stood, "We are here. The Queen's Suite is here. There's a bookshelf that pushes into her room, but only from the tunnel. It cannot be opened by anyone from inside the chambers, which means that we will be able to see what is happening, and decide on the ideal moment to make our move."

Clark took several feet forward, then pressed on a loose stone in the wall. Several stones fell loose, which provided a small opening below. Clark crouched down, and slowly pulled a sword out from the hole in the wall. David almost let out a gasp of wonderment. The sword sparkled with diamonds embedded into the handle. Clark handed it to David. He was speechless.

"That sword was carried by King Theodore, seven generations ago. The Royal fables say that King Theodore's sword was one that no man could defeat. It was used to defend the Royal Crest, his nation, and his people. This is the only weapon we have right now. We must use it wisely. It might seem foolish to think that we have any chance of defeating men with modern day machine guns, but the weapons of the Kingdom never go out of date."

David stared at the sword and took a deep breath. He didn't have a clue how to use it, but he had no choice. Every moment that they stood standing here was another moment that Hope desperately needed their help. He wrapped the ancient sheath about his waist, and slipped the sword inside. "For Princess Hope, and for the Kingdom of Tarsurella. Let's go."

David and Clark took huge strides forward, and soon their trot turned into a full-blown gallop. They quickly approached the turn that led into the Queen's secret library within her chambers.

Clark turned off his flashlight App. But before the light flickered out and darkness enveloped them, David caught a glimpse of the faux book shelf standing before them. His heart pounded, knowing that Hope was on the other side. They were so close!

As Clark slowly pulled a book out from the shelf, a tiny shaft of light from the other room came pouring through. David drew closer and peered through the peep hole. He blinked, his eyes trying to readjust to the new scene. He frantically searched the room–Princess Hope was nowhere to be seen! He felt himself begin to panic. What had happened to her? Where was she? Suddenly, his eyes caught the odd image of something heaped upon the ground. Suddenly, it registered. Hope was lying on the floor! David reached for the lever to open the door.

Clark's strong arm grabbed hold of David's wrist, and blocked him from making a sudden movement.

"Son, be still," Clark whispered in an authoritative tone.

At that very moment, the main doors flew open, and an unwanted character stepped inside. David felt Clark's grip relax on his wrist. David struggled to catch his breath. That was too close. He had nearly blown their cover and gotten them all killed.

"What are you doing on the floor?!" Smashman yelled at a helpless Hope, "I told you to put on the dress!"

David's chin tensed up. He felt his hand grip the handle to King Theodor's sword with an unforgiving grasp. *If that man even dared to—*

"I will not," Hope spoke quietly from the floor. Her voice wasn't much louder than a whisper, "I will not do what you say."

All at once, he grabbed her by her hair, and dragged her to a standing position. Hope let out a yelp, which ripped at David's insides. He felt as though his heart was being run through a paper-shredder.

"Steady," Clark whispered, "stay steady."

David clenched his teeth. This was impossible to watch. All he knew was that the second Clark gave the signal, he would dash into the room and slice the evil man apart!

"There are two ways we can do this, Your Highness," he snarled at her, "the easy way, or the hard way. I would suggest you choose wisely!"

Hope trembled from weakness. She could barely hold herself up and her body was throbbing from such deep pain in her ribs. Still, she did the only thing she knew to do. She continued to speak scripture. "God sits enthroned above the circle of the earth. All of the men below are like grasshoppers. The Lord goes out like a mighty man, like a man of war he stirs up his zeal, He cries, He shouts aloud, He shows Himself mighty against his foes. The Word of God is quick and powerful, sharper than any double edged sword—"

Smashman pushed her backwards, causing her to tumble onto the bed. "Fine!" he shouted, "If you won't wear the dress, I will put it on for you!" He tore her sheer sleeve, leaving a frightening rip in the chiffon material.

"Stop!" she cried, "Get away from me!" She attempted to push him away, but to no avail. He pinned her, and made clear the devastating reality that he was much stronger than she. Any attempts to stop him would be fruitless.

"You will obey me!" he shouted, lifting up his arm to hit her again, "I am your master!"

David couldn't bear to watch any longer. An electrical bolt of rage burst through his entire being, and within a split second, every part of him was on fire with it. Without warning, he pulled the lever, and the secret door flew open. David charged forward with a determined shout.

Smashman saw him coming, rolled off the bed, and ducked out of the way.

The momentum from his lunge caused David to keep flying forward, and he nearly smashed into the wall. The move was extremely un-elegant, and nowhere near the slick, James Bond image that one might hope to portray when bursting in to save the damsel in distress.

Clark raced in behind him like a bullet, and swiftly grabbed Hope off the bed.

When David turned to regain his footing, Smashman was waiting there for him, ready to live up to his name. His iron fist smashed into David's face. The blow was so shocking and intense that David nearly blacked out as his head slammed into the wall.

He felt his footing fail, as he slipped down the wall. By the time Smashman turned around, Clark already had Hope out of the room, and the secret door shut behind them.

The enraged man let out a barbaric cry of frustration as he pounded on the locked bookshelf door, then reached for the gun in his belt.

David saw the blurry figure standing before him, aiming directly at him. Before he processed what was happening, it was too late.

Smashman fired at his enemy. Satisfied with his aim, he shouted, "That is for stealing my Queen!" Then his heavy boots turned and started running.

Chapter 21 - Too Close

"Millie, Jillian, come on we're getting out of here!" Clark called.

Jillian let out a gasp as her hands flew up to her face. "Hope!"

Jillian couldn't believe the sight before her eyes. Her poor sister looked as though she had been through cruel and unusual punishment, "Oh my goodness, is she okay?! What happened? Is she hurt?" Jillian rushed to grab her sister's hand.

Clark, who still held the limp Princess in her arms, didn't have time to answer her questions. "Your sister is going to be okay. But we need to leave. Right now."

Millie let out a whimper. This was all too much! Who had hurt her sister? "Clark, I'm scared! What's happening?"

"Millie, do you remember what I told you about being brave? Courage is not the absence of fear. It's just deciding that something else is more important. And right now, you being brave enough to follow me and leave the castle is way more important than any fear that you feel. Can you do that for me, Mil? Can you be brave?"

Millie nodded her head, even though she felt terror all over, "Yes."

He quickly led them through the dark quarters and Hope let out a moan. She felt Jillian grab her hand, she just didn't have the energy to say anything. "I love you Hope. It's gonna be okay," Jillian whispered.

Hope squeezed her hand, and sent that love right on back to her.

"Where's David?" Hope asked through cracked lips.

Clark kept his pace up, running into the kitchen to use the final escape pod that he hoped was left.

"Clark, *where* is David?" Hope lifted her head and made her voice more firm this time.

Clark unlatched a steel opening in the kitchen floor and breathed a sigh of relief. The escape pod was indeed still there. "Come on girls," he urged Millie and Jillian to climb in, "take a seat and fasten your seatbelts quickly."

They obeyed.

"Wait!" Hope choked as he gently lowered her below the floor, and set her down in the co-pilot's chair, "You're not just leaving him, are you? Clark, you couldn't! A man never leaves a soldier behind."

"Your Highness, this young man cannot be your concern right now." He hit a big red button that powered up the engine. A display of lights started to dance on the dashboard.

"That man is audaciously cold-blooded and heartless!" Hope cried, "If we leave David, he will die back there! And what about Asher?"

"Your Highness, we must get you out of here! You are the pawn that he wants. Trust me, once you've been extracted from the premises, everyone else will be much safer."

"You don't mean that," Hope shook her head, fighting back tears. "You're just telling me what you think I want to hear. But I don't. I know the truth." With one final lurch of energy, she stretched across the dashboard and hit the 'Power Down' button. Everything started to reverse and shut down again. "Go get David."

Clark groaned within himself. What was he to do?! He had to get Hope and the girls out of here, but it wasn't right to disobey her command. He lowered his voice in humility, "I will go find him, if that's what you truly want. But," he paused, having trouble forming the words, "you must be prepared for the worst."

He turned the engine back on, and the lights did their special dance again. "If I'm not back in five minutes, go without me."

"But Clark—"

"I mean it." He looked Hope straight in the eye, and she knew that he was dead serious. "Everything is set on auto-pilot, it will take you directly to your safe destination. Don't try to play the hero. You're the one that everyone is after. Don't wait for me."

He reached into the backseat and kissed Millie on the hand, "I love you girls. Both of you. I always have, and I always will. No matter what."

"Oh Clark, don't leave us!" Millie fought back tears, "I don't think I can be brave without you!"

It took everything within Clark's being to tear himself away from that sweet little girl. He loved her more than life itself. Still, he let go of her hand, and knew that his Royal duties called. "I love you. Goodbye."

And with that, he ducked out of the pod.

After several long and painful hours of staring at the cuckoo-clock, Mrs. Drakos announced that it was time for lunch to be served.

"Thank you, Mrs. Drakos," Chasity tried her best to be gracious, "I cannot express enough gratitude to you for taking me in like this, and treating me so sweetly in this time of crisis. As soon as peace and righteousness is restored to the Kingdom, I'll do everything within my power to honor you for your humble service."

"Oh my!" Mrs. Drakos's cheeks flushed red, flattered by the Royal complement, "Your Highness, it is our honor! Truly! I have no greater joy than to see you fed and cared for! I only wish that this visit were not because of such awful circumstances. Nevertheless, my husband and I will see to it that your time in Greece is as blessed, relaxing, and delicious as possible!"

Chasity stepped into the kitchen. The counter was loaded with authentic Greek food. The cuisine that Mrs. Drakos spoiled her with was absolutely divine! In ordinary circumstances, her mouth would be watering from all of these heavenly delicacies. But today her stomach was in knots, and thinking about eating only made her feel nauseous.

"Come, come Your Highness, have a seat!" Mrs. Drakos motioned toward the table. Chasity sat down. Hanson and Lance stood awkwardly against the back wall in the kitchen. The tiny house was so cramped, it made their ever-looming presence feel even more awkward.

"Boys, come have a seat!" Mrs. Drakos invited them, "There is plenty of food to go around!"

"No thank you, ma'am," Lance shook his head and stood firm. He had his sunglasses on inside, and Mrs. Drakos thought it was ridiculous.

"They're not trying to be rude, but it's against Royal protocol for them to dine with us," Chasity explained.

"Well pish-posh!" Mrs. Drakos exclaimed, as she grabbed Lance's hand, "You're not in The Palace, you are in my home! Scoot your little self into that chair, prepare yourself a plate, and *do* take those foolish sunglasses off!"

Lance obeyed her commands. What else was he to do?! She was like a bossy grandmother who knew exactly what she wanted! And if he didn't listen to her, she probably had a wooden paddle hanging somewhere in the laundry room!

Mrs. Drakos turned to Hanson, and her sharp blue eyes shone into his. Without saying a word, he followed Lance and sat down.

After their plates were piled high with pita bread, octopus, triopita, and gyros, Mr. Drakos prayed, and then announced, "Opa! Dig in!"

Chasity stared down at her napkin. She couldn't stop thinking about her family. Far too many hours had passed without hearing anything. She glanced upward, and found Hanson staring at her. "Excuse me," she said quietly, "I need some fresh air." She suddenly pushed herself away from the table and ran out the back door.

Hanson groaned and stood up, disappointed that he would have to step away from this tantalizing meal. "Sorry," he apologized to Mrs. Drakos before taking off after Princess Chasity.

As soon as he stepped outside, he could see that Chasity was already making her way down to the beach. She scurried down the steep steps, with Hanson following quickly after her.

"Your Highness!" he called. "Stop!"

She whipped around, her hair violently blowing across her face, thanks to the sea breeze. "Just let me go, okay?! I need like five minutes of privacy without you being my shadow!" Her angry voice tore at him, "Is that seriously too much to ask?!"

"Princess, you know the rules," Hanson tightened his jaw, and his voice, "I cannot allow you out of my sight. Especially not right now."

"Fine," she snapped, knowing perfectly well that he wouldn't leave her alone, "just let me get a ten-second lead, and *don't* talk to me."

She knew she was being bossy and bitterly cruel, but she didn't care! Being around Hanson 24/7 was like having the oxygen sucked from her lungs. Sure, he had saved her life. Sure, she needed to be protected. But he was the most irritating, unfriendly, snarky, crass, unfeeling, and unthoughtful person she had ever met! Sure, he was charming, and devastatingly handsome, but she didn't care anymore. She didn't care about anything. All she wanted, more than anything, was to know that her family was safe. That they would all be together again. That they were still alive.

She walked against the bitter wind, taking monstrous steps until she reached the shore. She ignored the complaint in her ankle. Then she kicked off her shoes and walked faster. They were only slowing her down.

The massive waves which crashed upon the rocks beside her

were like a pounding reminder that everything she'd ever known had spun completely out of control. Her universe had fallen off its axis, and just like the wind and waves that tore at her now, there was nothing she could do about it. All she could do was stand, keep walking forward, and refuse to fall over. The merciless elements would *not* take her down. She refused to drown in this ocean of emotion; yet, angry tears streamed down her face as she silently cried.

She felt the desperate need for a life boat to come save her. "Oh God," she whispered, "help."
Next thing she knew, her cries were audible. Her shoulders were shaking, and her whole body responded to the devastating trauma that had just ripped through her life.

Hanson sensed her sudden distress, and did the only thing he knew that could comfort a Princess— no, a heartbroken girl— in a moment like this: be a friend. He slowly approached from behind, and placed his arm around her. Chasity was lost in such a storm of tears and fears, that she didn't even recognize his presence. It wasn't until he gently lifted her head and drew it to his chest, that she realized what was happening. "*Shh*," he attempted to comfort her, "it's okay. You're gonna be okay."

She accepted his open invitation to grieve, and without thinking, she threw herself deeper into his comforting embrace. "I, I can't do this!" she choked, "I can't lose them! Not again! I need them! All of them! If even one of them is dead, I, I–"

Hanson didn't have any words. So he just held her. He slowly stroked her hair, attempting to keep the strands out of her face that the wind blew in every direction. After several minutes, he knew he had to shake her out of this. If she didn't stop now, there might not be a way to settle her down later.

"Come on, you're shivering." He pulled back as he noticed her bare arms, "Let's get you out of this wind."

Chasity sniffled. Her throat hurt, and her nose ached, thanks to the massive tear-fest that had just flooded her sinuses. She followed Hanson's lead as they turned to climb the bank of tall boulders. He bare toes slid on the slippery, slimy moss that covered the rocks. He grabbed her hand to help the Princess keep her footing. After overcoming several obstacles, they finally reached a small cave and ducked inside.

Hanson sat down and took off his black jacket. "Here," he said as he draped it around her shoulders, "You need it more than I do."

Chasity lowered beside him and shivered one last time. They could still see the ocean from the opening in the cave, but now they were guarded from the blustery wind.

Chasity dabbed her eyes, blotting up the mascara that was probably all over her face by now. Without warning, she was arrested by a deep embarrassment.. "I'm so sorry that you had to see that," she tried to laugh it off. "I'm sure it's not very often that you get front row seats to witness the dramatic viewing of a complete, emotional breakdown!"

"It's no big deal," Hanson shrugged, eyes staring off toward the sea, "I'm here for you."

"Yeah, I know." Chasity sounded irritated, "It's your job."

"No," he paused and turned to look at her, "I mean it. I'm really here for you."

Chasity met his gaze. She could feel the compassion radiating out of him. For the first time since he had arrived at The Palace, Hanson finally felt real to her.

Hanson had always been a dark, puzzling, and ever-looming mystery of questions, drama and frustrating unknowns; but now, as they sat here together like two completely normal people, Chasity saw him in a light that she had never seen him in before–real.

"Who *are* you, Hanson Fletcher?" Chasity asked slowly. "I see you every day. You watch me eat, read, walk and talk with my sisters, but I have no idea who you are. Your past, your family, your passions? I don't even know your middle name!"

Hanson suddenly broke their gaze and turned his head toward the ocean again, "We can't talk about this."

"Why?" Chasity pleaded, "Because of some stupid, ancient rule that says Royalty is supposed to have nothing to do with the personal affairs of their hired hands? How ridiculous and outdated is that?" she laughed in frustration. "We can't even have a normal conversation, because of all these pointless, precautionary regulations! You're not even allowed to call me by my first name! Don't you find that incredibly demeaning? You're a *person*, Hanson. A real, living, breathing human being, who has thoughts and feelings and emotions, and you're expected to behave like some sort of brain-washed military robot! Doesn't that drive you crazy?"

"Of course it does!" Hanson snapped, raising his voice at the Princess, "This whole job is maddening! Do you think this is what I signed up for? Do you think this is what I had in mind for my life? I was chosen for The Security Academy when I was in middle school. I didn't have a normal childhood. I didn't play soccer with friends, or watch cartoons every Saturday morning while stuffing my face with Lucky Charms. I was raised with one purpose: to protect and defend the Royal Crown. Now I'm here, and there are rules, and they stink but this is my *life*, Chasity. And there's nothing you can do to change that."

Chasity bit her bottom lip, and folded her hands into her lap. "I'm so sorry. I had no idea."

"I don't want your pity," he spoke quickly.

"Maybe not," she replied, "but you do need something. You need what I needed just moments ago, when I was a total mess and my whole world was crashing down around me. I needed a friend. I needed a shoulder to cry on, and to simply know that someone cared. So now I'm offering the same to you, Hanson. I'm not just your Princess. I'm your friend. Anytime you need me, I'm here."

Hanson boiled over with frustration, and wanted to pull the hair right out of his head, "What don't you get about this situation? Did you not hear anything I just said?! We cannot be friends! We can't sit here and have these conversations, and act like we've known each other for years. I can't get close to you."

"Hanson, you don't have to follow those stupid rules!" she argued. "We're sitting here on an Island in Greece, completely alone! Nobody back at Headquarters is going to know if you talked to me or not, or if you call me by my first name. The Kingdom is in utter turmoil, and our lives and destinies as we know them have been altered forever. If it is a crime for us to be friends, then let me be the one to take the blame. Whatever terrifying punishment they're threatening you with, I will see to it that I receive it instead of you."

"Chasity, listen to me," Hanson spoke slowly as his voice quivered, "I'm not the person you think I am."

Chasity locked eyes with him once more.

He continued, "This weekend, I was confronted with a terrible, horrific choice to make. I had to make a decision that nobody should ever be forced to. Believe me when I say these words. You don't want to be friends with me. You *can't* be friends with me. My backstory is ugly and shattered and complicated, and you getting involved will only put your own life in danger. The less you know about me, the better."

"I don't understand," Chasity spoke quietly.

"I had to choose," he sighed heavily, "between you, your family, and my loyalty to the Crown; and the people that I deeply care about. An agonizing threat forced me to decide which was more important—my family, friends, and everything I've ever known? Or you. But I couldn't do it.
I couldn't bring myself to betray the Crown." He reached into the pocket of his jacket which was still resting around Chasity's shoulders, and pulled out a small electronic chip, "My hands were shaking as I tried to do it. But I couldn't."

"This doesn't make any sense," Chasity replied. "Hanson, what are you saying?"

He handed her the small chip. "Here. I want you to throw this into the ocean. I'm giving this to you, as a symbol of my loyalty. I couldn't imagine what your life would be like if I would've done this. I never would've been able to forgive myself. It's my duty to protect you, no matter what the cost. Now, I don't know what kind of destruction is awaiting me at home. But you have to know, Chasity, as much as I tried to fight it, the answer always came back to you. I choose you. And I'll continue to choose you, every single time." He slowly reached for her hand.

As Hanson touched her, Chasity felt an exciting spark of electricity bolt through her.

His other hand reached for her cheek as he drew his face toward hers. Hanson felt himself being drawn in by her sweet and magnetic presence. As much as this beautiful, frustrating, brilliant young woman had driven him crazy, this forced decision caused him to realize that she was worth fighting for. Every time he put up his shield of defense against Chasity's transcendent beauty and alluring charm, she managed to do something else that knocked him defenseless. He could feel every wall crumbling from around his heart.

Chasity could barely remember how to breathe as Hanson continued to speak, "If things were different, if I had met you on a holiday by the sea, or at a polo match, or horseback riding at the local stables, it wouldn't be like this. *I* wouldn't be like this. I would want to be your friend. Heck, I would want to talk to you like all of the time." He laughed nervously, "I would send you notes, and call to ask for your help on homework, and offer to carry your books, and take you out for pizza, and probably drive you crazy because I would never leave you alone. If you gave me the time of day, looked my direction, or texted me back, I would seal those memories in my mind. I would lay awake at night and think about you. Your eyes, your adorable laugh, and your sassy little temper." He smiled, "I would be entranced by your beauty, your love for life, your kindness, and your heart for everyone around you. But it's not different," Hanson's gaze saddened. "And it never will be. So I can't think about you this way, and I *won't*. Because I could never put you in that much danger."

"Danger?" Chasity echoed. Her heart had melted from his words, "What could possibly be dangerous about this? You keep saying that you're trying to protect me. But protect me from what?"

"Me," he breathed, letting go of her hand, hating that things had to be this way. "Chasity, I'm like an explosive. If you get too close, I can't protect you anymore."

She leaned in closer as an invisible force drew her in. "Have you ever thought about the fact," she spoke slowly as she reached to touch his hair, "that I don't want to be protected?"

Hanson could feel himself crumbling. He weakened, as flashes of hormones shot through his body, suggesting all sorts of things that he knew he shouldn't be thinking. Yet he was. Her nearness was overwhelming. Here she was, in his arms, a moment that he never dared to dream would be possible. He inched even closer, ready to give her what she was asking for. A kiss.

As their faces drew closer, the whole earth was silent. Even the thundering waves pounding on the sand stopped and held their breath.

Chasity closed her eyes, carelessly abandoning herself to the fate of whatever beautiful thing was going to happen next.

Just seconds before their lips were to meet, Hanson pulled away and bolted to his feet.

"I uh, we– um," Hanson struggled to find his footing and return to the real world. There was no way he could let this happen! Was he crazy? How did he even allow things to get this far? Where was his brain?! "We need to get back to the house," he spoke in an even tone. "They'll be expecting us."

Chasity sat there in shock, wondering what had just happened. Wasn't he just about to kiss her?!

She wasn't sure if she was angry or relieved. A strange devastation crashed into her chest, as her heart suffered the sting of rejection. Confusion ensued.

"Um, yeah," Chasity said slowly, wiping off her hands and

pulling herself to a standing position, "right." She struggled to regain her composure.

Chasity cleared her throat, attempting to act as if nothing had happened. She tucked a stray piece of hair behind her ear, "Let's go."

Chapter 22 – True Hero

Laney nervously dug beneath her nails. Zac quietly tapped on The Palace floor with his drumsticks. Justin ran anxious fingers through his hair. "Sooo, if we ever get out of here," he started slowly, "do you think we'll write a song about this?"

His wacky thought couldn't help but bring a little bit of laughter to the group.

"How long do you think we've been here?" Laney asked. "It feels like we've been trapped in this room for an eternity. My stomach is begging for food."

Kitty glanced at her watch, joining in on the band's conversation. "Twenty-two hours. I can't even think about food, my stomach is freaking out. Isn't anyone else sick from worrying about David? I can only pray that he's found Hope and that they somehow found a way out of here."

Laney sighed heavily. She had been trying not to worry about her friend, trying to keep the mood light. But how could she not be gravely concerned? Had he been caught while trying to escape in the hallway? She hadn't heard any gunshots. But The Palace was so ginormous. Anything could have happened.

And what would happen to them? Would they be trapped here for days? If Tarsurella wasn't brave enough to face the situation, wouldn't the U.S. Army come after them? How could it be that they had been trapped here for so long, and nobody had done anything about it yet? Would they starve to death? Would they ever see their parents, their friends, and their homes again? Laney shook her head. She had to stop thinking like that. It would only bring on a panic attack.

Suddenly, a loud rumbling was heard in the distance, and the floor started shaking. Kitty gasped, "Helicopters! They're coming for us!"

Sure enough, within seconds, the whole sky was flooded with Royal aircraft. The Palace grounds swarmed with helicopters landing in the lawn, and armed men raced onto the scene.

Several gunshots were heard, as evil shouts came from the men who held them captive. All at once, in a frantic fury of chaotic gunfire, screams were heard as every terrified soul ducked and covered their heads.

One guard called to another, barking out a command in Arabic to begin shooting the prisoners. "Smashman lost the Princess! It's all over!" he shouted. But to the ears of the terrified citizens, their unknown language disguised the purpose of their murderous cries. "Take as many lives as you can, before your own! For Smashman, and for Allah!"

Laney froze in horror, as the men started shooting captives on the North side of the room. Her entire body went numb with fear, as she saw several bodies drop to the ground.

"Run, run, go, go!" Justin called out, seeing an opening at the door nearest to them.

Laney didn't move. She didn't know if she should scream or cry. Her head was spinning. The violent scene unfolding before her eyes made her stomach churn.

"Laney, come on!" Justin shouted, grabbing her hand and pulling her limp body along. Next thing she knew, she was in the hallway, and United States soldiers were flooding in by the hundreds.

"Kids, follow me! This way, come on!" a U.S. soldier called to them. "Stay behind us, we will get you out of here!"

Six other servicemen surrounded them like a shield as they raced through the hallway. Within seconds, they burst through the side doors which led them outdoors. Laney gasped for air, still holding Justin's hand, far too afraid to let go. "Oh, dear God!" she cried, tears streaming from her face, "Thank you God! Oh my, we're free!"

They led them to a helicopter and helped each band member, as well as Bailee and Kitty, hop up to safety. Laney watched in amazement as floods of civilians came from inside The Palace, and were each led to the life-giving haven of heroic helicopters. "Thank you!" Laney cried, not even bothering to hold back the tears as she looked into the eyes of the brave soldier who had led them out, "Th-thank you so much!"

He could hardly hear her over the whirl of the helicopter, but still he yelled back, "You guys are safe now!" He gave her a strong, fatherly look of reassurance, "We're going to get you back home to your families, don't you worry!" He then turned to the pilot, "Let's get this thing off the ground!"

"But what about David?" Bailee asked.

"Oh my gosh, David!" Laney gasped as the helicopter began to rise. "Sir, we have a friend, he's still in there! David Carter, he's still in the building!"

"I'm sorry, miss, but we can't go back now!" he called back, "My orders were to fill this copter, and get them to safety, which is exactly what we're doing!"

"But we can't just leave him!" Laney cried out, "It's David!"

But there was no point in arguing with him. They were already in the air and vacating the premises. Laney turned to look over her shoulder. The beautiful Palace, which used to be such a vision of spectacular awe-invoking beauty, now looked like a cold and heartless torture chamber. As they flew away, it grew smaller and smaller, fading into the distance.

"David? David? Son, can you hear me?" the calming voice spoke to David, and slowly his eyes blinked open. The face before him was blurry.

David moaned. His right hand clung to his left shoulder. A wave of intense pain crashed over him, as his arm screamed, reminding him of what had happened just moments ago, before he slipped out of consciousness. He tightened his jaw and kicked his foot, wanting to find a way to release his body from the wicked pain that shook him.

"He's still with us!" Clark declared to the nurse who knelt down beside him, then he spoke firmly to David, "Son, you need you to keep your eyes open! Stay awake, look at me."

David blinked again. He fought with everything inside to keep himself going. He couldn't give up. He wouldn't give up. Not until he knew. "Where?" he whispered, mustering up what little strength he could find, "Where is she? Is she okay?"

"*Shhh*," Clark directed him again, "save your strength. We need to get you downstairs."

"I've stopped the bleeding for the time being," the nurse reported, tightening the wrap around his shoulder, "but we need to move quickly and get him to the medical transport as swiftly as possible."

Clark carefully bent over to pick him up, cautiously making sure not to bump his arm. With a grunt, he lifted the young man into his arms, and headed toward the door.

"All of the enemy threats have been disarmed and removed," the nurse explained. "The coast is clear for us to move through The Palace."

Clark didn't have to be told twice. He walked rapidly down the hallway.

"David!" Princess Hope called out from the other end of the hallway, "Oh my gosh, is he okay?!" She tried to run toward them, but she couldn't move fast enough. Even with Jillian and Millie's support, she struggled.

"Your Highness!" Clark gasped as he stopped to turn around. What was she doing here?! He quickly barked orders at a nearby American soldier to whisk David to the medical helicopter. The soldier obeyed.

"What are you doing?!" Clark demanded, "I told you to leave in the escape pod!"

The nurse abruptly rushed to her aid, examining her for signs of broken bones. Clark quickly scooped her up, even though Hope wanted to fight him. "You shouldn't even be walking!"

"Sir, she has at least one broken rib, if not more," the nurse reported, "We need to go, now."

Hope was hurting, but that didn't stop her mouth from working, "I couldn't just leave! Royalty never leaves a man behind. Especially when it's someone who just saved your life! I sent the escape pod, but we weren't in it. I knew that if everyone thought I had escaped safely from The Palace, they would send troops to rescue everyone else who remained. Is he alright? Is David going to be okay?"

"How could you be so foolish?!" Clark continued with his emotional rebuke, "You not only put your life in danger, but the lives of your younger sisters! That could have been disastrous!"

"But we're okay, Clark!" Millie piped up. She and Jillian were taking huge steps, trying to keep up with Clark's monstrous strides.

Clark let out a frustrated sigh as they reached the courtyard and spotted the helicopter, "Thank God you girls are safe. But next time, do *exactly* as you are told. Things could have gone a heck of a lot worse than they did."

"Addison!" Bridget cried, flinging out her arms and embracing her brother. Addison's arms enveloped her, as his nose was buried in her head of curls. She smelled strongly of Cherry Blossom Shampoo, just like she always did. Normally, the smell drove him nuts. But today, he tried not to cry. She was safe. He squeezed her tighter, and she let out a giggle. "Bro, can't breathe!"

"I don't care!" he teased, finally letting her go, and kissing her on the forehead.

"My turn, my turn!" Willie came bounding into the room.

Addison got down on his knees, as Willie tackled him in a bear hug. "Awe, that's my little man!"

Addison ruffled his wild mane of red hair, and memorized every freckle on his pale thin face. Again, he tried not to cry.

Deborah held out a box of Kleenex, which she had already been using. Bridget reached for a tissue and dabbed her eyes, "I love you guys so much. Ugh, and I'm not even wearing waterproof mascara."

Addison laughed. For the first time in twenty-three hours, he laughed. It was a true, genuine laugh. One that came from the core of his being. He had honestly forgotten what it felt like. He forgot what it was to smile. What it felt like for his family to be reunited. To feel peace, and to know that everything was going to be okay. It was a feeling that he never wanted to lose again.

Now that Bridget and Willie had joined Addison in his temporary place of refuge, he could breathe a little bit easier.

"Where's Daddy?" Willie asked, his innocent face turning to ask Deborah the all-important questions, "When can I see him, and Hope and Chasity and Jillian and Asher and Millie?"

Deborah took a deep breath, "Your daddy is still in his secret hiding place. Don't worry though, because he is perfectly safe. Millie and Jillian will be here soon, just in time for dinner actually! The rest of your siblings are going to stay in their secret locations just a little bit longer, until it's time for everyone to go home."

"How long?" Willie looked confused.

"Just long enough," Deborah offered a reassuring smile then tactfully changed the subject, "How do chicken nuggets sound for dinner?"

"Yum!" Willie burst out, "I love chicken nuggets!"

"Then let's go get all washed up for dinner!" Deborah grabbed his hand, "Come now, you want to be clean for when Millie and Jillian get here!"

Willie cheerfully followed her out of the room, skipping and talking about how he wanted extra ketchup tonight.

Addison gave his sister another hug. "I love you, sis."

"Oh Addi, I was so scared." Bridget spoke, her voice quaking a little. "I was terrified, just thinking about losing one of you—"

"But you didn't." Addison pulled back from the hug, and looked her directly in the eyes, "You didn't lose any of us. And you're not going to. Because we're family, and we stick together, and no matter what happens, we're always going to be here for each other."

Bridget sighed and fell backwards onto the couch, "I have the worst migraine ever. I didn't think it was possible to feel this terrible. I feel like I got hit by a locomotive. And I wasn't even there!" Bridget popped back up, "Oh, Addison. Hope, our poor Hope, did you see her?! Did you see that video?!"

Addison sighed and plopped down beside her. The thought brought something like a ten-thousand-pound weight onto his shoulders. "Bridget, I can't even think about it. It drives me so beyond mad."

Bridget let out angry tears, "If that freak of a man hurt her, I am going to—"

"Sis, stop." Addison grabbed her hands, "Hate isn't going to fix anything. I know you're angry. I'm angry too, believe me! But just like worrying, regretting, or blaming yourself, hating the enemy isn't going to get us anywhere. Hope is okay now. We have to be thankful for what we've got."

"Thankful?!" Bridget choked, "Do you hear yourself? Your Kingdom just got hijacked by tyrants, citizens were murdered, and your little sister was abused by monsters from the pit of a nightmare! Addison, they wrecked us! Our lives are *never* going to be the same again. Ever."

Addison sighed as a mournful silence settled over the room. Bridget was right. The darkness that had overtaken their lives wasn't over yet.

"Your Highness, and Princess Bridget," a security guard entered the room as he bowed, then nodded toward Bridget, "I have an update from the Security Team. I was told to wait and relay it to you when Prince Willie was occupied elsewhere. It has been requested that he does not hear this piece of information. Though we've searched the entire palace, your brother, Prince Asher, has not been found among the others. He's missing."

After dinner, Willie enjoyed a bubble bath and was tucked into bed. Exhausted, Bridget excused herself and went to bed early as well, which left Addison all alone with his thoughts once again.

A solemn-faced Deborah opened the door with a large box in her arms, "Your Highness, I know you are in much distress. We all are. But you may like something else to occupy your mind while we wait to receive updates." She carefully set the box down on the triangle-shaped coffee table, "The young maidens who attended your ball wrote you letters and cards, congratulating you on your Coronation. We asked them to share messages of good cheer, filled with merriment. I know that right now it all feels quite meaningless, but perhaps it will get your mind off things, at least for a few moments, until we receive further word about Prince Asher."

"Thank you, Deborah," Addison replied. He knew that Deborah cared about him, and was only trying to help. But this was the last thing that he wanted to think about at this moment.

He ran frustrated fingers through his hair, and maneuvered his body in the chair. He struggled to find a more comfortable position, but it was pointless. He pinched the bridge of his nose, an anxious characteristic he had inherited from his Father.

Finally, he sighed and reached for the box of letters. He grabbed the first one off the pile. The pink envelope had his name written in glitter. He flipped it around, only to find a red-lipstick-kiss pressed flirtatiously onto the back of it. He sighed again, and tossed the envelope aside. He could already tell, that one wouldn't be worth reading.

He dug deeper into the box. His hands found another letter, in a plain white envelope. His name was written in boring black ink, and didn't look quite so forward in attempts to capture his heart.
His fingers slowly opened it. Addison read:

Your Royal Highness, Prince Addison of Tarsuerlla,

I hope this letter finds you well. By the time you read this (if you ever do) you will be the crowned King of Tarsurella. Congratulations! Some people might think that you didn't have to work very hard to be in the position you are today. In fact, I used to be one of those people. Before my first trip to The Palace, I thought you were a pompous, stuck up, self-absorbed jerk who floated around in his pool and sipped on his Pepsi, while the rest of the world suffered and died just miles away from your comfortable palace.

I have since learned that I was completely wrong in my judgement of you. Who could've known, that all along I was the one being a pompous, self-absorbed jerk? In a strange twist of events, I now feel like the bad guy. Even though my ill opinion of you probably wouldn't bother you in the least, I must ask for your forgiveness. The Bible says to "confess your sins one to another," and even though you would never have known the dark state of my judgmental heart, I just wanted to make sure that I left Tarsurella with a clean conscience.

I hope that you can find it in your heart to forgive me! I truly admire your kind character and compassion for others, and I believe that you will make the finest King that Tarsurella has ever seen.

Many blessings on you and your Kingdom,
~Vanessa

Addison couldn't help but smile. He was deeply struck by Vanessa's humility and tenderness to share everything she had.

Addison read the letter once more, then tucked it into his pocket. He knew very little about Vanessa; her background, her faith, her dreams, her personality. But perhaps it would be wise to take some time to get to know her better. It seemed as though she had a lovely heart. The thought of it gave Addison an inkling of hope for the future.

The following day, Hope's long eyelashes fluttered open. She let out a half-groan, half-yawn, and rolled over onto her side. When she turned, her body dramatically disagreed with her newfound position. She let out a yelp, shocked to feel the pain. She had forgotten how sore she was. A nurse quickly came to her aid, helping her rearrange her pillows, and pouring a fresh glass of orange juice. "Is the pain bothering you greatly? Would you care for more pain reliever?"

"No, thank you," Hope replied in a groggy voice, struggling to collect her thoughts. The pain meds they had given her last night had really knocked her out and made her feel disoriented. She felt as though she had been sleeping for days. "What time is it?"

"Half-past noon," the nurse replied without missing a beat. "Do you feel up to eating some lunch?"

"Not exactly," she sighed. "Where is my family?"

"I will inform them that you're awake, and I'm sure some of them will be in to see you shortly. We're going to keep an eye on that rib of yours, and once we are confident that it is healing nicely, we will send you back home. Until then, our fine Military Hospital will take good care of you. Here are some magazines, a selection of your favorite novels, an assortment of snacks, and some music for your listening pleasure. The TV works as well," the nurse lowered her voice to a mournful tone, "but every channel is blasting with news of the past events, and that may not be something you're ready to relive yet."

"Thank you," Hope replied as she reached for her glass of orange juice. She winced. The nurse was right. The past few days had been nothing short of horrific. Suddenly, she remembered the last thought that had been so heavy on her heart before she fell asleep. "Where is David Carter? Is he okay?"

"I don't have details about that particular individual, but I will inquire about him on your behalf."

Hope anxiously waited, flipping through several magazine pages, trying to get her mind off the lingering questions that tormented her. Was David okay? Did he make it to the hospital? Was he still–no, she wouldn't go there. She *couldn't* go there. Surely David was still alive.

A few moments later, the nurse entered and said, "There's someone here to see you, Your Highness."

Hope felt her breath catch as she saw his figure walk through the door. She didn't even care about how bad her hair looked, or the fact that she hadn't brushed her teeth in a while. It didn't matter that she was in a nerdy hospital gown and wasn't wearing any deodorant. Her heart swelled with compassion and gratitude for the young man that stood in the doorway. His left shoulder was bulked up with an awkward cast which made half of him look like the Hulk.

David tiptoed inside gawkily, unsure of what to say. "Uh, good morning. Or afternoon," he chuckled, then his smile disappeared, "or whatever it is. How are you feeling?"

"A little sore. But my goodness, I should be asking you the same question!" Hope shook her head in wonderment and disbelief, "Thank God, you're alive."

"Yeah," David forced a laugh as he sat down in the arm-chair beside her bed, trying to keep the mood light, "It gives a whole new meaning to the phrase, 'a shot in the arm'."

Hope smiled, but she didn't laugh. It was far too serious. "I'm just glad you're okay. I mean, really. Truly. It's like, I don't even know what to say." Hope looked away for a moment, fingering the edge of her blanket, struggling to express what was on her heart. "When I saw you crash through the wall and come to rescue me with that sword, it's like you were God's warrior of deliverance for my salvation!" She looked directly at him, attempting to convey the passion behind her words, "The Lord only knows what would've happened if you and Clark hadn't found me. So thank you. My words sound like such a lame attempt at what I'm truly trying to tell you. I just…" Hope didn't want to get all sappy and dramatic, but it was happening anyway. "David, you saved my life."

Now it was David's turn to talk.

He opened his mouth, when suddenly the Princess's siblings flooded into the room. "Hope! Hope! Hope!" Their rambunctious shouts shot through the doorway as Willie and Millie raced in, climbing onto her bed.

"I brought you a stuffed elephant!" Willie proudly proclaimed. "Cozy animals always make me feel better!"

"Yeah, but it was my idea!" Millie wanted to make sure that Hope knew who was behind the brilliant gift.

"Careful, careful!" Bridget cautioned, as the kids went to hug their big sister, "Hope is in a lot of pain right now, gentle hugs, you don't want to hurt her!"

"Aww, it's okay," Hope laughed, relishing in the feeling of their wiggly little arms being wrapped all around her, "This is a good kind of pain."

Bridget sat a beautiful vase of lilacs on the counter beside Hope's bed, "Dad and Addison send you these flowers along with all of their love. They wish they could be here, but they couldn't, for security reasons."

As Bridget embraced her sister, she fought back tears. "Oh Hope," her voice shook as she spoke, "Praise Jesus that you're okay."

Clark was the last to enter the room. David heard his footsteps and looked up. Clark set his strong hand on his shoulder, "I think it might be time for you to leave."

David nodded, suddenly feeling awkward for being in the room with the Royals. Both Bridget and Hope were shedding happy tears, and it was like a Hallmark moment that he had no business being a part of. He stood up and wished that he could say something else to Hope before he left, but she was too busy reuniting with her siblings. Clark was right. He had done his part, Hope was safe, and now he must bow-out respectfully. As David turned to leave, he felt Clark's hand on his shoulder once more. He stopped and looked at him.

"Thank you," Clark spoke, his eyes moist, "you're a true hero, son."

Chapter 23 – Not on the Menu

"Oh, Your Highness, come quickly, come quickly! The King is addressing the nation!" Mrs. Drakos called for the Princess. Chasity was still finishing up her breakfast, and she hated to leave warm pancakes sitting on her plate, but she knew that more important matters were at hand. She wiped her face and scurried into the living room where Mrs. Drakos's tiny TV set was standing on an old wooden crate.

A solemn newscaster spoke from The Palace grounds.

"It's less than forty-eight hours since the tragic, shocking, and terrifying events at The Palace took place, and the Kingdom of Tarsurella is still in mourning. Eight dead, dozens wounded, and the city is still reeling with fear and despair. As you can see, The Palace is still abandoned. In fact, it looks like a haunting ghost town.

"The only people permitted to be on The Palace grounds are FBI agents who are searching the castle for clues as to what *really* happened the night of Prince Addison's Coronation. There are still very little details as to how this attack unfolded, who was behind it, and how the enemy gained access. We will keep you updated as more information is unveiled within the coming hours.

"With young Prince Asher still missing, authorities and Palace guards are working tirelessly to uncover as much information as they possibly can. The Head of Royal Security told us, and I quote, 'Last night everyone was safely removed from the premises, and those who were in need of medical care were airlifted to nearby facilities. We've released security squads and bomb dogs to thoroughly search the land for further threats.' End of quote.

"Today, the King will address his heartbroken nation with

words of comfort, and hopefully fill his people in on more of the story. Millions will be watching all around the world, as we grieve together with the victims of this catastrophic terrorist event.

"Prince Addison has passed this duty onto his Father, one last time. Because of the fact that Addison's official crowning ceremony never took place, it is unsure whether the title of King has been officially passed onto him yet, or if he is still holds the position of Prince. Many believe that this will be the King's last public speech, before he passes everything on to Addison. Addison will not be speaking tonight, for security reasons."

Soon, the face of their beloved father appeared. The poor soul looked as though he had aged overnight. Chasity was confident that he hadn't slept a wink, as the heavy burden for his nation weighed down on him.

The King opened his mouth, and words of grace poured out. He spoke scriptures of comfort and strength, reminding the world of God's faithfulness. He offered his sorrow and sympathy to families who had lost their loved ones, and praised the United States for sending in troops and assisting them in their final defeat of the terrorists. He praised a young American named David Carter, and a faithful member of the kitchen staff, Clark Myers, for rescuing his precious daughters. He admired and encouraged all of the heroes who acted bravely, including the terrorized guests who were held captive for so many hours. He charged his people to take courage, and to remember their ancient roots as they rebuild the Kingdom of Tarsurella. A Kingdom of hope, strength, security, and joy. A Kingdom that was sowing tears, but would one day reap a harvest of laughter.

"Sorrow lasts for a night, but joy comes in the morning!" the King declared. "King David did not write those words in vain. He had been through some things. King David lost loved ones, and friends, and fought many bloody battles. Sometimes they won, and sometimes they lost. But He trusted the God of his forefathers; the God of Abraham, Isaac, and Jacob! He knew that He worshiped and served a covenant God, a God who proved faithful to his forefathers, and would never break His promises.

"We all know that Tarsurella was founded upon the Bible, and was built by a long legacy of Kings and Queens who believed the Word of God to be true. I believe that if God was faithful to our ancestors in the midst of fiery trials and challenging persecutions, He will be faithful to us! Take courage, O Kingdom, and know that God hears your cries! He is crying with us, keeping track of every tear shed by this beloved nation, and the nations around the world. He keeps every tear in a bottle, and in His perfect timing, He turns them all into diamonds. He is turning us into diamonds. Through this refinement, our nation will only come out stronger and more beautiful. We will come out as gold, refined by flame, but not consumed!

"Pressed, but not crushed. Persecuted, but not abandoned. Struck down, but not destroyed. We are a blessed people, because the victory has been promised! Let the enemies of Tarsurella hear and tremble; we will not give way to fear! We will not allow you to trample our nation, nor steal our courage! As a Kingdom, we will rise together as one! In unity we will encourage, strengthen one another, and carry each other through this storm. As a kingdom under God, we will triumph!"

The King ended his speech, and Mrs. Drakos quickly turned off the TV.

"He's right!" Mrs. Drakos spoke. "In times such as this we only have one place to which we can turn–our God, the solid rock of Jesus Christ. Faithful He has been, faithful He will be!"

"Yes, we have to keep reminding ourselves of that," Chasity agreed quietly. "It's so easy to forget that He is still in control." She turned to Lance and Hanson, "Any word yet on when we can return home?"

"Not yet," Hanson spoke. "My prediction is that it will be awhile. The Kingdom is still unsteady, and The Palace hasn't even been cleared yet. Even after it is, they will probably have you stay here awhile longer, just to be extra cautious."

Chasity resisted the urge to smile. His response was so casual, and instead of saying 'Your Highness' he had said, 'you'. It was a small change, but his casual attitude spoke volumes to her.

"So, if we are here for several more weeks," Chastity started slowly, "what are we going to do with ourselves? Mr. And Mrs. Drakos, please don't take this the wrong way, you have been so gracious and I appreciate your hospitality very much, but the past few days have been filled with nothing but waiting and eating. It would be so refreshing to get out for a run. Or a swim in the ocean! Or perhaps I could even go down to the market and buy some new clothes."

"Oh my cupcakes, you're right!" Mrs. Drakos responded. "We haven't even provided you with an ample supply for a Royal wardrobe, how foolish of us! Mr. Drakos, what were we thinking?!"

"Oh, please no," Chasity quickly spoke, "It's not your fault at all! We've kind of been on lockdown." She glanced at her security guards again, "Is there even a *slim* chance of letting me go out for a bit?"

"I'll call Headquarters and see what our options are," Hanson replied, then excused himself from the discussion to talk to Jackson.

Chasity could definitely use a change of pace. The past few days had been unbearable. Especially after the crazy turn of events with Hanson. Following their intimate moment in the cave, things had been beyond awkward. She couldn't even look him in the eye. They needed an opportunity to get away and talk about what had happened, but being stuck inside the house playing cards and working puzzles with Mrs. Drakos did not give place for that.

When Hanson announced that they had permission to go to town for several hours, Chasity was relieved.

"It's a small fishing village where not many people speak English," Hanson explained, sharing the new information he had just received. "It's highly unlikely that any of the locals will recognize you as being part of the Royal Family. Jackson says it's currently the safest place in the world for you to be."

"The only way to get to town is on foot," Mr. Drakos spoke. "We do not own a car."

"That's not true!" Mrs. Drakos corrected him. "There are two old motorbikes out in the shed! Ralph and I used to drive them around back in our glory days! You are more than welcome to use them!"

"Thank you!" Chasity proclaimed.

Fifteen minutes later, they were cruising through Greece on a pair of baby-blue mopeds. Of course, Hanson had insisted on driving, just to be safe. Chasity strongly protested, but it was to no avail. Although she was determined that she would drive on the way back. There was no way she would miss out on an opportunity like that! How often did she get to drive a moped around Greece? Never!

The sea-foam-green coastline waved at them as they cruised by. Chasity felt her breath catch. It was all so beautiful! With the ocean on one side, and rolling hills and robust vineyards on the other, she couldn't believe how spectacular the scenery was. "This is amazing!" she shouted.

Hanson sped up and their moped shot forth at a crazy speed, leaving Lance in the dust. "Faster Lance!" Chasity called over her shoulder.

"These roads are really curvy!" Lance proclaimed cautiously, "Do you see how steep these hills and drop-offs are? One wrong move, and we're in the ocean! Better safe than sorry!"

"Oh, come on," Chasity laughed, "You're not even that close to the edge! And I think I just saw a turtle pass you!"

Ten minutes later, the scenery had changed, and they were in the middle of cobblestone streets with happy market men attempting to sell their smelly fish. They decided to pull off to the side of the street, find a good place to park, and get off to walk.

"This village is so adorable!" Chasity spoke. "It's like something you'd read about in a children's fairy tale book. Just look at the ancient architecture! I wish I had a camera, so I could capture some of these moments for Millie. She would *love* this."

The threesome spent the afternoon exploring the town, drifting in and out of small hole-in-the-wall shops. While Chasity browsed for her new wardrobe, Lance and Hanson stood outside, keeping an eye out for any signs of impending danger, wearily glancing at their watches.

"Dude, how long does it take for her pick out a couple of new outfits?" Lance vented. They weren't normally allowed to share their personal thoughts while on duty, because everything they said was recorded and hooked up to the main security system. But here in Greece, all of their conversations were off the record.

Hanson sighed, "When girls go shopping, it's like they step into another world. They lose track of time and check out of reality. Honestly, we could be here for hours."

Even though he spoke casually, his mind was still on high alert. His studious eyes scanned the crowd, glancing from one person to the next. Everyone who bustled about on the streets all appeared as though they had somewhere very important to be. The occasional shouts in English of "get out of the way!" and "move your goats!" rose and fell over the crowd. Hanson didn't feel like there were any impending threats against the Princess, but still, he wouldn't let his guard down. Even though Jackson believed that no one knew the Princess was in Greece, he still cautioned him to keep his eye out for any suspicious activity.

"I've never been in Greece before," Lance said, "It would be a great vacation place. Maybe someday when I'm retired, I'll come back here on holiday."

"What about Christmas vacation?" Hanson asked. "Why do you have to wait until you're retired to come back?"

"Oh. Good point."

Hanson fought to keep his mind under control and focused on the task at hand. It was all too easy to let his thoughts drift. His mind wanted to carry him to places where he wasn't supposed to go. He was dreadfully worried about his mother, about Lilly, and the innocent souls who had happened to be in the wrong place at the wrong time. What had happened the morning after the Coronation? Could his father have followed through with the vicious threats? Or was he too surprised by the terror attacks? Was he waiting until Hanson returned home, to discover that the chip was gone, and then pull the trigger on his loved ones? Oh, how he wished he could call his mom! They had zero communication with anyone except the Security Team, and working overtime hours was beginning to take a toll on him. He shook his head. He couldn't allow himself to think about it. It was all too overwhelming. He had to stay focused on the task at hand...

"Hanson?! Hanson Fletcher?!" a female voice proclaimed before overwhelming him with a hug.

Hanson struggled to keep his footing as the girl crashed into him. Not because she was heavy, but because he couldn't believe what was happening. "Lilly?!" His voice changed from shock to pure joy, "How in the world did you—what are you doing here?"

"Oh, my stars, I'm so glad you're okay!" Lilly's red curls bounced as she drew away from the hug, "I can't believe you're here! Oh, you poor dear, you made it through the attacks at The Palace! I was worried sick about you! I tried calling your cell like a million times, but nothing ever went through. Ugh, I'm so glad you're okay!" She squeezed him again.

"Yeah, of course!" Hanson returned the embrace, still completely puzzled by what was happening, "But why are you—?"

"My family has a home here! It's kind of like a safe house, for emergencies, you know? After the attack we were all so badly shaken, Dad insisted we leave the country for a while. Why are you here?"

Hanson shook his head in disbelief. He couldn't believe that she was standing in front of him. She was alive! "Oh, um…" he struggled to reply, as his thoughts raced. Perhaps this meant that his mom had been left unharmed as well! Maybe his dad decided not to follow through with the terrible threats! Maybe it was all just big talk and no action.

"Royal duties," Lance spoke up, then popped his hand out. "Pleased to meet you. The name is Lance."

"Lilly Chesterfield," Lilly tossed a flirtatious grin his way, then set her sights back on Hanson. "So this means you're here with the Princesses?"

"*Shhh*," Hanson placed a hand on her shoulder, in hopes to quiet her, "Um, we're trying to keep things on the DL."

"Oh, I totally get it." Lilly playfully motioned the action of zipping her lips. "Your secret is safe with me. So do you want to go grab lunch? I'm absolutely starving!"

"Um, I'm kind of working," he replied.

"Such a tough job you have!" Lilly laughed, "Standing around in Greece, looking totally bae. The Greek boys have nothing on you, Hanson Fletcher."

Lance's eyes widened. This beautiful girl was hardcore flirting with his friend. Maybe he could step in, and move things along a bit…

"The Princess is shopping," Lance explained, "and from what I've heard, women take a while to decide on what they like. I'm sure you two have plenty of time to go grab a snack and catch up."

"Lance, I can't leave my post," Hanson argued.

"Sure you can! Look around you. Nothing is happening. Jackson said the Princess will be perfectly safe here. I'll stay with her the whole time. You, my man, need to go out and enjoy yourself for a bit. Besides, you can't leave this lovely lady just waiting here, hungry as she is!"

Lilly laughed, "Your short little friend is right! It'll take fifteen minutes to run across the road, find a deli, and get caught up. And if Her Royal Highness is looking for shoes, I might even dare to say that you have a good forty-five before she's done."

Hanson stuck his hands in his pockets, then finally gave in to the temptation. "Half-an-hour and I *have* to be back. Got it?"

"Yay!" Lilly squealed, doing a little skip, jumping up to peck him on the cheek, then clinging to his arm, "I've missed you like mad!"

Hanson laughed as he grabbed her hand, remembering all the crazy, fun times they'd had together. He motioned to the road, realizing that they now had to cross it, "Ready to make a dash for it?"

Chasity mindlessly flipped through a rack of clothes. Her heart was plagued with endless thoughts about Hanson. They were running through her brain like a movie that she couldn't control. The heavy questions weighed on her soul.

What would've happened if he'd actually kissed her? And why didn't he? Why was he so afraid of building a relationship? What were these terrible consequences that he kept referring to? And what was all that talk about betrayal, and making a choice, and the strange computer chip?

Deep down, Chasity knew better than to be thinking like this. She couldn't have a relationship with Hanson. She wasn't raised to believe in her culture's practice of frivolously dating around. She had heard her Father speak many times, "The only time any daughter of this King will enter into a formal relationship, will be with the intention of prayerfully exploring the possibility of marriage."

And Hanson sure didn't seem like Royal husband material. Or did he? Chasity frowned. *Stop!* She chided herself, *You know absolutely next to nothing about this guy! You cannot give him your heart.*

Chasity wished that her mom was here. Talking with her about this would make things so much easier. She remembered her mother's words, when they used to have conversations about saving her heart, for one special man. "Don't waste your time dating young paupers who don't know how to properly cherish your heart." She had told her, "Wait for the man that God has for you! Wait for a true Prince! He will cherish and love you for all of your days. Until then, be content to rest in your singlehood, and seek after God with all of your heart!"

Chasity knew that her mother was right. Her timeless advice was solid gold. She knew in her *head* that she should abide by her mother's wisdom, but her heart ached for something else.

Chasity suddenly realized that she hadn't been making much progress, and decided to check out. After paying for her purchases and stepping outside, the sunlight kissed her face and greeted her with a warm smile. She spotted Lance, but Chasity continued searching the crowd for Hanson.

"Um," Chasity started slowly, "Is it just me, or is someone

missing?"

"He's across the street, catching up with a friend," Lance explained casually.

"A friend?" Chasity echoed.

"Yes, Princess."

Chasity frowned. "Well did you see where they went?"

"Of course, right this way."

After crossing the congested street, they entered a deli several blocks away. Chasity was not mentally prepared for the scene that lay before her. Hanson sat across from a gorgeous, red-headed girl, leaning forward on the edge of his seat, zeroed into her eyes, obviously hanging on every word she said. As they stepped inside, Hanson let out a laugh and Chasity felt her stomach drop to the floor. She had never seen Hanson look so relaxed, so joyful, so at ease, and so totally infatuated. She bit her lip, attempting to ignore the swirling feelings of jealousy that rose up inside.

All at once, Hanson spotted them entering, "Oh hey!" he waved them over.

Chasity felt her eyebrows shoot up. Hanson had never 'oh hey'-ed her before. He was acting like he was off the clock, and life was good.

"This is my good friend, Lilly Chesterfield." Hanson introduced them.

"We've met," Chasity interjected. "At The Palace's stables, remember? And you were at the Coronation."

"Yes, absolutely!" Lilly nodded, "Wow, what a crazy time that was. Nobody saw any of that coming. I can't even imagine how hard this all must be for the Royal Family. First with Hope, and now with Asher missing."

Hanson glanced at his watch and determined that his free time was over. "Well, I'd better get back to work." He looked at Lilly sympathetically, "Duty calls." Chasity felt a sudden sting as he spoke. "But thank you for this! I had such a good time. I'll call you as soon as we get home."

"Good, I'm looking forward to it," Lilly agreed as she stood to her feet. "And stay safe, okay?" She stood on her tippy toes, and gave him a friendly peck on the cheek, "These are crazy times for the Kingdom; I don't want anything happening to you."

Lilly curtsied gracefully toward the Princess, "Your Highness, such a pleasure to see you again. The Royal Family is forever in my prayers."

Chasity knew she should say something, but she couldn't bring herself to do it.

"And thanks for letting me borrow your hunky security guard," Lilly winked at Hanson. "I think the boy needs to get out more often."

"Here, I'll walk you out," Hanson gently grabbed Lilly's arm and they headed for the door.

Chasity swallowed. Hard.

The two headed out the door, but Chasity continued to watch them through the deli windows.

"Mmm, everything looks so delicious here!" Lance said as he

explored the menu. "I have no idea how I'm going to decide! Greek food is the bomb."

Chasity peeked at the menu, but found her eyes drifting back to where Hanson and Lilly stood outside. Talking. Laughing. Playfully flirting with one another. Chasity felt like she was going to be sick.

"What sounds good to you?" Lance asked.

"Um," she glanced at the menu, then looked outside again, just in time for Hanson to give Lilly a hug, and in return, she kissed him on the cheek again. Chasity sighed, forcing herself to look away, "I don't think they have what I want here."

"Why, what do you want?" Lance asked.

Chasity felt her throat tighten up. But she wasn't talking about the food at all. "Something I'll never be able to have."

Chapter 24 – Rebuilding

"We have gathered very little evidence as to who's responsible for this crime. This was the most massive security breach this Kingdom has ever seen. But our suspect list continues to grow," Jackson told Addison solemnly, as they sat together at a table. "We have reason to believe that it was someone within the castle who took down the virtual firewall and allowed the enemy to infiltrate. Obviously, we would like to think that all of our friends, family, and staff members would be morally incapable of such a crime. But we must take a second look at every suspect who causes us to ask questions. Are there any other people who are close to you, whom you have reason to believe may want to do ill against the Throne?"

Addison ran frustrated fingers through his hair. He glanced at Bridget, who sat beside her.

"Jacob is on our suspect list." Jackson said.

Bridget tried not to flinch. She knew it was coming. Even though it had been months ago, her heart still hurt every time someone mentioned his name.

"Although he wasn't at The Palace during the hours our security leak happened, it is possible that he had previously gathered information, passwords, or codes from you during a previous visit. He may have shared that information with others, for a very hefty sum."

Bridget suddenly felt the need to defend herself, as if Jackson was accusing her of somehow playing a part in this. "I never told him anything!" she snapped. "I might have been in love with him, but I wasn't stupid!"

"Bridget, it's okay," Addison attempted to calm her down, knowing that this was such a tender wound for his sister. "Jackson isn't accusing you."

"That's sure what it sounds like!" she continued. "As if I was some sort of ditzy blonde who was so blinded by his charms, I just opened up and told him all of the passwords and codes."

"Your Highness, we know you would never do such a thing intentionally. You, as well as anyone, understand the importance of The Palace's security. But it is my responsibility to leave no stone unturned with this case. Which happens to include, like it or not, the possibility of Jacob having received some sort of top-secret information from you."

"Well, he didn't." Bridget spoke much too quickly, and crossed her arms, "Are we done here?"

Jackson nodded calmly. "Thank you for your time, Princess."

She popped out of her chair before Jackson had even finished his sentence, and allowed the door to shut rather loudly behind her.

"I'm sorry," Addison apologized on her behalf, "this is just really hard for her. She thought that Jacob was the guy she was going to spend the rest of her life with. She still hasn't healed from it all."

"I completely understand," Jackson sympathized, "but I still have to do my job."

"I know," Addison nodded, "and I'll try my best to help her understand that."

"I'm sure you will," Jackson almost smiled. "Just one of the many reasons why you make such a wise leader. And perhaps more importantly, a loving brother."

"Is there anything else we can do for her?" Addison asked, feeling deeply concerned. "I feel like Bridget just needs to get away. To have a change of pace, and scenery. Everything is right up in her face now. Especially after all of this. She needs to allow her soul some time to heal."

Jackson nodded slowly, "That is a wise thought, Your Highness. Actually, there is a safe haven in Alaska that has been recently established. The cover is a beautiful ranch, about 100 miles north of Anchorage. There's a wonderful family in our Undercover Royal Protection Program who would happily host her."

"Hmm. Maybe it's worth checking into. Don't mention anything to her about it, though. I'd like to research the location and family more thoroughly, before we make any decisions to offer Bridget that possibility."

Millie clung to her big sister's hand with a grip that expressed just how afraid she truly was.

Bridget lovingly stroked Millie on the head, rearranging some stray pieces of hair that had fallen out of place. "Sweetie, why don't you go check out your room? We're home now."

Two days had passed, and the Security Team finally deemed

The Palace safe to return. Bridget, Hope, Jillian, Millie and Willie walked through the familiar halls, excited to hug their Father who would be returning that evening. Chasity would return within the next few days as well. But their family was not yet complete. Asher was still missing.

The news headlines never stopped buzzing about Prince Asher's mysterious disappearance. For the last forty-eight hours, the whole world could talk about no other topic. Everyone speculated about what had happened to the young Royal. Had he been captured by escaping terrorists? Was he being held captive somewhere in a foreign country? Had the terrorists killed him and hid the body? TNN had dozens of opinions about the scenario, but nobody had any facts. The UN had been working tirelessly to unravel the mystery and find Prince Asher, but they were still left with more questions than answers. Bridget couldn't bear to think about it. Every hour that passed without new information about Asher was like an extended form of torture. Bridget continually prayed for her brother, the UN, and everyone involved with the rescue mission, but her heart grew tired from the wait. She tried to stay present and attentive to her current situation, her young siblings, and their emotional needs, but it was devastatingly draining.

"Can I sleep in your bed tonight," Millie asked, "just in case there are any more bad guys in The Palace?"

"Honey, we already talked about this. Jackson and the Security Team are taking good care of us. The Palace is safe now! You're perfectly protected, and don't need to worry about anything. They won't let anything bad happen to you."

"That's what they said before!" Millie argued, clearly still traumatized by everything that had happened, "But then the bad guys came!"

"I know, honey. But nothing like that is ever going to happen again. There's no reason to be afraid, because God protected us and everyone is safe now!"

Millie suddenly burst out in tears, "Not Asher!"

Bridget sent pleading eyes to Hope for help. What could she possibly say now? How could she even begin to comfort Millie, when Bridget felt like crying herself?

"It's okay Millie!" Hope squeezed her hand, "You can stay with me. I'm not going to leave you. Remember what Clark told you, about being brave? We're all worried about Asher, but we have to continue to be brave for him. The best way we can do that, is to keep praying and trusting God, even when we don't feel like we can."

Millie sniffed, "It's just so hard."

"I know," Hope wiped away her baby sister's warm tears with her index finger, "That's enough crying for now. You should be excited–we get to see Daddy tonight! I'd say that calls for a huge celebration! How does dinner, chocolate cake, board games and a movie sound?"

Millie sniffled one last time, attempting to switch mental gears, "That's good. But what if we skipped dinner and just ate chocolate cake? And ice cream!?"

Hope laughed, "Now *that* sounds like our joyful Millie is back!"

"Does that mean yes on the ice cream?!" Millie shot triumphant fist bumps into the air.

"I don't know, I guess we'll have to go talk to Clark," she winked.

"Mr. Pork Chops!" she gasped, suddenly remembering a thought of utmost importance. "Let's go get him! I haven't seen him in days, he must miss me terribly!"

After Hope and Millie retrieved Mr. Pork Chops from her bedroom and had a joyful reunion with her massive collection of stuffed animals, the twosome led several wagons full of their stuffed friends downstairs to the kitchen. Halfway there, Willie discovered what was going on, and wanted to join in on the fun. He grabbed a green wagon, loaded it up with his Legos, and joined the parade.

Clark smiled and looked up from the onions he was chopping, as soon he heard Millie. "Well what do we have here? Looks like quite the party going on!"

Millie told Clark all about their planned festivities for the evening, and he thought a chocolate cake sounded like a splendid idea. He invited his two favorite kids to help mix the cake and lick the beaters.

Hope smiled, grateful for Clark and his kind heart. He truly went above and beyond, and entirely out of his way for Millie and Willie. He had a heart of gold, and Hope thought that he should be honored for it. He had assisted David in her rescue, and she hadn't properly thanked him for it yet. But she would. Now simply wasn't the right time. She would avoid talking about those traumatic events around the little ones.

Hope glanced around the kitchen, zooming out of the conversation before her and tunneling into her own thoughts. Life was *so* strange. Just a few days ago, she was trapped in an unthinkable nightmare, and a secret passageway beneath this very kitchen led to her escape pod. Now, it was as if everything was back to normal, and this kitchen lined with cooking utensils, serving pans, and stainless steel appliances was just that, a bland kitchen again. She observed that the staff was scarce, and only a few workers labored to prepare their evening meal. Bridget had told her that the majority of workers were undergoing a very intensive screening process. Several of them had even been pegged as suspects, and the bulk of their staff wouldn't be allowed to return to work until after the Security Team left no stone unturned. Hope shuddered from a phantom shiver that crawled up her spine. "Jackson and the team believe there was a traitor," Bridget had told her. "The attack had to have come from somewhere within."

How awful and unsettling was that thought?! One of their very own workers, selling their family out, handing them over to a demonic terrorist group who had torn their whole world apart. Rage boiled within her blood as she thought about the heartless traitor who did such a thing. They would discover whoever this wretched worm of a person was, and justice would be served. Hope shook her head, and tried to set her mind on happier things. She couldn't continue thinking about what had happened; it was far too overwhelming.

Hope refocused on Clark and the kids, and was at peace to see them so content and enjoying themselves. But soon, another thought fluttered into her mind. David. She had so much more to say to him. When she thought about the awkward way random words had tumbled out of her mouth at the hospital, she wanted to kick herself! Could she have been any more of a dork? One moment he was there, and then when she looked up, he was gone.

What had been on his mind? Why did he leave so quickly? As soon as Hope had the opportunity, she had asked her nurse about him again, but she reported that he had been discharged. That evening, after her family had said goodnight and left her alone in her hospital room, she had decided to Google him. Yes, yes, the whole concept of Googling someone seemed extremely freaky and stalker-ish, but Hope couldn't stop herself. Perhaps it was the pain medication causing her to act so loopy. But once she typed in his name, an over-abundance of headlines shouted at her. They told her everything that she already knew. David Carter, the lead singer of *Kennetic Energy,* who had been held hostage with his bandmates at The Tarsurellian Palace, was rescued by helicopter and delivered to a military hospital.

She had read the comments from his distressed fans, and kept scrolling across the hashtag #PrayForDavid. Their community of fans poured out such radical love for their favorite band, that Hope couldn't have imagined how heartbroken they would've been if something had happened to him. If only his flamboyant fangirls knew the rest of the story—that he had risked his very *life* to rescue Hope—their obsession for him would sky rocket.

Now, just thinking about David made her heart melt into a helpless little puddle of giddy emotions. There were so many questions that she had for him. So many unknowns. Why had he put everything on the line, just to save her? How did he find her, how did he escape from where they were being held hostage, and why was it so important to him? She wanted to believe that this meant something more than the fact that David was just a good guy, or that he had wanted to perform a notable deed of honor. After all, hadn't he written a song for her? Hadn't he acted all sweet and shy and slightly smitten?

Hope tried to hide the goofy smile that plastered itself across her face, but apparently she wasn't doing a very good job of it. When Clark saw her, he raised an eyebrow, then tried to hide his own smile and commented, "Looks like Hope is really excited about that cake."

"Huh?" Hope asked, unsure of what Clark had just said.

"The cake," he grinned. "You must be very excited about it. From the smile on your face, you clearly have some delightful thought dancing through your mind. It must be chocolate, right?"

"Yes!" Hope forced a laugh and tried to go along with it, "Of course. Super excited about that cake. Can't wait." She stepped closer to where the group was happily licking their beaters.

"Now, we will pop this little fella' in the oven, and I need my junior chefs to collect my icing tools. I'll teach you two how to make homemade cream cheese frosting."

"Yummy!" Millie exclaimed, "I can't wait! Where are your tools?"

Clark motioned to a cupboard across the kitchen, and the two raced to find it. As Clark opened the oven, he spoke, "David is recovering well. He flew back to the States, and his school threw a huge homecoming party for him and the band. Everyone's relieved that they're safe and back home."

Hope tried to hide her surprise. How had Clark known that she was *just* thinking about him? Or was it simply a goofy coincidence? Nevertheless she was grateful for this new information. "Oh. Well, that's good. Must be nice for them to be back. Thank you for the update, I hadn't heard anything."

"I thought you might appreciate knowing," Clark closed the oven and wiped his hands on his apron, "seeing as how he's the guy who saved your life and everything."

Hope detected a teasing twinkle in his eye as he spoke to her. "So did you!" she quickly burst out, "And I was going to thank you! I mean, I wanted to, but I didn't want to say anything in front of the kids and–"

Clark laughed, "Oh please, Your Highness, no thanks needed. My job is to protect and honor the Royal Crest. It is my pleasure to serve you in whatever ways I may. But we all know who the true hero in this story is–David," he winked. "I was just his sidekick. When the story is told to your great-grandkids, generations from now, he will be remembered as the valiant knight in shining armor, riding in to rescue his fair lady!"

Hope laughed, feeling herself blushing, "Whatever."

Clark shrugged playfully, "Okay, try and deny it, but that kind of valiant spunk is a rare thing found in young men these days. I would know, I have a son of my own. David was willing to put everything on the line for you. And if you ask me, that kind of love and sacrifice runs a whole lot deeper than those nonsensical songs he sings on the radio about first crushes, and whatnot."

Hope felt her eyes grow wide, shocked at the words that came out of his mouth. Millie and Willie came running back, talking to Clark both at the same time. Hope was speechless. What could she say now?! She placed sassy hands on her hips, "Well," she scolded Clark playfully, "I'm going to go for a walk."

Clark just grinned at her, and Hope truly didn't mind that he believed David was interested in her. If she could trust anyone in The Palace, it would most certainly be Clark.

"Your Highness!" Jackson suddenly burst into The Royal Boardroom, where King Addison was in the middle of a meeting with several staff leaders from the Security Team. "We've just received word on Prince Asher."

Addison felt his breath catch. The whole room went silent, as Addison struggled to read the expression on Jackson's face. *Is everything okay? Is he alive?!*

"Our team just completed a rescue mission from an underground prison in Yemen," Jackson spoke quickly. "The terrorist leaders who held him captive have been killed. Asher has been flown to a United States Army medical camp in the Middle East. All of his vitals are stable, but he's being treated for the abuse he received while being in captivity."

"Oh, thank You, God!" Addison cried out, feeling all of his raw emotions suddenly bubble up. The men in the room started applauding, letting out a wild shout of victory.

"The battle belongs to the Lord!" one of them called out.

Addison was so relieved, he didn't even know what to say. "Have you told the others?" Addison asked, knowing that his family would be overjoyed to hear the news.

"Not yet," Jackson replied. "There is something else we need to discuss. Something we are gravely concerned about."

Addison felt the air being sucked out of his lungs, once again. The relief he had felt was now gone. "What?" He didn't even want to ask, "What now?"

"Our men completed their entire scanning process of our firewall, and uncovered some disturbing news. As we suspected, the security leak happened from within." Jackson placed a manila folder onto the table, and opened it up, revealing the top-secret contents inside. "This is Muhamad Rakhsha, a notorious warlord whom the United States has been trying to capture for the last twelve years." Addison frowned at the ugly face of the man who had snuffed out innocent lives, extinguishing them like candles by the breath of his wickedness.

"Muhamad had several accounts on popular worldwide gaming sites. Websites which Prince Asher frequented. Muhamad played under the username of Smashman008. Asher was well acquainted with Smashman, and we have hundreds of logged hours recorded on file, with many conversations between the two of them. We found nothing overly suspicious until we read the last several months of conversations. They grew more and more disturbing. Now, before I show you this, Your Highness, I want to warn you that there are many ill words spoken about you. This will no doubt be painful for you to read, but this is the reality of the situation."

Jackson dug deeper into the folder and handed Addison a printed page of a conversation between Asher and Smashman. Addison struggled to read the words.

Smashman008: Nice score! U R champion!

GameBoy360 (Asher): Thx dude. At least I'm good at something, you know? I suck at everything else in life.

Smashman008: Yeah right. I'm sure U rock!

GameBoy360: Not compared to my jerk older brother. Everything I do is never good enough for him or the family. But it's not like I care anymore.

Smashman008: Sounds like you're sick of being in his shadow?

GameBoy360: So sick. Sometimes I just want to shoot him.

Smashman008: Why don't U? LOL.

Gameboy360: Haha. I wish.

Smashman008: Ever thought of doing something to get back @ him? Like a prank?

Gameboy360: Sounds fun. He has a big party coming up in a few weeks that would be the perfect time to mess up his life. LOL. Any ideas?

Smashman008: U could mess w/the electronics. Shut down the lights, stop the music, etc. I know a killer code that can do that.

Gameboy630: Send it over, man!

Smashman008:
smashman008filecode300electakeover.html

Gameboy360: THX.

Addison looked up at Jackson, "Did Asher click on it?"

Jackson nodded, "Yes. The link Smashman sent him required him to log in from his system database, which gave Smashman our PI number, and from there the hacking began. Once Prince Asher clicked on that link, Smashman was into our system without us knowing, and within several weeks he was able to bug it, tap all the lines, and know every move we were going to make, before we made it. He knocked out the firewall, and made his move."

"So, Asher is responsible for this?" Addison asked, already knowing the truth. "The hacking, the takeover, the violence, the terror, the shootings, and every life that was lost? All because my kid brother started talking to a stranger on the internet and venting about how much he can't stand me?"

Jackson nodded sadly, "All of the evidence is clear. Prince Asher is a federal criminal, for assisting a terrorist and providing him with a gateway into our system."

Addison suddenly stood up, unable to keep himself in his

chair. "I can't believe this! I mean, I knew that Asher was in a bad place, but I had no idea that he would do something so stupid!"

"We believe that it is best the worldwide press does not know the full story yet," Jackson said. "With your permission, I'm proposing we announce Prince Asher's safety, yet say nothing about his involvement in the crime. We will keep this under wraps for as long as possible, while we release a statement that says we are continuing to research the case."

Addison nodded, "Yes, I think that is best. If the world knew what actually happened, they would not respond favorably. When is he coming home?"

"Your Majesty, we found many more disturbing interchanges between the two. Prince Asher is in a very dark place. When reading through these conversations, we began to feel that perhaps his mind is not stable. We would like to ask your father's permission to send him to a rehabilitation center in Israel. If you would like to know more about why we are suggesting this, feel free to read through the conversations, but be warned, they are extremely dark. The young Prince needs help, Your Majesty."

Addison felt his heart crunch beneath the weight of it all. How had he not known that his brother was struggling so deeply? Had he really been so self-absorbed and focused on his own life that he hadn't been able to see what was truly going on?

"Very well," Addison agreed, "I trust your judgement. I'm sure Asher isn't going to be fond of the idea, but he needs to experience some inner healing. In fact, I think we all do. I'd like for you to see about making arrangements for Bridget to go to Alaska. And bring Chasity home as soon as possible." Addison sighed heavily, "It's time to start picking up the pieces, and begin rebuilding our lives."

Chapter 25 - The View

Vanessa handed her debit card to the smiley woman at the front desk. Vanessa resisted the temptation to bite her nails. It made her nervous to think of more money being charged to her account for a night's stay at The Palace. Even though she would soon be earning more than enough money to cover all of her expenses, it was hard for her not to cringe at the thought of it. There were still so many unknowns. Returning to The Palace so quickly after the terrorist attack made her nervous as well. Was it truly safe for Vanessa to be back in Tarsurella? Her parents were extremely concerned about her safety, despite reassurance from The Palace Security that all was well.

Even though she wouldn't be officially hired until January, when a majority of King Addison's staff would undergo a turnover, Vanessa had been asked to return for interviews, a further screening process, and more background checks. The decision of whether or not to hire her would be made within a matter of several weeks, and then a deposit would be made into her account to cover her expenses until she returned on January 1st.

Vanessa felt as though she had been walking through a strange dream. During the night of the Coronation, Addison's job proposal sent her soaring. Then moments later, when the gun shots shattered through the building, she was thankful to be in a room with a quick escape route. All forty of the guests who she was to be dining with that evening had dashed out of the building, terrified. In the moment, she wasn't even aware of how much God was truly watching out for her. Had she been in nearly any other room, she may have been captured with the rest. Or worse.

After the glorious daydream came an all-time low, as she returned home to the United States—crying in her parents' arms, watching the news in horror, and fervently praying for the Royal Family.

To say that she was shocked when The Palace called and asked her to come for an interview so soon, would be an understatement. She felt like everything was happening so fast! If The Palace chose to hire her, she would only have a few months to pack up the belongings in her childhood bedroom, find an apartment, and perhaps enroll in the Tarsurellian University.

In her original plans, her intention was to attend NYU, and she had been toying with the idea of taking a gap year. When her parents surprised her with the trip to Tarsurella right when enrollment for school would've been, she decided that a gap year spent traveling and exploring would serve her well.

Who knew that she would end up in a position like this! Life was wild and unpredictable, that's for sure. Yet, amidst all the craziness, Vanessa had a certain peace that everything would work out the way that it was meant to. She always clung to her life verse, Jeremiah 29:11, for peace of mind.

Especially on days like this.

"Welcome back, Miss Vanessa," the front desk worker's voice was warm. "His Royal Highness has been expecting you. I've been instructed to buzz him up as soon as you arrive. You will be staying in The Queen's Suite. Quite the honor!"

"What?" Vanessa exclaimed. "There's no way I can afford that! I'd like a regular guest room, like before, please."

"Oh, it will be at no extra cost to you, dear. The economy guest rooms are unavailable right now, since our staffing is still low. Very few of the maids are back to work yet. But His Majesty insisted that you stay in The Queen's Suite. It's upstairs, where the Royal Family lives. Quite the lucky duck, you are!" The woman winked at her.

"But," Vanessa continued to protest, totally confused by what was happening, "there must be some sort of misunderstanding. Why would they want me to stay in—"

"Vanessa!" a voice called from behind.

Vanessa twirled around, surprised to see Addison walking toward her with a small entourage, which included an important-looking woman wearing high heels and a tan dress, and several men dressed in business suits.

"I'm so glad you made it!" Addison smiled. "How was your flight?"

Vanessa struggled to find her words, slightly overwhelmed at what was happening. Addison was the King now, but he didn't wear a crown on his head. Besides the black tuxedo and shiny blue tie, he still looked like the same guy. Vanessa didn't know if she should bow, or curtsey, or shake his hand, or just stand there awkwardly.

"Oh! It was good," she spat out, "I think. The flight attendant passed out chocolate chip cookies with macadamia nuts, so that was a plus." Vanessa wanted to scold herself for her mindless rambling. Surely the King did not care about what kind of cookies she ate.

"My dad should be getting here in a few minutes, then we're going to a quick meeting before dinner, but I'd love it if you could dine with us." Addison motioned toward the stairs, "Dinner will be upstairs in the Family Room; just kind of a casual thing."

Vanessa was once again taken off guard by his abundant

hospitality. "Of course! I, um," she glanced at her blue jeans and Captain America T-shirt, "Should I dress up?"

"No!" Addison laughed, "Not at all. Don't worry, I'll ditch the suit and tie. Just wear whatever you're comfortable in. See you at six!"

Vanessa nodded, still not fully processing everything that was happening. "Right. Sure thing."

Addison headed down the hall, disappearing as quickly as he had shown up.

"Oh my, how exciting!" the front desk worker squealed. "Dinner with the Royal Family! I'm sure this is none of my business, but it must be awfully surreal to have the young King smitten with you."

"Huh?" Vanessa choked, followed by fake laughter, "No, no, no. I'm here for an interview, for a job. I'm applying for a position on the Helping the Homeless Committee."

"Sure you are," the lady laughed. "The staff turnover isn't until January. Interview week is usually the first week of December! You're just a tad bit early, my dear."

Vanessa felt her heart beat pick up. Addison wasn't actually *interested* in her, was he? Sure, there had been times that she felt a possible spark of romance in the air. Like when they danced together at The Ball. But Addison danced with lots of girls, at lots of balls. And Vanessa was no different than any of the others. The boy was bombarded with beautiful ladies, always throwing themselves at his feet. The guy would have to be crazy to be attracted to her! That couldn't even be possible. Could it?

Vanessa shook her head, trying to rid her brain of such

insane thoughts, and focused on the task at hand. She needed to get checked into her room, change her clothes, and prepare for her professional dinner meeting; the most important interview of her life.

David Carter still wasn't ♛ used to this kind of attention. The Welcome Home party that awaited *Kennetic Energy* was one of unparalleled, epic proportions.

The whole school erupted in cheers as David and his band walked through the doors. The administration declared a reprieve from classes, and Principal Oak gave David a special assembly and a ribbon of honor, praising him for being a hometown hero. The local news jumped at the chance to chat with their homegrown celebrity.

But their town wasn't the only city in America talking about David's historic rescue of the Royal Princess. Hollywood was also buzzing about it. *Pop Culture Highlights* came to David's house to do an exclusive interview. *Shining Star Magazine* asked for a photoshoot paired with all the juicy details. Brian Mecrest called and asked the band to perform on the hit talent show, American Rival. *Kennetic Energy*'s designated PO Box for fan mail was bursting with letters, cards, and gifts.

"We've never had so many booking requests!" Laney squealed as she twirled around in the swirly chair next to David's desk. She pushed herself away from his laptop and struggled to grasp the reality of what was happening. "If I accept all these touring requests, we are going to be booked for the next sixteen months. We need to buy a bus."

David lay sprawled out on his twin bed, listening to Laney's excited rambling, but not fully processing what she was saying. He spun a small, cloth basketball in his hand, then popped it into the net hanging over his closet door. The ball swooshed through the net that had been hanging there since he was five years old.

"David, did you hear me?" Laney asked, rebounding the ball mid-air as it dropped toward the ground. She tossed it back to him, "Our lives have radically changed. Nothing is ever going to be the same again."

"Yeah, pretty cool," David spoke half-heartedly as he caught the ball.

"I'm not hearing much enthusiasm in your voice," Laney chided him. "What's your problem? You should be on top of the world right now! Our music career is hotter than it's ever been, and you're the guy that everyone is talking about! So what gives?"

David sighed, unsure of how to express himself. "I don't know. But you don't come out of an experience like that as the same person."

"Yeah, I know, I was there!" Laney replied. "We were all in that room together. It was terrible, and I hope that I never have to see anything like that in my life, ever again. But it's over, David. We have to move on now. Life is giving us so many epic opportunities and reasons to be happy!"

"Do you think we'll ever go back to Tarsurella?" he asked.

"Who knows," Laney shrugged, "but let's talk American Rival. Can you believe that we're going to be performing?! I can't wait to meet Brian! I am literally not going to be able to sleep until this happens."

"How do you think the Royals are working through all of this?" David asked. "I mean, it's got to be really hard for them. First their home gets invaded by terrorists, then their brother is missing. And now they're expected to just carry on with life as usual?"

Laney sighed, trying to change the subject he was focused on, "What are you going to wear? I think we should switch up our look a little bit. I mean, we don't want to be too predictable with our stage appearance. We should stay a little bit edgy, and totally current. I want to take some risks, maybe we could try something wild, like…"

David wasn't listening to a word Laney was saying. His thoughts were still an ocean away, in Tarsurella.

David's cell phone started ringing, so he perched himself up to glance at the I.D. His eyes did a double take. The Royal Office of the Kingdom of Tarsurella was calling him! His hands began to sweat as he hurried to swipe his screen.

"Hello?" he asked quickly, trying to keep his voice as calm as possible.

"Hello, is this David Carter?" a friendly voice asked on the other end of the line.

"Yes," David attempted to put on his most professional-sounding voice, despite all the nervous energy he was feeling, "this is him." In a matter of seconds, David's mind raced with many possibilities. *Did Princess Hope have a message for him? Did she want to see him again? Did she—*

"King Addison was deeply touched by, and is forever grateful for your act of selfless heroism. He wishes to honor you with the bestowal of the Royal Crest. He has asked to host a regal ceremony for you, Clark Myers, and several other men and women who he believes to be exceptional heroes. The King desires to give reward and honor to whom it is due. He is requesting your appearance at an event, to be held at The Palace two weeks from Saturday. He would like your parents to attend as well. The occasion will be small, yet formal."

David was speechless. His heart sped up as the exciting reality crashed over him–he would get to see Hope again! "Of, of course," he stuttered, "absolutely, we will be there. Thank you, thank you so much! Please let His Royal Majesty know that the honor is all mine. I'm completely blown away by the fact that he would want me to come."

"Wonderful! We will arrange for your travel, and I'll be contacting you with further details soon. Thank you for your time, Mr. Carter."

David thanked her again before hanging up. He tossed his phone onto the bed, and shot up to his feet. A fresh burst of excited energy animated David once more, making him appear completely different than he did just minutes before. Laney raised her eyebrows, noting the sudden change.

"What were you saying about getting new clothes?" David asked with a sly grin, "I need to decide what I'm going to wear."

When Laney's confused look didn't disappear, David explained with a grin, "I'm going back to Tarsurella."

Vanessa took a deep breath before leaving The Queen's Suite. The day had been quite surreal, not to mention completely unbelievable! Here she was, staying in the gloriously beautiful Queen's Suite, a sacred place where tourists were never invited to tread.

It left her breathless to think that the Queen previously lived her daily life here. Her hands shook nervously as she got ready at the vanity, applying a fresh layer of lip-gloss. She couldn't help but feel like a Royal herself, as she added a few streaks of rosy pink blush to her face. She was tempted to take pictures of the stunning room, to capture some memories of this spectacular opportunity. But somehow it just didn't feel right to do it. She knew that the late Queen's Suite was extremely special to the family.

She left the suite dressed in her periwinkle maxi-dress and white jean jacket, and slowly made her way down the hall. Addison told her to dress casually, but she wanted to make a good impression during the interview. The walls were adorned with a scrapbook-esque display of family photographs. The carpeted floors in the hallway gave this section of The Palace an entirely different feel than the fancy marble floors on the first floor. Much of the decor was not uncommon to what you would find in a normal home, and it made Vanessa smile. It was actually kind of cozy!

With a sudden flash of her imagination, she could picture Prince Addison as a little boy dashing down the hallway, as the Queen held a mug of warm peppermint tea in her hand, and kept a watchful eye on her child. The memories that were made in this home were just as real and genuine as those made in any other home. Vanessa felt another twinge of guilt in her gut, as she remembered how much she used to disdain even the thought of this seemingly-uppity family. Oh, how wrong she had been.

She passed several rooms, searching for the Family Room. She wasn't sure what to expect, but when she saw little Willie jumping up and down on the sofa, she knew she had arrived at the right place. She felt like a strange outsider stepping into such an adorable little scene.

Willie had thrown large couch cushions all over the room,

and was hopping across them. "Don't fall in the lava!" he warned his sister.

Millie screamed as she jumped over two cushions at once, "Ahh! An alligator almost bit me!"

"That's so unrealistic," Jillian called from the nearby kitchen table where she carefully arranged the silverware. "It's impossible for alligators to survive in lava."

"But these are lava-gators!" Millie argued. "They can live in lava, and they breathe out fire, like dragons! Willie, look out, there's one right there–he's throwing fire at you!"

Jillian sighed and rolled her eyes. "They are so juvenile."

Hope laughed, "And *you* need to go back to being eleven!"

"I'm jumping as fast as I can!" Willie shouted. "But I think it's gonna eat my leg!" Willie attempted to jump to safety, but accidently bumped into Vanessa who had just stepped inside.

"Umph! A person!" he declared.

Everyone stopped what they were doing to see who had entered the room. Vanessa stood there awkwardly, unsure of what to say. "Uh, hi."

"It's Vanessa, right?" Bridget slapped a smile onto her face and walked over to greet her, "Great to see you again!"

Vanessa was surprised by Bridget's smile, and couldn't quite read if it was fake or genuine. Their last interaction hadn't gone too well.

"Yes!" Vanessa breathed, trying to stay calm and afloat in the midst of her sea of nerves. She felt like little Willie, trying to jump from one island of safety to another, one word at a time. "King Addison invited me. He's interviewing me for a new position at The Palace." Vanessa was sure to add that in there. Perhaps it would help Bridget dismiss any other notions that she was interested in her brother.

"You're pretty!" Millie complemented her. "Are you going to marry Addison? He's looking for a wife, you know!"

Vanessa's face turned flush red as she laughed nervously. "Oh my goodness, you're so cute." That was all she could think to say to the little girl.

"Do you like chocolate cake?" Millie asked, "I hope so, because we made a super yummy one for tonight! Me and Clark, that is. Clark is our chef, and he makes the best desserts ever!"

"I helped too!" Willie chimed in.

"Yeah, and if you don't like cake, I can eat your piece," Millie generously offered to Vanessa.

Just then, Addison walked in. Vanessa was surprised to see that he was wearing a pair of jeans and a light blue Aeropostale shirt. The colors made his blue eyes pop, and she had never noticed how striking they were before. She glanced at the others and realized that most of the Royal Family was wearing sweatpants or jeans, or in Willie's case, no pants at all. She suddenly felt extremely overdressed. Addison had told her ahead of time, but somehow dressing casual didn't make sense until now.

"Hey, I hope you're hungry," Addison smiled. "I've been hearing rumors about how good this dinner is supposed to be."

"And we get ice cream too!" Millie gave herself a running start, then threw herself into Addison's arms. Vanessa smiled, quietly admiring the special way that Addison had with young children. Millie looked at Vanessa, "Do you like ice cream?"

"Are you kidding?" Vanessa laughed, "Ice cream is my middle name!"

"Yeah, it's pretty much all you need in life, huh kiddo?" Addison asked Millie, adding to Vanessa's joke.

"Well, that and chocolate cake, Mr. Pork Chops, and Clark, and my daddy, and camping!" Millie grinned. "Addi, when are we going to go camping? Can we go tomorrow? Vanessa, you can come with us! You can sleep in my tent!"

"Alright, the burgers are almost done!" the retired King announced as he walked in from the balcony where he had been manning the grill. "Is everything else ready? Let's get this BBQ started!"

"Yep!" Jillian gave him two thumbs up. "The table is set, the condiments are out, and I think we're all starving."

In a suddenly flurry of activity, everyone gathered around the table and started talking at once. Vanessa couldn't help but laugh at the chaos. As an only child, their family dinner table was very quiet. The loud and rambunctious scene of chatter and laughter made her smile.

"Dad, I'd like you to meet Vanessa," Addison told his father before he ducked back out the door to grab his burgers.

Vanessa did a slight curtsey, unsure of how to greet the King who wore a black T-Shirt that said "Grill Master". "It's a pleasure to meet you, Your Majesty."

"Oh please, call me Steve," the King grinned. "We don't bring any of that formal stuff upstairs. Can you tell by the stains on this old shirt?" he laughed. "It's our honor to have you in our home, so please just relax, make yourself at home, and enjoy!"

Vanessa nodded. It was easier said than done. She was dinning with the *Royal Family*. "Thank you, Sir."

The King raised a teasing eyebrow.

"I mean, Steve!" she quickly recovered, letting out a laugh.

"That's better," he winked before turning to return to his burgers.

"Your dad is so nice," Vanessa said, thinking out loud.

"Yeah, he's got a great heart," Addison handed Vanessa a paper plate. Millie accidently squirted Willie with ketchup, and the two started to squabble. Vanessa couldn't help but laugh again. Maybe relaxing and having fun wouldn't be nearly as challenging as she thought it would be!

Once everyone decorated their hamburgers and added an abundance of chips to their plates, they all bowed their heads to pray. Addison led them in a thoughtful prayer, then it was time to dig in.

"So Vanessa, do you do a lot of traveling?" Hope asked before taking a bit bite of her hamburger.

"Not as a young child, but I've always had a desire to get out and explore. Mom said I was bitten by the wanderlust bug," Vanessa laughed at the memory "But during my Senior Year, we took a trip out West to all of the big national parks. Then, after I graduated they surprised me with a trip to Europe.

They had been saving up for it for years. I was so elated."

"Ohhh, I've never been to any of the parks in the U.S.," Hope said. "That would be really fun!"

"So Dad," Bridget perked up, purposefully changing the conversation, "Las Stephan is designing a new wedding gown line. He asked if I want to be his exclusive spokesperson and model for the brand."

"Hmm," the late King replied thoughtfully, "doesn't it help to be married before becoming a spokesperson for marriage?"

"It's not for marriage, Dad, it's for the gowns. You don't have to be married to model a wedding gown. You should see the dresses, they are gorgeous!"

"Do you have a wedding dress?" Millie asked Vanessa. "When you marry Addison, can I be the flower girl?"

The entire table fell silent.

Addison laughed nervously, "I'm so sorry," he apologized to Vanessa on behalf of his little sister, "Millie overhears way too much from episodes of *Say Yes to the Dress*. Weddings are kind of an obsession around here." Addison tossed an obviously condemning glance in Bridget's direction.

"I can't help it!" Bridget threw her hands up in surrender and laughed. "They're just so beautiful. The lace, the flowers, the men in tuxes, the cake, the fancy dishes, it all makes me totally start fangirling."

"Cake!" Millie cried. "Everybody eat fast, so we can get to dessert faster!"

Vanessa giggled as the lively conversation continued.

Throughout the meal, she managed to steal several shy glances at Addison and she enjoyed seeing him so relaxed. He was clearly in his element. It was obvious that spending time with his family was something that brought him great joy, and Vanessa guessed that if she were to ask him, he would much rather be with his family than in the office. At first, Vanessa had tried to violently ward off any thoughts that suggested he was handsome. But now, as he laughed at Millie's goofy antics, patiently wiped ketchup and mustard off Willie's face, and playfully teased his sisters, Vanessa couldn't help but find him attractive. It was like he was wearing his big, beautiful heart on his sleeve and she absolutely loved the view.

Chapter 26 – Letting Go

Chasity gazed thoughtfully out the window as their private jet-liner left Greece. It was bittersweet for her to leave such a beautiful place. She was excited about getting home to see her father and siblings, and to be reassured of the fact that everyone was secure again. Yet, at the same time, she knew that in some sort of strange way she would miss the little house on the seashore. Mr. and Mrs. Drakos had been such generous hosts, despite the non-ideal conditions that sent her there. Mr. and Mrs. Drakos highly encouraged her to come back and visit. She loved the idea, and knew that their beach would always hold a special place in her heart.

Chasity pulled her thoughts from below and focused on what was happening in their plane. Hanson and Lance were playing a card game called Peanut. Hanson was explaining the rules, and Lance listened eagerly, preparing with a game face that told her he was ready to dominate. But nobody had warned the poor boy that Hanson's Peanut-playing reflexes were so fast, and that he was surely about to get creamed. After two rounds, Lance declared that Hanson was cheating, and after a small squabble, the game finally ended.

Hanson walked back from where he had been playing, and sat down in the open seat beside Chasity. He stared forward, not even daring to look at her as he spoke,

"I've requested to be repositioned within The Palace," he spoke in an official and unfeeling tone. "Jackson is reviewing my request, and considering promoting me to the Security Tower. I should know soon."

"What?" Chasity breathed, feeling an unwelcome wave of panic and sadness wash over her. "Why?"

Hanson looked at her. His eyebrows popped up. He didn't say

anything, but his response was heard loud and clear. It was because of her.

Chasity bit her lip and asked quietly, "Because of what happened on the beach?"

Hanson sighed, "There were many factors that went into the reasoning behind my decision."

Chasity nodded, even though she wasn't satisfied with his answer. "I was raised to believe that the truth should always be spoken, even if it stings a little bit. I don't want you to lie to me Hanson. I need to ask you something. And you have to answer this, otherwise the next few years of my life are going to be spent wondering and speculating, and I just can't put myself through that kind of pointless torture. So I need you to answer me as honestly and genuinely as you can, okay? Do you see any hope at all of us having any kind of future, um," the last word lingered on her tongue before it finally came out, "together?"

Hanson felt something inside his heart ache, knowing that she wasn't going to like the answer. Hey, he didn't even like the answer. But still, it's just the way things were, and they both needed to be okay with it.

"I think you already know what I'm going to say," Hanson replied. "You know how I feel about you, and you also know the reasons why this can never work. But I guess the future is still unknown I guess. I mean, who knows, maybe years from now, like way down the road, I'll be working another job and you'll miraculously still be single, and we'll stumble upon each other during a happenchance meeting at a café in Paris."

Chasity almost smiled at the thought. Even though she was fighting the urge to cry, his words sounded so sweet and full of whimsy, and promise. "Well," she replied, quickly deciding

[374]

to change the subject, "if they *do* decide to promote you to upstairs, you'll have to sneak me up there to play chess sometime."

The puzzled look on Hanson's adorable face tempted Chasity to laugh, despite the turmoil that she felt inside.

"The Royals are not allowed in the Tower," Chasity continued. "But we always hear stories about it. The biggest rumor is that there's a lot of chess playing going on up there."

"Well that sounds riveting," Hanson joked sarcastically, "but at least it will be more entertaining than watching you read."

Chasity laughed again.

"I'm serious!" Hanson continued with a playful grin. "Watching you read was like watching the grass grow. And it takes so long for you to get through one page! There were times when I wondered if you were re-reading the same page over and over again."

"Hey now!" Chasity shot back, "Don't make fun of my freakishly slow reading skills. Hope is a speed reader, but I like to take my time. It helps me get into the story better, and really soak in everything that is happening."

"You do a lot of things slowly," he laughed. "It takes you ten years to eat dessert."

Chasity shook her head with a laugh, "It's not fair. You know all of these quirky, embarrassing things about me, and I have absolutely nothing on you. Before you get reassigned, you have to at least tell me three embarrassing things about yourself that nobody knows. Then you can go down in history as the *one* security guard in my life who I actually knew something about!"

"That's so lame," Hanson laughed, "I'm not gonna do that."

"Humor me," Chasity's big blue eyes pleaded.

Once they got off this plane and returned to The Palace, everything would be changing. He would be working in a completely different unit, and the only time he would likely see Chasity would be on the big screen security monitors. This might be last time he would ever have a real conversation with her.

He sighed. "So, when I was three years old, my parents enrolled me in preschool and there was this super-pretty girl I had a huge crush on. I wanted to share my animal crackers with her, so I asked her to meet me out under the jungle gym, but it was right after naptime and I had just had an.... uhh... accident. The teacher helped me take care of it super quick so that none of the other kids knew, but of course they called my parents. So at recess, my mom rushed to the school and came running onto the playground yelling, 'Here are your Pullups, Hanson!' Needless to say, all the kids thought it was hilarious, and I never got to share my animal crackers with her."

"Oh, you poor dear!" Chasity giggled, "That must've been so traumatic. How did you ever get over it?"

"I didn't," Hanson replied with a perfectly straight face. "That's why I'm still completely freaked out to go on dates. Or eat animal crackers."

Chasity's eyes widened, for a moment thinking he was serious, then read the mischievous undertone in his eyes. She laughed, "You're a mess."

"Yeah, when Lilly and I talk about it today, she said it left a very lasting impression on her." He laughed, "And I don't think that's a good thing."

Chasity's smile disappeared. Lilly was the animal cracker girl? He'd known her *that* long? Chasity sighed. She had to let this thing go. Before he did any further damage to her already-shattering heart, she needed to release him once and for all. Who was she trying to fool? Hanson was right. A relationship between them would never work. Any irrational thought of the future working out in their favor was just a daydream, and she had to force herself to stop thinking about it. Hanson was like the morning dew. He simply wasn't going to last. Like Peter Pan appearing in Wendy's life for several magical moments, he would soon return to *Neverland* with all the other lost boys. What was the purpose of entertaining something in her mind that she wouldn't be able to attain?

All at once Chasity realized that the thought of a future without Hanson seemed devastating. Somehow this guy owned much more real estate in her heart than she had intended to give up. How had he snuck in there so quickly?

The cruel reality was that Hanson was not hers to have, nor would he ever be. Hanson had become a precious idol, and the realization of that fact suddenly jolted her awake. *Neverland* was only a dream, and she had no intention of ever living there. So why was she playing around like this?

As her mind listed all the reasons as to why her fantasy needed to end, her heart continued to whisper things that she wanted to believe were true. *Lord help me!* she prayed quietly. *Forgive me for making him an idol that I have coveted. I must let go and release him to You.*

"I don't want you to wait for me," Chasity spoke quietly.

"Huh?" Hanson asked. She had so quickly changed the course of their discussion again, it was challenging to keep up.

"In that café. In Paris. We both know that I'm not going to show up. Our lives are heading down two very different paths and," Chasity felt tears surfacing, "I'm not going to be there."

Hanson nodded as his throat tightened up.

Chasity sniffled, trying to regain her composure, "I think it's good that you're headed upstairs. The promotion will be great for you. Who knows? Maybe new doors will open for you! Whatever happens, I wish you all the best."

Hanson couldn't stand to sit beside her any longer. His heart was being crushed. Finally he stood up, nodded and said, "Thank you, Your Highness."

A few hours later, Vanessa was still laughing. The family had just finished an amusing game of *Sing, Act, Draw* and Vanessa couldn't remember a time when her sides had hurt so much! He face was aching from smiling so excessively.

"I can't believe that was supposed to be a bunny rabbit!" Hope burst out in giggles.

Jillian tried to defend herself, but her own giddy laughter overpowered her words, "Hey, it's a lot harder than it looks!"

"Oh my, what an evening this has been!" The retired King laughed once more then glanced at his watch, "But, it's somebody's bedtime."

"Oh Daddy, can't we please stay up a bit longer?!" Millie pleaded, hopping into his lap. "This is the first night we've all been together!"

"It's almost ten-thirty," he replied. "I've already given you two extra hours. And tomorrow is a school day."

Millie sighed happily and hugged her Father, "I love you, Daddy. I don't ever want us to be separated again."

He returned the hug and planted a kiss on her forehead. "Neither do I, my sweet Millie."

Hope pulled herself off the couch and stood with an outstretched hand toward Millie. "Come on, little munchkin, let's go get ready for bed. We can have a slumber party tonight."

"I get to sleep in your room?!" Millie perked up, "Yay! Can Willie and I skip baths, too?"

Addison chuckled quietly from where he sat next to Vanessa, with a sleeping boy in his arms. "I don't think Willie would make it into the tub tonight. I'd better go tuck him in."

"Oh no," the former King protested, rising to his feet before Addison, "I'll take him. You stay here and continue visiting with your lovely company."

Addison shuffled the floppy boy into his father's arms, "Thanks, Dad."

"It's been a pleasure getting to know you, Miss Vanessa," the King spoke with a twinkle in his eye, "And I sure hope that we will be seeing more of you in the future."

Vanessa laughed, "Well, if Addison decides to hire me, then perhaps you will."

After Hope and the children exited, Bridget popped up from where she was lounging in the easy chair. "Does anyone want waffles? I'm totally craving them right now." She headed toward the freezer.

"I'm still stuffed," Vanessa giggled, "I don't think I could eat another bite!"

"Yeah, me too," Addison agreed as he slipped his hands into his pockets.

"Um, I should probably get going," Vanessa said, not wanting to overstay her welcome. "It's getting late, and I'm sure you have a long day tomorrow, running the country and all."

A flash of disappointment, as quick as white lightening, passed through Addison's eyes. "Yeah, of course." He cleared his throat, reminding himself of tomorrow's long "to-do" list. "Your official interview with the board is tomorrow at one. Deborah will check in with you tomorrow morning with details."

"Oh," Vanessa nodded, tugging softly at the end of her jacket sleeve, "Wow, suddenly I'm super nervous."

"Oh, no, don't worry about it!" Addison tried to reassure her, "You'll do amazing! Just be yourself, and I'm sure the board will see why you'll make such a valuable asset to our team."

Vanessa took a deep breath and smiled, "Thanks. I'm going to try my best, and we'll see what happens!"

Addison grinned, his eyes soaking up the sight. He felt like he was basking in the rays of Vanessa's inner light. Something about her just made him feel more alive. A moment of silence fell upon them, and Addison realized that he was just standing there looking at her with a goofy smile on his face.

"Oh, um, do you want me to walk you back to your room?"

"Oh, no that's okay," Vanessa replied, "I think I can make it back there okay." She threw a laugh onto the end of her sentence, attempting to make it sound less awkward, but it didn't work. She wanted to slap herself. Why was she acting so strange? And why was he looking at her with a smile that had the potential to make her knees melt? She shook her head, trying to put everything back into perspective, to keep first things first. The job. That's the only reason she was here. "See you tomorrow at one!" She offered a little wave before leaving.

Addison said goodbye and closed the door behind her. Still smiling, he walked toward the kitchen and found his hands drumming nervously on the countertop.

"Time to spill your guts, mister." Bridget spoke mischievously as she popped a pair of waffles into the toaster.

"What do you mean?" Addison laughed, even though he knew exactly what she was talking about.

"You are totally into her!" Bridget retorted. "I've never seen you that smitten before in my life! But do you really know that much about her? I mean, what's her middle name? What's her favorite color? Does she like coffee better, or tea? Is she a cat person, or a dog person? Does she crack her knuckles? Does she carry a deep-seated hatred towards your monarchy, and desire to see the downfall of our nation?"

"Whoa, Bridg," Addison's tone shifted, "where's that coming from?"

"Listen, I know I have no right to barge in on your personal life, but I've heard things about this girl from inside sources. And trust me, she's not all that her pearly white smile appears to be."

"And just who are these sources that you speak of?" Addison adamantly crossed his arms.

"My best friends. And they care about you just as much as I do. They would never lie to us." Bridget matter-of-factly stated her case, "Vanessa's intentions are not pure. And this isn't just coming from hearsay. Weeks ago, when we had our little tennis match, you should've heard her spewing off all this hate speech against the Crown. She could only speak of democratic freedoms, and how cruel and unthinkable we were for ruling everyone with our iron fist."

"Perhaps her perspective has changed?" Addison suggested. "Otherwise, I don't think she would've flown across the ocean for this job interview."

Bridget laughed bitterly, frustrated that her brother was blinded to the full picture. "Can't you see what's going on here?!" she raised her voice with passion. "This girl is just like the rest of them! She's got you under some sort of love spell, preying on your mind and emotions, as you helplessly fall into her trap; then when you least expect it, her true colors will show, and you'll be left with nothing but heartbreak from the betrayal, and utter embarrassment!"

Addison took a deep breath, struggling to keep his voice calm. He wanted to defend Vanessa and her character, but he knew that verbally attacking his sister would only further escalate the conversation. "Could it be," he started slowly, "that the problem you have with Vanessa actually has nothing to do with her? Maybe this situation is just bringing up negative memories from the past. Memories pertaining to Jacob."

"This has nothing to do with Jacob!" she snapped back. "This is just me, a concerned sister, worried about you entering into a relationship with someone you know absolutely nothing about!"

"Well then, I'll get to know her," Addison smiled. "I'm not going to rush anything."

"So are you going to ask to court her?" Bridget asked with a raised brow.

"I can't say that the thought hasn't crossed my mind. But right now obviously is not a good time. If I pursue a relationship with her, or any girl, I want to do it the right way. I want my head and my heart to be all in, without being distracted and pulled in a thousand different directions. But the Kingdom is still in turmoil. I've got so much on my plate, and I just wouldn't be able to give Vanessa, or anyone, the adequate time needed to pursue and get to know her. Picking up the pieces of a broken nation is a huge undertaking," he sighed.

Bridget didn't bother to hide her relief. "I think that's wise," she nodded. "You're smart to stick this chick on the backburner. Your family and your country are the ones who really need you right now."

"Speaking of family," Addison decided to change the subject. "We need to talk about Asher."

"Oh no," Bridget's voice fell as her waffles popped up, "did something else happen? Are the injuries worse than they thought?" The last Bridget had heard, her brother was safe and being treated in an army hospital in the Middle East. The whole family was beyond relived. But Addison hadn't revealed the whole story yet.

"Asher is fine, physically anyway. He's receiving some of the

[383]

best treatment in the world. But Jackson showed me some emails from a chat room on one of his video games." Addison sighed again, "I don't even know how to tell you this. We all knew that Asher was struggling, but it's way worse than we thought. It's bad, sis. The mental and emotional turmoil that he's in caused him to do some crazy things. He let Smashman into The Palace."

Bridget bit her lip. An icy sheet of bitterness froze across the lake of her normally life-filled eyes. "He betrayed us?" she asked in a single breath.

Addison hesitated, "Betrayal seems like a really strong word. And I don't think Asher knew the weight of what he was opening us up to. The actual link that opened the door for the enemy to come in, was clicked on innocently. So there's a fine line here, between what he did knowingly, and what he had no control over. But there was so much animosity and hate coming from Asher in these game room conversations, that the motives to hurt us somehow were pretty clear. You could pick this story apart in a hundred different ways, which is what the Security Team has been doing, but they seem to keep coming back to the same conclusion—Asher is a federal criminal."

"I want to cry, but I can't," Bridget said. "It's like I don't feel anything anymore. I'm so numb."

Addison stretched out his arms to hug her.

"No!" she snapped back, "I don't want your comfort! I told you, I'm not sad about this. It is what it is. Life stinks, and we can't do anything about it."

Addison was taken aback by her harsh reaction. "Bridg, it's okay to be upset about this. We've been through so much these past few weeks, but you're acting as if it hasn't had any effect on you. Don't let your heart become so stone cold that you don't feel pain anymore."

Bridget's eyebrows shot up in offence, "What, you're expecting me to have this big, dramatic meltdown, like I did when Jacob betrayed us? You know what, Addison? I don't care anymore. It's just like, why even bother? People are always going to be jerks, and life is always going to be disappointing, and you just have to learn to deal with it. If my not crying is disturbing to you, then maybe you should consider the fact that I've grown up a little bit!"

"Why are you putting on this mask?" Addison argued, "I know you're just as heartbroken as I am! You don't have to try and act tough. There's a healing process that we're all going to have to go through. We need to be real with each other and talk about this stuff."

"Talking doesn't change anything," she snapped again, grabbing her waffles out of the toaster, and heading for the door, "which is why I'm done with this conversation."

"You forgot the syrup!" Addison called after her.

"That's what room service is for," she grumbled, then slammed the door behind her.

"Clark, Clark!" Millie burst into the kitchen, calling for one of her most cherished people in the world. "I have some exceptionally exciting news!"

Hope gingerly trailed behind her sister who had run ahead of her. This morning at the breakfast table, Addison told Millie about the banquet and ceremony that he planned to host for Clark, David, and others who had played such heroic roles. Millie was thrilled that Clark would receive such an honor, and asked if she could be the one to announce it to Clark.

Hope carried a bouquet of roses in her hand with the official invitation, because Mille thought a man wouldn't appreciate flowers. Still, Addison asked that they be given with the announcement. The purpose of this event was to bestow honor upon Clark, and to express their deep gratitude. Hope was humbled to be a part of it and thought it was important that he know just how much they appreciate him. Not simply because of his leadership skills during The Palace takeover, but also because of his everyday caring and loving heart.

Hope would be fibbing to herself if she didn't admit she was crazy excited about David coming back. She couldn't wait to talk to him. She hadn't a clue what she would tell him, and it made her giddy and nervous just thinking about it, but nevertheless she still couldn't wait.

"Well, good morning!" Clark's tone was cheerful.

"Addison is throwing you a party!" Millie announced. "There's going to be a big, yummy dinner, and you get the day off, and Addi is going to give you a Royal Crest for being so brave!"

"Whoa, whoa, what's all this now?" Clark laughed, trying to keep up with Millie who speedily gushed out her words.

Clark's face softened as Hope approached and handed him the official invitation, "King Addison is requesting your presence at a banquet, held to honor you and the other selfless souls who acted so heroically during the days of the attack."

Clark's hands trembled just slightly as he opened the envelope.

Hope continued, "Your whole family is invited. You will receive the whole weekend off, as well as a special stay in one of our luxury suites. The King would like you to take unlimited dips in the pool, horseback rides, golf games, and pretty much anything else that you'd find enjoyable around here."

Clark's eyes sparkled as tears pressed to the edges, "Thank you."

"No, thank you." Hope replied quietly. "Truly, this is the least we could do for you. Some of us might not even *be* here right now if it weren't for you."

"Well, God sure is faithful, isn't he?" Clark glanced at the rose bouquet attempting to change the subject, "I'd better get a vase for those flowers. They sure are pretty."

"You like flowers?" Millie asked in a shocked voice.

"Of course I do!" Clark replied. "I love how happy these flowers are going to make my wife. And a happy wife means a happy life!"

"I didn't know you had a wife!" Millie gasped. "Why didn't you ever tell me?"

"Millie," Hope scolded her, "it's not proper to butt into people's personal lives. Clark, where would I find a vase?"

Clark smiled at Millie before replying to Hope, "Perhaps you'll meet her at the banquet. Three rows down, bottom shelf to your left."

"Oh, yes!" Millie was truly excited by the idea. "I'm going to make her a card. I'll draw something super special on the front. Do you think she would like a picture of Pork Chops eating cupcakes?"

Clark let out a hearty belly laugh, "Yes, I'm sure she would love it."

Chapter 27 – Alaskan Adventure

"Are you sure you have enough clothes?" Hope laughed at Bridget as she launched herself onto her Cheetah print suitcase, trying to close it up tight.

"Are you kidding me?" Bridget asked, slightly out of breath from her effort, "I'm going to be in Alaska. The closest store is like an hour away. She stood up and nervously gnawed on her sparkly index nail. "Now I'm wondering if I have enough shoes."

Hope glanced at the six other ginormous suitcases piled up and waiting patiently by Bridget's bedroom door. "Um, I think you should be good," Hope giggled. "You're not going to need a store. If anyone in your village needs shoes, they can come and see you."

Bridget sighed as she put anxious hands on her hips, "I don't know, maybe this is a bad idea."

"Bridg, don't second-guess yourself." Hope walked up to her sister and wrapped her in a hug, "The only thing bad about this situation is the fact that I'm going to miss you like crazy. But other than that, Addison's idea was amazing."

Bridget sighed. When Addison first told her about the Royal Safe House in Alaska, she couldn't imagine herself going there. I mean, why would she? All of her friends were in Tarsurella. If she wasn't here she would miss so many parties, fashion shows, meet-and-greets, concerts, and other fabulous events. She was the socialite of Tarsurella and the belle of every ball! If she went AWAL everyone would make a huge deal out of it. But the longer she thought about it, the idea started to grow on her.

Addison gave her an information packet about the tiny village in Alaska and the host family that she would be staying with. The village wasn't big on media, Wi-Fi, or sometimes (depending on the weather) even electricity! Addison reminded her that most of the folks around there wouldn't even have a clue who she was. Suddenly, her interest was sparked. *Going to a world where nobody knows who I am? A world where I can walk around outside without a flock of cameras or security guards following me? Sounds like bliss.*

As much as Bridget loved her jet-set fashionista lifestyle, since Addison's Coronation things just hadn't been the same. Her conversations with Bailee and Kitty felt dull and shallow. Talk of things like designer clothes and European boys were making her crazy! As much as she tried to distract herself with these things, her mind always wandered back to Asher and the disasters that followed on that terrible night. She had attempted to do several interviews, but everyone was asking about how their family was "recovering" and how she was handling the trauma. Bridget was *so* over it. She didn't want to think about it, but everyone kept bringing the nightmare up and throwing it into her face. The discussion either revolved around sparkly jewelry or traumatic gunfire, and she didn't want to talk about either one of those topics.

Going to a place where nobody knew who she was sounded adventurous and exciting. It was what she had been asking her father for permission to do, even before the Coronation! He agreed with Addison's idea, and Bridget was shocked that he was actually going to let her go! For once in her life, a brand new chapter of the beautiful unknown was about to unfold.

"I'll miss you too!" Bridget hugged her back. "Are you sure you don't want to come with me?"

"Yeah," Hope nodded, "I feel like my place is here right now. Besides, I can't miss the banquet."

"You're so brave," Bridget sighed, looking at her sister with admiration. "I honestly don't know how you do it. I mean, doesn't it bother you that everyone at that dinner is going to be talking about what happened? It's like you're going to be forced to relive it all over again."

"Of course it will be hard," Hope agreed, "but at the same time, I have so much peace. As terrible as everything was, I still felt God's presence right there with me, all the way through. I knew I couldn't give in to fear, and God helped me do that. But instead of looking back at all the bad things that happened, we're going to celebrate the good stuff! That's what the purpose of Addison's banquet is, to bestow glory and honor on those it is due."

Bridget was blown away by the purple mountaintops. As her flight neared the airport in Anchorage, she soaked in the view. Her eyes feasted on the refreshing sight of miles and miles of luscious green pine tree tops with pristine blue rivers winding through them.

As they neared the city, tall buildings sparkled in the sunshine. *Enjoy these buildings,* Bridget told herself silently with a smile, *because this will be the last you get to see of a big city for a while!*

The host family, who was scheduled to pick her up, would be taking her to a tiny village four-and-a-half hours away from civilization. As apprehensive as she was about the idea of having spotty cell service in a land where moose and wolves were known to run wild, she was still excited about the adventure awaiting her. It was like nothing she had ever done before. The idea of such a fresh start energized her.

As soon as they landed, Bridget descended from the airplane, wheeling two massive suitcases behind her. A butler who had flown with her worked on gathering the rest of her luggage.

Inside the airport, Bridget searched for the couple who was supposed to be picking her up. Her eyes scanned the moving crowd. She knew from her information packet that their names were Becky and Donald Henderson, and she hoped to recognize them from their photo.

"Do you see them?" Bridget asked her security guard who was looking around as well.

"Oh my gosh, it's Princess Bridget!" a little brown-haired girl with bouncy curls gasped as she tugged on her mom's jacket. "Take a picture, I want to meet her!"

The tired mom looked up, and Bridget waved politely at her, giving them permission to approach her. As exhausted as Bridget was from traveling, she could never say no to her excited fans. They were just so sweet!

The little girl skipped toward her, dragging her mom by the hand. Bridget hugged her, signed her Alaskan tourist hat, and posed for a photo. After they said goodbye, Bridget turned to her guard. "I thought nobody was going to recognize me here."

"Anchorage is a big tourist hub," he replied. "The excitement should die down once you reach the village."

Bridget bit her lip as a worried expression ate up her face. She sure hoped so. That was the whole reason she was coming to Alaska! She didn't want the trip to turn into a giant meet-and-greet.

"Princess?" a female voice called from behind.

Bridget let out an exasperated sigh, prepared to see yet

another excited fan. But when she turned around, Becky Henderson was standing there.

"Oh, hello!" Bridget was relieved as she recognized her features from the family's photograph.

Becky took several large strides forward and offered her a hand to shake, "I'm Becky, it's such a pleasure to meet you!"

"You too!" Bridget grinned. "Thank you so much for your hospitality, it was so kind of you to invite me here."

After a few more formalities and running through details with her guard, he was finally ready to release her. "We will miss you, Your Highness. Stay safe."

"Thank you," Bridget smiled, unable to hide the excitement that she felt. For the first time in her *life* she would be out in the real world without a security guard breathing down her neck! She was finally free!

She walked away with Becky, hauling all of her bags and suitcases along with them. A strange feeling washed over her as they navigated their way through the airport. She was completely alone. No guards, no assistants, no family members, no handmaidens.

"It's a good thing I brought the truck," Becky spoke, "I don't think all this stuff would've fit in my little car."

Bridget suddenly felt slightly embarrassed. Had she gone completely overboard with her packing? She couldn't think of anything to say in return, so she just continued walking. It was enough of a struggle to haul everything along without running into people. By the time they reached the parking lot, Bridget was completely out of breath. Bridget glanced at Becky, who lifted her luggage into the forest-green truck without even breaking a sweat. Bridget tried to hide the fact that she was completely wiped out, but once they got in the truck Becky said, "You look exhausted. Long flight?"

"It was a good ten hours," Bridget replied, glancing at herself in the side mirror. She shuddered, thinking she looked like a total mess.

"Well, that's not bad," Becky replied in a perky tone. "It must be nice having a private jet. No layovers or flight changes. That cuts off a huge chunk of travel time."

"Yes, I suppose."

"Are you hungry?" Becky asked. "We can drop through McDonalds and grab you something. I'm in the mood for a McCoffee. It'll help keep me awake on the ride home."

"Um," Bridget had never eaten at McDonalds before. She'd heard her American friends rave about their french fries, "sure, thank you."

"No problem!" Becky slowly backed out of their parking spot, then quickly cut the wheel to get her truck straightened out. She placed it in Drive and joined the traffic parade trying to get out of the airport parking lot.

"I want you to make yourself feel completely at home," Becky said as her truck crawled along. "I know that you've been through a lot lately, and you're in need of a change of pace. Well, Alaska will be just that for you. Life on the ranch is loaded with hard work, but every second is absolutely worth it. I always say that being up here in the middle of such beautiful wildlife, you can't get much closer to God, Himself. It's the perfect place for a retreat. Alaska is like the ultimate getaway. You can unplug from everything."

"Not my blow dryer I hope," Bridget remarked questioningly. "Addison said electricity can be spotty up here, so…"

Becky laughed, "Yes, we have electricity at the ranch. The only time we have power outages are during really bad snowstorms. What I meant by unplugging was shutting off our phones, getting away from the numbingly-fast pace of this world, and stepping outside. Taking a breath. Learning to feel again. This has been so good for our son, Liam. I can't imagine living anywhere else, trying to raise children in this iPhone-obsessed world. Living out here has instilled such a wonderful love for God's creation in Liam. He'll be more than happy to take you out canoeing, or biking, while the weather is still nice."

Bridget remembered seeing photos of the thirteen-year-old boy in her information packet. Becky and Donald only had one child.

"You're in for a real treat!" Becky continued talking, "You'll find there aren't any malls or movie theaters out where we live, but there are so many other enjoyable things that young people find to do for entertainment. Horseback riding, trail hiking, white water rafting…"

Bridget struggled to keep her eyes open as Becky chattered on. She tried to focus on the words being spoken, but her mind kept drifting to another place. She thought of her fluffy bed back home, and the pillows that completely enveloped her everything as she plopped down. Ahh, there was nothing like the feeling of stretching out after a tiring day and…

Bridget's head wobbled slightly in the bouncing truck as she drifted off to sleep.

Bridget rolled over and kept her eyes glued shut. She knew it was morning, but she wasn't ready to leave her bed yet. *I'm going to stay here all morning,* she thought blissfully. *I have absolutely no responsibilities. Then I'm going to go to the spa and–* Bridget's eyes shot open.

The dark, log-walled room was not her familiar Palace bedroom. The reality of the situation shocked her, as she had completely forgotten where she was!

"Alaska," she breathed, trying to steady herself. "This is real."

She was so exhausted last night from her trip, that when Becky gently woke her and said they had arrived, Bridget tumbled inside to bed, too tired to even care what the room looked like.
But now, she was seeing it in the morning light, and the sight was sadly disappointing. There was one small window to her left, with a dingy brown curtain hanging over it. Across from her bed was a painting with a happy family of deer hanging out by a bubbling brook. And to her right there was nothing but her brown, wooden bedroom door. Blech! The entire room in size was smaller than her closet! To be fair, she had a freakishly large walk-in closet. But she was pretty sure that her temporary quarters were smaller than the size of most average people's closets.

Bridget groaned and reached for her cell phone. It was patiently waiting for her on the wooden bed-stand. Her eyes widened as she read the time. 2:03? She had slept in much later than she intended to! *Well, that's rude,* she thought to herself, *the first day at your host family's house and you didn't even show up for breakfast. Or lunch.*

Bridget suddenly realized that she was ravenously hungry and knew the only way to cure that was to get herself out of bed. She reached for the door handle but suddenly stopped herself. She couldn't go out there looking like this. She had no clue where the bathroom was, so she changed into a grey tank, her red and black plaid checked shirt, and black jeans, throwing her tangled mane up into a messy bun.

She quietly made her way down the tiny hallway and into the family room. The house was completely silent. She assumed that everyone was out working. She glanced upward and noticed the giant moose head hanging over the stone fireplace. The lodge-style living room was also extremely dark with stained wood, and Bridget found it rather depressing. She was all about bright colors and flashy lighting; everything this room *wasn't*. This room lacked a feminine touch. Bridget started a mental "to-do" list in her head. The first item on it, was to redecorate her temporary bedroom, then maybe offer a few suggestions for the rest of the house. It was in desperate need of a facelift.

She snooped around the kitchen cabinets, awkwardly opening and closing every door to see what she could find. It felt strange rummaging through the cupboards of a stranger's house. But Becky told her to make herself at home, right?

"Looking for something in particular?" a voice called from behind.

Bridget did a little jump as she twirled around, touching a surprised hand to her chest. She was completely shocked to hear that someone else was in the room! She was even more shocked to see a young, muscular, good looking, man standing there.

"Oh, I'm sorry," he chuckled, "I didn't mean to scare you."

She took a deep breath, "No, I'm fine. I just didn't know anyone else was in here. For a second I thought the moose head was talking to me." She laughed nervously in the presence of the young guy. She noticed his handsome appearance and assumed that he must be one of the ranch workers.

His blue eyes sparkled with a bit of mystery and whimsy as he replied, "I'm Liam. Nice to meet you." He offered a hand in her direction, "It's Bridget, right?"

Bridget thought it was a funny coincidence that he had the same name as Becky's and Donald's son. But what was even more surprising, was the fact that he did not address her as Princess. It was Bridget. Just Bridget.

"Yeah," she smiled slowly as she shook his hand in return, "so, do you work here?"

Liam laughed, "I guess you could say that. My parents run the place."

A puzzled expression plagued Bridget's beautiful face. Wait, was this the son of Becky and Donald? It couldn't be! The photograph that she saw was a scrawny little kid with a face full of zits. This guy was no puny thirteen-year-old! He had to be at least nineteen, if not older.

"Mom and Dad sent me in here to check on you," he explained, "Wanted to make sure that you actually woke up some time before dinner."

"Oh," Bridget's cheeks flushed red, "sorry, I didn't mean to sleep in so late."

"No worries, you had a long trip," his enchanting smile reappeared. "After you eat, I can show you around the ranch. Do you ride?"

Bridget studied his face. He had such a sweet smile, dazzling eyes, and a firm, chiseled jaw. His kind personality seemed just as endearing. Was this what Addison had in mind for her when he shipped her up North? Did he know that this ruggedly handsome wilderness guide was waiting to show her around the land, take her horseback riding, and attempt to steal her heart? She frowned as she grew angry with the whole situation. Liam seemed so sure of himself. So confident that she would sigh and say, "Yes, I'd love to go riding with you." But if Liam thought that's how this story was going to go, he was in for a surprise ending. There was no way that she would let this guy get anywhere near her heart. He carried the same deceptive façade that all the other guys did. Knee-melting smiles on the outside, but inside they were ravenous wolves. She had seen it all before, and there was no way she was going to fall for it again.

"Actually I–" she started to refuse his offer, when another voice entered the room.

"Afternoon!" Becky called from where she had walked in the back sliding screen door. "How did you sleep?"

"Just fine, thanks." she quickly replied.

"I see you've met our son, Liam," Becky spoke. "Have you had breakfast yet? I suggested that he take you on a horseback ride. That way you can see the property, explore some of the trails, and get your first real glimpse of everything that Alaska has to offer! Sound good?"

Oh great. She couldn't refuse now. Becky was expecting her to go with him. "Sure," Bridget clenched her teeth as she spoke, "why not."

Before long, she was seated in a western saddle atop a horse named Appalo. Liam and his horse, Bruce, were blazing ahead on the trail. Liam glanced over his shoulder to make sure Bridget and Appalo were keeping up. Bruce's gait was set at a steady trot, but his strides were much bigger than Appalo's. "It looks like you've done a lot of riding?" Liam asked. He noticed how comfortable Bridget appeared to be.

"Yeah, we were all raised on horses." Bridget's tone wasn't very friendly. Her brisk reply gave Liam the hint that she wasn't in a particularly chatty mood at the moment. He didn't mind. The familiar yet spectacular scene was far too beautiful to spoil with forced conversation. He was content to soak in the glorious views that surrounded them, in silence.

Bridget couldn't believe how breath-taking Alaska's beauty was. The thick, luscious pine trees were a vibrant shade of green that Bridget hadn't known even existed. The pristine air was clear, and it made every breath smell like nature's sweet candy. The winding trail zig-zagged toward a sparkly lake. A gentle breeze stirred her hair.

Bridget took another deep breath, and could feel herself relaxing even more. Ms. Becky was right. This would be the *perfect* place to unplug and unwind. A majestic bird call was heard, followed by an osprey swooping over the lake. Bridget was tempted to pull out her iPhone and snap a picture, but somehow she felt it would ruin the moment.

Several feet down the trail another woodland creature made its grand appearance. "Oh, my goodness, a moose!" Bridget gasped, shocked at how big it was. The ginormous creature lifted its head from where it took a drink in the lake, and turned to look at them.

"*Shh, shhh,*" Liam quickly hushed her, as he halted his horse to a stop. Bridget stopped also. The moose continued to stare at them, until finally he decided that it was okay for them to be there. He turned back to the water and continued his afternoon drink.

Liam made a clicking noise with his tongue, giving Bruce permission to start moving again. When he did, the Moose made a fearful dash for the woods.

"Wow!" Bridget breathed, watching the big furry creature run away. "Look at the size of his antlers! Do they ever attack?"

"Only if they feel threatened," Liam replied.

"I can't believe we've only been out here twenty minutes, and I'm already completely at a loss for words. This is beyond magnificent."

Liam smiled. "Yeah, Alaska has a charming way of pulling out all the stops for its visitors. Just wait until you see it from the canoe. It'll give you a whole 'nother perspective."

"We're going canoeing?" she asked.

"I mean, if you want to," Liam said. "There's a nice place to launch out, about fifteen minutes from here. We usually park our horses there and enter the mouth of the river. Looks like it'll be a pretty gentle ride. No big rapids today. Are you up for it?"

Bridget shrugged, "Sure."

Half an hour ago she would have turned him down. But something about being out here beneath the clear blue sky, with so many amazing creatures and sights to be seen, made her want to explore what was around the next river bend. *Besides*, she thought, *what else am I going to do? Sit in the dark in my tiny room and attempt to connect to their spotty Wi-Fi? As long as I'm here, I might as well get the whole Alaskan experience.*

Fifteen minutes later they dismounted their horses, tied them to a post, and Liam lifted a large green canoe out of a shed. The launching area was nice, with a picnic table and a fire pit.

"Is this part of your property as well?" Bridget asked, assuming that they had built the shed.

"Yup!" Liam replied as he neared the water with the canoe lifted atop his head. He lowered it onto the shore. Then, he walked back toward Bruce, reached into his saddle bag and pulled out a package of Pringles, Oreos, pretzels, and gummy worms.

Bridget raised a suspicious eyebrow. Was this turning into a picnic? Was he thinking he was going to impress her by providing all this improv food? Did he want her to think that he was witty and charming? If he was trying to make her think those things, it certainly wasn't working. In fact, she felt like he was trying *way* too hard to impress her. She chose not to say anything as they crawled into the canoe. He gave her a quick paddling lesson, and then they were off.

Bridget relished the moments of peace and tranquility. After several minutes of paddling in silence and soaking up the view, Liam finally spoke. "So what's the scenery like in Tarsurella? Are you ever able to get out and explore like this?"

Bridget laughed, "Not so much. Just the size of my Security Team alone would scare away any wildlife."

"This will probably be a huge adjustment for you, huh? I don't know much about life in a monarchy, but I get the feeling that your time here will be like a classic fish-out-of-water tale."

"I haven't been *that* far removed from reality, you know." Bridget took offence at his comment, "Just because I grew up in a palace doesn't mean I don't know how to row, or ride, or work hard and get dirt under my nails."

Liam laughed.

"Why are you laughing?" Bridget could feel herself growing upset with him.

"I'm sorry," he couldn't hide the smirk in his smile, "but from what I've read about you, it's hard to imagine the girl who spends her days in The Royal Spa, fitting in around here. It's like you've been living in some kind of fairy tale world. With maids and cooks and butlers and a walk in closet and your own private jet, it's just comical to imagine you with dirt under your nails."

Bridget's face grew angry. First he wanted to impress her, and now he wanted to attack her character?! "You don't know anything about me," Bridget snapped. "All you know is what you read in magazines and yet you make these snap judgements about how superficial and spoiled I am! You have no right to talk to me like this, because you have no idea what I've been through."

Liam was surprised. He stopped paddling. He had been completely unaware of the fact that his playful teasing would step on such a sore spot in her soul. "Wow, I'm so sorry," Liam's voice softened as he genuinely apologized, "I had no intention of offending or hurting you with my words. I should've been more sensitive to the place you must be in emotionally. I know that you've been through a lot, especially these past few weeks."

Bridget scooted awkwardly in the canoe. His apology was so sweet and heartfelt. Now she felt like a monster for ripping his head off like that. "I'm sorry, too," she replied quietly, "I shouldn't have snapped at you. I'm sure you didn't mean to make me mad on purpose. It's just," Bridget could feel tears forming in her eyes as her throat tightened up. *Don't do it!* she scolded herself. *You can't cry in front of him, he'll think you're a total baby.* "It's been hard."

Liam nodded understandingly. "My mom always tells me that hurt people, hurt people. And I think sometimes the level to which we are offended or jump on other people's backs, can be a really good mirror of where our own heart is at." He reached to open up the bag of pretzels. "Pain can make us do crazy things sometimes."

Bridget remembered the way that she exploded on Addison when he told her about his interest in Vanessa, and also about what Asher had done. A deep remorse settled over her as she suddenly realized what a pathetic state her heart was in. She could still feel the knives of betrayal from those she loved most, lodged into her soul. Her heart was bleeding, and she didn't know how to stop it. The best way she knew to avoid the pain was by becoming numb to it. But in the process of numbing herself, she had become insensitive to the feelings of those around her as well.

Liam threw a few pretzels into the water. Bridget looked at her quizzically, so Liam explained, "The ducks love them."

Bridget looked at a floating pretzel which quickly grew soggy. Then she turned her gaze toward the horizon. The river was as still as glass, and appeared to go on for a never-ending stretch of eternity. "How long is this river?" she asked, changing the subject.

"Twenty-seven miles."

Several ducks flew in overhead, making their adorable little quacking sounds as they announced their landing, and shouting to their friends, "Free food!"

"So, what do you do for fun around here?" Bridget asked, curious to know more about Liam. "I mean, besides working on the ranch and doing things outdoors? Where do you hang out with your friends? What's around here? Shopping, bowling, laser tag?"

Liam laughed. "We have a Wal-Mart twenty minutes from here. But that's not exactly the ideal hangout place. If you want to do anything like that, you have to head back to Anchorage. For me, my life pretty much revolves around being outdoors. Campfires, capture the flag, trail riding, four-wheelers."

Bridget couldn't hide the surprise on her face. "Okay, but what about your social life? Like, where do you go to meet people and hang out?"

"My parents host a Bible study home group that meets in our house every Sunday and Wednesday night. Most of my friends come to that."

"So, do you hang out with other people at school?" Bridget asked.

"Actually, I was homeschooled, and I'm not attending college right now," Liam smiled as he answered.

Bridget crossed her arms. "I'm starting to think that you're just as unbelievably sheltered as I am."

Liam laughed, "So maybe we have more in common than you thought we did."

"Actually, I'm getting a little bit claustrophobic. Here I thought I was coming to a big beautiful place where nobody would know my name or care about my status. A place where I could just walk into the store, or mingle at a coffee shop with some amazing people. But it turns out I've actually come to a place where there are *no* people!" Bridget felt like her wide and spacious dream of life in Alaska was starting to close in on her. It was just as tiny, constricting, and trapping as her new bedroom.

Liam laughed again, "Why is that such a big deal to you? Socializing, getting out, meeting new people?"

"Liam, I'm a nineteen-year-old girl! The desire to socialize pumps through my blood! *I* am the reason that they developed texting!"

"You're a Christian, right?" Liam questioned. "Your desire for man's approval and acceptance doesn't need to be a driving force in your life. Your relationship with God and intimacy with Him can be enough to fill you up and satisfy that desire, no matter where you are in the world."

"Oh my gosh," Bridget felt like jumping out of the boat. Why was this guy always trying to dig deep and unravel the secrets of her heart? "You're acting like you think you're my therapist or something! Where is this stuff coming from?"

"The Bible says your conversation should be seasoned with salt," Liam replied. "So as long as we're just going to sit here and watch the ducks eat pretzels, we might as well talk about something worth-while, right?"

Bridget flinched. Hadn't she *just* been complaining about how shallow all of her conversation was getting back at home? But why was he wanting to go so deep, so fast? There's no way she would trust him. She wasn't going to unlock the chains on the door of her heart, and give him a peek at what was happening inside. He didn't need to know that she was bleeding. He didn't need to know that she was afraid and broken, and terrified to ever trust anyone ever again. He didn't need to know how angry she was with Asher, and maybe even with God, for allowing all of this to happen. Yet, as much as she wanted to keep her poker face on, she had the strangest feeling that somehow he already knew.

"Alright then," her eyes intensified as she fixed her gaze on him, "tell me something interesting and salt-worthy. Since you seem to know so much about me, I think it's only fair that I get the same info about you. Who are you? What's your frame of reference for offering me all of this life advice?"

Liam smiled. "I thought you'd never ask." His smiled disappeared as he returned to a dark and painful memory, "When I was six, after watching my step-dad beat up my birth mom, I was placed into foster care. I lived in Washington State for a few years, bouncing around from home to home, until I was thirteen. I was placed in the custody of a juvenile detention center, after taking a baseball bat to my step-dad's car. I was really close to taking it to his head, before the cops came."

Bridget lifted a shocked hand up to her face. What in the *world?* She couldn't even imagine.

"Thankfully, my patrol officer called Donald and Becky who lived in Washington at the time, and were toying with the idea of moving to Alaska. Donald had an amazing track record of working with troubled teens, and he prayed about inviting me into their home. God told him yes. And I know it was God because it would've been insane otherwise; I was such a punk. They introduced me to Jesus and forced me to go to church, but I didn't want anything to do with it. I was still hanging out with the wrong crowd of friends, and so messed up in my head. I still hated my step-dad's guts, and swore that if I ever had the chance, I would kill him.

"Donald and Becky weren't seeing any positive changes, so

they decided that I needed a little bit more drastic life-change. We all moved up to Alaska, and I was miserable. Until one day, I was out here on this river, and I had an encounter that changed me forever. God spoke to my heart and crashed over me with His unbelievable love and peace. I had never experienced anything like it before, and I just lost it. I never wept so much in my life. It was like, all of these toxic emotions and fears and hurts came pouring out of me, and God filled me up with His liquid love. I've never been the same since that day, and I can't help but be completely in awe of Him. I would apologize for being passionate, but I can't. I'm not ashamed of who I am, nor of seeing the pain in your eyes and wanting to help you heal. Bridget, God's brought you here for an amazing purpose. He wants to do a miracle in your heart, and set you free from all the chains that have been tied to your soul."

"Thank you," Bridget whispered, trying to fight back the tears, "thank you for sharing that." Her voice returned to its normal volume, "It means a lot to me to hear that. I would've never thought that you had such a wild past. Honestly, hearing your story gives me hope for my brother, Asher. He, um…"

Bridget sucked in a deep breath of air, but it still didn't stop the tears.

"He betrayed us."

Bridget quickly brushed the tears away and tried to recompose herself, "I don't know how he got in such a bad place, but it's so scary. I'm worried sick about him. The Security Team worked so hard to discover how the terrorists got into The Palace, and it turns out that Asher is completely responsible. You just never expect that the people you love the most, would turn and hurt you the most."

"Kinda feels like a knife straight through your heart, doesn't it?"

Bridget's lip quivered. How could he *know* this? How did he know exactly how she was feeling?
"It wasn't just him, though," she continued. "I had, um, a really close friend who did the same thing. Actually, I was completely in love with him. I trusted him with everything. My heart, my future… and he took advantage of it."

"Have you been able to forgive them?" Liam asked.

Bridget shrugged, "I don't know. I mean, a thing like that is nearly unforgiveable."

"I hated my step-dad for *so* many years," Liam said. "After everything he had done to me and my mom, I never thought I'd be able to forgive him. But then Jesus came along. And that changed everything. He told me that my sins were just as unforgiveable as my step-dad's were. That in my heart, I was just as evil and wicked as he was. And guess what? Jesus chose to forgive me anyway. Then I came to a verse in Matthew that says, if I don't forgive the people who have hurt me, then God won't forgive my sins either. All of a sudden, I realized that harboring un-forgiveness and hatred in my heart toward my step-dad wasn't hurting him, but it was killing me. I was consumed with this bitter poison, and God wanted to remove it from my heart. Here I thought that my step-dad had stabbed me with this awful knife, but I was the one who continued to hold it there. God wanted to remove it and heal the wound."

"But is forgiving him really going to change anything?" Bridget asked. "I mean, it won't go back in time and change what happened."

"It might not change what happened," Liam replied, "but it

can change what happened in *your* heart. Do you really want to keep walking around through life with a forced smile on your face, while you continue to bleed to death on the inside?"

"I want to forgive him," Bridget sighed, "I really do. But then, how am I ever going to trust him again? Do you trust your step-dad?"

"I can honestly say that I love my step-dad. I pray for him, and I want the best for him. But would I trust him with a woman that I loved, or with my kids? No way. But that doesn't mean that I don't trust other Godly men. There was a time in my life when I didn't just hate my step-dad, I hated any male figure in authority. But Donald, my new dad, helped me to learn to trust again. He showed me what the heart of our Heavenly Father looks like, and that He would never hurt or abuse me. He only wants the absolute best for me, and He does for you too. When Asher, your brother, and these other guys from your past hurt you, it didn't just affect the way that you feel about them, it changed the way that you feel about everyone, am I right? You used to trust people with a naïve, childlike innocence, but now you've built up these protective, massively huge walls to keep everybody out. Forgiveness isn't just going to change the way you view what happened. It's so much deeper than that. It's gonna change the way that you see God, His heart for you, and the people around you. It's going to release those knives, and help you to see clearly again. You'll learn how to trust again. You'll even learn how to love again."

Bridget could feel her heart melting as he spoke. Liam was like a messenger sent from Heaven. She knew that he was absolutely right. God *did* have a purpose in sending her here. And it wasn't to party and socialize. It was to have her heart healed and her skewed vision restored. Ever since Jacob had betrayed her, things just hadn't been the same inside. But she never realized how terribly off everything was, until right now.

"I want to," she could feel the tears again, "I really, really want to. But I'm so afraid. I'm not even sure if I can trust God right now, let alone anyone else."

"Bridget, you were created for love," Liam spoke, tapping into the heart of their Heavenly Father and bringing down words straight from Him, "God created you for a spectacular purpose: to live and abide in His love, to bask in the affection that He has for you, then to pour out that love for others. You are perfect in His sight. He adores you, and would never want to harm you. But we live in a fallen world, and people are going to be evil, and offences are going to come. But that doesn't change God's heart or character. The fact that terrorists infiltrated the walls of The Palace, and cruddy guys jumped over the walls of your heart, doesn't mean that God ever changed the way that He feels about you. Not even for one second! Nobody had to teach you how to love. But someone taught you how to be afraid. God wants to restore you and bring you back to that place of carefree fearlessness again. You're His daughter, Bridget. He created your heart, and He is more than able to heal it."

Chapter 28 – Wisdom

Hope tried to distract herself with a magazine, but her eyes kept drifting to the clock. Earlier today she asked the front desk what time David and his parents would be arriving. She was told that their ETA was 4:00. Her leg bounced nervously from where she lounged on her bed, propped up with pillows. If the front desk was right, David and his family would be here by now. It was 4:05.

Hope closed her magazine and considered wandering downstairs to see if he just *happened* to still be checking in. It wouldn't be strange if she ran into him casually like that, would it?

She decided to leave the comforts of her bed and venture downstairs. Before exiting her room, she glanced in the mirror, quickly doing a hair check. As she floated down the staircase she felt giddy as she thought about what it would be like to see him again.

When she landed at the bottom, she was disappointed to find no one at the front desk. David was nowhere to be seen. She snatched one of the mints from the desk, unwrapped it and popped it in her mouth. She placed her hands on her hips and sighed. What should she do now? Wait for him to come downstairs? Frequent some of the most popular tourist areas such as the pool, the tennis courts, and the riding stables? No, that would just be freaky and stalker-ish.

She could call his room and make an appointment of some sort to see him. No, that would be way too forward. Perhaps her only option was to wait until tomorrow evening during the banquet. She suddenly felt a wave of anxiousness crash over her. She needed to find someone else to talk to and occupy her thoughts.

She turned on her heel and quickly ascended the stairs again. She knocked on the door of her sisters' suite, and Darcy's friendly bark was heard inside.

The door opened, and Chasity stood in front of Hope. "Hey!" she grinned, "What's up?"

"Oh, nothing much," she tried to act chill about it as she stepped inside and petted Darcy on the head, "just came to see what you girls are up to."

"Ugh, you're not missing anything too exciting," Jillian spoke from where she stood in their mini-living room, "Just trying to decide what to wear to the banquet tomorrow night. It's too bad sneakers and jeans are against the dress code."

Hope laughed as she saw the pile of clothes tossed all over the couch. "Oh yes, I can see that you are in serious need of my expertise!"

Fifteen minutes later the decision about what Jillian was going to wear was finally made. "Thanks," Jillian let out a sigh of relief, "now that we've gotten that annoying little detail out of the way, I can finally relax. How does popcorn sound?" Jillian headed toward their kitchenette before waiting for a response from her sisters.

"I'll pass," Hope said.

"Popcorn sounds perfect," Chasity answered, "and I'm sure Lance wants some too."

All the girls looked at Lance who stood in the corner by the window-seat. Hope laughed, "Goodness, you're so quiet, I totally forgot that you're in here!"

Lance gave a simple thumbs up.

"You feed your security guy snacks?" Hope laughed.

"Yep, we've gotta keep 'em happy!" Chasity laughed. "That's a long time to go without food. We don't want 'em to get hangry!"

Hope noticed that there was only one guard on duty, but she didn't find it particularly unusual. "So, are you guys excited about tomorrow night?" Hope asked, carefully easing her way into the conversation.

"Of course!" Jillian gushed, "I might be acting like a total fangirl, but I won't lie about the fact that I'm excited to see David Carter again!" She giggled.

"What about you?" Chasity asked, "Are you excited?"

"Um," Hope struggled with what to say, "No? I mean, kind of? But not too excited. I mean it's just another banquet right? It should be, um...You know, I should probably go figure out what I'm gonna wear. Time's getting short!" Hope made a beeline for the door. "See you girls at dinner!"

They chorused their "See ya later," and Hope closed the door behind her. She took a deep breath, as dozens of thoughts raced across her mind all at once. She needed to talk to someone. She had to get this whole jumbled mess figured out. What was going on? Was she actually in love with David? Or was it just a silly crush? Should she tell her sisters? Should she tell him? Should she force herself to get over it? The tension in her mind was nearly unbearable. She started pacing down the hall.

Who should I talk to? she asked herself. *Bridget, the girl with all the answers, has terrible cell service. Addison is swamped with Royal responsibilities. Dad is still working frantically to help Addison get caught up on it all. My handmaidens are still on leave from The Palace. Who can I trust?*

A face suddenly popped into her head.

Clark. Someone she could trust with her life! She imagined him lounging by the pool with his family, soaking up the rays of sunshine of his glorious vacation. No, she couldn't bother him. Besides, it would be extremely improper to discuss matters like this with a staff member.

She sighed, resigning to the fact that she would just have to figure this out on her own. She returned to her room, and noticed that the old phone mounted on the wall was flashing with messages. She had lots of friends that were trying to get in touch with her. But she didn't feel like talking to any of them. She reluctantly placed the phone up to her ear, and clicked the first message.

"Afternoon, Your Highness," the recorded message from the front desk spoke, "here are your messages. Dial one to hear Bonsent Ranaldo, requesting to speak with you. Dial two, Kristina Cash, asking about you attending a fundraiser dinner. Dial three, Kitty Kittredge, asking about Princess Bridget. Dial four, Stefan requesting a wardrobe fitting. Dial five, Head Cook Clark requesting–" Hope didn't allow the machine to finish. She quickly pressed number five to hear the recorded message from Clark.

"Good afternoon, Princess," Clark's deep voice spoke, "It's about 3:10 and I have a request for you. Please don't feel pressured to do this, I just thought that it would be a nice opportunity for you to meet my family. We will be meandering around the gardens this afternoon, so if you care to join us for a few moments, that would be great. If not, I completely understand. Have a great rest of your day."

Hope hung up and smiled. Perhaps the opportunity for her to speak with him was opening up after all!

She ventured out to the gardens, keeping her eyes peeled for signs of Clark. She walked around for a while, then sat on a bench. They had probably left already.

Hope sighed, feeling like she'd been running around in anxious circles all day long. She closed her eyes and tried to settle her heart.

Lord, I am so sorry. I feel like a nervous dog chasing its tail. I'm getting nowhere. I have all these worries floating around in my mind, and I haven't even stopped to talk to You about it! You have been so faithful to take care of me my whole life long. If I can trust You with my safety and protection, surely I can trust You with the matters of my heart. Lord, I think I might truly be in love with David Carter. But the most devastating truth is that I cannot be! I know that now isn't the time in my life where I should be focused on relationships and romance, but David has awakened feelings inside of my soul that I didn't even know I had. What should I do? Please send me some guidance, Lord! Make the path straight before me. Show me what to do.

"Amen," she whispered. Her eyes fluttered open. She decided just to sit and listen for a few moments. A gentle breeze rustled through the trees, and some cheery birds sang a happy tune.
She cocked her head slightly as she peered up the trail. There was a figure walking toward her. Or was it two? They were holding hands. As they neared, Hope recognized them as Clark and his never-before-seen wife.

"Clark!" she smiled as she stood up. "Lovely day for a walk, isn't it?"

"Ah, good afternoon, Your Highness," Clark grinned.

"I just heard your message a few minutes ago," she quickly spoke. "Sorry I didn't get here sooner."

"Oh no, this is wonderful," he smiled. "I want you to meet my wife and the love of my life, Elizabeth."

"How do you do, Your Highness?" The kind-looking brunette woman curtsied.

"It's a pleasure to meet you! Thank you," Hope replied before turning to Clark. "Where's the rest of your family?"

"My son just ran off to play putt-putt golf with some of the other kids," Clark replied, "I'm sorry he isn't here, but maybe he'll have an opportunity to meet you at the banquet."

"Yes, that would be wonderful," Hope spoke halfheartedly, her mind already on another matter. "Um, what I'm about to ask is a little bit informal. But, uh, do you mind if I speak to you about something?"

Clark's eyebrows shot up. "Why of course not, Princess."

"Do you need me to leave?" Elizabeth asked politely

"Oh no!" Hope reassured her, "You can stay. In fact, it might be helpful to have a woman's perspective on this. I um, I need some advice."

Clark still looked confused, but he slowly sat down on the bench beside Hope, and Elizabeth joined him.

"I'm sorry," Hope quickly apologized, "I know this might seem a little bit awkward and unprofessional, but today I was asking myself who I trust the most. Like, who do I know is always going to be there for me and always have my best interest in mind? Who is most likely to make me smile on a bad day, and has proven that they'll risk *everything* just to protect me and my family? I know that serving the Crown is part of your job, but I have this feeling deep down that even if you didn't work for us, and you were just some random guy I met out on the street," Hope laughed, "that you would still care. Your kindness and compassion is so evident, Clark, and I just want you to know that I appreciate that."

Elizabeth had tears welling up in her eyes. It made her heart soar to hear her husband being praised for his golden heart. She, out of anyone, knew just how loyal, loving, and upright her husband was.

"Well, thank you," Clark nodded. "I feel very unworthy of the words that you've attached to my name, but I do appreciate you going the extra mile just to tell me all of this. You're a very special woman, Princess Hope, and much like your name, you do give me *hope* that the unfading qualities of virtue, purity, and kindness will still be found in this next generation."

Hope's smile grew bigger, "Thank you. As you both very well know, my mother died several years ago. There are so many things that I wish to ask her, but cannot. And my Father, well he's still extremely busy trying to help Addison set things in order for the big shift coming in January. And I guess I'm just in need of some parental guidance." She looked at Elizabeth, already trusting her and having no clue why, "So, would you two mind standing-in as parents for a moment? I've got a problem and I could really use some sound advice on what to do."

Elizabeth squeezed her hand, "Absolutely, honey. We're all ears."

♛

As Addison straightened his tie, he felt a sudden lurch of

anxiety. Another big event was only moments away, and the thought of it made him feel uneasy. Was it unwise to plan another banquet so soon after the disasters that broke out at the last one?

He shook his head and chose to regain control over his thoughts. *No,* he told himself, *it's not going to be like this. I'm trusting God. I can't control what happens, but He can. I'm going to trust in His peace and believe that everything is going to work out exactly like it's supposed to. God, I give You my worries and anxiety. Help me to have Your perspective and believe that everything is perfectly fine when I surrender it into Your hands.*

Addison sighed, suddenly feeling better. Everything would be more than okay. He wouldn't allow trauma of the past to dictate the hope of his future. Tonight they were celebrating all of the good that had come out of that terribly ugly situation. They would rejoice in the beauty that was found in the midst of ashes; the hearts that bravely stood and fought. Yes, God's hand was clearly upon them. Even though they couldn't see it while everything was happening, God was still present and working in their midst. They had much to celebrate tonight! God's goodness hadn't failed them, and it never would. He could fully trust and allow his heart to be at peace.

Addison smiled as he thought of Vanessa. She had returned to the United State once again. He wanted to ask her to stay for the banquet, but knew it wasn't quite the right thing to do. She needed to return home to pack and prepare for the huge life change that was coming her way. In January she would be back here, for good. Addison had decided to hire her. He was solidly pleased with the decision. In fact, he was more than pleased. He was nearly to the point of a little bit giddy and absent-minded!

In His eyes, Vanessa was an absolute gem. Not only would the entire Kingdom benefit from her energetic presence in the boardroom and her passion on the streets, but he felt that having Vanessa here would make him a better King. And a better man. Vanessa had opened up a deep chamber inside of Addison's heart that unleashed a whole new world of possibilities. She made him believe that anything was possible. Her infectious energy, unbridled passion, kind heart, and spunky passion were all qualities that Addison couldn't get out of his head. Vanessa was a treasure that he wanted to pursue. And perhaps, if she felt the same way about him, the two could someday join together in joy and unity, to change their Kingdom in ways that nobody had ever dreamed of before.

It was an electrifying thought. Could Vanessa be his wife someday? If it could possibly be true, or even if it was just a fantasy, it was still enough to launch Addison out of bed every morning and get him moving with a vigorous hope and expectation for the future!

A knock was heard on Addison's door, followed by its opening. A head popped in. "May I come in?"

"Hey Dad," Addison smiled, "sure thing. I was just getting ready to head downstairs."

"Addison, I wish to speak with you for a few moments. Things have been wildly busy these past few weeks, but I've been wanting to share something that's been on my heart for quite some time now."

Addison could tell by the expression on his face that this discussion might take a few moments. Addison motioned toward the couch in his room, and they sat down together.

The proud father placed a steady hand on his son's arm, "Addison," he choked up, as misty tears fogged his eyes, "you have made me a proud, proud man. Ever since you were a young boy, it has been my heart's cry that God would grant me the wisdom to raise you in such a way that would honor the Lord, bestow love on your family, and bless this nation. When you became King, I had full confidence in the fact that God has equipped you for such a time as this. And indeed, He did. You have had to walk through something that no leader would ever want to endure. Not only was your nation targeted and terrorized, but your very family was shaken to the core. And yet, through it all, you remained faithful. Your relationship with the Lord has grown and strengthened, and you've emerged from this fire as a man of integrity, purity, faith and honor. Like Shadrach, Meshach, and Abednego, you walked through the fires of hell, and were not burned. There is not even the smell of smoke on your jacket! I couldn't possibly be more proud of you, son."

Addison couldn't hold back the evidence of his emotion. His father's words were supposed to be a joyful blessing, but they felt like a heavy weight, for he felt he did not deserve the glory of them.

"But Dad," Addison choked, "I'm not the man you think I am. The terrorist invasion shook me to the very core. It caused me to question my faith, and everything that I believe in. I wasn't strong and unshakable. The fires completely consumed me. Now I feel even more inadequate to rule Tarsurella than I did before. All I've ever wanted is for you to

[421]

be proud of me. But I can't be you, Dad. I just can't."

"Oh Addison," he replied compassionately, "I would never want you to be me. And no one is expecting you to be, except yourself! You have placed so many unnecessary burdens on your shoulders that I would never want for you to carry. Jesus said that His yolk is easy and His burden is light. He wants to carry the lion's-share of your cares and responsibilities. Your job is to merely obey His leading, and trust in the fact that He will take care of everything. Can't you see, my dear son? The flames didn't destroy you. They simply removed everything that was impure and unfitting in your life. It burned away the fear, the distrust, and the desire to have control. Now you stand on the other side, feeling stripped of everything you once were. But that is good! Now the Potter can begin again with your heart. He can mold and shape you into everything that He desires for you to be. Even though He is not yet finished with you, or any of us, I know that just like me, He is a proud, proud Father. Let the weight go, Addison. Your Heavenly Father loves you, and so do I. You don't have to prove anything to anybody. You are a fine King and a Godly man. But more than that, you are my son."

Addison allowed the words to crash over his soul like a rainstorm of healing floodwaters. He embraced his father, and the reality of those words sunk in deeper. He basked in the simple truth that his father loved him. He didn't have to earn anything, or prove anything. His dad was already proud of him. What more could he want?

Addison smiled as the hug ended, "Well, as long as we're taking this time to be super sappy and emotional," he chuckled, "I have something to tell you. With your permission, honor, and blessing, Dad, I believe I may have found the woman I want to pursue."

Chapter 29 – The Choice

David Carter entered the banquet room, accompanied by his Mother. His palms were still sweaty. Even after becoming a "National Hero," some things never changed. Like his nerves.

David's eyes darted around the room, searching for any sight of Hope. His past twenty-four hours of being at The Palace, yet not being able to see the Princess, had been rather torturous. It was like standing in the midst of a mouth-watering candy store, while being forbidden to taste any of it. Finally, his invisible restraints had been lifted. He would be free to talk to Hope and express the things that he had been longing to say for weeks. Maybe. That is, if they ever had the opportunity to talk alone. At public events like this, a time for chatting privately might not show itself. But David sincerely wished that it would.

"Oh my," Mrs. Carter gasped as she soaked in the stunning scenery, "just look at that chandelier. It must have cost a fortune!"

David nodded, but didn't bother to look up. He was scanning the long table, searching the faces that were already seated. He saw military personnel and their wives, and random children scattered about, but there was no sign of any of the Royals. He saw Clark approaching them with his wife. They all exchanged greetings, and his mom enjoyed speaking with the Head Cook and his wife. David tried to stay focused on their conversation, but his eyes continued to drift.

A few moments later, he saw her.

Hope entered the room wearing an evening gown that put the

fancy chandelier to shame. The glistening dress sparkled, but Hope's face shone far brighter.

At that moment, David had trouble hiding a smile of his own. He was positive he had never seen anyone so beautiful in his life. She smiled kindly as she greeted the guests that flocked about her. She absolutely glowed amidst the people and the soft lighting. David mentally prepared himself to approach her. But much too soon, the Master of Ceremonies called the room to attention.

"Good evening," the important-looking man welcomed the small crowd. David was relieved to find that it was a relatively intimate gathering. It was nothing like the massive gala that The Ball was. Sure, everything was stunning and regal, but it seemed a little bit on the DL with the pomp and circumstance. "On behalf of King Addison of Tarsurella, I would like to welcome you all. The King is thrilled to host this party in honor of the men and women who deserve recognition, glory, and every expression of heartfelt thanksgiving we can bestow upon them. Men and women who have encouraged and inspired us all. King Addison believes that by the end of the evening, you will feel the same way about these special guests as He does. They are truly heroes among us. Please take your seats, then we will welcome King Addison to the table, which will be followed by the National Anthem."

David sat in his designated chair. His assigned seat at the banquet table was next to his Mom, Clark, and Clark's son. He watched as Hope and her sisters gathered at another table, just a few yards away from them.

After the King entered, they all rose to sing the National

Anthem, Addison shared a few words, prayed over the food, and the first course was revealed on silver platters.

Hope noted David's presence. He was just as handsome as always, dressed to the hilt in his fancy black suit and tie ensemble. She took a deep breath as she lifted her spoon full of onion soup, and released a small blow. After talking with Clark and Elizabeth, she finally knew what she must do. Now would be perhaps the most difficult part—waiting until after dinner was finished.

Seven courses later, they were all stuffed. "That was pretty good!" Millie announced after finishing her dessert, "But I could tell that Clark didn't make it. Everything he does is so much yummier!"

Hope laughed. "True. But don't you think Clark deserved a vacation today?"

"Ooh yes!" Millie said, "But if I was the one throwing the party for him, it would be totally different! We would have a big, blow-up bounce house in the foyer, and we'd blow bubbles, and roller-skate *inside*. Then we'd have a huge white wall where we could make a painting for Clark, and use whatever colors we want to! Then we could drain the pool and pour Jell-O in there, and swim around in it!"

"Oh my," Jillian laughed, even though, in her opinion, her little sister was being completely immature. How could she not love the little nut? "Maybe we should ask Addison to put you on the event planning committee! Our parties would be crazy!"

As the volume of conversation and laughter rose in The

Royal Dining Room, The Master of Ceremonies stood up again to get everyone's attention. "Now that we are all finished with this fabulous meal, I ask that we begin to congregate in The Ball Room. There, King Addison will present our honored guests with his prepared speech, gifts, and for those whom have been chosen ahead of time, the Royal Crest. As you all know, the Royal Crest is the highest honor that can be given in Tarsurella! This is a very exciting and momentous event. But please, no flash photography or selfie sticks, thank you."

"What's a selfie stick?" Millie asked.

Hope laughed again, as she began to gather her dress and push herself away from the table, "I'm so thrilled that you don't know what that is." She touched Millie's cheek, "Stay eight forever, okay? And keep on having the time of your life."

Mille shrugged, "Okey-doke!"

Hope smiled as she stood up, relieved to see that Millie was readjusting into Palace life so nicely. The first few days after they had returned home, Hope was worried about her. Millie would not leave her side, and insisted that she never be alone. But now, her childlike faith and carefree personality was rekindled, and Hope was confident that it wouldn't be long until Millie was back to her same old, fearless little self.

Hope headed with the crowd out of The Royal Dining Room. Once in the hallway, several guests were vying for her attention. She stopped to kindly chat with each of them. Millie had grown tired of waiting for her, and had skipped on ahead into The Ball Room. Hope bid her guests goodbye and went to catch up with Millie. Hope felt a gentle touch on her arm, and she slowly turned around.

"Princess?" the voice asked.

"David!" Hope breathed happily, "It's so good to see you again!"

"You too," he tried not to blush, but it wasn't working. He was never any good at hiding his feelings. "You look, uh, absolutely beautiful."

"Oh my goodness, thank you!" It was Hope's turn to blush. "So do you! I mean, uh. You look nice. I mean…you know what I mean." She laughed nervously.

"I've been wanting to talk to you," David said quickly. "I didn't really get to say everything I–"

"David, we need you backstage!" one of the Palace workers told him. "We're about to start!"

Hope frowned. Sometimes she really hated time and the limits it placed on one's life. She felt like Cinderella, always getting cut off by that silly clock.

"I wish to speak to you, too," she replied quickly, "so meet me out on the Garden Terrace, after the ceremony. It's right outside of the East Ball Room, past the wishing well fountain. You can't miss it."

"Got it," he grinned. "See you soon."

Chasity applauded and cheered with the crowd as Addison placed an icy blue sash on each of the men lined up at the front. The sashes were embroidered with the Royal Crest. Chasity had never seen the Royal Crest given to anyone before. It was a spectacular thing to see so many deserving souls receiving it all at once. Addison had just finished speaking about why he was giving it to each person, and it caused Chasity's heart swell with joy.

David the popstar, Clark the cook, John the construction worker, Anthony the military man, and so many others, had all played a pivotal role in defending, rescuing, and winning back their beloved Palace. They had so much to be thankful for! As Addison had put it, "Everyday heroes were among them," and it was a blessing to be able to recognize them in this way.

Next, Addison asked for the Security Team members who had been on duty the night of the attack, to come forward. Chasity couldn't help but smile as Hanson lined up beside all of the rest. He held his head high with pride, as Addison spoke most highly of their service. She hoped that he knew how truly amazing he was, and that he would be truly happy in his profession.

Chasity sighed, wondering what Hanson's future would have in store.

It's okay, Chasity told herself, *I've made my peace. I've let him go.*

And she had. Sure, she had shed some ugly tears over it. But it was time for a new chapter in her life to be written. Hanson had consumed so many of the pages in her heart, that a few days ago she struggled to think about a future without him.

But now she rested in the fact that her story wasn't ending. It was only just beginning. Hanson would go on to become, hopefully, an honored and respected guard upstairs; working in the Tower, keeping a careful eye on her and the rest of the Royals. And she would continue to live her life, just as she did before that devastatingly handsome young guard knocked on her bedroom door. She didn't know what the next chapter held in store for her, but she was filled with a fresh hope and excitement as she thought about all of the unknowns. She was ready to find out.

After the ceremony ended, Hanson returned to his new station. Chasity breathed deeply as she watched him leave the room.

Just like that, it was all over. Most likely, she may never see him again.

Chasity smiled as a strange, bittersweet peace washed over her, *I trust You, God. I trust You with the keys of my heart. Go ahead and write Your story. Do whatever it is that You have planned for my life. I think I'm finally ready this time.*

Once again The Ball Room was filled with excited chatter as violins played sweetly in the background. Hope longed to escape to the terrace as quickly as she could, but a mob of people surrounded her. She tried to sweetly excuse herself, but she knew that social engagements like this could run long. Attempting to leave small-talk conversations was always a challenge.

Half an hour later, she finally made her way to the Garden Terrace. David was waiting there.

"I'm so sorry!" she gushed, rushing onto the balcony, trying not to trip over the massive skirt of her dress. "Have you been waiting long?"

"Not at all," he replied sweetly, "I've actually only been here for a minute. I thought I was going to be the one who left you waiting."

"Oh yes, I'm sure everyone wanted to talk to you," she smiled, "being the big superstar on campus that you are."

David shook his head, "I'm still not used to it. All the attention is just strange. I still just feel like the geeky white guy from Kentucky who likes to write songs and play in a garage band with his best friends. Everyone's treating me like I'm something completely different, but I'm still the same guy."

"I believe it," Hope nodded.

"So how do you deal with it?" David asked. "I mean, you've been under the limelight ever since you were born. What makes you feel and stay normal when everyone is telling you that you're some big superstar?"

"I guess I've never really thought about it before," Hope replied thoughtfully as she drew near to the balcony's edge and looked over. The entire garden was lit up below. "This is just my life. I've never known anything else. I suppose this is my normal."

David sighed. He looked at her white-glove-clad hands, and wanted to reach for them. Everything about her was amazing. He wanted to tell her, but didn't know how to express what he was feeling.

"I want to tell you something," he started slowly, "but I don't have my guitar. So I feel at a total loss for words. It's like, if I open up my mouth right now, I'm going to sound like a babbling fool who can't even think straight. But if I don't say what's been burning on my heart, I'm never going to be able to forgive myself."

Hope looked away from the garden, and into his eyes. She took a deep breath, praying for courage. "David, wait."

He did. His quietness was Hope's que to continue. "I think I know what you're going to say." She started slowly, "I know exactly how you feel." She felt her voice quiver with nervousness. She continued anyway. "I've been experiencing the same thing these past few weeks. So many thoughts, emotions, and words that have just been exploding on the inside. So many things I want to tell you. It's confusing, yet beautiful and terrifying all at the same time. If I could, I would just un-jar everything that's inside of me and let it explode onto you like some sort of bursting fountain or firework. But I can't allow myself to do that, David. And neither can you. You can't take the lid off of what you're feeling."

"Why?" he asked frantically, his eyes searching hers for hidden answers. "I know I'm not crazy. Whatever is going on between us, it's real. You just admitted that you're feeling all of these things, and neither of us can deny this electricity in the air. Hope, I love you. And I'm not afraid to tell you that."

"Oh David," she whispered, trying to keep herself from crying, "I believe you. But look at us!" She backed away from him, tying to keep her head above water. She had to keep her perspective straight. "We're still so young. We barely even know one another. We can't possibly know if what we're feeling is love, can we? I mean, truly? We were thrown into a life-threatening situation that caused us to feel things that elevated our simple crushes into something much more intense. But, at the end of the day, that's all it is. That's all it can be. A crush. The reality of the situation is that we're two completely different people, living entirely different lives. Your place is in the United States, touring, performing for your fans, doing what you love. And my place is here in Tarsurella, with my family, continuing my education and waiting to see what else God has in store for me."

David felt himself grow angry with Hope's words. It wasn't what he wanted. He loved her. And it wasn't a silly, fifteen-second crush that you write a pop song about. It was deep, and real, and consumed every part of him. But still, he had to respect her opinion.

His jaw tightened. "Is that really what you want?" he asked cautiously. If she said yes, then he would respectfully back down. She was a strong-willed girl, and if her mind was made up, then it would be all over between them.

But if she said no, he was prepared to forget everything and kiss her right then and there. The late autumn air and the twinkling starlight was teasing him. Her beauty had him completely captivated.

Hope could feel the war between her head and her heart intensify. Of *course* that wasn't what she wanted! The electric pull between them was so real. She wanted to kiss him just as much as he did her. But then what? He would fly home, and she would stay here, and they'd only see each other every few months? He would continue to be chased down by obsessed fangirls, and she would receive hate mail for being his beloved girlfriend. They needed more time to get to know one another. As friends. Without the pressure of a possible romance.

After praying, then talking to Clark and Elizabeth, Hope knew what she had to do. Clark and Elizabeth's words confirmed what she felt like God was already telling her. She was counseled to wait.

"Oh, to be young and in love," Elizabeth had told her. "It's a most exciting thing! But it can also be devastatingly dangerous if you make the wrong choices. When you're emotionally or physically intertwined with someone, and connected so deeply, you cannot see clearly anymore. It's a most difficult choice to make, but the choice to wait for God's best is one of the most important decisions you'll ever make in your life. Clark and I waited for each other. We were best friends all throughout High School. Clark asked me to date him, several times, but I continued to turn him down. Not because I didn't like him. But because I valued the possibility of our future much too highly. I didn't want us to mess anything up by diving in prematurely. We were not ready for marriage, so why would we tempt ourselves like that? And if it happened to be that Clark *wasn't* the man God had for me, I didn't want to spend all of my love and affection on that man, only to have the leftovers of my broken heart to give to the next one. Does this make sense?"

Hope remembered Elizabeth's words and clung to them. She knew they were true. She had to believe that if she gave this up right now, there would be something better in store in the future. She would open up and release him, and if he truly loved her, then he would be back someday. She had to believe that.

"David," she breathed, "I would love to remain friends. But I can't be your girlfriend. Not yet, anyway. We still have so much to learn about one another before we could even think about dating!" She laughed, trying to lighten up the moment, "Like, what's your favorite movie snack? Or, what part of the Oreo do you eat first? The cookie or the cream? How could we possibly build a long-lasting relationship without knowing these things about one another?" she joked.

[434]

David nodded, accepting the crushing blow of defeat. "I understand. I will step down, and respectfully resign to the place that I probably should have remained in the first place." He grabbed her hand and humbly bowed, "Your Highness, have a lovely evening. Blessings on you and your Kingdom."

"David," she spoke in a saddened tone, "you're not my Royal subject. I said I want to be friends. I don't want to banish you from my world forever!"

David attempted to force a smile onto his face, but it was to no avail. "Goodbye, Hope."

Hope watched, breathless and without any words as he turned to leave the balcony. She wanted to call for him to stay, but knew that it would be pointless.

After all, wasn't *she* the one who had let him go?

Chapter 30 – Clear Sky, Clear Heart

Bridget had only been in Alaska for several days, but the fresh air seemed to be working miracles.

Somehow, her heart was lighter. She didn't know if it was due to the fact that she wasn't running around attempting to meet the demands of her crazy schedule, or the newfound lack of distance between her and the midnight sky. Bridget gazed up toward Heaven in wonderment. The inky black blanket of darkness stretched as far as her eyes could see. Yet every few inches, twinkling lights pierced through the black backdrop, displaying a majestic sight. The galaxies above were thick and colorful, and served as a vivid reminder as to how absolutely tiny and insignificant she was.

"If you think this is cool, just wait until the Northern Lights happen," Liam's voice invaded her quiet thoughts. "That's when God completely shows off."

Bridget continued staring wistfully into the sky, "I believe it." She adjusted her glance and pulled her forest-green blanket closer to her chest. She opened her mouth, ready to complain about the frigid temperature, but instead decided to make her way closer to the blazing campfire. She approached the flames, where a group of woodsy-looking, bundled-up teens were seated in a circle around the fire.

Rebecca was passing out marshmallows and graham crackers. Bridget had never been to a legit campfire night before. This group of locals were the community of young adults that Liam had been talking about; their youth group.

Bridget entered the scene unnoticed, and couldn't help but smile as she slipped into a camp-chair. The dark atmosphere was illuminated by dancing flames which lit up the grins and laughter coming from the rowdy bunch. Although she had made microwave s'mores with her sisters, this would be her first s'more around a real campfire. She tried not to appear like a total novice as she grabbed a poker and placed her marshmallow onto its end. She quickly realized that nobody was watching her, and the reality was thrilling.

After casual conversation and rich sweets, Donald gently led the group into a Bible study about forgiveness.

Bridget felt her heart sting as he spoke. She couldn't even hear what Donald was saying, due to the fact that her heart was pounding so loudly with conviction. She hadn't forgiven Asher. She hadn't forgiven Jacob. She hadn't even forgiven Addison for being interested in a girl, just because she felt like he shouldn't be. Bridget fought back tears. The wretched feeling of sin weighed heavy upon her soul as she struggled to make things right in her mind. *Lord, forgive me!* She thought frantically and sincerely, *My heart has been so messed up! I've been holding these offences harshly against those who hurt me, thinking that somehow perhaps I would feel better. But I don't. I feel terrible. I see now that Liam was right. I'm the one who is drinking poison. And if I don't get rid of this, it's going to suck all the life out of me. But I can't! I don't know how! I don't know how I can possibly love them again. I don't know how to forgive Jacob for ripping my heart apart. I don't know how to forgive Asher for everything that he did. But I want to. Lord, help me. There's no way that I can forgive them on my own!*

Bridget couldn't sit in her seat any longer. She didn't want to be rude, but the pulling on her heart was stronger than the desire to please her host family. All at once, she stood up and walked several feet away from the group. She turned on her cell phone flashlight, and continued walking. In the wide open air, she felt as if she could walk forever. But she didn't.

She made sure that she was out of earshot of the group, and quickly searched through her text messages. Addison had sent her one earlier that day. Surprisingly, it had actually come through. She pressed on the number that he sent her within the message, and waited in suspense as it rang.

For a few dreadful moments, she thought that perhaps the call would not go through.

Finally, a voice picked up on the other end.

"Baghdad U. N. Underground Hospital, how may I direct your call?"

"Hello," Bridget kept her tears at bay, "this is Princess Bridget. I've called to speak with Asher."

"Yes, Your Highness, one moment please."

A few moments later her voice came back on the line. "I'm sorry, Your Highness, but the young Prince is currently not taking any calls."

"Put it through anyway," Bridget asserted, "I need to speak with him."

"Very well, Your Highness," the woman aided her request.

"I said I'm not taking calls," a grumpy voice came on the line.

"Asher!" Bridget's voice resounded through the wide open air, "Thank God! You have no idea how good it is to hear your voice!"

Asher didn't reply.

"Listen, bud, you have to know something." Bridget took a deep breath, "Addison told me what you did. And I don't know whether this was all just a huge, terrible mistake, or if you actually purposed in your heart to hurt us. Whether your intentions were innocent or terribly evil, from where I stand, it still looks horrific. And honestly, after everything that Hope and the rest of us walked through, I wanted someone to blame. So I blamed you. I was so angry, and broken. And I was getting cold! And numb. Not just towards you, but toward everyone! But I can't do that anymore, Asher. I won't do that anymore. You know why? Because this life is too short to walk around allowing bitterness to corrode our souls. And I want to know what it feels like to live again. To trust again. To love again. So with the Lord's help, and only by His grace, I'm going to say this. And mean it." Bridget closed her eyes and slowly spoke the powerful words, "I forgive you, Asher."

"Like I care." Asher's response was cold and cruel. "Save your breath for someone who does." And with that, the line went empty.

Bridget continued her heartfelt confession, aware of the fact that Asher wasn't listening anymore, "And I love you," she sighed. "God's gonna pull you out of this dark place. Just like He's doing with me."

"So, what did you think of our little campfire get-together last night?" Liam asked as he tossed a saddle onto its proper rack.

Bridget popped her head up from where she scooped a bucket of corn into the feeding trough. If any of her sisters had seen her at that moment, they wouldn't have believed the sight. Princess Bridget, who was born with a silver spoon in her mouth and raised in designer diapers, was doing chores in a barn at seven in the morning!

Yes, chores. Her maids would be floored. The press would be pulling their hair out. Nobody had ever seen this side of

Bridget before. Strangely enough, Bridget was adjusting to the gentle flow of life in Alaska fairly quickly. Sure, she severely missed many things about her home—electricity that never had power outages, showers that never ran out of hot water, and siblings who made every meal loud and colorful—yet something about being in Alaska just felt right.

"Probably not quite up to par with the big city parties you're used to, huh?" Liam grinned.

"Correct," Bridget laughed. "It was nothing like back home. But that's why it was so perfect. I know this is probably going to sound super cheesy and fabricated, but every ounce of it is true. God did a miracle in my heart last night."

Liam's smile stayed put, "Oh yeah?"

Bridget nodded as she spoke slowly, "I called Asher last night. I told him that I forgave him."

"How did he respond?"

"He acted like he didn't care," Bridget replied, "but I think it's all part of his façade. Like mine used to be, until God broke through the iron walls around my heart and finally got through to me. I'm gravely concerned about Asher, but I have to have hope that he's going to be okay. If the Lord is able to rescue me out of all my sinful messes, then I know he can do the same for Asher."

"Amen," Liam nodded, "God is going to work in your brother's heart."

"Asher isn't the only person I forgave," she continued. "As I prayed, the Lord led me through some old, really painful memories, and helped me to finally let go of everything that happened with Jacob. I even called my big brother, Addison.

Before we left, we had kind of a blowup, and I completely chewed him out over this girl that he may be interested in. But I was so muddled up in the mess of my own toxic heart, I couldn't even see straight! If Addison believes that there's something beautiful and noble about this girl, then maybe I need to give her a second chance."

"We all deserve second chances," Liam agreed, "and sometimes we even need third, or fourth, or fifth chances. So what about me?" he probed, "Do I get a second chance?"

"Whatever do you mean?" Bridget laughed.

"I couldn't help but notice that, when you arrived, you kind of already hated my guts." Liam replied.

"That's not true!" Bridget laughed.

Liam's eyes suggested otherwise.

"Okay, maybe I was a bit stand-off-ish." she admitted with a grin. "Your first impression wasn't a very good one. But can you blame me? I thought you were acting like this big, hunky, know-it-all wilderness guy, who planned to prey on the shallow, rich girl from the big city, getting his laughs out of all the ways she couldn't do anything Alaska expected of her."

"Hunky?" Liam echoed, "Ah, maybe your first impression of me wasn't all that bad after all."

Bridget's eyes widened, surprised by the fact that word fell out of her mouth. Did she really say that? She decided to play it off and roll her eyes. "Did I mention egotistical and narcissistic? Because that was definitely supposed to be part of the previous description."

Liam laughed, "Well, I hope that you'll stick around here long enough for you to gain a true and honest opinion of my character, before heading home."

"Yeah," Bridget smiled, secretly admiring him from a distance, "I don't think that will be a problem."

Chapter 31 – Happily Ever After

"Camping, camping, we're finally going camping!" Millie sang at the top of her lungs.

"We've been out here for two hours, and she still hasn't stopped singing that goofy song," Jillian sighed as she glanced at Addison, "Make her stop?"

Addison grinned from where he was bent over a hodgepodge of muddled metal bars, plastic tent pegs, and a green canvas. "Two hours?" Addison laughed, "Surely it hasn't been that long. Our tent is still on the ground."

Hope studied the instructions with a puzzled expression. "Too bad Bridget isn't here. I know she's only been in Alaska for a short time, but from the tone of her texts, it sounds like she's turning into a real Girl Scout."

Addison laughed, "All the girl told me was that she made her own s'mores over an outdoor fire. That hardly sounds like Girl Scout qualifications."

"These tents are gonna take forever to set up," Jillian observed. "If they're not up by dark, I'm going back to sleep in the castle."

"Oh, come on now, where's your sense of adventure?" Addison teased, "If this was real camping, there'd be no indoor plumbing. And no fluffy beds waiting for us just a few yards away."

"But this *is* real camping!" Millie insisted with passion and fervor. "We are in the middle of the Australian outback, with wild lions roaming throughout the land! We have to fend for our survival!"

"Lions?" Hope giggled, "Australia doesn't have lions. How about wild kangaroos?"

"Oh yeah?" Addison questioned in a child-like tone. "Who says there aren't any lions out here? The people who say there aren't any lions around these parts must not be telling the truth, because I think one is about to pounce on Millie!" Addison let out his most ferocious sounding roar, and playfully bounded toward his kid sister. Millie let out a joyful scream, and ran in the opposite direction. Addison chased her, hands up with vicious claws, purposefully allowing her to remain a few steps ahead of him.

If causal onlookers were to partake the unfolding scene, they may have shook their heads, wondering why the King was running around the backyard with his little sister when there were far more important matters to attend to. More uppity members of the Royal Staff found it foolish, and were sure to express their opinion to the young King, reminding him that he couldn't afford to take an afternoon off. "The nation is still recovering from terrible losses! You're trying to regain the trust of your people, and the eyes of the whole world are upon you!"

Addison respectfully made up his own mind, and turned aside from their "counsel." "I believe that the core of our nation is made up right here. In this palace. With this family. We are the heartbeat of Tarsurella. And from this hub, the entire world is impacted and affected. Like a native tree, we must let our roots go deep before we spread our branches out and give aid to others. What happens if I neglect the core of this country? Everything else will suffer. Cancel all of my plans, and reschedule my meetings. Today, Millie's wish is coming true. We're going camping."

Millie continued screeching as Addison chased her across the back yard. Past the bubbling brook and playful fountain, stood a tall and ancient oak tree. In the boughs of the strong wooden centerpiece, sat a cheerful treehouse. The very same treehouse that Addison used to play in during his younger years.

"I'm safe, I'm safe!" she shouted, as she reached the bottom rung of the treehouse ladder.

"*Rawr!*" Addison snatched her from the ladder, and twirled her around, before gently tackling her on the ground. She released infectious giggles as the lion tickled her.

"I surrender, I surrender!" she called out between bursts of violent laughter.

Addison laughed and let the tickling subside. He leaned up against the tree's great trunk, with Millie in his lap. She took deep breaths and refilled her lungs with oxygen.

"I love when you play with me." She gave him a tight hug, "Thank you for making the whole family go camping together."

"And thank you," he playfully tapped her on the nose, "for giving me a reason to get out of that stuffy office! Do you want to know a secret?"

"Yes!" she perked up, "I love, love, love, secrets! And I'm really good at keeping them!"

Addison's expression questioned her, "You mean, you won't even tell Mr. Pork Chops?"

Millie shamefully looked at the grass, as she considered the possibility, "Pork Chops won't tell anyone!"

"Millie, I'm serious." Addison allowed his tone to match his eyes, "What I'm about to tell you is something that I've never told *anyone* before. You have to promise that you won't even tell Pork Chops."

Millie pursed her lips then took a deep breath, determined to keep her brother's secret. "I promise."

"You remember Miss Vanessa, right?

Millie's eyes lit up, "Of course! Is she coming camping with us?"

"No," Addison was pleased to see that Millie had taken such a liking to her, "but she interviewed for a new job here at The Palace. And I officially decided that I'm going to give it to her."

"Yay!" Millie was nearly as excited as he was, "Does this mean she'll be living here with us?"

"Oh no, she'll get an apartment, somewhere downtown. But I'm sure we'll be seeing a lot of her. I'm going to call and let her know that she got the job. But here's the real secret: I'm a little bit nervous."

"You? Nervous?" Millie asked, "Why?"

Addison wasn't sure what to tell the spunky little girl. He liked Vanessa. He liked her a lot.

Last night Bridget had called him, all the way from Alaska, in the middle of the night. The phone call was quite unexpected. His sister gave a heartfelt apology for her wrongs, and gave Addison and Vanessa her blessing. "Life is so short," she sniffed, "and none of us know how long we have here on this earth. Faith, family, and love are the only truly eternal things that we have in this life. I want you to be happy! And I trust you, Addison. I know that you wouldn't even be giving this girl the time of day if you didn't see something truly special in her. Whatever you decide to do, to pursue a relationship or not, I want you to know that I am completely behind you."

Addison recalled her words before telling Millie, "Miss Vanessa is very special. And I want to get to know her better. I want to spend time chatting, and hanging out, and truly getting to hear more of her heart. When she moves here in January, if things go well and she's even a fraction of the amazing woman that I think she is, then some things might start to change around here."

"You mean," Millie's jaw dropped, "You're going to marry her?"

Addison laughed, "Now, let's not get carried away and put the Royal wedding carriage before the horse of a foundational friendship. I haven't even told Vanessa how I feel about her yet! And I won't, for a while anyway. We need to give her time to get adjusted to life here in Tarsurella, and see if she likes life at The Palace. It will take some getting used to, but change isn't always bad. Sometimes, change can be amazing."

"Well, what are you waiting for?!" Millie proclaimed as she reached into Addison's pocket and pulled out his cell phone, "Let's get this show on the road! Call Miss Vanessa and let her know that she got the job!"

Addison laughed once more and scrolled through his contacts for her number.

Meanwhile, in the Watch Tower, Hanson couldn't help but smile at the scene. Little Millie was like a jack-in-the-box of pure adorableness, just pouncing out at every given opportunity. King Addison appeared to be quite smitten with whomever this young woman was.

Hanson leaned back in his black office chair and sighed. Life in the Tower was different. Now he felt like a spy in the tree, eavesdropping on all sorts of forbidden conversations, gaining an aerial view of everything that happened in the lives of the Royals.

The security screen flashed to another scene, where the retired King attempted to make a campfire with three of his girls; Hope, Chasity, and Jillian. Little Willie was bounding around the yard, collecting sticks and throwing them for their happy Golden Retriever.

"Ah, we couldn't have asked the good Lord for a more beautiful day!" the elder King announced, "But I do believe that our glorious fall season is fading into the background, and winter is on its way!"

Hope shivered as she hugged her plaid pink and brown sweater, "That fire is going to feel amazing. Any luck yet, Pops?"

Her father sighed from where he crouched over on his knees, frowning at the fire pit. "Starting a fire from scratch was never one of my strong points," he chuckled. "Your dear mother always used to say that if we were ever forced to live out in the wilderness on our own, and it was up to me to provide food, warmth, and shelter, we wouldn't survive." He glanced at Addison's pathetic piles of jumbled up tents, "I fear I have passed that quality on to my son as well."

Chasity approached one of the nearby security guards and asked for a lighter.

"Thank you," Chasity grinned at the guard.

Hanson felt himself flinch. Just a few weeks ago that could've been him handing her the lighter. It shouldn't matter to him. And Hanson still didn't know why it mattered, but it did. It mattered that someone else was standing where he used to. It mattered that Chasity was safe and protected and cared for, even if it was something as silly and nonsensical as building her a fire in her backyard. Whatever she needed, Hanson wanted to do it. He knew that his desire to see her shielded and tended to ran far deeper than his job description. His fierce loyalties to Chasity were dangerously bordering the line of insanity. He had grown far too attached, and as much as he wished otherwise, he knew that keeping his distance was crucial. They had said their goodbyes, made their peace, and parted ways. He couldn't go back.

Hanson sighed, dumbfounded by the series of events and the way they unfolded over the previous months. From the first day of work, when he had gotten pounded by his father in the alleyway with his bullying henchmen and his fierce threats, until this very moment, so much had happened. He never could've imagined that his father's words would have swayed him so intensely. Who could've known that he was only inches away from betraying the Crown? That tiny little chip could have been the very seed to forever destroy the nation of Tarsurella.

Instead, something had stopped him. Maybe it was providence. Perhaps it was fate. Hanson wasn't sure if he believed in all of that, but he did know one thing to be true—his affections for Chasity were greater than any thought he gave to himself, his family, and even his life-long Lilly. As intensely committed as he was to protecting his family and friends, somehow Chasity's sweet smile, sassy charm, and entrancing laughter had trumped it all. Chasity had saved her entire Kingdom, without even knowing it.

Thankfully, Mr. Fletcher's murderous threats had only proved to be a ludicrous farce. Hanson's family, friends, and the random strangers who could've been at the wrong place at the wrong time, had all been left unharmed. Hanson could only hope that Mr. Fletcher decided the risk wasn't worth taking, and had moved onto the harassing of some other innocent soul, far, far away. Surely this was what happened. But as much as Hanson wanted to believe this to be true, he still felt an undertone of dread clouding the back of his mind. Mr. Fletcher was like a sly snake. He still may be waiting to strike at a moment when Hanson least expected it.

"Did I miss anything exciting?" A guard named Jason entered the Security Tower, from where he had previously excused himself to refill his coffee mug.

Hanson glanced at his co-worker. "Nope. Not unless you count the fact that the former King finally got the fire started."

"Oh, riveting!" Jason laughed jokingly. "Hey, have you heard of that band from the States? *Kennetic Energy*? They played at The Coronation Ball, and the lead singer rescued Princess Hope during the disaster?"

"Of course I've heard of them," Hanson laughed. "I might work in a Tower, but I don't live under a rock."

"They just dropped a new single this morning. Get this. It's called *Hope*."

Hanson shrugged. "Total coincidence, right?"

"Must be. There's no way they would've had time to write and record it since they were here last. Want to take a listen?"

"Sure, pop it in," Hanson gave his consent. One of the perks about working the Tower was that they were able to listen to music, as long as it played quietly in the background and wasn't distracting them from their job. It was something Hanson was never able to do while working the ground.

"Just a small town boy who's been on a ride, midnight dreams flash before my eyes, blinded by the bright lights of a Hollywood party at twilight," David started crooning through their stereo system, *"I blink twice to make sure that she's real, 'Cause the vision before me is so surreal, Now I've never seen an angel before, Until she stepped through that open door."*

Hanson tapped his fingers on the counter to match the beat. It was super catchy.

"Now I'm hovering, I'm stuttering, butterflies are fluttering, I'm trying to act smooth as glass, but I know this act ain't gonna last, I'm covering, discovering, that I'm a fool whose chokin' on his words, She'll think that I'm absurd, but I've gotta say these words, Baby, you have to know I've lost all hope, I've lost all hope, I've lost all hope."

In the very same moment, on the other side of the world, Vanessa bopped her head along to the new song floating through her radio airwaves. She wasn't crazy about pop music, but this song was almost good.

She lifted a green cardigan up to her mirror, examining what it did to her skin tone. Then, she lifted a sweater of the same design up with her other hand, but this one was a mustard yellow. She alternated between the two, wondering which she should get rid of. She didn't need this many clothes, when some people in their very own community were struggling to stay warm.

She tossed the green one into a cardboard box on her bed labeled 'Giveaway.'

She dug through her closet, going deeper into the jungle of material. She stopped when her eyes fell upon the gown she had worn to Addison's Coronation. The gown in which she danced with him. She ran her fingers across the precious material and sighed. That moment felt like a lifetime away.

Just then. Her phone started ringing. It was a number from The Tarsurellian Palace!

Vanessa scrambled to grab the phone off her bed, and lifted it to her ear. "Hi, uh, hello?" She cleared her throat.

"Hi there! This is King Addison's personal secretary!" The little girlish voice giggled. Vanessa questioned the number as she pulled her phone back again and glanced at it. Was this a prank call?
It did not sound like Deborah.

"It's Millie!" she proclaimed. "You remember me, right?"

"Why, of course!" Vanessa laughed, "How could I not? You, my dear, are entirely impossible to forget."

"I have some exciting news!" Millie gushed, "My brother decided to hire you!"

Vanessa was so shocked that the phone slipped out of her hand. As it smacked on the hardwood floor, she missed Millie's contingent sentence, "And he's in love with you!"

Addison's face turned white, shocked that Millie had blurted out such news. "Hand me the phone!" Addison quickly grabbed the phone from his sister's grasp. "No!" he frantically explained, "I am so sorry, she doesn't know what she's talking about. She's just being, uh, cute. You know how kids are. But I'm still serious. About the job, I mean. Hello? Are you there? Vanessa?"

[452]

It took a full second for Vanessa to realize that the phone had dropped. She dashed down to floor to pick it up, "I'm so sorry! I'm here! Wait, what?"

The two were speaking at the same time, and neither could understand the other. Vanessa laughed, "I could be totally wrong here, but I *think* you're trying to tell me that I got the job?"

"Yes!" Addison grinned, relived to know that she was still on the line. "Uh, Deborah is going to send you all the details." Addison quickly tried to cover up his awkward tone. "I can't wait to see you. I mean work with you. It's going to be great to have you on board."

"Yeah! Wow. You too. I mean, wow. Thank you!" Vanessa gushed, "I don't even know what to say!"

"Neither does Addison!" Millie giggled as she grabbed the phone back, "That's all for now, see you in January!"

With a sudden click, the noise proclaimed that their conversation had ended. Vanessa tossed her phone onto the bed as Vanessa let out a victory shout, "Mom! Dad! I got the job! I got the job! I'm moving to Tarsurella!"

And with that, Vanessa turned up the radio and started dancing around her bedroom like a popstar wannabe. Her childlike joy and victorious elation brought out a side of her personality that was rarely ever expressed, or seen in public. Still, her childhood collection of stuffed animals sitting on the shelf had quite the view of Vanessa's one-girl dance party.

David's voice blasted through her bedroom, *"Now I'm hovering, I'm stuttering, butterflies are fluttering, I'm trying to act smooth as glass, but I know this act ain't gonna last, I'm covering, discovering, that I'm a fool whose chokin' on his words, She'll think that I'm absurd, but I've gotta say these words, Baby, you have to know I've lost all hope, I've lost all hope, I've lost all hope."*

When the song ended, Vanessa flopped backwards onto her bed, with her phone clutched to her chest, completely breathless.

"David Carter might have lost his hope," Vanessa smiled to herself as she spoke, "but I think I've finally found mine."

Coming Soon! *The Tales of Tarsurella: The Rebellion*

Get a special sneak peek at the next book!

She should have been able to use a dozen different words to describe the snowy scene. Sparkling. Mystical. Romantic. Her poetic mind should have been able to describe the splendid sight of each dainty snowflake tumbling in an effortless free fall. But her congested brain was far too occupied to afford such whimsical luxuries. Wistfully gazing out the window and soaking in the Tarsurellian scenery wasn't something she had time for.

Her parents had been pursuing her on the matter. "Send us post cards!" they chimed. "Take pictures, and record everything that happens to you!" It was a nice goal–in theory–to meticulously document every detail of her first year spent abroad, far away from her family. But her schedule was far too demanding for that.

Her friends back in the States wanted to know every nitty-gritty update. She had only been gone for a month, but they were constantly badgering her for more information. "What does The Palace look like inside?" they asked. "What does the European backdrop feel like?

Vanessa Bennett simply laughed when confronted with such questions. "It's just Europe. Not Disney World. The winter here is just as cold, and bitter, and frigid as it is in New York. Snowfall around the castle doesn't magically turn into diamonds. No matter where you live, cold is cold! It stings your ears and hurts your nose, and makes your chest ache."

But tonight, Vanessa was far from the blustery winds. She

was safely folded inside the heartbeat of the castle. Her very favorite room. The Queen's Library. Nestled into a snuggly window seat, big crimson cushions embraced her. Vanessa's small little frame was nearly gobbled up by the abundance of lush pillows. She held a thoughtless hand to her cheek, completely immersed in her project, conclusively unaware of the time. Her stiff shoulders had been in the same position for hours. Scattered papers, colorful highlighters, dull pencils, and tiny eraser dust filled her space.

Her turquoise mug of steaming hot-chocolate had turned into a cold pool of forgotten liquid. Mini white marshmallows bobbed on top, hoping to perhaps still catch her attention.

But there was no chance of that happening.

She didn't even notice the howling winds which slammed against the towering cathedral-style windows. When Vanessa first arrived at The Palace, she was in awe of the intricate craftsmanship of every bronze frame. But now, she was not even observant enough to notice that the sun had disappeared, and the unwelcome darkness of a cold winter's night was setting in.

A sudden voice burst through the hushed library, quickly jolting Vanessa's thoughts away from her work.

"Are you ready for the party?!"

Vanessa's eyes darted upward, recognizing the familiar high-pitched voice. She smiled as the welcome interruption came bounding toward her.

Spunky, eight-year-old Millie skipped across the library, her light brown hair bouncing. Her short bob cut was fresh and hopeful, a very springy choice for the dead of winter. Vanessa subconsciously reached for her own dark hair, aware that it had grown several inches. She needed a cut soon, as well.

Millie catapulted herself into the bay window beside Vanessa. Vanessa tried not to wince as she sat on several important papers.

"Party?" Vanessa echoed playfully, choosing not to stress over her wrinkled-up notes, "I wasn't aware of any upcoming shindigs. What's the special occasion?"

Vanessa's brain was overcrowded with information. What would they be celebrating this week? Was it Pork Chop's, Millie's beloved stuffed pig's birthday? Had Millie lost another tooth? There were always many, *many* reasons for Millie to party. Vanessa had become accustomed to Millie's festive pattern of living life. The little girl was an unbridled package of boundless energy. Her unquenchable zest for daily life and quirky little ways were endearing and refreshing. Millie had grown quite attached to Miss Vanessa within just a few short weeks, and Vanessa felt the same way about her.

Millie's blue eyes widened as she spilled the obvious, "Asher is coming home!"

Oh. Right. How had Vanessa forgotten? Well, she hadn't really. But she had never paused to consider the fact that Asher's homecoming might bring about an official party, Royal Family style. She shook her head and laughed at her absentmindedness, "Of course! That party! Well, I bet you're super excited to see him."

Vanessa's throat constricted slightly. Of course the family would be thrilled to see their brother. But there was no doubt that his return would be a bit like eating chocolate-covered dandelions. There was still a bitter, unwelcome after-taste lingering in the air, at the mention of his name. After all the traumatic events that had taken place just months earlier, Vanessa found herself anxious at the idea of his return.

The young Prince Asher was an important counterpart of their family, and surely they must have missed him in his absence. But for Vanessa, she never thought twice of the empty space at their dinner table. Suddenly, it dawned on her. She hadn't noticed, because she had been sitting in his seat...

Read the entire first chapter of *The Rebellion* at www.livylynnblog.com!

Check out these other titles by Livy Lynn Jarmusch!

Secrets of Royalty

Welcome to the Worthlessness Camp.

A nightmarish place where helpless captives are held by chains. Here, an orphaned girl grows tired of her tears and desires to escape from the place of her fears. But the powers of darkness are far too strong for her. Suddenly, a glimmer of hope is seen on the horizon. Who is this Prince on a white horse, galloping in to save the day?

As you dive into this allegorical fairy-tale, experience the relentless love of a passionate Prince, who rescues this helpless captive and sweeps her into the royal courts of His Kingdom. But happily ever after has not yet arrived, and this grand rescue is only the beginning. Does this orphan have the makings of a Princess inside of her? Will she become everything the Prince says she can be, and rule by His side? Or will the wicked villain continue to control her mind, her heart, and destroy her destiny?

As you travel throughout this story, you'll uncover the hidden Secrets of Royalty and rediscover what it truly means for you to be a Chosen Daughter of the Most High King! Following this epic tale is a 31 Day Devotional that will powerfully transform the way that you think about yourself, your relationship with God, and the world around you!

Regal Hearts:
The Unlikely Story of a Princess, a Popstar, an Amish Girl, and an Average Girl

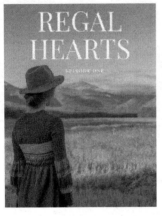

Following the dramatic birth of her royal daughters, the Queen of Bella-Adar is murdered by the merciless sword of an evil usurper. The helpless princesses are placed in the care of the URIA, an undercover organization who safely extracts and protects the girls from a tragic fate. Sixteen years later, Lena Bodner encounters a stranger who uncovers secrets from her past...

Read the first episode of Regal Hearts for FREE by visiting livylynnblog.com and subscribing to her free email updates!

Find these tiles and more at livylynnblog.com, on Amazon.com, or ask about them at your local bookstore!

Made in the USA
Middletown, DE
06 July 2017